WINDMILLS OF THE GODS

A master storyteller, Sidney Sheldon is the author of eighteen novels (which have sold over 300 million copies), over 200 television scripts, twenty-five major motion pictures and six Broadway plays, ranking him as one of the world's most prolific writers. His first book, *The Naked Face*, was acclaimed by the *New York Times* as 'the best first mystery novel of the year' and subsequently each of his highly popular books has hit No. 1 on the *New York Times* bestseller list.

For more about Sidney Sheldon, visit his website at www.sidneysheldon.com

Visit www.AuthorTracker.co.uk for exclusive information on Sidney Sheldon.

Books by Sidney Sheldon

SIDNEY SHELDON

Windmills of the Gods

HARPER

For Jorja

This novel is entirely a work of fiction.
The names, characters and incidents portrayed in it are
the work of the author's imagination. Any resemblance to
actual persons living or dead, events or localities is
entirely coincidental.

Harper
An Imprint of HarperCollins*Publishers*
77–85 Fulham Palace Road,
Hammersmith, London W6 8JB

www.harpercollins.co.uk

This paperback edition 2006
2

First published in Great Britain by
Fontana 1987

ISBN 978-0-00-789667-7

Set in Sabon by Palimpsest Book Production Limited,
Polmont, Stirlingshire

Printed and bound in Great Britain by
Clays Ltd, St Ives plc

We are all victims, Anselmo. Our destinies are decided by a cosmic roll of the dice, the whims of the stars, the vagrant breezes of fortune that blow from the windmills of the gods.

A Final Destiny H. L. Dietrich

PROLOGUE

Ilomantsi, Finland

The meeting took place in a comfortable, weather-proofed cabin in a remote, wooded area some 200 miles from Helsinki. The members of the Western Branch of the Committee had arrived discreetly at irregular intervals. They came from eight different countries, but their visit had been quietly arranged by a senior minister in the Valtioneuvosto, the Finnish Council of State, and there was no record of entry in their passports. Upon their arrival, armed guards escorted them into the cabin, and when the last visitor appeared, the cabin door was locked and the guards took up positions in the full-throated January winds, alert for any sign of intruders.

The members seated around the large, rectangular table were men in powerful positions, high in the councils of their respective governments. They had met before and under less clandestine circumstances, and they trusted one another because they had no choice. For added security, each had been assigned a code name.

The meeting lasted almost five hours, and the discussion was heated.

Finally, the chairman decided the time had come to call for a vote. He rose, standing tall, and turned to the man seated at his right. 'Sigurd?'

'Yes.'

'Odin?'

'Yes.'

'Balder?'

'We're moving too hastily. If this should be exposed, our lives would be –'

'Yes, or no, please?'

'No . . .'

'Freyr?'

'Yes.'

'Sigmund?'

'Nein. The danger –'

'Thor?'

'Yes.'

'Tyr?'

'Yes.'

'I vote "yes". The resolution is passed. I will so inform the Controller. At our next meeting, I will give you his recommendation for the person best qualified to carry out the motion. We will observe the usual precautions and leave at twenty-minute intervals. Thank you, gentlemen.'

Two hours and forty-five minutes later, the cabin

was deserted. A crew of experts carrying kerosene moved in and set the cabin on fire, the red flames licked by the hungry winds.

When the Palokunta, the fire brigade from Ilomantsi, finally reached the scene, there was nothing left to see but the smouldering embers that outlined the cabin against the hissing snow.

The assistant to the fire chief approached the ashes, bent down and sniffed. 'Kerosene,' he said. 'Arson.'

The fire chief was staring at the ruins, a puzzled expression on his face. 'That's strange,' he muttered.

'What?'

'I was hunting in these woods last week. There was no cabin.'

BOOK ONE

BOOK ONE

ONE

Washington, D.C.

Stanton Rogers was destined to be President of the United States. He was a charismatic politician, highly visible to an approving public, and backed by powerful friends. Unfortunately for Rogers, his libido got in the way of his career. Or, as the Washington mavens put it: 'Old Stanton fucked himself out of the Presidency.'

It was not that Stanton Rogers fancied himself a Casanova. On the contrary, until that one fatal bedroom escapade, he had been a model husband. He was handsome, wealthy, and on his way to one of the most important positions in the world, and although he had had ample opportunity to cheat on his wife, he had never given another woman a thought.

There was a second, perhaps greater irony: Stanton Rogers' wife, Elizabeth, was social, beautiful and intelligent, and the two of them shared a common interest in almost everything, whereas

Barbara, the woman Rogers fell in love with and eventually married after a much-headlined divorce, was five years older than Stanton, pleasant-faced, rather than pretty, and seemed to have nothing in common with him. Stanton was athletic; Barbara hated all forms of exercise. Stanton was gregarious; Barbara preferred to be alone with her husband or to entertain small groups. The biggest surprise to those who knew Stanton Rogers was the political differences. Stanton was a liberal, while Barbara had grown up in a family of arch-conservatives.

Paul Ellison, Stanton's closest friend, had said. 'You must be out of your mind, chum! You and Liz are practically in the *Guinness Book of Records* as the perfect married couple. You can't throw that away for some quick lay.'

Stanton Rogers had replied tightly, 'Back off, Paul. I'm in love with Barbara. As soon as I get a divorce, we're getting married.'

'Do you have any idea what this is going to do to your career?'

'Half the marriages in this country end in divorce. It won't do anything,' Stanton Rogers replied.

He had proved to be a poor prophet. News of the bitterly fought divorce was manna for the press, and the gossip papers played it up as luridly as possible, with pictures of Stanton Rogers' love nest, and stories of secret midnight trysts. The newspapers kept the story alive as long as they could, and when the furore died down, the powerful friends who had backed Stanton Rogers for the Presidency quietly disappeared. They found a new white knight to champion: Paul Ellison.

Ellison was a sound choice. While he had neither Stanton Rogers' good looks nor his charisma, he was intelligent, likeable and had the right background. He was short in stature, with regular, even features and candid blue eyes. He had been happily married for ten years to the daughter of a steel magnate, and he and Alice were known as a warm and loving couple.

Like Stanton Rogers, Paul Ellison had attended Yale and was graduated from Harvard Law School. The two men had grown up together. Their families had adjoining summer homes at Southampton, and the boys swam together, organized baseball teams, and later, double-dated. They were in the same class at Harvard. Paul Ellison did well, but it was Stanton Rogers who was the star pupil. As editor of the *Harvard Law Review*, he saw to it that his friend Paul became assistant editor. Stanton Rogers' father was a senior partner in a prestigious Wall Street law firm, and when Stanton worked there summers, he arranged for Paul to be there. Once out of law school, Stanton Rogers' political star began rising meteorically, and if he was the comet, Paul Ellison was the tail.

The divorce changed everything. It was now Stanton Rogers who became the appendage to Paul Ellison. The trail leading to the top of the mountain took almost fifteen years. Ellison lost an election for the Senate, won the following one, and in the next few years became a highly visible, articulate law-maker. He fought against waste in government and Washington bureaucracy. He was a populist, and believed in international détente. He was asked to give the nominating speech for the incumbent pres-ident running for re-election. It was a brilliant, impas-sioned speech that made everyone sit up and take notice. Four years later, Paul Ellison was elected President of the United States. His first appointment was Stanton Rogers as Presidential Foreign Affairs Adviser.

Marshall McLuhan's theory that television would turn the world into a global village had become a reality. The inauguration of the forty-second President of the United States was carried by satel-lite to more than 190 countries.

In the Black Rooster, a Washington, D.C., hang-out for newsmen, Ben Cohn, a veteran political reporter for the *Washington Post*, was seated at a table with four colleagues, watching the inaugura-tion on the large television set over the bar.

'The son-of-a-bitch cost me fifty bucks,' one of the reporters complained.

'I warned you not to bet against Ellison,' Ben Cohn chided. 'He's got the magic, baby. You'd better believe it.'

The camera panned to show the massive crowds

10

gathered on Pennsylvania Avenue, huddled inside their overcoats against the bitter January wind, listening to the ceremony on loudspeakers set up around the podium. Jason Merlin, Chief Justice of the United States Supreme Court, finished the swearing-in oath, and the new President shook his hand and stepped up to the microphone.

'Look at those idiots standing out there freezing their asses off,' Ben Cohn commented. 'Do you know why they aren't home, like normal human beings, watching it on television?'

'Why?'

'Because a man is making history, my friends. One day all those people are going to tell their children and grandchildren that they were there the day Paul Ellison was sworn in. And they're all going to brag "I was so close to him I could have touched him."'

'You're a cynic, Cohn.'

'And proud of it. Every politician in the world comes out of the same cookie cutter. They're all in it for what they can get out of it. Face it, fellas, our new President is a liberal and an idealist. That's enough to give any intelligent man nightmares. My definition of a liberal is a man who has his ass firmly stuck in clouds of cotton wool.'

The truth was that Ben Cohn was not as cynical as he sounded. He had covered Paul Ellison's career from the beginning and, while it was true that Cohn had not been impressed at first, as Ellison moved up the political ladder, Ben Cohn

11

began to change his opinion. This politician was nobody's 'yes' man. He was an oak in a forest of willows.

Outside, the sky exploded into icy sheets of rain. Ben Cohn hoped the weather was not an omen of the four years that lay ahead. He turned his attention back to the television set.

'The Presidency of the United States is a torch lit by the American people and passed from hand to hand every four years. The torch that has been entrusted to my care is the most powerful weapon in the world. It is powerful enough to burn down civilization as we know it, or to be a beacon that will light the future for us and for the rest of the world. It is our choice to make. I speak today not only to our allies, but to those countries in the Soviet camp. I say to them now, as we prepare to move into the twenty-first century, that there is no longer any room for confrontation, that we must learn to make the phrase "one world" become a reality. Any other course can only create a holocaust from which no nation would ever recover. I am well aware of the vast chasms that lie between us and the Iron Curtain countries, but the first priority of this administration will be to build unshakeable bridges across those chasms.'

His words rang out with a deep, heartfelt sincerity. *He means it*, Ben Cohn thought. *I hope no one assassinates the bastard.*

* * *

In Junction City, Kansas, it was a pot-bellied stove kind of day, bleak and raw, and snowing so hard that the visibility on Highway 6 was almost zero. Mary Ashley cautiously steered her old station wagon towards the centre of the highway, where the snowploughs had been at work. The storm was going to make her late for the class she was teaching. She drove slowly, careful not to let the car go into a skid.

From the car radio came the President's voice: '. . . are many in government as well as in private life who insist that America build more moats instead of bridges. My answer to that is that we can no longer afford to condemn ourselves or our children to a future threatened by global confrontations and nuclear war.'

Mary Ashley thought: *I'm glad I voted for him. Paul Ellison is going to make a great President.*

Her grip tightened on the wheel as the snow became a blinding white whirlwind.

In St Croix, a tropical sun was shining in a cloudless, azure sky, but Harry Lantz had no intention of going outside. He was having too much fun indoors. He was in bed, naked, sandwiched between the Dolly sisters. Lantz had empirical evidence that they were not truly sisters. Annette was a tall, natural brunette, and Sally was a tall, natural blonde. Not that Harry Lantz gave a damn whether they were blood relatives. What was important was that they were both expert at what

13

they did, and what they were doing made Lantz groan aloud with pleasure.

At the far end of the motel room, the image of the President flickered on the television set.

'. . . because I believe that there is no problem that cannot be solved by genuine goodwill on both sides, the concrete wall around East Berlin and the Iron Curtain that surrounds the other Soviet Union satellite countries must come down.'

Sally stopped her activities long enough to ask, 'Do you want me to turn that fuckin' thing off, hon?'

'Leave it alone. I wanna hear what he has to say.'

Annette raised her head. 'Did you vote for him?'

Harry Lantz yelled, 'Hey, you two! Get back to work . . .'

'As you are aware, three years ago, upon the death of Romania's President, Nicolae Ceausescu, Romania broke off diplomatic relations with the United States. I want to inform you now that we have approached the government of Romania and its President, Alexandros Ionescu, and he has agreed to re-establish diplomatic relations with our country.'

There was a cheer from the crowd on Pennsylvania Avenue.

Harry Lantz sat upright so suddenly that Annette's teeth sank into his penis. 'Jesus Christ!' Lantz screamed. 'I've already been circumcised! What the fuck are you trying to do?'

'What did you move for, hon?'

14

Lantz did not hear her. His eyes were glued to the television set.

'One of our first official acts,' the President was saying, 'will be to send an Ambassador to Romania. And that is merely the beginning . . .'

In Bucharest, it was evening. The winter weather had turned unexpectedly mild and the streets of the late marketplaces were crowded with citizens lined up to shop in the unseasonably warm weather.

Romanian President Alexandros Ionescu sat in his office in Peles, the old palace, on Calea Victoriei, surrounded by half a dozen aides, listening to the broadcast on a short-wave radio.

'. . . I have no intention of stopping there,' the American President was saying. 'Albania broke off all diplomatic relations with the United States in 1946. I intend to re-establish those ties. In addition, I intend to strengthen our diplomatic relations with Bulgaria, with Czechoslovakia, and with East Germany.'

Over the radio came the sounds of cheers and applause.

'Sending our Ambassador to Romania is the beginning of a worldwide people-to-people movement. Let us never forget that all mankind shares a common origin, common problems, and a common ultimate fate. Let us remember that the problems we share are greater than the problems that divide us, and that what divides us is of our own making.'

*　　*　　*

15

In a heavily guarded villa in Neuilly, a suburb of Paris, the Romanian revolutionary leader, Marin Groza, was watching the President on Chaine 2 Television.

'. . . I promise you now, that I will do my best, and that I will seek out the best in others . . .'

The applause lasted fully five minutes.

Marin Groza said thoughtfully, 'I think our time has come, Lev. He really means it.'

Lev Pasternak, his security chief, replied, 'Won't this help Ionescu?'

Marin Groza shook his head. 'Ionescu is a tyrant, so in the end, nothing will help him. But I must be very careful with my timing. I failed when I tried to overthrow Ceausescu. I must not fail again.'

Peter Connors was not drunk – not as drunk as he intended to get. He had finished almost a fifth of Scotch when Nancy, the secretary he lived with, said, 'Don't you think you've had enough, Pete?' He smiled and slapped her.

'Our President's talkin'. You gotta show some respect.' He turned to look at the image on the television set. 'You communist son-of-a-bitch,' he yelled at the screen. 'This is my country, and the CIA's not gonna let you give it away. We're gonna stop you, Charlie. You can bet your ass on it.'

TWO

Paul Ellison said, 'I'm going to need a lot of help from you, old friend.'

'You'll get it,' Stanton Rogers replied quietly.

They were seated in the Oval Office, the President at his desk with the American flag behind him. It was their first meeting together in this office, and President Ellison was uncomfortable.

If Stanton hadn't made that one mistake, Paul Ellison thought, *he would be sitting at this desk instead of me.*

As though reading his mind, Stanton Rogers said, 'I have a confession to make. The day you were nominated for the Presidency, I was as jealous as hell, Paul. It was *my* dream, and you were living it. But do you know something? I finally came to realize that if I couldn't sit in that chair, there was no one else in the world I would want to sit there but you. That chair suits you.'

Paul Ellison smiled at his friend and said, 'To tell you the truth, Stan, this room scares the hell out of me. I feel the ghosts of Washington and Lincoln and Jefferson.'

'We've also had Presidents who –'

'I know. But it's the great ones we have to try to live up to.'

He pressed the button on his desk, and seconds later a white-jacketed steward came into the room.

'Yes, Mr President?'

Paul Ellison turned to Rogers. 'Coffee?'

'Sounds good.'

'Want anything with it?'

'No, thanks. Barbara wants me to watch my waistline.'

The President nodded to Henry, the steward, and he quietly left the room.

Barbara. She had surprised everyone. The gossip around Washington was that the marriage would not last out the first year. But it had been almost fifteen years now, and it was a success. Stanton Rogers had built up a prestigious law practice in Washington, and Barbara had earned the reputation of being a gracious hostess.

Paul Ellison rose and began to pace. 'My people-to-people speech seems to have caused quite an uproar. I suppose you've seen all the newspapers.'

Stanton Rogers shrugged. 'You know how they are. They love to build up heroes so they can knock them down.'

'Frankly, I don't give a damn what the papers say. I'm interested in what *people* are saying.'

'Quite candidly, you're putting the fear of God into a lot of people, Paul. The armed forces are against your plan, and some powerful movers and shakers would like to see it fail.'

'It's not going to fail.' He leaned back in his chair. 'Do you know the biggest problem with the world today? There are no more statesmen. Countries are being run by politicians. There was a time not too long ago when this earth was peopled with giants. Some were good, and some were evil – but, by God, they were giants. Roosevelt and Churchill, Hitler and Mussolini. Charles de Gaulle and Joseph Stalin. Why did they all live at that one particular time? Why aren't there any statesmen today?'

'It's pretty hard to be a world giant on a twenty-one-inch screen.'

The door opened and the steward appeared, bearing a silver tray with a pot of coffee and two cups, each imprinted with the Presidential seal. He skilfully poured the coffee. 'Can I get you something else, Mr President?'

'No. That's it, Henry. Thank you.'

The President waited until the steward had gone. 'I want to talk to you about finding the right Ambassador to Romania.'

'Right.'

'I don't have to tell you how important this is. I want you to move on it as quickly as possible.'

Stanton Rogers took a sip of his coffee and rose to his feet. 'I'll get State on it right away.'

* * *

In the little suburb of Neuilly, it was 2 a.m. Marin Groza's villa lay in ebon darkness, the moon nested in a thick layer of storm clouds. The streets were hushed at this hour, with only the sound of an occasional passer-by rippling the silence. A black-clad figure moved noiselessly through the trees towards the brick wall that surrounded the villa. Over one shoulder he carried a rope and a blanket, and in his arms was cradled an Uzi with a silencer and a dart gun. When he reached the wall, he stopped and listened. He waited, motionless, for five minutes. Finally, satisfied, he uncoiled the nylon rope and tossed up the scaling hook attached to the end of it until it caught on the far edge of the wall. Swiftly, the man began to climb. When he reached the top of the wall, he flung the blanket across it to protect himself against the poisoned-tip metal spikes embedded on top. He stopped again to listen. He reversed the hook, shifting the rope to the inside of the wall, and slid down into the grounds. He checked the balisong at his waist; the deadly Filipino folding knife that could be flicked open or closed with one hand.

The attack dogs would be next. The intruder crouched there, waiting for them to pick up his scent. There were three Dobermans, trained to kill. But they were only the first obstacle. The grounds and the villa were filled with electronic devices, and continuously monitored by television cameras. All mail and packages were received at the gatehouse and opened there by the guards. The doors of the villa were bomb-proof. The villa had its own water supply, and Marin Groza had a food taster. The villa was impregnable. Supposedly. The figure in black was here this night to prove that it was not.

He heard the sounds of the dogs rushing at him before he saw them. They came flying out of the darkness, charging at his throat. There were two of them. He aimed the dart gun and shot the nearest one on his left first, and then the one on his right, dodging out of the way of their hurtling bodies. He spun around, alert for the third dog, and when it came, he fired again, and then there was only stillness.

The intruder knew where the sonic traps were buried in the ground, and he skirted them. He silently glided through the areas of the grounds that the television cameras did not cover, and in less than two minutes after he had gone over the wall, he was at the back door of the villa.

As he reached for the handle of the door, he was caught in the sudden glare of half a dozen floodlights. A voice called out, 'Freeze! Drop your gun and raise your hands.'

The figure in black carefully dropped his gun and looked up. There were half a dozen men spread out on the roof, with a variety of weapons pointed at him.

The man in black growled, 'What the fuck took you so long? I never should have got this far.'

'You didn't,' the head guard informed him. 'We started tracking you before you got over the wall.'

Lev Pasternak was not mollified. 'Then you should have stopped me sooner. I could have been on a suicide mission with a load of grenades or a god-damn mortar. I want a meeting of the entire staff tomorrow morning, eight o'clock sharp. The dogs have been stunned. Have someone keep an eye on them until they wake up.'

Lev Pasternak prided himself on being the best security guard in the world. He had been a pilot in the Israeli six-day war and, after the war, had become a top agent in Mossad, one of Israel's five secret services.

He would never forget the morning, two years earlier, when his colonel had called him into his office.

'Lev, someone wants to borrow you for a few weeks.'

'I hope it's a blonde,' Lev quipped.

'It's Marin Groza.'

Mossad had a complete file on the Romanian dissident. Groza had been the leader of a popular Romanian movement to depose Alexandros Ionescu and was about to stage a coup when he had been betrayed by one of his men. More than two dozen underground fighters had been executed, and Groza had barely escaped the country with his life. France had given him sanctuary. Ionescu denounced Marin Groza as a traitor to his country and put a price on his head. So far half a dozen attempts to assassinate Groza had failed, but he had been wounded in the latest attack.

'What does he want with me?' Pasternak asked. 'He has government protection.'

'Not good enough. He needs someone to set up a fool-proof security system. He came to us. I recommended you.'

'I'd have to go to France?'

'It will only take you a few weeks.'

'I don't –'

'Lev, we're talking about a *mensch*. He's the guy in the white hat. Our information is that he has enough popular support in his home country to knock over Ionescu. When the timing is right, he'll make his move. Meanwhile, we have to keep the man alive.'

Lev Pasternak thought about it. 'A few weeks, you said?'

'That's all.'

The Colonel had been wrong about the time, but he had been right about Marin Groza. He was a thin, fragile-looking man with an ascetic air about him and a face etched with sorrow. He had an aquiline nose, a firm chin, and a broad forehead, topped by a spray of white hair. He had deep, black eyes, and when he spoke, they blazed with passion.

'I don't give a damn whether I live or die,' he told Lev at their first meeting. 'We're all going to die. It's the *when* that I'm concerned about. I have to stay alive for another year or two. That's all the time I need to drive Ionescu out of my country.'

23

He ran his hand absently across a livid scar on his cheek. 'No man has the right to enslave a country. We have to free Romania and let the people decide their own fate.'

Lev Pasternak went to work on the security system at the villa in Neuilly. He used some of his own men, and the outsiders he hired were checked out thoroughly. Every single piece of equipment was state-of-the-art.

Pasternak saw the Romanian rebel leader every day, and the more time he spent with him, the more he came to admire him. When Marin Groza asked Pasternak to stay on as his security chief, Pasternak did not hesitate.

'I'll do it,' he said, 'until you're ready to make your move. Then I will return to Israel.'

They struck a deal.

At irregular intervals, Pasternak staged surprise attacks on the villa, testing its security. Now, he thought: *Some of the guards are getting careless. I'll have to replace them.*

He walked through the hallways, carefully checking the heat sensors, the electronic warning systems, and the infrared beams at the sill of each door. As he reached Marin Groza's bedroom, he heard a loud crash, and a moment later Groza began screaming out in agony.

Lev Pasternak passed Groza's room and kept walking.

THREE

Headquarters for the Central Intelligence Agency is located in Langley, Virginia, seven miles south-west of Washington, D.C. At the approach road to the Agency is a flashing red beacon on top of a gate. The gatehouse is guarded twenty-four hours a day, and authorized visitors are issued coloured badges giving them access only to the particular department with which they have business. Outside the grey seven-storey headquarters building, whimsically called the 'Toy Factory', is a large statue of Nathan Hale. Inside, on the ground floor, a glass corridor wall faces an inner courtyard with a land-scaped garden dotted with magnolia trees. Above the reception desk a verse is carved in marble:

And ye shall know the truth and
the truth shall set ye free.

The public is never admitted inside the building, and there are no facilities for visitors. For those who wish to enter the compound 'black' – unseen – there is a tunnel that emerges onto a foyer facing a mahogany elevator door, watched around the clock by a squad of grey-flannelled sentries.

In the seventh-floor conference room, guarded by security aides armed with snub-nosed .38 revolvers under their business suits, the Monday morning executive staff meeting was under way. Seated around the large, oak table were Ned Tillingast, Director of the CIA; General Oliver Brooks, Army Chief of Staff; Secretary of State Floyd Baker; Pete Connors, Chief of Counterintelligence; and Stanton Rogers.

Ned Tillingast, the CIA Director, was in his sixties, a cold, taciturn man, burdened with maleficent secrets. There is a light branch and a dark branch of the CIA. The dark branch handles clandestine operations, and for the past seven years, Tillingast had been in charge of the 4500 employees working in that section.

General Oliver Brooks was a West Point soldier who conducted his personal and professional life by the book. He was a company man, and the company he worked for was the United States Army.

Floyd Baker, the Secretary of State, was an anachronism, a throw-back to an earlier era. He was of southern vintage, tall, silver-haired and distinguished-looking, with an old-fashioned gallantry. He was a man who wore mental spats. He owned a chain of influential newspapers around the country, and was reputed to be enormously wealthy. There was no one in Washington with a keener political sense, and Baker's antennae were constantly tuned to the changing signals around the halls of Congress.

Pete Connors was black-Irish, a stubborn, bulldog of a man, hard-drinking and fearless. This was his last year with the CIA. He faced compulsory retirement in June. Connors was Chief of the Counterintelligence staff, the most secret, highly compartmentalized branch of the CIA. He had worked his way up through the various intelligence divisions, and had been around in the good old days when CIA agents were the golden boys. Pete Connors had been a golden boy himself. He had taken part in the coup that restored the Shah to the Peacock Throne in Iran, and he had been involved in Operation Mongoose, the attempt to topple Castro's government, in 1961.

'After the Bay of Pigs, everything changed,' Pete mourned. The length of his diatribe usually depended upon how drunk he was. 'The bleeding hearts attacked us on the front pages of every newspaper in the world. They called us a bunch of lying, sneaking clowns who couldn't get out of our own way. Some anti-CIA bastard published the names of our agents, and Dick Welch, our Chief of Station in Athens, was murdered.'

Pete Connors had gone through three miserable marriages because of the pressures and secrecy of his work, but as far as he was concerned, no sacrifice was too great to make for his country.

Now, in the middle of the meeting, his face was red with anger. 'If we let the President get away with his fucking people-to-people programme, he's going to give the country away. It has to be stopped. We can't allow –'

Floyd Baker interrupted. 'The President has been in office less than a week. We're all here to carry out his policies and –'

'I'm not here to hand over my country to the damned commies, Mister. The President never even mentioned his plan before his speech. He sprang it on all of us. We didn't have a chance to get together a rebuttal.'

'Perhaps that's what he had in mind,' Baker suggested.

Pete Connors stared at him. 'By God, you agree with it!'

'He's my President,' Floyd Baker said firmly. 'Just as he's yours.'

Ned Tillingast turned to Stanton Rogers. 'Connors has a point. The President is actually planning to *invite* Romania, Albania, Bulgaria, and the other communist countries to send their spies here posing as cultural attachés and chauffeurs and secretaries and maids. We're spending billions of dollars to guard the back door, and the President wants to throw open the front door.'

General Brooks nodded agreement. 'I wasn't consulted, either. In my opinion, the President's plan could damn well destroy this country.'

Stanton Rogers said, 'Gentlemen, some of us

28

may disagree with the President, but let's not forget that the people voted for Paul Ellison to run this country.' His eyes flicked across the men seated around him. 'We're all part of the President's team and we have to follow his lead and support him in every way we can.' His words were followed by a reluctant silence. 'All right, then. The President wants an immediate update on the current situation in Romania. Everything you have.'

'Including our covert stuff?' Pete Connors asked.

'Everything. Give it to me straight. What's the situation in Romania with Alexandros Ionescu?'

'Ionescu's riding high in the saddle,' Ned Tillingast replied. 'Once he got rid of the Ceausescu family, all of Ceausescu's allies were assassinated, jailed, or exiled. Since he seized power, Ionescu's been bleeding the country dry. The people hate his guts.'

'What about the prospects for a revolution?'

Tillingast said, 'Ah. That's rather interesting. Remember a couple of years back when Marin Groza almost toppled the Ionescu government?'

'Yes. Groza got out of the country by the skin of his butt.'

'With our help. Our information is that there's a popular groundswell to bring him back. Groza would be good for Romania and, if he got in, it would be good for us. We're keeping a close watch on the situation.'

Stanton Rogers turned to the Secretary of State. 'Do you have that list of candidates for the Romanian post?'

Floyd Baker opened a leather attaché case, took some papers from it, and handed a copy to Rogers. 'These are our top prospects. They're all qualified career diplomats. Each one of them has been cleared. No security problems, no financial problems, no embarrassing skeletons in the closet.'

As Stanton Rogers took the list, the Secretary of State added, 'Naturally, the State Department favours a career diplomat, rather than a political appointee. Someone who's been trained for this kind of job. In this situation, particularly. Romania is an extremely sensitive post. It has to be handled very carefully.'

'I agree.' Stanton Rogers rose to his feet. 'I'll discuss these names with the President and get back to you. He's anxious to fill the appointment as quickly as possible.'

As the others got up to leave, Ned Tillingast said, 'Stay here, Pete. I want to talk to you.'

When Tillingast and Connors were alone, Tillingast said, 'You came on pretty strong, Pete.'

'But I'm right,' Pete Connors said stubbornly. 'The President is trying to sell out the country. What are we supposed to do?'

'Keep your mouth shut.'

'Ned, we're trained to find the enemy and kill him. What if the enemy is behind our lines – sitting in the Oval Office?'

'Be careful. Be very careful.'

Tillingast had been around longer than Pete Connors. He had been a member of Wild Bill

Donovan's OSS before it became the CIA. He, too, hated what the bleeding hearts in Congress were doing to the organization he loved. In fact, there was a deep split within the ranks of the CIA between the hard-liners and those who believed the Russian bear could be tamed into a harmless pet. *We have to fight for every single dollar*, Tillingast thought. *In Moscow, the Komitet Gosudarstvennoi Bezopasnosti – the KGB – trains a thousand agents at a time.*

Ned Tillingast had recruited Pete Connors out of college, and Connors had turned out to be one of the best. But in the last few years, Connors had become a cowboy – a little too independent, a little too quick on the trigger. Dangerous.

'Pete – have you heard anything about an underground organization calling itself Patriots for Freedom?' Tillingast asked.

Connors frowned. 'No. Can't say that I have. Who are they?'

'So far they're just a rumour. All I have is smoke. See if you can get a lead on them.'

'Will do.'

An hour later, Pete Connors was making a phone call from a public booth at Hain's Point.

'I have a message for Odin.'

'This is Odin,' General Oliver Brooks said.

Riding back to the office in his limousine, Stanton Rogers opened the envelope containing

31

the names of the candidates for the ambassadorship and studied them. It was an excellent
list. The Secretary of State had done his homework. The candidates had all served in Eastern
and Western European countries, and a few of
them had additional experience in the Far East
or Africa. *The President's going to be pleased*,
Stanton thought.

'They're dinosaurs,' Paul Ellison snapped. He
threw the list down on his desk. 'Every one of
them.'

'Paul,' Stanton protested, 'these people are all
experienced career diplomats.'

'And hide-bound by State Department tradition.
You remember how we lost Romania three years
ago? Our experienced career diplomat in Bucharest
screwed up and we were out in the cold. The pin-
striped boys worry me. They're all out to cover
their asses. When I talked about a people-to-people
programme, I meant every word of it. We need to
make a positive impression on a country that at
this moment is very wary of us.'

'But if you put an amateur in there – someone
with no experience – you're taking a big risk.'

'Maybe we need someone with a different kind
of experience. Romania is going to be a test case,
Stan. A pilot run for my whole programme, if
you will.' He hesitated. 'I'm not kidding myself.
My credibility is on the line. I know that there
are a lot of powerful people who don't want to

see this work. If it fails, I'm going to get cut off at the knees. I'll have to forget about Bulgaria, Albania, Czechoslovakia, and the rest of the Iron Curtain countries. And I don't intend for that to happen.'

'I can check out some of our political appointees who –'

President Ellison shook his head. 'Same problem. I want someone with a completely fresh point of view. Someone who can thaw the ice. The opposite of the ugly American.'

Stanton Rogers was studying the President, puzzled. 'Paul – I get the impression that you already have someone in mind. Do you?'

Paul Ellison took a cigar from the humidor on his desk and lit it. 'As a matter of fact,' he said slowly, 'I think I may have.'

'Who is he?'

'She. Did you happen to see the article in the current issue of *Foreign Affairs* called "Détente Now"?'

'Yes.'

'What did you think of it?'

'I thought it was interesting. The author believes that we're in a position to try to seduce the communist countries into coming into our camp by offering them economic aid –' He broke off. 'It was a lot like your inaugural speech.'

'Only it was written six months earlier. She's published brilliant articles in *Commentary* and *Public Affairs*. Last year I read a book of hers on

33

Eastern European politics, and I must admit it helped clarify some of my ideas.'

'All right. So she agrees with your theories. That's no reason to consider her for a post as impor –'

'Stan – she went further than my theory. She outlined a detailed plan that's fascinating. She wants to take the four major world economic pacts and combine them.'

'How can we –?'

'It would take time, but it could be done. Look, you know that in 1949, the Eastern bloc countries formed a pact for mutual economic assistance, called COMECON, and in 1958 the other European countries formed the EEC – the Common Market.'

'Right.'

'We have the Organization for Economic Cooperation and Development, which includes the United States, some Western bloc countries and Yugoslavia. And don't forget that the third world countries have formed a non-aligned movement that excludes us.' The President's voice was charged with excitement. 'Think of the possibilities. If we could combine all these plans and form one big marketplace – my God, it could be awesome! It would mean *real* world trade. And it could bring peace.'

Stanton Rogers said cautiously, 'It's an interesting idea, but it's a long way off.'

'You know the old Chinese saying, "A journey

of a thousand miles starts with but a single step . . ."'

'She's an amateur, Paul.'

'Some of our finest ambassadors have been amateurs. Anne Armstrong, the former Ambassador to Great Britain, was an educator with no political experience. Perle Mesta was appointed to Denmark, Clare Boothe Luce was Ambassador to Italy. John Gavin, an actor, was the Ambassador to Mexico. One-third of our current ambassadors are what you call "amateurs".'

'But you don't know anything about this woman.'

'Except that she's damned bright, and that we're on the same wavelength. I want you to find out everything you can about her.' He picked up a copy of *Foreign Affairs* and glanced at the table of contents. 'Her name is Mary Ashley.'

Two days later, President Ellison and Stanton Rogers breakfasted together.

'I got the information you asked for.' Stanton Rogers pulled a paper from his pocket. 'Mary Elizabeth Ashley, Twenty-Seven Old Milford Road, Junction City, Kansas. Age, almost thirty-five, married to Dr Edward Ashley – two children, Beth twelve, and Tim ten. Chairman of the Junction City Chapter of the League of Women Voters. Assistant Professor, East European Political Science, Kansas State University. Grandfather born in Romania.' He looked up. 'The more I've thought about this, the more sense it makes. She probably knows more about Romania than most ambassadors know about the countries they're going to serve in.'

'I'm glad you feel that way, Stan. I'd like to have a full security check run on her.'

'I'll see that it's done.'

FOUR

'I disagree, Professor Ashley.'

Barry Dylan, the brightest and youngest of the students in Mary Ashley's political science seminar, looked around defiantly. 'Alexandros Ionescu is worse than Ceausescu ever was.'

'Can you give us some facts to back up that statement?' Mary Ashley asked.

There were twelve graduate students in the seminar being held in Kansas State University's Dykstra Hall. The students were seated in a semi-circle facing Mary. The waiting lists to get into her classes were longer than any other professor's at the University. She was a superb teacher, with an easy sense of humour and a warmth that made being around her a pleasure. She had an oval face that changed from interesting to beautiful, depending on her mood. She had the high cheek-bones of a model and almond-shaped, hazel eyes. Her hair was dark and thick. She had a figure that made her female students envious, and the males fantasize, yet she was unaware of how beautiful she was.

Barry was wondering if she was happy with her husband. He reluctantly brought his attention back to the problem at hand.

'Well, when Ionescu took over Romania, he cracked down on all the pro-Groza elements and re-established a hardline, pro-Soviet position. Even Ceausescu wasn't that bad.'

Another student spoke up. 'Then why is President Ellison so anxious to establish diplomatic relations with him?'

'Because we want to woo him into the Western orbit.'

'Remember,' Mary said, 'Nicolae Ceausescu also had a foot in both camps. What year did that start?'

Barry again. 'In 1960 when Romania took sides in the dispute between Russia and China to show its independence in international affairs.'

'What about Romania's current relationship with the other Warsaw Pact countries, and Russia in particular?' Mary asked.

'I'd say it's stronger now.'

Another voice. 'I don't agree. Romania criticized Russia's invasion of Afghanistan, and they criticized the Russians' arrangement with the EEC. Also, Professor Ashley –'

The bell sounded. The time was up.

Mary said, 'Monday we'll talk about the basic factors that affect the Soviet attitude towards

Eastern Europe, and we'll discuss the possible consequences of President Ellison's plan to penetrate the Eastern bloc. Have a good weekend.'

Mary watched the students rise and head for the door.

'You, too, Professor.'

Mary Ashley loved the give and take of the seminars. History and geography came alive in the heated discussions among the bright young graduate students. Foreign names and places became real, and historical events took on flesh and blood. This was her fifth year on the faculty of Kansas State University, and teaching still excited her. She taught five political science classes a year in addition to the graduate seminars, and each of them dealt with the Soviet Union and its satellite countries. At times she felt like a fraud. *I've never been to any of the countries I teach about*, she thought. *I've never been outside the United States.*

Mary Ashley had been born in Junction City, as had her parents. The only member of her family who had known Europe was her grandfather, who had come from the small Romanian village of Voronet.

Mary had planned a trip abroad when she received her Master's Degree, but that summer she met Edward Ashley, and the European trip had turned into a three-day honeymoon at Waterville, 55 miles from Junction City, where Edward was taking care of a critical heart patient.

'We really must travel next year,' Mary said to Edward shortly after they were married. 'I'm dying to see Rome and Paris and Romania.'

'So am I. It's a date. Next summer.'

But that following summer Beth was born, and Edward was caught up in his work at the Geary Community Hospital. Two years later, Tim was born. Mary had taken her Ph.D. and gone back to teaching at Kansas State University, and somehow the years had melted away. Except for brief trips to Chicago, Atlanta and Denver, Mary had never been out of the State of Kansas.

One day, she promised herself. *One day* . . .

Mary gathered her notes together and glanced out of the window. Frost had painted the window a winter grey, and it was beginning to snow again. Mary put on her lined leather coat and a red, woollen scarf and headed towards the Vattier Street entrance, where she parked her car.

The campus was huge, 315 acres, dotted with 87 buildings, including laboratories, theatres and chapels, amid a rustic setting of trees and grass. From a distance, the brown limestone buildings of the University resembled ancient castles, with turrets at the top, ready to repel enemy hordes. As Mary passed Denison Hall, a stranger with a Nikon camera was walking towards her. He aimed the camera at the building and pressed the shutter. Mary was in the foreground of the picture. *I should have got out of his way*, she thought. *I've spoiled his picture.*

One hour later, the negative of the photograph was on its way to Washington, D.C.

Every town has its own distinctive rhythm, a life pulse that springs from the people and the land. Junction City, in Geary County, is a farm community (population 20,381), 130 miles west of Kansas City, priding itself on being the geographical centre of the continental United States. It has a newspaper – the *Daily Union* – a radio station, and a television station. The downtown shopping area consists of a series of scattered stores and gas stations along 6th Street and on Washington. There is a Penney's, the First National Bank, a Domino Pizza, Flower Jeweller's, and a Woolworth's. There are fast food chains, a bus station, a menswear shop, and a liquor store – the type of establishments that are xeroxed in hundreds of small towns across the United States. But the residents of Junction City loved it for its bucolic peace and tranquillity. On weekdays, at least. Weekends, Junction City became the Rest and Recreation Centre for the soldiers at nearby Fort Riley.

Mary Ashley stopped to shop for dinner at Dillon's Market on her way home and then headed north towards Old Milford Road, a lovely residential area overlooking a lake. Oak and elm trees lined the left side of the road, while on the right side were beautiful houses variously made of stone, brick or wood.

The Ashley house was a two-storey stone house set in the middle of gently rolling hills. The house had been bought by Dr Edward Ashley and his bride thirteen years earlier. It consisted of a large living room, a dining room, library, breakfast room and kitchen downstairs and a master suite and two additional bedrooms upstairs.

'It's awfully large for just two people,' Mary Ashley had protested.

Edward had taken her into his arms and held her close. 'Who said it's going to be for only two people?'

When Mary arrived home from the University, Tim and Beth were waiting to greet her.

'Guess what?' Tim said. 'We're going to have our pictures in the paper!'

'Help me put away the groceries,' Mary said. 'What paper?'

'The man didn't say, but he took our pictures and he said we'd hear from him.'

Mary stopped and turned to look at her son. 'Did this man say why?'

'No,' Tim said, 'but he sure had a nifty Nikon.'

On Sunday, Mary celebrated – although that was not the word that sprang to mind – her thirty-fifth birthday. Edward had arranged for a surprise party for her at the country club. Their neighbours, Florence and Douglas Schiffer, and four other couples were waiting for her. Edward was as delighted as a small child at the look of amazement on Mary's face when she walked into the club and saw the festive table and the happy birthday banner. She did not have the heart to tell him that she had known about the party for the past two weeks. She adored Edward. *And why not? Who wouldn't?* He was attractive and intelligent and caring. His grandfather and father had been doctors, and it had never occurred to Edward to be anything else. He was the best surgeon in Junction City, a good father, and a wonderful husband.

As Mary blew out the candles on her birthday cake, she looked across at Edward and thought: *How lucky can a lady be?*

Monday morning, Mary awoke with a hangover. There had been a lot of champagne toasts the night before, and she was not used to drinking alcohol. It took an effort to get out of bed. *That champagne done me in. Never again*, she promised herself.

She eased her way downstairs and gingerly set about preparing breakfast for the children, trying to ignore the pounding in her head.

'Champagne,' Mary groaned, 'is France's vengeance against us.'

Beth walked into the room carrying an armful of books. 'Who are you talking to, Mother?'

'Myself.'

'That's weird.'

'When you're right, you're right.' Mary put a box of cereal on the table. 'I bought a new cereal for you. You're going to like it.'

Beth sat down at the kitchen table and studied the label on the cereal box. 'I can't eat this. You're trying to kill me.'

'Don't put any ideas in my head,' her mother cautioned. 'Would you please eat your breakfast?'

Tim, her ten-year-old, ran into the kitchen. He slid into a chair at the table and said, 'I'll have bacon and eggs.'

'Whatever happened to good morning?' Mary asked.

'Good morning. I'll have bacon and eggs.'

'Please.'

'Aw, come on, Mom. I'm going to be late for school.'

'I'm glad you mentioned that. Mrs Reynolds called me. You're failing maths. What do you say to that?'

'It figures.'

'Tim, is that supposed to be a joke?'

'I personally don't think it's funny,' Beth sniffed.

He made a face at his sister. 'If you want funny, look in the mirror.'

'That's enough,' Mary said. 'Behave yourselves.'

Her headache was getting worse.

Tim asked, 'Can I go to the skating rink after school, Mom?'

'You're already skating on thin ice. You're to come right home and study. How do you think it looks for a college professor to have a son who's failing maths?'

'It looks okay. You don't teach maths.'

They talk about the terrible twos, Mary thought grimly. *What about the terrible nines, tens, elevens and twelves?*

Beth said, 'Did Tim tell you he got a "D" in spelling?'

He glared at his sister. 'Haven't you ever heard of Mark Twain?'

'What does Mark Twain have to do with this?' Mary asked.

'Mark Twain said he has no respect for a man who can only spell a word one way.'

We can't win, Mary thought. *They're smarter than we are.*

She had packed a lunch for each of them, but she was concerned about Beth, who was on some kind of crazy new diet.

'Please, Beth, eat all of your lunch today.'

'If it has no artificial preservatives. I'm not going to let the greed of the food industry ruin my health.'

Whatever happened to the good old days of junk food? Mary wondered.

Tim plucked a loose paper from one of Beth's notebooks. 'Look at this!' he yelled. '"Dear Beth, let's sit together during study period. I thought of you all day yesterday and –"'

'Give that back to me!' Beth screamed. 'That's

mine.' She made a grab for Tim, and he jumped out of her reach.

He read the signature at the bottom of the note. 'Hey! It's signed Virgil. I thought you were in love with Arnold.'

Beth snatched the note away from him. 'What would you know about love?' Mary's twelve-year-old daughter demanded. 'You're a child.'

The pounding in Mary's head was becoming unbearable.

'Kids – give me a break.'

She heard the horn of the school bus outside. Tim and Beth started towards the door.

'Wait! You haven't eaten your breakfasts,' Mary said.

She followed them out into the hallway.

'No time, Mother. Got to go.'

' 'Bye, Mom.'

'It's freezing outside. Put on your coats and scarves.'

'I can't. I lost my scarf,' Tim said.

And they were gone. Mary felt drained. *Motherhood is living in the eye of a hurricane.*

She looked up as Edward came down the stairs, and she felt a glow. *Even after all these years*, Mary thought, *he's still the most attractive man I've ever known.* It was his gentleness that had first caught Mary's interest. His eyes were a soft grey, reflecting a warm intelligence, but they could turn into twin blazes when he became impassioned about something.

'Morning, darling.' He gave her a kiss. They walked into the kitchen.

'Sweetheart – would you do me a favour?'

'Sure, beautiful. Anything.'

'I want to sell the children.'

'Both of them?'

'Both of them.'

'When?'

'Today.'

'Who'd buy them?'

'Strangers. They've reached the age where I can't do anything right. Beth has become a health food freak, and your son is turning into a world-class dunce.'

Edward said thoughtfully, 'Maybe they're not our kids.'

'I hope not. I'm making oatmeal for you.'

He looked at his watch. 'Sorry, darling. No time. I'm due in surgery in half an hour. Hank Cates got tangled up in some machinery. He may lose a few fingers.'

'Isn't he too old to still be farming?'

'Don't let him hear you say that.'

Mary knew that Hank Cates had not paid her husband's bills in three years. Like most of the farmers in the community, Hank Cates was suffering from the low farm prices and the Farm Credit Administration's indifferent attitude towards the farmers. A lot of them were losing farms they had worked on all of their lives. Edward never pressed any of his patients for money, and many of them paid him with crops. The Ashleys had a cellar full of corn, potatoes and wheat. One farmer had offered to give Edward a cow in payment, but when Edward told Mary about it, she said, 'For heaven's sake, tell him the treatment is on the house.'

Mary looked at her husband now and thought again: *How lucky I am.*

'Okay,' she said. 'I may decide to keep the kids. I like their father a lot.'

'To tell you the truth, I'm rather fond of their mother.' He took her in his arms and held her close. 'Happy Birthday, plus one.'

'Do you still love me now that I'm an older woman?'

'I like older women.'

'Thanks.' Mary suddenly remembered something. 'I've got to get home early today and prepare dinner. It's our turn to have the Schiffers over.'

Bridge with their neighbours was a Monday night ritual. The fact that Douglas Schiffer was a doctor and worked with Edward at the hospital made them even closer.

Mary and Edward left the house together, bowing their heads against the relentless wind. Edward strapped himself into his Ford Granada, and watched Mary as she got behind the wheel of the station wagon.

'The highway is probably icy,' Edward called. 'Drive carefully.'

'You, too, darling.'

She blew him a kiss, and the two cars drove away from the house, Edward heading towards the hospital, and Mary driving towards the town of Manhattan, where the University was located, 16 miles away.

Two men in an automobile parked half a block from the Ashley house watched the cars leave. They waited until the vehicles were out of sight.

'Let's go.'

They drove up to the house next door to the Ashleys. Rex Olds, the driver, sat in the car while his companion walked up to the front door and rang the bell. The door was opened by an attractive brunette in her middle thirties.

'Yes? Can I help you?'

'Mrs Douglas Schiffer?'

'Yes . . . ?'

The man reached into his jacket pocket and pulled out an identification card. 'My name is Donald Zamlock. I'm with the Security Agency of the State Department.'

'Good God! Don't tell me Doug has robbed a bank!'

The agent smiled politely. 'No, ma'am. Not that we know of. I wanted to ask you a few questions about your neighbour, Mrs Ashley.'

She looked at him with sudden concern. 'Mary? What about her?'

'May I come in?'

'Yes. Of course.' Florence Schiffer led him into

the living room. 'Sit down. Would you like some coffee?'

'No, thanks. I'll only take a few minutes of your time.'

'Why would you be asking about Mary?'

He smiled reassuringly. 'This is just a routine check. She's not suspected of any wrong-doing.'

'I should hope not,' Florence Schiffer said indignantly. 'Mary Ashley is one of the nicest persons you'll ever meet.' She added, '*Have* you met her?'

'No, ma'am. This visit is confidential, and I would appreciate it if you kept it that way. How long have you known Mrs Ashley?'

'About thirteen years. Since the day she moved in next door.'

'Would you say that you know Mrs Ashley well?'

'Of course I would. Mary's my closest friend. What –?'

'Do she and her husband get along well?'

'Next to Douglas and me, they're the happiest couple I've ever known.' She thought a moment. 'I take that back. They *are* the happiest couple I've ever known.'

'I understand Mrs Ashley has two children. A girl twelve and a boy ten?'

'That's right. Beth and Tim.'

'Would you say she's a good mother?'

'She's a *great* mother. What's –?'

'Mrs Schiffer, in your opinion, is Mrs Ashley an emotionally stable person?'

'Of course she is.'

'She has no emotional problems that you are aware of?'

'Certainly not.'

'Does she drink?'

'No. She doesn't like alcohol.'

'What about drugs?'

'You've come to the wrong town, Mister. We don't have a drug problem in Junction City.'

'Mrs Ashley is married to a doctor?'

'Yes.'

'If she wanted to get drugs –'

'You're way off base. She doesn't do drugs. She doesn't snort, and she doesn't shoot up.'

He studied her a moment. 'You seem to know all the terminology.'

'I watch *Miami Vice*, like everybody else.' Florence Schiffer was getting angry. 'Do you have any more questions?'

'Mary Ashley's grandfather was born in Romania. Have you ever heard her discuss Romania?'

'Oh, once in a while she'll tell stories her grandfather told her about the old country. Her grandfather was born in Romania but he came over here when he was in his teens.'

'Have you ever heard Mrs Ashley express a negative opinion about the present Romanian government?'

'No. Not that I can remember.'

'One last question. Have you ever heard Mrs

Ashley or Dr Ashley say anything against the United States government?'

'Absolutely not!'

'Then in your estimation, they're both loyal Americans?'

'You bet they are. Would you mind telling me –?'

The man rose. 'I want to thank you for your time, Mrs Schiffer. And I'd like to impress upon you again that this matter is highly confidential. I would appreciate it if you didn't discuss it with anyone – not even your husband.'

A moment later he was out of the door. Florence Schiffer stood there staring after him. 'I don't believe this whole conversation took place,' she said aloud.

The two agents drove down Washington Street, heading north. They passed a billboard that read: 'Enjoy yourself in the land of Ah's.'

'Cute,' Rex Olds grunted.

They went by the Chamber of Commerce and the Royal Order of the Elks building, Irma's Pet Grooming and a bar called 'The Fat Chance'. The commercial buildings came to an abrupt end.

Donald Zamlock said, 'Jesus, the main street is only two blocks long. This isn't a town. It's a pit stop.'

Rex Olds said, 'To you it's a pit stop, and to me it's a pit stop, but to these people it's a town.'

Zamlock shook his head. 'It's probably a nice

place to live, but I sure as hell wouldn't want to visit here.'

The sedan pulled up in front of the State Bank and Rex Olds went inside.

He returned twenty minutes later. 'Clean,' he said, getting into the car. 'The Ashleys have seven thousand dollars in the bank, a mortgage on their house, and they pay their bills on time. The president of the bank thinks the doctor is too soft-hearted to be a good businessman, but as far as he's concerned, he's a top credit risk.'

Zamlock looked at a clipboard at his side. 'Let's check out a few more names and get back to civilization before I begin to moo.'

Douglas Schiffer was normally a pleasant, easygoing man, but at the moment there was a grim expression on his face. The Schiffers and the Ashleys were in the middle of their weekly bridge game, and the Schiffers were 10,000 points behind. For the fourth time that evening, Florence Schiffer had reneged.

Douglas Schiffer slammed down his cards. 'Florence!' he exploded, 'which side are you playing on? Do you know how much we're down?'

'I'm sorry,' she said nervously. 'I – I just can't seem to concentrate.'

'Obviously,' her husband snorted.

'Is anything bothering you?' Edward Ashley asked Florence.

'I can't tell you.'

They all looked at her in surprise. 'What does *that* mean?' her husband asked.

Florence Schiffer took a deep breath. 'Mary – it's about you.'

'What about me?'

'You're in some sort of trouble, aren't you?'

Mary stared at her. 'Trouble? No. I – what makes you think that?'

'I'm not supposed to tell. I promised.'

'You promised who?' Edward asked.

'A federal agent from Washington. He was at the house this morning asking me all kinds of questions about Mary. He made her sound like some kind of international spy.'

'What kind of questions?' Edward demanded.

'Oh, you know. Was she a loyal American? Was she a good wife and mother? Was she on drugs?'

'Why the devil would they be asking you questions like that?'

'Wait a minute,' Mary said excitedly. 'I think I know. It's about my tenure.'

'What?' Florence asked.

'I'm up for tenure at the University. The University does some sensitive government research on campus, so I suppose they have to check everyone pretty thoroughly.'

'Well, thank God that's all it is.' Florence Schiffer breathed a sigh of relief. 'I thought they were going to lock you up.'

'I hope they do,' Mary smiled. 'At Kansas State.'

'Well, now that that's out of the way,' Douglas

Schiffer said, 'can we get on with the game?' He turned to his wife. 'If you renege one more time, I'm going to put you over my knee.'

'Promises, promises.'

FIVE

Abbeywood, England

'We are meeting under the usual rules,' the chairman announced. 'No records will be kept, this meeting will never be discussed, and we will refer to one another by the code names we have been assigned.'

There were eight men inside the library of the fifteenth-century Claymore Castle. Two armed men in plainclothes, bundled up in heavy overcoats, kept vigil outside, while a third man guarded the door to the library. The eight men inside the room had arrived at the site separately, a short time earlier.

The chairman continued. 'The Controller has received some disturbing information. Marin Groza is preparing a coup against Alexandros Ionescu. A group of senior army officers in Romania has decided to back Groza. This time he could very well be successful.'

Odin spoke up. 'How would that affect our plan?'

'It could destroy it. It would open too many bridges to the West.'

Freyr said, 'Then we must prevent it from happening.'

Balder asked, 'How?'

'We assassinate Groza,' the chairman replied.

'That's impossible. Ionescu's men have made half a dozen attempts that we know of, and they've all failed. His villa seems to be impregnable. Anyway, no one in this room can afford to be involved in an assassination attempt.'

'We wouldn't be directly involved,' the chairman said.

'Then how?'

'The Controller discovered a confidential dossier that concerns an international terrorist who's for hire.'

'Abul Abbas, the man who organized the hijacking of the *Achille Lauro*?'

'No. There's a new gun in town, gentlemen. A better one. He's called Angel.'

'Never heard of him,' Sigmund said.

'Exactly. His credentials are most impressive. According to the Controller's file, Angel was involved in the *Sikh Khalistan* assassination in India. He helped the *Macheteros* terrorists in Puerto Rico, and the *Khmer Rouge* in Cambodia. He's master-minded the assassination of half a dozen army officers in Israel and the Israelis have offered a million-dollar reward for him, dead or alive.'

'He sounds promising,' Thor said. 'Can we get him?'

'He's expensive. If he agrees to take the contract, it will cost us two million dollars.'

Freyr whistled, then shrugged. 'That can be handled. We'll take it from the general fund we've set up.'

'How do we get to this Angel person?' Sigmund asked.

'All his contacts are handled through his mistress, a woman named Neusa Muñez.'

'Where do we find her?'

'She lives in Argentina. Angel has set her up in an apartment in Buenos Aires.'

Thor said, 'What would the next step be? Who would get in touch with her for us?'

The chairman replied, 'The Controller has suggested a man named Harry Lantz.'

'That name sounds familiar.'

The chairman said drily, 'Yes. He's been in the newspapers. Harry Lantz is a maverick. He was thrown out of the CIA for setting up his own drug business in Viet Nam. While he was with the CIA, he did a tour in South America, so he knows the territory. He'd be a perfect go-between.' He paused. 'I suggest we take a vote. All those in favour of hiring Angel please raise your hands.'

Eight well-manicured hands went into the air.

'Then it's settled.' The chairman rose. 'The meeting is adjourned. Please observe the usual precautions.'

It was a Monday, and Constable Leslie Hanson was having a picnic in the greenhouse on the castle's grounds, where he had no right to be. He was not alone, he later had to explain to his superiors. It was warm in the greenhouse, and his companion, Annie, a buxom country lass, had prevailed upon the good constable to bring a picnic hamper.

'You supply the food,' Annie giggled, 'and I'll supply the dessert.'

The 'dessert' was five feet six inches, with beautiful, shapely breasts and hips that a man could sink his teeth into.

Unfortunately, in the middle of dessert Constable Hanson's concentration was distracted by a limousine driving out of the castle gate.

'This bloody place is supposed to be closed on Mondays,' he muttered.

'Don't lose your place,' Annie coaxed.

'Not likely, pet.'

Twenty minutes later, the constable heard a second car leaving. This time he was curious enough to get up and peer out of the window. It looked like an official limousine, with darkened windows that concealed the passengers.

'Are you comin', then, Leslie?'

'Right. I just can't figure out who could be in

the castle. Except for tour days, it's closed down.'

'Exactly what's going to happen to me, love, if you don't hop it.'

Twenty minutes later when Constable Hanson heard the third car leave, his libido lost out to his instincts as a policeman. There were five more vehicles, all limousines, all spaced twenty minutes apart. Because one of the cars stopped long enough to let a deer run by, Constable Hanson was able to note the licence-plate number.

'It's supposed to be your bloody day off,' Annie complained.

'This could be important,' the constable said. And even as he said it, he wondered whether he was going to report it.

'What were you doing at Claymore Castle?' Sergeant Twill demanded.

'Sight-seeing, sir.'

'The castle was closed.'

'Yes, sir. The greenhouse was open.'

'So you decided to sight-see in the greenhouse?'

'Yes, sir.'

'Alone, of course?'

'Well, to tell the truth –'

'Spare me the grotty details, Constable. What made you suspicious of the cars?'

'Their behaviour, sir.'

'Cars don't behave, Hanson. Drivers do.'

'Of course, sir. The drivers seemed very cautious. The cars left at intervals of twenty minutes.'

'You are aware, of course, that there are probably a thousand innocent explanations. In fact, Hanson, the only one who doesn't seem to have an innocent explanation is yourself.'

'Yes, sir. But I thought I should report this.'

'Right. Is this the licence number you got?'

'Yes, sir.'

'Very well. Be off with you.' He thought of one witticism to add. 'Remember – it's dangerous to throw stones at people if you're in a glass house.' He chuckled at his *bon mot* all morning.

When the report on the licence plate came back, Sergeant Twill decided that Hanson had made a mistake. He took his information upstairs to Inspector Pakula and explained the background.

'I wouldn't have bothered you with this, Inspector, but the licence-plate number –'

'Yes. I see. I'll take care of it.'

'Thank you, sir.'

At SIS headquarters, Inspector Pakula had a brief meeting with one of the senior heads of the British Secret Intelligence Service, a beefy, florid-faced man, Sir Alex Hyde-White.

'You were quite right to bring this to my attention,' Sir Alex smiled, 'but I'm afraid it's nothing more sinister than trying to arrange a Royal vacation trip without the press being aware of it.'

'I'm sorry to have bothered you about this, sir.' Inspector Pakula rose to his feet.

'Not at all, Inspector. Shows your branch is on its toes. What did you say the name of that young constable was?'

'Hanson, sir. Leslie Hanson.'

When the door closed behind Inspector Pakula, Sir Alex Hyde-White picked up a red telephone on his desk. 'I have a message for Balder. We have a small problem. I'll explain it at the next meeting. Meanwhile, I want you to arrange for three transfers. Police Sergeant Twill, an Inspector Pakula, and Constable Leslie Hanson. Spread them out a few days. I want them sent to separate posts, as far from London as possible. I'll inform the Controller and see if he wants to take any further action.'

In his hotel room in New York, Harry Lantz was awakened in the middle of the night by the ringing of the telephone.

Who the hell knows I'm here? he wondered. He looked blearily at the bedside clock, then snatched up the phone. 'It's four o'fucking clock in the morning! Who the –?'

A soft voice at the other end of the line began speaking, and Lantz sat upright in bed, his heart beginning to pound. 'Yes, sir,' he said. 'Yes, sir . . . No, sir, but I can arrange to make myself free.' He listened for a long time. Finally he said, 'Yes, sir.

I understand. I'll be on the first plane to Buenos Aires. Thank you, sir.'

He replaced the receiver, reached over to the bedside table and lit a cigarette. His hands were trembling. The man he had just spoken to was one of the most powerful men in the world, and what he had asked Harry to do . . . *What the hell is going down?* Harry Lantz asked himself. *Something big.* The man was going to pay him $50,000 to deliver a message. It would be fun going back to Argentina. Harry Lantz loved the South American women. *I know a dozen bitches there with hot pants who would rather fuck than eat.*

The day was starting out great.

At 9 a.m. Lantz picked up the telephone and dialled the number of Aerolineas Argentinas. 'What time is your first flight to Buenos Aires?'

The 747 arrived at the Ezeiza Airport in Buenos Aires at 5 p.m. the following afternoon. It had been a long flight, but Harry Lantz had not minded it. *Fifty thousand dollars for delivering a message.* He felt a surge of excitement as the wheels lightly kissed the ground. He had not been to Argentina for almost five years. It would be fun to renew old acquaintances.

As Harry Lantz stepped out of the plane, the blast of hot air startled him for a moment. *Of course. It's summer here.*

During the taxi ride into the city, Lantz was

amused to see that the graffiti scrawled on the sides of buildings and sidewalks had not changed. *Plebiscito las pelotas* (Fuck the Plebiscite). *Militares, Asesinos* (Army, Assassins). *Tenemos hambre* (We are hungry). *Marihuana na libre* (Free pot). *Droga, sexo y muncho rock* (Drugs, sex and rock 'n' roll). *Juicio y castigo a los culpables* (Trial and punishment for the guilty).

Yes, it was good to be back.

Siesta was over and the streets were crowded with people lazily walking to and from appointments. When the taxi arrived at the Hotel El Conquistador in the heart of the fashionable Barrio Norte sector, Lantz paid the driver with a million peso note.

'Keep the change,' he said. Their money was a joke.

He registered at the desk in the huge, modern lobby, picked up a copy of the *Buenos Aires Herald* and *La Prensa*, and let the assistant manager show him to his suite. Sixty dollars a day for a bedroom, bathroom, living room and kitchen, air-conditioned, with television. *In Washington, this set-up would cost an arm and a leg*, Harry Lantz thought. *I'll take care of my business with this Neusa broad tomorrow, and stay around a few days and enjoy myself.*

It was more than two weeks before Harry Lantz was able to track down Neusa Muñez.

His search began with the city telephone directories. Lantz started with the places in the heart of the city: Plaza Constitución, Plaza San Martin, Barrio Norte, Catalinas Norte. None of them had a listing for a Neusa Muñez. Nor was there any listing in the outlying areas of Bahia Blanca or Mar del Plaza.

Where the hell is she? Lantz wondered. He took to the streets, looking up old contacts.

He walked into La Biela, and the bartender cried out, '*Señor* Lantz! *Por dios* – I heard you were dead.'

Lantz grinned. 'I was, but I missed you so much, Antonio, I came back.'

'What are you doing in Buenos Aires?'

Lantz let his voice grow pensive. 'I came here to find an old girl friend. We were supposed to get married, but her family moved away and I lost track of her. Her name is Neusa Muñez.'

The bartender scratched his head. 'Never heard of her. *Lo siento.*'

'Would you ask around, Antonio?'

'*Por qué no?*'

Lantz's next stop was to see a friend at police head-quarters.

'Lantz! Harry Lantz! *Dios! Qué pasa?*'

'Hello, Jorge. Nice to see you, *amigo.*'

'Last I heard about you, the CIA kicked you out.'

Harry Lantz laughed. 'No way, my friend. They begged me to stay. I quit to go into business for myself.'

'*Si?* What business are you in?'

'I opened up my own detective agency. As a matter of fact, that's what brings me to Buenos Aires. A client of mine died a few weeks ago. He left his daughter a bundle of money, and I'm trying to locate her. All the information I have on her is that she lives in an apartment somewhere in Buenos Aires.'

'What's her name?'

'Neusa Muñez.'

'Wait here a moment.'

The moment stretched into half an hour.

'Sorry, *amigo*. I can't help you. She is not in our computer or in any of our files.'

'Oh, well. If you should come across any information about her, I'm at the El Conquistador.'

'*Bueno.*'

The bars were next. Old familiar haunts. The Pepe Gonzalez and Almeida, Café Tabac.

'*Buenas tardes, amigo. Soy de los Estados Unidos. Estoy buscando una mujer. El nombre es* Neusa Muñez. *Es una emergencia.*'

'*Lo siento, señor. No la conozco.*'

The answer was the same everywhere. *No one has ever heard of the fucking broad.*

Harry Lantz wandered around La Boca, the colourful waterfront area where one could see old ships rusting at anchor in the river. No one around there knew of Neusa Muñez. For the first time,

Harry Lantz began to feel he might be on a wild goose chase.

It was at the Pilar, a small bar in the barrios of Flores, that his luck suddenly changed. It was a Friday night, and the bar was filled with working men. It took Lantz ten minutes to get the bartender's attention. Before Lantz was half way through his prepared speech, the bartender said, 'Neusa Muñez? *Si.* I know her. If she wishes to talk to you, she will come here *mañana*, about midnight.'

The following evening, Harry Lantz returned to the Pilar at eleven o'clock, watching the bar gradually fill up. As midnight approached, he found himself getting more and more nervous. What if she did not show up? What if it was the wrong Neusa Muñez?

Lantz watched as a group of giggling young women came into the bar. They joined some men at a table. *She's got to show up*, Lantz thought. *If she doesn't, I can kiss the fifty grand goodbye.*

He wondered what she looked like. She had to be a stunner. He was authorized to offer her boyfriend, Angel, a cool two million dollars to assassinate someone, so Angel was probably up to his ass in millions. He would be well able to afford a beautiful young mistress. Hell, he could probably afford a dozen of them. This Neusa had to be an actress or model. *Who knows, maybe I can have a little fun with her before I leave town. Nothing like com-bining business and pleasure*, Harry Lantz thought happily.

The door opened and Lantz looked up expectantly. A woman was walking in alone. She was middle-aged and unattractive, with a fat, bloated body and huge, pendulous breasts that swayed as she walked. Her face was pockmarked, and she had dyed blonde hair, but her dark complexion indicated *mestizo* blood inherited from an Indian ancestor who had been bedded by a Spaniard. She was dressed in an ill-fitting skirt and sweater meant for a much younger woman. *A hooker down on her luck*, Lantz decided. *But who the hell would want to fuck her?*

The woman looked around the bar with vacant, listless eyes. She nodded vaguely to several people and then pushed her way through the crowd. She walked up to the bar.

'Wanna buy me a drink?' She had a heavy Spanish accent, and up close she was even more unattractive.

She looks like a fat, unmilked cow, Lantz thought. *And she's drunk.* 'Get lost, sister.'

'Esteban say you are lookin' for me, no?'

He stared at her. 'Who?'

'Esteban. The bartender.'

Harry Lantz still could not accept it. 'He must have made a mistake. I'm looking for Neusa Muñez.'

'*Si. Yo soy* Neusa Muñez.'

But the wrong one, Harry Lantz thought. *Shit!*
'Are you Angel's friend?'

She smiled drunkenly. *'Si.'*

Harry Lantz recovered swiftly. 'Well, well.' He
forced a smile. 'Can we go to a corner table and
talk?'

She nodded indifferently. 'Ess okay.'

They fought their way across the smoky bar,
and when they were seated, Harry Lantz said, 'I'd
like to talk about –'

'You buy me a rum, *si*?'

Lantz nodded. 'Sure thing.'

A waiter appeared, wearing a filthy apron, and
Lantz said, 'One rum and a Scotch and soda.'

Muñez said, 'Make mine a double, huh?'

When the waiter left, Lantz turned to the woman
seated beside him. 'I want to meet with Angel.'

She studied him with her dull, watery eyes.
'Wha' for?'

Lantz lowered his voice. 'I have a little present
for him.'

'Si? What kin' a presen'?'

'Two million dollars.' Their drinks arrived.
Harry Lantz raised his glass and said, 'Cheers.'

'Yeah.' She downed her drink in one gulp. 'Wha'
for you wanna give Angel two million dollars?'

'That's something I'll discuss with him
in person.'

'Tha's not possible. Angel, he don' talk to
nobody.'

'Lady, for two million dollars –'

69

'Kin I have 'nother rum? A double, huh?'

My God, she already looks like she's about to pass out. 'Sure.' Lantz summoned the waiter and ordered the drink. 'Have you known Angel a long time?' He made his tone casual.

She shrugged. 'Yeah.'

'He must be an interesting man.'

Her vacant eyes were fixed on a spot on the table in front of her.

Jesus! Harry Lantz thought. *It's like trying to have a conversation with a fucking wall.*

Her drink arrived, and she finished it in one long swallow.

She has the body of a cow and the manners of a pig. 'How soon can I talk to Angel?'

Neusa Muñez struggled to her feet. 'I tol' you, he don' talk to nobody. *Adios.*'

Harry Lantz was filled with a sudden panic. 'Hey! Wait a minute! Don't go.'

She stopped and looked down at him with bleary eyes. 'Wha' you wan'?'

'Sit down,' Lantz said slowly, 'and I'll tell you what I want.'

She sat down heavily. 'I need a rum, huh?'

Harry Lantz was baffled. *What the fuck kind of man is this Angel? His mistress is not only the ugliest broad in all of South America, but she's a lush.*

Lantz did not like dealing with drunks. They were too unreliable. On the other hand, he hated the thought of losing his $50,000 commission. He watched as Muñez gulped her drink. He wondered how many she had had before coming to meet him.

Lantz smiled and said reasonably, 'Neusa, if I can't talk to Angel, how can I do business with him?'

'Ess simple. You tell me what you wan'. I tell Angel. If he say *si*, I tell you *si*. If he say *no*, I tell you *no*.'

Harry Lantz distrusted using her as a go-between, but he had no choice. 'You've heard of Marin Groza.'

'No.'

Of course she hadn't. Because it wasn't the name of a rum. This stupid bitch was going to get the message all wrong and screw up the deal for him.

'I need a drink, huh?'

He patted her fat hand. 'Certainly.' He ordered another double rum. 'Angel will know who Groza is. You just say Marin Groza. He'll know.'

'Yeah? Then wha'?'

She was even stupider than she looked. What the fuck did she think Angel was supposed to do for two million dollars? Kiss the guy? Harry Lantz said carefully, 'The people who sent me want him blown away.'

She blinked. 'Wha's "blown away"?'

Christ! 'Killed.'

'Oh.' She nodded indifferently. 'I'll ass' Angel.' Her voice was beginning to slur even more. 'Wha' you say the man's name is?'

71

He wanted to shake her. 'Groza. Marin Groza.'

'Yeah. My baby's outta town. I'll call him tonight 'n meet you here tomorrow. Kin I have 'nother rum?'

Neusa Muñez was turning out to be a nightmare.

The following evening, Harry Lantz sat at the same table in the bar from midnight until four in the morning, when the bar closed. Muñez did not appear.

'Do you know where she lives?' Lantz asked the bartender.

The bartender looked at him with innocent eyes. *'Quien sabe?'*

The bitch had fouled everything up. How could a man who was supposed to be as smart as Angel get hooked up with such a rum dummy? Harry Lantz prided himself on being a pro. He was too smart to walk into a deal like this without first checking it out. He had cautiously asked around, and the information that impressed him most was that the Israelis had put a price of a million dollars on Angel's head. A million bucks would buy a lifetime's worth of booze and young hookers. Well, he could forget about that and he could forget about his $50,000. His only link to Angel had been broken. He would have to call The Man and tell him he had failed.

I won't call him yet, Harry Lantz decided. *Maybe she'll come back here. Maybe the other bars will run out of rum. Maybe I should have had my ass kicked for saying yes to this fucking assignment.*

SIX

The following night at eleven o'clock, Harry Lantz was seated at the same table in the Pilar, intermittently chewing peanuts and his fingernails. At 2 a.m. he saw Neusa Muñez stumble in the door, and Harry's heart soared. He watched as she made her way over to his table.

'Hi,' she mumbled, and slumped into a chair.

'What happened to you?' Harry demanded. It was all he could do to control his anger.

She blinked. 'Huh?'

'You were supposed to meet me here last night.'

'Yeah?'

'We had a date, Neusa.'

'Oh. I went to a movie with a girl frien'. There's this new movie, see? Ess 'bout this man who falls in love with this fuckin' nun an' –'

Lantz was so frustrated he could have wept. *What could Angel possibly see in this dumb, drunken bitch? She must have a golden pussy*, Lantz decided. 'Neusa – did you remember to talk to Angel?'

She looked at him vacantly, trying to understand the question. 'Angel? *Si.* Kin I have a drink, huh?'

He ordered a double rum for her and a double Scotch for himself. He needed it desperately. 'What did Angel say, Ñeusa?'

'Angel? Oh, he say yeah. Ess okay.'

Harry Lantz felt a surge of relief. 'That's wonderful!' He no longer gave a damn about his messenger boy mission. He had thought of a better idea. This drunken bitch was going to lead him to Angel. One million dollars reward money.

He watched her slop down her drink, spilling some of it down her already soiled blouse. 'What else did Angel say?'

Her brow knit in concentration. 'Angel, he say he wanna know who your people are.'

Lantz gave her a winning smile. 'You tell him that's confidential, Neusa. I can't give him that information.'

She nodded, indifferent. 'Then Angel say to tell you to fuck off. Kin I have a rum 'fore I go?'

Harry Lantz's mind started working at top speed. If she left, he was sure he would never see her again. 'I'll tell you what I'll do, Neusa. I'll telephone the people I'm working for, and if they give me permission, I'll give you a name. Okay?'

She shrugged. 'I don' care.'

'No,' Lantz explained patiently, 'but Angel does. So you tell him I'll have an answer for him by tomorrow. Is there some place I can reach you?'

'I guess so.'

He was making progress. 'Where?'

'Here.'

Her drink arrived, and he watched her gulp it down like an animal.

Lantz wanted to kill her.

Lantz made the telephone call collect, so it could not be traced, from a public telephone booth on Calvo Street. It had taken him one hour to get through.

'No,' the Controller said. 'I told you that no names are to be mentioned.'

'Yes, sir. But there's a problem. Neusa Muñez, Angel's mistress, says he's willing to make a deal, but he won't move without knowing who he's dealing with. Naturally, I told her I had to check it out with you first.'

'What is this woman like?'

The Controller was not a man to play games with. 'She's fat and ugly and stupid, sir.'

'It's much too dangerous for my name to be used.'

Harry Lantz could feel the deal slipping away from him. 'Yes, sir,' he said earnestly. 'I understand. The only thing is, sir, Angel's reputation is based on his being able to keep his mouth shut. If he ever started talking, he wouldn't last five minutes in his business.'

There was a long silence. 'You have a point.' There was another silence, even longer. 'Very well.

You may give Angel my name. But he is never to divulge it, and never to contact me directly. He'll work only through you.'

Harry Lantz could have danced. 'Yes, sir. I'll tell him. Thank you, sir.' He hung up, a big grin on his face. He was going to collect the $50,000.

And then the million-dollar reward.

When Harry Lantz met Neusa Muñez late that evening, he immediately ordered a double rum for her and said, happily, 'Everything's set. I got permission.'

She looked at him indifferently. 'Yeah?'

He told her the name of his employer. It was a household word, and he expected her to be impressed.

She shrugged. 'Never heard'a him.'

'Neusa, the people I work for want this done as quickly as possible. Marin Groza is hiding out in a villa in Neuilly, and –'

'Where?'

God Almighty! He was trying to communicate with a drunken moron. He said patiently, 'It's a little town outside of Paris. Angel will know.'

'I need 'nother drink.'

An hour later, Neusa was still drinking. And this time Harry Lantz was encouraging her. *Not that she needs much encouragement*, Lantz thought. *When she's drunk enough, she's going to lead me to her boyfriend. The rest will be easy.*

He looked over at Neusa Muñez staring filmy-eyed into her drink.

It shouldn't be hard to catch Angel. He may be tough, but he can't be very bright. 'When is Angel coming back to town?'

She focused her watery eyes on him. 'Nex' week.'

Harry Lantz took her hand and stroked it. 'Why don't you and I go back to your place?' he asked softly.

'Okay.'

He was in.

Neusa Muñez lived in a shabby, two-room apartment in the Belgrano district of Buenos Aires. The apartment was messy and unkempt, like its tenant. When they walked through the door, Neusa made straight for the little bar in the corner. She was unsteady on her feet.

'How 'bout a drink?'

'Not for me,' Lantz said. 'You go ahead.' He watched as she poured out a drink and downed it. *She's the most ugly, repulsive bitch I've ever met*, he thought, *but the million dollars is going to be beautiful.*

He looked around the apartment. There were some books piled on a coffee table. He picked them up, one by one, hoping to get an insight into Angel's mind. The titles surprised him: *Gabriela*, by Jorge Amado; *Fire From The Mountain*, by Omar Cabezas; *One Hundred Years of Solitude*, by Garcia

Marquez; *At Night The Cats*, by Antonio Cisneros. So Angel was an intellectual. The books did not fit with the apartment or the woman.

Lantz walked over to her and put his arms around her huge, flabby waist. 'You're damned cute, do you know that?' He reached up and stroked her breasts. They were the size of watermelons. Lantz hated big-breasted women. 'You've got a really great body.'

'Huh?' Her eyes were glazed.

Lantz's arms moved down and stroked her fat thighs through the thin cotton dress she wore. 'How does that feel?' he whispered.

'Wha'?'

He was getting nowhere. He had to think of an approach that would get this amazon into bed. But he knew he had to make his move carefully. If he offended her, she might go back and report him to Angel, and that would be the end of the deal. He could try to sweet talk her, but she was too drunk to know what he was saying.

As Lantz was desperately trying to think of a clever gambit, Neusa mumbled, 'Wanna fuck?'

He grinned in relief. 'That's a great idea, baby.'

'Come on 'n the bedroom.'

She was stumbling as Lantz followed her into the small bedroom. It contained one closet with the door ajar, a large unmade bed, two chairs and a bureau with a cracked mirror above it. It was the closet that caught Harry Lantz's attention. In it he glimpsed a row of men's suits hanging on a rack.

Neusa was at the side of the bed, fumbling with the buttons on her blouse. Under ordinary circumstances, Harry Lantz would have been at her side, undressing her, caressing her body and murmuring exciting indecencies into her ear. But the sight of Muñez sickened him. He stood there watching as her skirt dropped to the floor. She was wearing nothing under it. Naked, she was uglier than when dressed. Her huge breasts sagged, and her protruding stomach shook like jelly as she moved. Her fat thighs were a mass of cellulite. *She's the grossest thing I've ever seen*, Lantz thought. *Think positively*, Lantz told himself. *This will be over in a few minutes. The million bucks will last forever.*

Slowly, he forced himself to get undressed. She was propped up in bed, like a leviathan, waiting for him, and he crawled in beside her.

'What do you like?' he asked.

'Huh? Choc'late. I like choc'late.'

She was drunker than he had thought. *That's good. It will make things easier.* He began to caress her flabby, fish-white body. 'You're a very pretty woman, hon. You know that?'

'Yeah?'

'I like you a lot, Neusa.' His hands moved down towards the hairy mound between her fat legs, and he began to make small, titillating circles. 'I'll bet you live an exciting life.'

'Huh?'

'I mean – being Angel's girl friend. That must

be really interesting. Tell me, baby, what's Angel like?'

There was a silence, and he wondered if Neusa had fallen asleep. He inserted his fingers in the soft, damp cleft between her legs, and felt her stir.

'Don't go to sleep, sweetheart. Not yet. What kind of man is Angel? Is he handsome?'

'Rich. Angel, he's rich.'

Lantz's hand continued its work. 'Is he good to you?'

'Yeah. Angel's good t' me.'

'I'm going to be good to you, too, baby.' His voice was soft. His problem was that everything was soft. What he needed was a million-dollar erection. He started thinking about the Dolly sisters and some of the things they had done to him. He visualized them working on his naked body with their tongues and fingers and nipples, and his penis began to grow hard. He quickly rolled over on top of Neusa and inserted himself into her. *God, it's like sticking it in a fucking pudding*, Harry Lantz thought. 'Does that feel good?'

'Ess okay, I guess.'

He could have strangled her. There were dozens of beautiful women around the world who were thrilled by his lovemaking, and this fat bitch was saying *Ess okay, I guess*.

He began moving his hips back and forth. 'Tell me about Angel. Who are his friends?'

Her voice was drowsy. 'Angel got no fren's. I'm his fren'.'

'Of course you are, babe. Does Angel live here with you, or does he have his own place?'

Neusa closed her eyes. 'Hey, I'm sleepy. When you gonna come?'

Never, he thought. *Not with this cow*. 'I already came,' Lantz lied.

'Then le's go to sleep.'

He rolled off her and lay at her side, fuming. *Why couldn't Angel have had a normal mistress? Someone young and beautiful and hot-blooded.* Then he would have had no trouble getting the information he needed. But this stupid bitch –! Still . . . there were other ways.

Lantz lay there quietly for a long time, until he was certain Neusa was asleep. Then he carefully arose from the bed and padded over to the closet. He switched the closet light on and closed the door so the light would not awaken the snoring behemoth.

There were a dozen suits and sports outfits hanging on the rack, and six pairs of men's shoes on the floor. Lantz opened the jackets and examined the labels. The suits were all custom-made by Herrera, Avenue La Plata. The shoes were made by Vill. *I've hit the jackpot!* Lantz gloated. *They'll have a record of Angel's address. I'll go to the shop first thing in the morning and ask a few questions.* A warning sounded in his mind. *No. No questions.* He had to be more clever than that. He was, after all, dealing with a world-class assassin. It would be safer to let Neusa lead him to Angel. *Then all*

I have to do is tip off my friends in the Mossad and collect the reward. I'll show Ned Tillingast and the rest of the fucking CIA bunch that old Harry Lantz hasn't lost his touch. All the bright boys have been chasing their asses trying to find Angel, and I'm the only one smart enough to pull it off.

He thought he heard a sound from the bed. He carefully peeked out of the closet door, but Neusa was still asleep.

Lantz turned out the closet light and walked over to the bed. Muñez's eyes were closed. Lantz tiptoed to the bureau and began looking through the drawers, hoping to find a photograph of Angel. That would be a help. No luck. He crept back into bed. Neusa was snoring loudly.

When Harry Lantz finally drifted off to sleep, his dreams were filled with visions of a white yacht crowded with beautiful, naked girls with small, firm breasts.

In the morning when Harry Lantz awakened, Neusa was gone. For an instant, Lantz panicked. Had she already left to meet Angel? He heard noises in the kitchen. He hurried out of bed and slipped into his clothes. Neusa was at the stove.

'*Beunos dias,*' Lantz said.

'Wan' coffee?' Neusa mumbled. 'I can't fix no breakfast. I got 'n appointment.'

With Angel. Harry Lantz tried to hide his excitement. 'That's fine. I'm not hungry. Why don't you go and keep your appointment and we'll meet for dinner tonight.' He put his arms around her, fondling her pendulous breasts. 'Where would you like to have dinner? Nothing but the best for my girl.' *I should have been an actor*, Lantz thought.

'I don' care.'

'Do you know Chiquin on Cangallo Street?'

'No.'

'You'll like it. Why don't I pick you up here at eight o'clock? I have a lot of business to attend to today.' He had no business to attend to.

'Okay.'

It took all his willpower to lean over and kiss Neusa goodbye. Her lips were flabby and wet and disgusting. 'Eight o'clock.'

Lantz walked out of the apartment and hailed a taxi. He hoped Neusa was watching from the window.

'Turn right at the next corner,' he instructed the driver.

When they had turned the corner, Harry Lantz said, 'I'll get out here.'

The driver looked at him in surprise. 'You wish to ride only one block, *señor*?'

'Right. I have a bad leg. War wound.'

Harry Lantz paid him, then hurried back to a tobacconist's shop across from Neusa's apartment building. He lit a cigarette and waited.

Twenty minutes later, Neusa came out of the apartment building. Harry watched as she waddled down the street, and he followed her at a careful distance. There was no chance of his losing her. It was like following the *Lusitania*.

Neusa Muñez seemed to be in no hurry. She moved down Florida Street, past the Spanish Library, and plodded along the Avenida Cordoba. Lantz watched as she walked into Berenes, a leather shop on San Martin. He stood across the street and observed her chatting with a male clerk. Lantz wondered whether the shop could be a connection with Angel. He made a mental note of it.

Neusa came out a few minutes later carrying a small package. Her next stop was at a *heladeria* on Corrientes, for an ice cream. She walked down San Martin, moving slowly. She seemed to be strolling aimlessly with no particular destination in mind.

What the hell happened to her appointment? Lantz wondered. *Where is Angel?* He did not believe Neusa's statement that Angel was out of town. His instincts told him that Angel was somewhere nearby.

Lantz suddenly realized that Neusa Muñez was not in sight. She had turned a corner ahead and disappeared. He quickened his step. When Lantz rounded the corner, she was nowhere to be seen. There were small shops on both sides of the street, and Lantz moved carefully, his eyes searching everywhere, fearful that Neusa might see him before he saw her.

He finally spied her in a *fiambreria*, a delicatessen, buying groceries. Were they for her, or was she expecting someone at her apartment for lunch? Someone named Angel.

From a distance, Lantz watched Neusa enter a *verduleria* and buy fruit and vegetables. He trailed her back to her apartment building. As far as he could tell, there had been no suspicious contacts.

Harry Lantz watched Neusa's building from across the street for the next four hours, moving around to make himself as inconspicuous as possible. Finally he decided that Angel was not going to show up. *Maybe I can get some more information out of her tonight*, Lantz thought, *without fucking her*. The idea of having to make love to Neusa again sickened him.

In the Oval Office at the White House, it was evening. It had been a long day for Paul Ellison. The entire world seemed to be composed of committees and councils and urgent cables and conclaves and sessions and he had not had a moment to himself until now. Well, *almost* to himself. Stanton Rogers was sitting across from him, and the President found himself relaxing for the first time that day.

'I'm keeping you from your family, Stan.'

'That's all right, Paul.'

'I wanted to talk to you about the Mary Ashley investigation. How is it coming?'

'It's almost completed. We'll have a final check

86

on her by tomorrow or the next day. So far it looks very good. I'm getting excited about the idea. I think it's going to work.'

'We'll make it work. Would you like another drink?'

'No, thanks. Unless you need me for anything else, I'm taking Barbara to an opening at the Kennedy Center.'

'You go ahead,' Paul Ellison said. 'Alice and I are due to entertain some relatives of hers.'

'Please give my love to Alice,' Stanton Rogers said. He rose.

'And you give mine to Barbara.' He watched Stanton Rogers leave. The President's thoughts turned to Mary Ashley.

When Harry Lantz arrived at Neusa's apartment that evening to take her out to dinner, there was no answer to his knock. He felt a moment of consternation. Had she walked out on him?

He tried the door, and it was unlocked. Was Angel here to meet him? Perhaps he had decided to discuss the contract face to face. Harry assumed a brisk, businesslike manner and walked in.

The room was empty. 'Hello.' Only an echo. He went into the bedroom. Neusa was lying across the bed, drunk.

'You dumb –' He caught himself. He must not forget that this stupid, drunken broad was his gold mine. He put his hands on her shoulders and tried to rouse her.

She opened her eyes. 'Wha'sa matter?'

'I'm worried about you,' Lantz said. His voice throbbed with sincerity. 'I hate to see you unhappy, and I think you're drinking because someone is making you unhappy. I'm your friend. You can tell me all about it. It's Angel, isn't it?'

'Angel,' she mumbled.

'I'm sure he's a nice man,' Harry Lantz said soothingly. 'You two probably had a little mis-understanding, right?'

He tried to straighten her out on the bed. *It's like beaching a whale*, Lantz thought.

Lantz sat down beside her. 'Tell me about Angel,' Lantz said. 'What's he doing to you?'

Neusa stared up at him, bleary-eyed, trying to focus on him. 'Le's fuck.'

Oh, Jesus! It was going to be a long night. 'Sure. Great idea.' Reluctantly, Lantz began to undress.

When Harry Lantz awoke in the morning alone in bed, memories came flooding into his brain, and he felt sick to his stomach.

Neusa had awakened him in the middle of the night. 'You know wha' I wan' you to do to me?' she mumbled. She told him.

He had listened in disbelief, but he had done the things she asked him to do. He could not afford to antagonize her. She was a sick, wild animal, and Lantz wondered whether Angel had ever done those things for her. The thought of what he had gone through made Lantz want to vomit.

He heard Neusa singing off-key in the bathroom. He was not sure he could face her. *I've had enough*, Lantz thought. *If she doesn't tell me this morning where Angel is, I'm going to his tailor and shoemaker.*

He threw back the covers and went in to Neusa. She was standing in front of the bathroom mirror. Her hair was in fat curlers, and she looked, if possible, even more unattractive than before.

'You and I are going to have a talk,' Lantz said firmly.

'Sure.' Neusa pointed to the bathtub full of water. 'I fix a bath for you. When you're finish', I fix breakfast.'

Lantz was impatient, but he knew he must not press too hard.

'You like omelettes?'

He had no appetite. 'Yeah. Sounds great.'

'I make good omelettes. Angel teach me.'

Lantz watched as she started to take the huge, lumpy curlers out of her hair. He stepped into the bathtub.

Neusa picked up a large, electric dryer, plugged it in, and began drying her hair.

Lantz lay back in the warm tub thinking: *Maybe I should get a gun and take Angel myself. If I let the Israelis do it, there'll probably be a fucking inquiry into who gets the reward. This way there won't be any question. I'll just tell them where to pick up his body.*

Neusa said something, but Harry Lantz could barely hear her over the roar of the hair dryer.

'What did you say?' he called out.

Neusa moved to the side of the tub. 'I got a presen' for you from Angel.'

She dropped the electric hair dryer into the water and stood there watching as Lantz's body twitched in a dance of death.

SEVEN

President Paul Ellison put down the last security report on Mary Ashley and said, 'Not a blemish, Stan.'

'I know. I think she's the perfect candidate. Of course, State isn't going to be happy.'

'We'll send them a crying towel. Now let's hope the Senate will back us up.'

Mary Ashley's office in Kedzie Hall was a small, pleasant room lined with bookcases crammed with reference books on Middle European countries. The furniture was sparse, consisting of a battered desk with a swivel chair, a small table at the window, piled with examination papers, a ladder-back chair, and a reading lamp. On the wall behind the desk was a map of the Balkans. An ancient photograph of Mary's grandfather hung on the wall. It had been taken around the turn of the century, and the figure in the photograph was standing in a stiff, unnatural pose, dressed in the clothes of the period. The picture was one of Mary's treasures. It had been her grandfather who had instilled in her a deep curiosity about Romania. He had told her romantic stories of Queen Marie, and baronesses and princesses; tales of Albert, the Prince Consort of England, and Alexander II, Tsar of Russia, and dozens of other thrilling characters.

Somewhere in our background there is royal blood. If the revolution had not come, you would have been a princess.

She used to have dreams about it.

Mary was in the middle of grading examination papers when the door opened and Dean Hunter walked in.

'Good morning, Mrs Ashley. Do you have a moment?' It was the first time the Dean had ever visited her office.

Mary felt a sudden sense of elation. There could be only one reason for the Dean coming here himself: He was going to tell her that the University was giving her tenure.

'Of course,' she said. 'Won't you sit down?'

He sat down on the ladder-back chair. 'How are your classes going?'

'Very well, I think.' She could not wait to relay the news to Edward. He would be so proud. It was seldom that someone her age received tenure from a university.

Dean Hunter seemed ill at ease. 'Are you in some kind of trouble, Mrs Ashley?'

The question caught her completely off guard. 'Trouble? I – No. Why?'

'Some men from Washington have been to see me, asking questions about you.'

Mary Ashley heard the echo of Florence Schiffer's words: *Some federal agent from Washington . . . He was asking all kinds of questions about Mary. He made her sound like some kind of international spy . . . Was she a loyal American? Was she a good wife and a good mother . . . ?*

So it had not been about her tenure, after all. She suddenly found it difficult to speak. 'What – what did they want to know, Dean Hunter?'

'They inquired about your reputation as a professor, and they asked questions about your personal life.'

'I can't explain it. I really don't know what's going on. I'm in no kind of trouble at all. As far as I know,' she added lamely.

He was watching her with obvious scepticism.

'Didn't they tell you *why* they were asking questions about me?'

'No. As a matter of fact, I was asked to keep the conversation in strict confidence. But I have a loyalty to my staff, and I felt it only fair that you should be informed about this. If there is something I should know, I would prefer to hear it from you. Any scandal involving one of our professors would reflect badly on the University.'

She shook her head, helplessly. 'I – I really can't think of anything.'

He looked at her a moment, as though about to say something else, then nodded. 'So be it, Mrs Ashley.'

She watched him walk out of her office and wondered: *What in God's name could I have done?*

Mary was very quiet during dinner. She wanted to wait until Edward finished eating before she broke the news of this latest development. They would try to figure out the problem together. The children were being impossible again. Beth refused to touch her dinner.

'No one eats meat any more. It's a barbaric custom carried over from the caveman. Civilized people don't eat live animals.'

'It's not alive,' Tim argued. 'It's dead, so you might as well eat it.'

'Children!' Mary's nerves were on edge. 'Not another word. Beth, go make yourself a salad.'

'She could go graze in the field,' Tim offered.

'Tim! You finish your dinner.' Her head was beginning to pound. 'Edward –'

The telephone rang.

'That's for me,' Beth said. She leaped out of her chair and raced towards the telephone. She picked it up and said seductively, 'Virgil?' She listened a moment, and her expression changed. 'Oh, sure,' she said disgustedly. She slammed down the receiver and returned to the table.

'What was that all about?' Edward asked.

'Some practical joker. He said it was the White House calling Mom.'

'*The White House?*' Edward asked.

The telephone rang again.

'I'll get it,' Mary said. She rose and walked over to the telephone. 'Hello.' As she listened, her face grew grim. 'We're in the middle of dinner, and I don't happen to think this is funny. You can just – what? . . . Who? The President?' There was a sudden hush in the room. 'Wait a – I – oh, good evening, Mr President.' There was a dazed expression on her face. Her family was watching her, wide-eyed. 'Yes, sir. I do. I recognize your voice. I – I'm sorry about hanging up a moment ago. Beth thought it was Virgil, and – yes, sir. Thank you.' She stood there listening. 'Would I be willing to serve as *what*?' Her face suddenly flushed.

Edward was on his feet, moving towards the phone, the children close behind him.

'There must be some mistake, Mr President. My name is Mary Ashley. I'm a professor at Kansas State University, and – You read it? Thank you, sir . . . That's very kind of you . . . Yes, I believe it is . . .' She listened for a long time. 'Yes, sir, I agree. But that doesn't mean that I . . . Yes, sir. Yes, sir. I see. Well, I'm certainly flattered. I'm sure it's a wonderful opportunity, but I . . . Of course I will.

I'll talk it over with my husband and get back to you.' She picked up a pen and wrote down a number. 'Yes, sir. I have it. Thank you, Mr President. Goodbye.'

She slowly replaced the receiver and stood there in shock.

'What in God's name was that all about?' Edward demanded.

'Was that *really* the President?' Tim asked.

Mary sank into a chair. 'Yes. It really was.'

Edward took Mary's hand in his. 'Mary – what did he say? What did he want?'

Mary sat there, numb, thinking: *So that's what all the questioning has been about.*

She looked up at Edward and the children and said slowly, 'The President read my book and the article of mine in *Foreign Affairs* magazine, and he thought they were brilliant. He said that's the kind of thinking he wants for his people-to-people programme. He wants to nominate me as Ambassador to Romania.'

There was a look of total disbelief on Edward's face.

'*You? Why you?*'

It was exactly what Mary had asked herself, but she felt that Edward could have been more tactful. He could have said, *How wonderful! You'd make a great ambassador*. But he was being realistic. *Why me, indeed?*

'You haven't had any political experience.'

'I'm well aware of that,' Mary responded

96

tartly. 'I agree that the whole thing is ridiculous.'

'Are you going to be the Ambassador?' Tim asked. 'Are we moving to Rome?'

'Romania.'

'Where's Romania?'

Edward turned to the children. 'You two finish your dinner. Your mother and I would like to have a little talk.'

'Don't we get a vote?' Tim asked.

'By absentee ballot.'

Edward took Mary's arm and led her into the library. He turned to her and said, 'I'm sorry if I sounded like a pompous ass in there. It was just such a –'

'No. You were perfectly right, Edward. Why on earth *should* they have chosen me?'

When Mary called him Edward, he knew he was in trouble.

'Honey, you'd probably make a great ambassador, or ambassadress, or whatever they call it these days. But you must admit it came as a bit of a shock.'

Mary softened. 'Try thunderbolt.' She sounded like a little girl. 'I still can't believe it.' She laughed. 'Wait until I tell Florence. She'll die.'

Edward was watching her closely. 'You're really excited about this, aren't you?'

She looked at him in surprise. 'Of course I am. Wouldn't you be?'

Edward chose his words carefully. 'It *is* a great honour, honey, and I'm sure it's not one they would offer lightly. They must have had good reason for choosing you.' He hesitated. 'We have to think about this very carefully. About what it would do to our lives.'

She knew what he was going to say, and she thought: *Edward's right. Of course he's right.*

'I can't just leave my practice and walk out on my patients. I have to stay here. I don't know how long you'd have to be away, but if it really means a lot to you, well, maybe we could work out some way where you could go over there with the children and I could join you whenever –'

Mary said softly, 'You crazy man. Do you think I could live away from you?'

'Well – it's an awfully big honour, and –'

'So is being your wife. Nothing means as much to me as you and the children. I would never leave you. This town can't find another doctor like you, but all the government has to do to find a better ambassador than me is to look in the yellow pages.'

He took her in his arms. 'Are you sure?'

'I'm positive. It was exciting being asked. That's enough for –'

The door flew open and Beth and Tim hurried in. Beth said, 'I just called Virgil and told him you're going to be an ambassador.'

'Then you'd better call him back and tell him I'm not.'

'Why not?' Beth asked.

'Your mother has decided she's going to stay here.'

'Why?' Beth wailed. 'I've never been to Romania. I've never been anywhere.'

'Me, neither,' Tim said. He turned to Beth. 'I told you we're never going to escape from this place.'

'The subject is closed,' Mary informed them.

The following morning Mary dialled the telephone number that the President had given her. When an operator answered, Mary said, 'This is Mrs Edward Ashley. I think the President's assistant – a Mr Greene – is expecting my call.'

'One moment, please.'

A male voice on the other end said, 'Hello. Mrs Ashley?'

'Yes,' Mary said. 'Would you please give the President a message for me?'

'Certainly.'

'Would you please tell him that I'm very, very flattered by his offer, but my husband's profession ties him down here, so I'm afraid it would be impossible for me to accept. I hope he understands.'

'I'll pass on your message,' the voice said noncommittally. 'Thank you, Mrs Ashley.' The line went dead.

Mary slowly replaced the receiver. It was done. For one brief moment, a tantalizing dream had been offered her. But that was all it was. A dream.

This is my real world. I'd better get ready for my fourth period history class.

Manama, Bahrain

The whitewashed stone house was anonymous, hidden among dozens of identical houses, a short walk from the *souks*, the large, colourful outdoor markets. It was owned by a merchant sympathetic to the cause of the organization known as the Patriots for Freedom.

'We will need it for only one day,' a voice over the telephone told him.

It was arranged. Now the chairman was speaking to the men gathered in the living room.

'A problem has arisen,' the chairman said. 'The motion that was recently passed has run into difficulty.'

'What sort of difficulty?' Balder asked.

'The go-between we selected – Harry Lantz – is dead.'

'Dead? Dead, how?'

'He was murdered. His body was found floating in the harbour in Buenos Aires.'

'Do the police have any idea who did it? I mean – can they connect this to us in any way?'

'No. We're perfectly safe.'

Thor asked, 'What about our plan? Can we go ahead with it?'

'Not at the moment. We have no idea how to reach Angel. However, the Controller gave Harry Lantz permission to reveal his name to him. If

Angel is interested in our proposition, he will find a way to get in touch with him. All we can do now is wait.'

The banner headline in the Junction City *Daily Union* read: JUNCTION CITY'S MARY ASHLEY DECLINES AMBASSADORSHIP.

There was a two-column story about Mary, and a photograph of her. On KJCK, the afternoon and evening broadcasts carried feature stories on the town's new celebrity. The fact that Mary Ashley had rejected the President's offer made the story even bigger than if she had accepted it. In the eyes of its proud citizens, Junction City, Kansas, was a lot more important than Bucharest, Romania.

When Mary Ashley drove into town to shop for dinner, she kept hearing her name on the car radio.

'. . . Earlier, President Ellison had announced that the ambassadorship to Romania would be the beginning of his people-to-people programme, the cornerstone of his foreign policy. How Mary Ashley's refusal to accept the post will reflect on –'

She switched to another station.

'. . . is married to Dr Edward Ashley, and it is believed that –'

Mary switched off the radio. She had received at least three dozen phone calls that morning from friends, neighbours, students and curious strangers. Reporters had called from as far away as London and Tokyo. *They're building this up all out of proportion*, Mary thought. *It's not my fault that the President decided to base the success of his foreign policy on Romania. I wonder how long this pandemonium is going to last? It will probably be over in a day or two.*

She drove the station wagon into a Derby gas station and pulled up in front of the self-service pump.

As Mary got out of the car, Mr Blount, the station manager, hurried over to her. 'Mornin', Mrs Ashley. An ambassador lady ain't got no call to be pumpin' her own gas. Let me give you a hand.'

Mary smiled. 'Thanks. I'm used to doing it.'

'No, no. I insist.'

When the tank was filled, Mary drove down Washington Street and parked in front of the Shoe Box.

'Mornin', Mrs Ashley,' the clerk greeted her. 'How's the ambassador this mornin'?'

This is going to get tiresome, Mary thought. Aloud, she said, 'I'm not an ambassador, but I'm fine, thank you.' She handed him a pair of shoes. 'I'd like to have Tim's shoes re-soled.'

The clerk examined them. 'Ain't these the ones we did last week?'

Mary sighed. 'And the week before.'

Mary's next stop was at Long's Department Store. Mrs Hacker, the manager of the dress department, said to her, 'I jest heard your name on the radio. You're puttin' Junction City on the map. Yes, sir.

I guess you and Eisenhower and Alf Landon are Kansas' only political big shots, Mrs Ambassador.'

'I'm not an ambassador,' Mary said patiently. 'I turned it down.'

'That's what I mean.'

It was no use. Mary said, 'I need some jeans for Beth. Preferably something in iron.'

'How old is Beth now? About ten?'

'She's twelve.'

'Land's sake, they grow so fast these days, don't they? She'll be a teenager before you know it.'

'Beth was born a teenager, Mrs Hacker.'

'How's Tim?'

'He's a lot like Beth.'

The shopping took Mary twice as long as usual. Everyone had some comment to make about the big news. She went into Dillon's to buy some groceries, and was studying the shelves when Mrs Dillon approached.

'Mornin', Mrs Ashley.'

'Good morning, Mrs Dillon. Do you have a breakfast food that has nothing in it?'

'What?'

Mary consulted a list in her hand. 'No artificial sweeteners, no sodium, fats, carbohydrates, caffeine, caramel colouring, folic acid or flavourites.'

Mrs Dillon studied the paper. 'Is this some kind of medical experiment?'

'In a sense. It's for Beth. She'll only eat natural foods.'

'Why don't you just put her out to pasture and let her graze?'

Mary laughed. 'That's what my son suggested.' Mary picked up a package and studied the label. 'It's my fault. I never should have taught Beth how to read.'

Mary drove home carefully, climbing the winding hill towards Milford Lake. It was a few degrees above zero, but the wind chill factor brought the temperature down to well below zero, for there was nothing to stop the winds from their biting sweep across the endless plains. The lawns were covered with snow, and Mary remembered the previous winter when an ice storm had swept the county and the ice snapped the power lines. They had no electricity for almost a week. She and Edward made love every night. *Maybe we'll get lucky again this winter*, she grinned to herself.

When Mary arrived home, Edward was still at the hospital. Tim was in the study watching a science fiction programme. Mary put away the groceries and went in to confront her son.

'Aren't you supposed to be doing your homework?'

'I can't.'

'And why not?'

'Because I don't understand it.'

'You're not going to understand it any better

by watching *Star Trek*. Let me see your lesson.'

Tim showed her his fifth grade mathematics book. 'These are dumb problems,' Tim said.

'There are no such things as dumb problems. There are only dumb students. Now let's take a look at this.'

Mary read the problem aloud. 'A train leaving Minneapolis had one hundred and forty-nine people on board. In Atlanta more people boarded the train. Then there were two hundred and twenty-three on the train. How many people boarded in Atlanta?' She looked up. 'That's simple, Tim. You just subtract one hundred and forty-nine from two hundred and twenty-three.'

'No, you don't,' Tim said glumly. 'It has to be an equation. One hundred and forty-nine plus n equals two hundred and twenty-three. n equals two hundred and twenty-three minus one hundred and forty-nine. n equals seventy-four.'

'That's dumb,' Mary said.

As Mary passed Beth's room, she heard noises. Mary went in. Beth was seated on the floor, cross-legged, watching television, listening to a rock record, and doing her homework.

'How can you concentrate with all this noise?' Mary shouted.

She walked over to the television set and turned it off and then turned off the record player.

Beth looked up in surprise. 'What did you do that for? That was George Michael.'

Beth's room was wallpapered with posters of musicians. There was Kiss and Van Halen, Motley Crue and Aldo Nova and David Lee Roth. The bed was covered with magazines: *Seventeen* and *Teen Idol* and half a dozen others. Beth's clothes were scattered over the floor.

Mary looked around the messy room in despair. 'Beth – how can you live like this?'

Beth looked up at her mother, puzzled. 'Live like what?'

Mary gritted her teeth. 'Nothing.'

She looked at an envelope on her daughter's desk. 'You're writing to Rick Springfield?'

'I'm in love with him.'

'I thought you were in love with George Michael.'

'I *burn* for George Michael. I'm in *love* with Rick Springfield. Mother, in your day didn't you ever *burn* for anybody?'

'In my day we were too busy trying to get the covered wagons across the country.'

Beth sighed. 'Did you know Rick Springfield had a rotten childhood?'

'To be perfectly honest, Beth, I was not aware of that.'

'It was awful. His father was in the military and they moved around a lot. He's a vegetarian, too. Like me. He's awesome.'

So that's what's behind Beth's crazy diet!

'Mother, may I go to a movie Saturday night with Virgil?'

'Virgil? What happened to Arnold?'

There was a pause. 'Arnold wanted to fool around. He's dorky.'

Mary forced herself to sound calm. 'By "fooling around", you mean –?'

'Just because I'm starting to get breasts the boys think I'm easy. Mom, did you ever feel uncomfortable about your body?'

Mary moved up behind Beth and put her arms around her. 'Yes, my darling. When I was about your age, I felt very uncomfortable.'

'I hate having my period and getting breasts and hair all over. Why?'

'It happens to every girl, and you'll get used to it.'

'No, I won't.' She pulled away and said fiercely, 'I don't mind being in love, but I'm never going to have sex. No one's going to make me. Not Arnold or Virgil or Kevin Bacon.'

Mary said solemnly, 'Well, if that's your decision . . .'

'Definitely. Mom, what did President Ellison say when you told him you weren't going to be his ambassador?'

'He was very brave about it,' Mary assured her. 'I think I'd better get dinner started.'

Cooking was Mary Ashley's secret *bête noire*. She hated to cook, and consequently was not very good at it, and because she liked to be good at everything she did, she hated it even more. It was a vicious circle that had partly been solved by having Lucinda come in three times a week to cook and clean the house. This was one of Lucinda's days off.

When Edward came home from the hospital, Mary was in the kitchen, burning some peas. She turned off the stove and gave Edward a kiss. 'Hello, darling. How was your day? Dorky?'

'You've been communicating with our daughter,' Edward said. 'As a matter of fact, it *was* dorky. I treated a thirteen-year-old girl this afternoon who had genital herpes.'

'Oh, darling!' She threw out the peas and opened a can of tomatoes.

'You know, it makes me worry about Beth.'

'You don't have to,' Mary assured him. 'She's planning to die a virgin.'

At dinner Tim asked, 'Dad, can I have a surf board for my birthday?'

'Tim – I don't want to rain on your parade, but you happen to live in *Kansas*.'

'I know that. Johnny invited me to go to Hawaii with him next summer. His folks have a beach house in Maui.'

'Well,' Edward said reasonably, 'if Johnny has a beach house, then he probably has a surf board.'

Tim turned to his mother. 'Can I go?'

'We'll see. Please don't eat so fast, Tim. Beth, you're not eating anything.'

'There's nothing here that's fit for human consumption.' She looked at her parents. 'I have an announcement to make. I'm going to change my name.'

Edward asked carefully, 'Any particular reason?'

'I've decided to go into show business.'

Mary and Edward exchanged a long, pained look.

Edward said, 'Okay. Find out how much you can get for them.'

EIGHT

In a scandal that had rocked the international secret service organizations, Mehdi Ben Barka, an opponent of King Hassan II of Morocco, was abducted from his exile in Paris and murdered with the help of the French Secret Service. It was following that incident that President Charles de Gaulle took the Secret Service from the control of the Premier's Office and placed it under the aegis of the Ministry of Defence. Thus it was that the current Minister of Defence, Roland Passy, was responsible for the safety of Marin Groza, who had been granted sanctuary by the French government. Gendarmes were stationed in front of the villa in Neuilly on twenty-four-hour shifts, but it was the knowledge that Lev Pasternak was in charge of the villa's inner security that gave Passy confidence. He had seen the security arrangements himself and was firmly convinced that the house was impregnable.

In recent weeks, rumours had been sweeping the diplomatic world that a coup was imminent; that

Marin Groza was planning to return to Romania; and that Alexandros Ionescu was going to be deposed by his senior military officers.

Lev Pasternak knocked on the door and entered the book-crammed library that served as Marin Groza's office. Groza was seated behind his desk, working. He looked up as Lev Pasternak came in.

'Everybody wants to know when the revolution is going to happen,' Pasternak said. 'It's the world's worst kept secret.'

'Tell them to be patient. Will you come to Bucharest with me, Lev?'

More than anything, Lev Pasternak yearned to return to Israel. *I'll only take this job temporarily*, he had told Marin Groza. *Until you're ready to make your move. Temporarily* had turned into weeks and months, and finally into three years. And now it was time to make another decision.

In a world peopled with pygmies, Lev Pasternak thought, *I have been given the privilege of serving a giant*. Marin Groza was the most selfless and idealistic man Lev Pasternak had ever known.

When Pasternak had come to work for Groza, he had wondered about the man's family. Groza would never speak of them, but the officer who had arranged for Pasternak to meet Groza told him the story.

'Groza was betrayed. The *Securitate* picked him up and tortured him for five days. They promised to free him if he would give them the names of his associates in the underground. He wouldn't

111

talk. They arrested his wife and his fourteen-year-old daughter and brought them to the interrogation room. Groza was given a choice: Talk or watch them die. It was the hardest decision any man ever had to make. It was the life of his beloved wife and child against the lives of hundreds of people who believed in him.' The man paused, then went on more slowly. 'I think in the end what made Groza decide the way he did was that he was convinced that he and his family were going to be killed, anyway. He refused to give them the names. The guards strapped him in a chair and forced him to watch his wife and daughter being gang-raped until they died. But they weren't through with Groza yet. When it was over and their bloody bodies were lying at his feet, they castrated him.'

'Oh, my God!'

The officer looked into Lev Pasternak's eyes and said, 'The most important thing for you to understand is that Marin Groza does not want to return to Romania to seek vengeance. He wants to go back to free his people. He wants to make certain that such things can never again happen.'

Lev Pasternak had been with Groza from that day on, and the more time he spent with the revolutionary, the more he came to love him. Now, he would have to decide whether to give up his return to Israel and go to Romania with Groza.

* * *

Pasternak was walking down the hallway that evening, and as he passed Marin Groza's bedroom door, he heard the familiar screams of pain ring out. *So it's Friday*, Pasternak thought. The day the prostitutes came. They were selected from England, North America, Brazil, Japan, Thailand, and half a dozen other countries, chosen at random. They had no idea what their destination was, or who they were going to see. They were met at Charles de Gaulle Airport, driven directly to the villa, and, after a few hours, taken back to the airport and put on a return flight. Every Friday night the halls resounded with Marin Groza's screams. The staff assumed that kinky sex was going on. The only one who knew what was really happening behind the bedroom door was Lev Pasternak. For the visits with the prostitutes had nothing to do with sex. They were a penance. Once a week Groza stripped himself naked and had a woman tie him to a chair and whip him mercilessly, until his blood flowed, and each time he was whipped he would see his wife and daughter being raped to death, screaming for help. And he cried out, 'I'm sorry! I'll talk. Oh, God, please let me talk . . .'

The telephone call came ten days after Harry Lantz's body was found. The Controller was in the middle of a staff meeting in the conference room when the intercom buzzer sounded.

'I know you asked not to be disturbed, sir, but there's an overseas call for you. It sounds urgent.

A Miss Neusa Muñez is calling from Buenos Aires. I told her –'

'It's all right.' He kept his emotions under tight control. 'I'll take the call in my private office.' He excused himself, went into his office, and locked the door. He picked up the telephone. 'Hello. Is this Miss Muñez?'

'Yeah.' It was a voice with a South American accent, coarse and uneducated. 'I got a message for you from Angel. He din' like the nosey messenger you sent.'

He had to choose his words carefully. 'I'm sorry. But we would still like Angel to go ahead with our arrangement. Would that be possible?'

'Yeah. He say he wanna do it.'

The man held back a sigh of relief. 'Excellent. How shall I arrange his advance?'

The woman laughed. 'Angel, he don' need no advance. Nobody cheats Angel.' Somehow the words were chilling. 'When the job is finished, he say you put the money in – wait a minute – I got it wrote down – here it is – the State Bank of Zürich. Tha's some place in Switzerland.' She sounded like a moron.

'I'll need the account number.'

'Oh, yeah. The number is – Jesus. I forgot. Hol' on. I got it here somewhere.' He heard the rustle of papers, and finally she was back on the telephone. 'Here it is. J-three four nine-zero seven seven.'

He repeated the number. 'How soon can he handle the matter?'

'When he's ready, *señor*. Angel say you'll know when 'ees done. You'll read 'bout it in the newspapers.'

'Very well. I'm going to give you my private telephone number in case Angel needs to reach me.'

He gave it to her slowly.

Tbilisi, Russia

The meeting was being held in an isolated dacha bordering on the River Kura.

The chairman said, 'Two urgent matters have arisen. The first is good news. The Controller has had word from Angel. The contract is moving forward.'

'That's *very* good news!' Freyr exclaimed. 'What's the bad news?'

'I'm afraid it concerns the President's candidate for the ambassadorship to Romania, but the situation can be handled . . .'

It was difficult for Mary Ashley to keep her mind on the class. Something had changed. In the eyes of her students, she had become a celebrity. It was a heady feeling. She could feel the class hanging on her words.

'As we know, 1956 was a watershed year for many of the Eastern European countries. With Gomulka's return to power, national communism emerged in Poland. In Czechoslovakia Antonin Mavorony led the Communist Party. There were

115

no major political changes in Romania that year . . .'

Romania . . . Bucharest . . . From the photographs Mary had seen, it had to be one of the most beautiful cities in Europe. She had not forgotten any of the stories her grandfather had told her about Romania. She remembered how terrified she had been as a little girl by his tales of the horrible Prince Vlad of Transylvania. *He was a vampire, Mary, living in his huge castle high in the mountains of Braşov, sucking the blood of his innocent victims.*

Mary was suddenly aware of a deep silence in the room. The class was staring at her. *How long have I been standing here day-dreaming?* she wondered. She hurriedly continued her lecture. 'In Romania, Gheorgiu-Dej was consolidating his power in the Workers' Party . . .'

The class seemed to go on endlessly, but mercifully, it was almost over.

'Your homework assignment will be to write an essay on the USSR's economic planning and management, describing the basic organization of the government organs, and the CPSU control. I want you to analyse the internal and external dimensions of Soviet policy, with emphasis on its positions on Poland, Czechoslovakia and Romania.'

Romania . . . Welcome to Romania, Madam Ambassador. Your limousine is here to drive you to your embassy. Her embassy. She had been invited to live in one of the most exciting capitals

116

of the world, reporting to the President, being in the centre of his people-to-people concept. *I could have been a part of history.*

She was roused from her reverie by the sound of the bell. Class was over. Time to go home and change. Edward would be back from the hospital early. He was taking her out to the country club for dinner.

As befitted an almost-Ambassador.

'Code Blue! Code Blue!' the crackling voice sounded over the loudspeaker throughout the hospital corridors. Even as the emergency crew began to converge on the ambulance entrance, the sound of an approaching siren could be heard. The Geary Community Hospital is an austere-looking, three-storey brown building perched on a hill on St Mary's Road in the southwest section of Junction City. The hospital holds 92 beds, has two modern operating rooms, and a series of examining rooms and administrative offices.

It had been a busy Friday, and the ward on the top floor was already filled with injured servicemen who had come to town from nearby Fort Riley, home of the First Infantry Division, known as The Big Red One, for their weekend R & R.

Dr Edward Ashley was sewing up the scalp of a soldier who had lost a bar fight. Edward Ashley had been a doctor at Geary Community Hospital for thirteen years, and before going into private practice, he had been an Air Force flight surgeon with the rank of captain. Several prestigious hospitals in large cities had tried to lure him away, but he preferred to stay where he was.

He finished with the patient he was working on, and looked around. There were at least a dozen soldiers waiting to be patched up. He heard the sound of the approaching ambulance siren. 'They're playing our song.'

Dr Douglas Schiffer, who was tending a gunshot wound victim, nodded. 'It looks like MASH in here. You'd think we were in some kind of war.'

Edward Ashley said. 'It's the only war they have, Doug. That's why they come into town every weekend and go a little nuts. They're frustrated.' He finished the last stitch. 'There you are, soldier. You're as good as new.' He turned to Douglas Schiffer. 'We'd better get down to emergency.'

The patient wore the uniform of a private, and he looked to be no more than eighteen years old. He was in shock. He was sweating profusely and his breathing was laboured. Dr Ashley felt his pulse. It was weak and thready. A splotch of blood stained the front of his uniform jacket. Edward Ashley turned to one of the paramedics who had brought in the patient.

'What do we have here?'

'A knife wound to the chest, doctor.'

'Let's see if his lung is collapsed.' He turned to a nurse. 'I want a stat chest x-ray. You've got three minutes.'

Dr Douglas Schiffer was observing the jugular vein. It was raised. He looked over at Edward. 'It's distended. The pericardium's probably been penetrated.' Which meant that the sac which protected the heart was filled with blood, pressing against the heart so that it could not beat properly.

The nurse who was taking the patient's blood pressure said, 'Blood pressure's dropping fast.'

The monitor measuring the patient's electro-cardiogram began to slow. They were losing the patient.

Another nurse hurried in with the chest x-ray. Edward scanned it. 'Pericardial tamponade.'

The heart had a hole in it. The lung was collapsed.

'Get a tube in him and expand the lung.' His voice was quiet, but there was no mistaking the urgency in it. 'Get an anaesthesiologist. We're going to open him up. Intubate him.'

A nurse handed Dr Schiffer an endotracheal tube. Edward Ashley nodded at him. 'Now.'

Carefully Douglas Schiffer began to push the tube into the unconscious soldier's windpipe. There was a bag at the end of the tube, and Schiffer began to squeeze it in a steady rhythm, ventilating the lungs. The monitor began to slow, and the curve on the monitor was completely flat. The smell of death was in the room.

'He's gone.'

There was no time to wheel the patient up to

the operating room. Dr Ashley had to make an instant decision.

'We're going to do a thoracotomy. Scalpel.'

The instant the knife was in his hand, Edward reached down and slashed it across the patient's chest. There was almost no blood, because the heart was trapped in the pericardium.

'Retractor!'

The instrument was put in his hands, and he inserted it into the patient's chest to spread the ribs apart.

'Scissors. Stand back!'

He moved closer so that he could reach the pericardial sac. He snipped the scissors into it, and the blood released from the imprisonment of the heart sac spurted out, hitting the nurses and Dr Ashley. Dr Ashley reached in and began to massage the heart. The monitor began to beep, and the pulse became palpable. There was a small laceration at the apex of the left ventricle.

'Get him up to the operating room.'

Three minutes later the patient was on the operating table.

'Transfusion – a thousand cc's.'

There was no time to match blood type, so 'O Negative' – the universal donor – was used.

As the blood transfusion began, Dr Ashley said, 'A thirty-two chest tube.'

A nurse handed it to him.

Dr Schiffer said, 'I'll close, Ed. Why don't you get cleaned up?'

Edward Ashley's surgical gown was stained with blood. He looked at the monitor. The heart was strong and steady.

'Thanks.'

Edward Ashley had showered and changed clothes and was in his office writing up the required medical report. It was a pleasant office, filled with bookcases containing medical tomes and athletic trophies. It contained a desk, an easy chair and a small table with two straight chairs. On the walls were his diplomas, neatly framed.

Edward's body felt stiff and tired from the tension he had just gone through. At the same time, he felt sexually aroused, as he always did after major surgery. *It's coming face to face with death that magnifies the values of the life force*, a psychiatrist had once explained to Edward. *Making love is the affirmation of nature's continuum. Whatever the reason, Edward thought,* I wish Mary were here.

He selected a pipe from the pipe rack on his desk, lighted it, and sank into the easy chair and stretched out his legs. Thinking about Mary made him feel guilty. He was responsible for her turning down the President's offer, and his reasons were valid. *But there's more to it than that*, Edward admitted to himself. *I was jealous. I reacted like a spoiled brat. What would have happened if the President had made me an offer like that? I'd probably have jumped at it. Jesus! All I could think of was that I wanted Mary to stay home and take care of me and the kids. Talk about your genuine male chauvinist pig!*

He sat there, smoking his pipe, upset with himself. *Too late*, he thought. *But I'll make it up to her. I'll surprise her this summer with a trip to Paris and London. Maybe I'll take her to Romania. We'll have a real honeymoon.*

The Junction City Country Club is a three-level, limestone building set in the midst of lush hills. The club has an eighteen-hole golf course, two tennis courts, a swimming pool, and a bar and dining room with a large fireplace at one end, a card room upstairs and locker rooms downstairs.

Edward's father had belonged to the club, as had Mary's father, and Edward and Mary had been taken there since they were children. The town was a closely knit community, and the country club was its symbol.

When Edward and Mary arrived, it was late, and there was only a sprinkling of guests left in the dining room. They stared, watching as Mary sat down, and whispered to one another. Mary was getting used to it.

Edward looked at his wife. 'Any regrets?'

Of course there were regrets. But they were castles-in-Spain regrets about the kind of glamorous, impossible dreams that everyone has. *If I had been born a princess; if I were a millionairess; if I received the Nobel Prize for curing cancer; if . . . if . . . if . . .*

Mary smiled. 'None, darling. It was a fluke that

122

they even asked me. Anyhow, there's no way I would ever leave you or the children.' She took his hand in hers. 'No regrets. I'm glad I refused the offer.'

He leaned across to her and whispered, 'I'm going to make you an offer you can't refuse.'

'Let's go,' Mary smiled.

In the beginning, when they were first married, their lovemaking had been fierce and demanding. They had a constant physical need for each other that could not be satisfied until they were both completely spent. The urgency had mellowed with time, but the emotions were still there, constant and sweet and fulfilling.

When they returned home now, they undressed without haste and got into bed. Edward held her close to him, then began to stroke her body gently, playing with her breasts, teasing the nipples with his fingers, moving his hand down towards the velvety softness.

Mary moaned with pleasure. 'That feels wonderful.'

She moved on top of him and began flicking her tongue down his body, feeling him become hard. When they were both ready, they made love until they were exhausted. Edward held his wife tightly in his arms. 'I love you so much, Mary.'

'I love you twice as much. Good night, darling.'

At three o'clock in the morning, the phone exploded into sound. Edward sleepily reached for the instrument and brought it to his ear. 'Hello . . .'

A woman's urgent voice said, 'Dr Ashley?'

'Yes . . .'

'Pete Grimes is havin' a heart attack. He's in pain somethin' awful. I think he's dying. I don't know what to do.'

Edward sat up in bed, trying to blink the sleep away. 'Don't do anything. Keep him still. I'll be there in half an hour.' He replaced the receiver, slid out of bed and started to dress.

'Edward . . .'

He looked over at Mary. Her eyes were half open. 'What's wrong?'

'Everything's fine. Go back to sleep.'

'Wake me up when you come back,' Mary mumbled. 'I think I'm going to feel sexy again.'

Edward grinned. 'I'll hurry.'

Five minutes later, he was on his way to the Grimes' farm.

He drove down the hill on Old Milford Road towards J Hill Road. It was a cold and raw morning, with a northwesterly wind driving the temperature well below zero. Edward turned up the car heater. As he drove, he wondered whether he should have called for an ambulance before he left the house. The last two 'heart attacks' Pete Grimes had had turned out to be bleeding ulcers. No. He would check it out first.

He turned the car onto Route 18, the two-lane highway that went through Junction City. The town was asleep, its houses huddled against the bitter, frigid wind.

When Edward came to the end of 6th Street, he made the turn that took him onto Route 57, and headed towards Grandview Plaza. How many times had he driven over these roads on hot summer days with the sweet smell of corn and prairie hay in the air, past miniature forests of cottonwood trees and cedars and Russian olive trees, and August haystacks piled up alongside the roads? The fields had been filled then with the odour of burning cedar trees that had to be regularly destroyed because they kept taking over the crops. And how many winters had he driven on this road through a frosted landscape with power lines delicately laced with ice, and lonely smoke from far-off chimneys? There was an exhilarating feeling of isolation, being encapsulated in the morning darkness, watching fields and trees fly silently past.

Edward drove as fast as possible, mindful of the treacherous road beneath the wheels. He thought of Mary lying in their warm bed, waiting for him. *Wake me up when you come back. I think I'm going to feel sexy again.*

He was so lucky. *I'll make everything up to her*, Edward promised himself. *I'll give her the damnedest honeymoon any woman ever had.*

Ahead, at the intersection of Highways 57 and 77 was a stop sign. Edward turned at Route 77, and as he started into the intersection, a truck appeared out of nowhere. He heard a sudden roar, and his car was pinned by two bright headlights racing towards him. He caught a glimpse of the giant five-ton Army truck bearing down on him, and the last sound he heard was his own voice screaming.

In Neuilly, it was Sunday and church bells pealed out across the quiet noon air. The gendarmes guarding Marin Groza's villa had no reason to pay attention to the dusty Renault cruising by. Angel drove slowly, but not slowly enough to arouse suspicion, taking everything in. Two guards in front, a high wall, probably electrified, and inside, of course, the usual electronic nonsense of beams, sensors and alarms. It would take an army to storm the villa. *But I don't need an army*, Angel thought. *Only my genius. Marin Groza is a dead man. If only my mother were alive to see how rich I have become. How happy it would have made her.*

In Argentina, poor families were very poor indeed, and Angel's mother had been one of the unfortunate *descamidos*. No one knew or cared who the father had been. Through the years Angel had watched friends and relatives die of hunger and sickness and disease. Death was a way of life, and Angel thought philosophically: *Since it is going to happen anyway, why not make a profit from it?* In the beginning, there were those who doubted Angel's lethal talents, but those who tried to put roadblocks in the way had a habit of disappearing. Angel's reputation as an assassin grew. *I have never failed*, Angel thought. *I am Angel. The Angel of Death.*

NINE

The snow-covered Kansas highway was ablaze with vehicles with flashing red lights that turned the frosty air blood-red. A fire truck, ambulance, tow truck, four highway patrol cars, a sheriff's car, and in the centre, ringed by headlights, the five-ton M871 Army tractor-trailer, and partially beneath it, Edward Ashley's crumpled car. A dozen police officers and firemen were milling around, swinging their arms and stamping their feet, trying to keep warm in the pre-dawn freeze. In the middle of the highway, covered by a tarpaulin, was a body. A sheriff's car was approaching, and as it skidded to a stop, Mary Ashley ran out of it. She was trembling so hard that she could barely stand. She saw the tarpaulin and started towards it.

Sheriff Munster grabbed her arm. 'I wouldn't look at him if I were you, Mrs Ashley.'

'Let go of me.' She was screaming. She shook loose from his grasp and moved towards the tarpaulin.

'Please, Mrs Ashley. You don't want to see what he looks like.'

He caught her as she fainted.

She woke up in the back seat of the sheriff's car. Sheriff Munster was sitting in the front seat, watching her. The heater was on, and the car was stifling.

'What happened?' Mary asked dully.

'You fainted.'

She suddenly remembered. *You don't want to see what he looks like.*

Mary stared out of the window at all the emergency vehicles and flashing red lights and thought: *It's a scene from hell.* In spite of the heat in the police car, her teeth were chattering.

'How did –' She found it difficult to get the words out. 'How did it h-happen?'

'Your husband ran the stop sign. An Army truck was comin' along 77 and tried to avoid him, but your husband drove right out in front of him.'

She closed her eyes and watched the accident happen in her mind. She saw the truck bearing down on Edward and felt his last second panic.

All she could think of to say was, 'Edward was a c-careful driver. He would n-never go through a stop sign.'

The sheriff said sympathetically, 'Mrs Ashley, we have eye-witnesses. A priest and two nuns saw it happen, and a Colonel Jenkins from Fort Riley.

They all said the same thing. Your husband ran the stop sign.'

Everything after that seemed to happen in slow motion. She watched Edward's body being lifted into the ambulance. Police were questioning a priest and two nuns, and Mary thought: *They're going to catch cold standing out there like that*.

Sheriff Munster said, 'They're takin' the body to the morgue.'

The body. 'Thank you,' Mary said politely.

He was looking at her strangely. 'I'd best get you back home,' he said. 'What's the name of your family doctor?'

'Edward Ashley,' Mary said. 'Edward Ashley is my family doctor.'

Later, she remembered walking up to the house and Sheriff Munster leading her inside. Florence and Douglas Schiffer were waiting for her in the living room. The children were still asleep.

Florence threw her arms around her. 'Oh, darling, I'm so terribly, terribly sorry.'

'It's all right,' Mary said calmly. 'Edward had an accident.' She giggled.

Douglas was watching her closely. 'Let me take you upstairs.'

'I'm fine, thank you. Would you care for some tea?'

Douglas said, 'Come on, I'm putting you to bed.'

'I'm not sleepy. Are you sure you wouldn't care for something?'

As Douglas led her upstairs into the bedroom, Mary said to him, 'It was an accident. Edward was in an accident.'

Douglas Schiffer looked into her eyes. They were wide and vacant. He felt a chill go through him.

He went downstairs to get his medical bag. When he returned, Mary had not moved. 'I'm going to give you something to make you sleep.' He gave her a sedative, helped her into bed, and sat at her side. An hour later, Mary was still awake. He gave her another sedative. Then a third. Finally, she slept.

In Junction City there are strict investigative procedures involved in the report of a 1048 – an injury accident. An ambulance is dispatched from the County Ambulance Service, and a sheriff's officer is sent to the scene. If Army personnel are involved in the accident, the CID – the Criminal Investigating Division of the Army – conducts an investigation along with the sheriff's office.

Shel Planchard, a plainclothes officer from the CID headquarters at Fort Riley, and the sheriff and a deputy were examining the accident report in the sheriff's office on 9th Street.

'It beats me,' Sheriff Munster said.

'What's the problem. Sheriff?' Planchard asked.

'Well, looky here. There were five witnesses to

the accident, right? A priest and two nuns, Colonel Jenkins and the truck driver, Sergeant Wallis. Every single one of them says Doc Ashley's car turned into the highway, ran the stop sign and was hit by the Army truck.'

'Right,' the CID man said. 'What's bothering you?'

Sheriff Munster scratched his head. 'Mister, have you ever seen an accident report where even *two* eye-witnesses said the same thing?' He slammed a fist against the papers. 'What bothers the hell out of me is that every one of these witnesses says *exactly* the same thing.'

The CID man shrugged. 'It just shows that what happened was pretty obvious.'

The sheriff said, 'There's somethin' else nigglin' at me.'

'Yeah?'

'What were a priest and two nuns and a colonel doin' out on Highway 77 at 4 a.m. in the mornin'?'

'Nothing mysterious about that. The priest and the sisters were on their way to Leonardville, and the colonel was returning to Fort Riley.'

The sheriff said, 'I checked with the DMV. The last ticket Doc Ashley got was six years ago for illegal parking. He had no accident record.'

The CID man was studying him. 'Sheriff, just what are you suggesting?'

Munster shrugged. 'I'm not suggestin' anythin'. I jest have a funny feelin' about this.'

'We're talking about an accident seen by five witnesses. If you think there's some kind of conspiracy involved, there's a big hole in your theory. If –'

The sheriff sighed. 'I know. If it wasn't an accident, all the Army truck had to do was knock him off and keep goin'. There wouldn't be any reason for all these witnesses and rigmarole.'

'Exactly.' The CID man rose and stretched. 'Well, I've got to get back to the base. As far as I'm concerned, the driver of the truck, Sergeant Wallis, is cleared.' He looked at the sheriff. 'Are we in agreement?'

Sheriff Munster said reluctantly, 'Yeah. It musta been an accident.'

Mary was awakened by the sound of the children crying. She lay still, her eyes tightly closed, thinking: *This is a part of my nightmare. I'm asleep, and when I wake up, Edward will be alive.*

But the crying continued. When she could stand it no longer, she opened her eyes and lay there, staring at the ceiling. Finally, reluctantly, she forced herself to get out of bed. She felt drugged. She walked into Tim's bedroom. Florence and Beth were there with him. The three of them were crying. *I wish I could cry*, Mary thought. *Oh, I wish I could cry.*

Beth looked up at Mary. 'Is – is Daddy really d-dead?'

Mary nodded, unable to speak the words. She sat on the edge of the bed.

'I had to tell them,' Florence apologized. 'They were going to go off to play with some friends.'

'It's all right.' Mary stroked Tim's hair. 'Don't cry, darling. Everything is going to be all right.'

Nothing was going to be all right again.

Ever.

The United States Army CID Command at Fort Riley is headquartered at Building Number 169, in an old limestone structure, surrounded by trees, with steps leading up to the porch of the building. In an office on the first floor, Shel Planchard, the CID officer, was talking to Colonel Jenkins.

'I'm afraid I have some bad news, sir. Sergeant Wallis, the driver of the truck that killed the civilian doctor –'

'Yes?'

'He had a fatal heart attack this morning.'

'That's a shame.'

The CID man said tonelessly, 'Yes, sir. His body is being cremated this morning. It was very sudden.'

'Unfortunate.' The Colonel rose. 'I'm being transferred overseas.' He allowed himself a small smile. 'A rather important promotion.'

'Congratulations, sir. You've earned it.'

* * *

Mary Ashley decided later that the only thing that saved her sanity was being in a state of shock. Everything that happened seemed to be happening to someone else. She was under water, moving slowly, hearing voices from a distance, filtered through cotton wool.

The funeral service was held at the Mass-Hinitt Alexander Funeral Home on Jefferson Street. It was a blue building with a white portico and a large white clock hanging above the entrance. The funeral parlour was filled to overflowing with friends and colleagues of Edward. There were dozens of wreaths and bouquets. One of the largest wreaths had a card that read simply: 'My deepest sympathy. Paul Ellison.'

Mary and Beth and Tim sat alone in the small family room off to one side of the parlour, the children red-eyed and still.

The casket with Edward's body in it was closed. She could not bear to think about the reason.

The minister was speaking: 'Lord, thou hast been our dwelling place. In all generations, before the mountains were brought forth, or ever thou hadst formed the earth and the world, ever from everlasting to everlasting, thou art God. Therefore, we will not fear, though the earth doth change, and though the mountains be shaken into the heart of the seas . . .'

She and Edward were in the small sailboat on Milford Lake.

'Do you like to sail?' he had asked her the first night they dated.

'I've never been sailing.'

'Saturday,' he said. 'We have a date.'

They were married one week later.

'Do you know why I married you, lady?' Edward teased. 'You passed the test. You laughed a lot and you didn't fall overboard.'

When the service ended, Mary and the children got into the long, black limousine that led the funeral procession to the cemetery.

Highland Cemetery on Ash Street is a vast park, with a gravelled road circling it. It is the oldest cemetery in Junction City, and many of the headstones have long since been eroded by time and weather. Because of the numbing cold, the graveside ceremony was kept brief.

'I am the resurrection and the life; he that believeth in me, though he were dead, yet shall he live; and whosoever liveth and believeth in me shall never die. I am he that liveth and was dead; and, behold, I am alive for evermore.'

Finally, mercifully, it was over. Mary and the children stood in the howling wind watching the casket being lowered into the frozen, uncaring earth.

Goodbye, my darling.

Death is supposed to be an ending, but for Mary Ashley it was the beginning of an unbearable hell. She and Edward had talked about death, and Mary had thought she had come to terms with it, but now death had suddenly assumed a reality that was immediate and terrifying. It was no longer a vague event that would happen on some far, distant day. There was no way to cope with it. Everything within Mary screamed to deny what had happened to Edward. When he died, everything wonderful died with him. The reality kept hitting her in fresh waves of shock. She wanted to be alone. She cowered deep within herself, feeling like a small, terrified child abandoned by an adult. She found herself raging against God. *Why didn't you take me first?* she demanded. She was furious with Edward for deserting her, furious with the children, furious with herself.

I'm a thirty-five-year-old woman with two children, and I don't know who I am. When I was Mrs Edward Ashley, I had an identity, I belonged to someone who belonged to me.

Time was spinning by, mocking her emptiness. Her life was like a runaway train over which she had no control.

Florence and Douglas and other friends stayed with her, trying to make things easier, but Mary wished they would go away and leave her alone. Florence came in one afternoon and found Mary in front of the television set watching a Kansas State football game.

'She didn't even know I was there,' Florence told her husband that evening. 'She was concentrating so desperately on that game.' She shivered. 'It was spooky.'

'Why?'

'Mary hates football. It was Edward who watched every game.'

It took Mary's last ounce of willpower to handle the detritus left by Edward's death. There was the will, and insurance, bank accounts and taxes and bills due and Edward's medical corporation and loans and assets and deficits, and she wanted to scream at the lawyers and bankers and account-ants to leave her in peace.

I don't want to cope, she wept. Edward was gone, and all anyone wanted to talk about was money.

Finally, she was forced to discuss it.

Frank Dunphy, Edward's accountant, said, 'I'm afraid the bills and death taxes are going to use up a lot of the life insurance money, Mrs Ashley. Your husband was pretty lax about his patients paying him. He's owed a lot of money. I'll arrange for a col-lection agency to go after the people who owe –'

'No,' Mary said fiercely. 'Edward wouldn't want that.'

Dunphy was at a loss. 'Well, then, I guess the bottom line is that your assets are thirty thou-sand dollars in cash and this house, which has a mortgage on it. If you sold the house –'

'Edward wouldn't want me to sell it.'

She sat there, stiff and rigid, holding in her misery, and Dunphy thought: *I wish to God my wife cared that much about me.*

* * *

137

The worst was yet to come. It was time to dispose of Edward's personal things. Florence offered to help her, but Mary said, 'No. Edward would have wanted me to do it.'

There were so many small, intimate things. A dozen pipes, a fresh can of tobacco, two pairs of reading glasses, notes for a medical lecture he would never give. She went into Edward's closet and ran her fingers over suits he would never wear again. The blue tie he had worn on their last night together. His gloves and scarf that kept him warm against the winter winds. He would not need them in his cold grave. She carefully put away his razor and toothbrushes, moving like an automaton.

She found love notes they had written to each other, bringing back memories of the lean days when Edward started his own practice, a Thanksgiving dinner without a turkey, summer picnics and winter sleigh rides, and her first pregnancy and both of them reading to Beth and playing classical music for her while she was in the womb, and the love letter Edward wrote when Tim was born, and the gold-plated apple Edward had given her when she began teaching, and a hundred other wonderful things that brought tears to her eyes. His death was like some cruel magician's trick. One moment Edward was there, alive, talking, smiling, loving, and the next moment he had vanished into the cold earth.

I'm a mature person. I have to accept reality. I'm not mature. I can't accept it. I don't want to live.

She lay awake through the long night, thinking how simple it would be to join Edward, to stop the unbearable agony, to be at peace. *We're brought up to expect a happy ending*, Mary thought. *But there are no happy endings. There's only death waiting for us. We find love and happiness, and it's snatched away from us without rhyme or reason. We're on a deserted space ship careening mindlessly among the stars. The world is Dachau, and we're all Jews.*

She finally dozed off, and in the middle of the night, her wild screams awakened the children, and they ran to her bedside and crawled into bed with her, hugging her.

'You're not going to die, are you?' Tim whispered.

Mary thought: *I can't kill myself. They need me. Edward would never forgive me.*

She had to go on living. For them. She had to give them the love Edward would not be able to give them. *We're all so needy without Edward. We need one another so terribly. It's ironic that Edward's death is harder to bear because we had such a wonderful life together. There are so many more reasons to miss him, so many memories of things that will never happen again. Where are you, God? Are you listening to me? Help me. Please help me.*

Ring Lardner said, 'Three out of three are going to die, so shut up and deal.' *I have to deal. I'm being terribly selfish. I'm behaving badly, as if I'm the only person in the world who is suffering. God isn't trying to punish me. Life is a cosmic grab-bag. At this moment, somewhere in the world, someone is losing a child, skiing down a mountain, having an orgasm, getting a haircut, lying on a bed of pain, singing on a stage, drowning, getting married, starving in a gutter. In the end, aren't we all that same person? An aeon is a thousand million years, and an aeon ago every atom in our bodies was a part of a star. Pay attention to me, God. We are all a part of your universe, and if we die, part of your universe dies with us.*

Edward was everywhere.

He was in the songs Mary heard on the radio, in the hills they had driven through together. He was in bed at her side when she awoke at sunrise.

Got to get up early this morning, honey. I have a hysterectomy and a hip operation.

His voice came to her clearly. She began to talk to him: *I'm worried about the children, Edward. They don't want to go to school. Beth says they're afraid that when they get home I won't be here.*

Mary went to visit the cemetery every day, standing in the icy air, mourning for what was lost to her forever. But it gave her no comfort. *You're not here*, Mary thought. *Tell me where you are. Please.*

She thought of the story by Marguerite Yourcenarl, 'How Want-Fo Was Saved'. It was the tale of a Chinese artist condemned to be put to death by his emperor for lying, for creating pictures of a world whose beauty was contradicted by reality. But the artist cheated the emperor by painting a boat and sailing away in it. *I want to escape, too*, Mary thought. *I can't stand it here without you, darling.*

Florence and Douglas tried to comfort her. 'He's at peace,' they told Mary. And a hundred other clichés. The easy words of solace, except that there was no solace. *Not now. Not ever.*

She would wake in the middle of the night and rush into the children's rooms to make sure they were safe. *My children are going to die*, Mary thought. *We're all going to die.* People were calmly walking the streets. *Idiots, laughing, happy – and they were all dying.* Their hours were numbered, and they wasted them playing stupid card games and going to silly movies and pointless football games. *Wake up!* she wanted to scream. *The earth is God's slaughterhouse, and we're his cattle. Didn't they know what was going to happen to them and to everyone they loved?*

The answer came to her, slowly, painfully, through the heavy black veils of grief. Of course they knew. Their games were a form of defiance, their laughter an act of bravado – a bravado born from the knowledge that life was finite, that everyone faced the same fate; and slowly her fear and anger melted and turned to wonder at the courage of her fellow human beings. *I'm ashamed of myself. I have to find my own way through the maze of time. In the end, each of us is alone, but in the meantime, we must all huddle together to give one another comfort and warmth.*

The Bible said that death was not a final ending; it was merely a transition. Edward would never leave her and the children. He was there, somewhere.

She carried on conversations with him. 'I talked to Tim's teacher today. His grades are improving. Beth is in bed with a cold. Remember how she usually gets them this time of the year? We're all having dinner over at Florence and Douglas' tonight. They've been wonderful, darling.'

And, in the middle of the black night, 'The Dean stopped by the house. He wanted to know whether I planned to go back to teaching at the University. I told him not now. I don't want to leave the children alone, even for a little while. They need me so much. Do you think I should go back one day?'

A few days later: 'Douglas got a promotion, Edward. He was made chief of staff at the hospital.'

Could Edward hear her? She did not know. Was there a God, and was there a hereafter? Or was it a fable? T. S. Eliot said: 'Without some kind of God, man is not even very interesting.'

* * *

President Paul Ellison, Stanton Rogers and Floyd Baker were meeting in the Oval Office. The Secretary of State said, 'Mr President, we're both getting a lot of pressure. I don't think we can hold off any longer on naming an Ambassador to Romania. I'd like you to look over the list I gave you and select –'

'Thanks, Floyd. I appreciate your efforts. I still think Mary Ashley would be ideal. Her domestic situation has changed. What was rotten luck for her may turn out to be good luck for us. I want to try her again.'

Stanton Rogers said, 'Mr President, why don't I fly out there and see if I can persuade her?'

'Let's try it.'

Mary was preparing dinner when the telephone rang, and when she picked it up, an operator said, 'This is the White House. The President is calling Mrs Edward Ashley.'

Not now, she thought. *I don't want to speak to him or anyone*.

She remembered how excited his call had once made her. Now it was meaningless. She said, 'This is Mrs Ashley, but –'

'Would you please hold?'

Moments later, the familiar voice came on the line. 'Mrs Ashley, this is Paul Ellison. I just want you to know how terribly sorry we are about your husband. I understand he was a fine man.'

'Thank you, Mr President. It was kind of you to send flowers.'

'I don't want to intrude on your privacy, Mrs Ashley, and I know it's been a very short time, but now that your domestic situation has changed, I'm asking you to reconsider my offer of an ambassadorship.'

'Thank you, but I couldn't possibly –'

'Hear me out, please. I'm having someone fly out there to talk to you. His name is Stanton Rogers. I would appreciate it if you would at least meet with him.'

She did not know what to say. How could she explain that her world had been turned upside down, that her life had been shattered? All that mattered now were Beth and Tim. She decided that in all courtesy, she would see the man and then refuse as gracefully as possible.

'I'll meet with him, Mr President, but I won't change my mind.'

There was a popular bar on the Boulevard Bineau that Marin Groza's guards frequented when they were not on duty at the villa in Neuilly. Even Lev Pasternak occasionally visited the bar. Angel selected a table in an area of the room where conversations could be overheard. The guards, away from the rigid routine of the villa, liked to drink, and when they drank, they talked. Angel listened, seeking the villa's vulnerable point. There was always a vulnerable point. One simply had to be clever enough to find it.

* * *

It was three days before Angel overheard a conversation that gave the clue to the solution of the problem.

A guard was saying, 'I don't know what Groza is doing to the whores he brings in there, but they're sure whipping the hell out of him. You should hear the screaming that goes on. Last week I got a look at the whips he keeps in his closet . . .'

And the next night. '. . . The hookers our fearless leader gets up at the villa are real beauties. They bring them in from all over the world. Lev arranges it himself. He's smart. He never uses the same girl twice. That way, no one can use the girls to get at Marin Groza.'

It was all Angel needed.

Early the following morning. Angel changed rental cars and drove a Fiat into Paris. The sex shop was in Montmartre, on the Place Pigalle, in the middle of a section populated by whores and pimps. Angel went inside, walking slowly along the aisles, carefully studying the merchandise for sale. There were shackles and chains and iron-studded helmets, leather pants with slits in front, penis massagers and joy jelly, inflatable rubber dolls and porno video tapes. There were male douches and anal cream and six-foot-long braided-leather whips with thongs at the end.

Angel bought a whip, paid cash for it and left.

The following morning, Angel brought the whip back to the shop. The manager looked up and growled, 'No refunds.'

'I don't want a refund,' Angel explained. 'I feel awkward carrying this around. I would appreciate it if you would mail it for me. I'll pay extra, of course.'

Late that afternoon, Angel was on a plane to Buenos Aires.

The whip, carefully wrapped, arrived at the villa in Neuilly the following day. It was intercepted by the guard at the gatehouse. He read the store label on the package, opened it and examined the whip with great care. *You would think the old man had enough of these already.*

He passed it through, and a guard took it to Marin Groza's bedroom closet, where he placed it with the other whips.

TEN

Fort Riley, the oldest Army fort in the United States, was constructed in 1853 when Kansas was still referred to as 'Indian Territory'. It was built to protect wagon trains from Indian war parties. Today it is used primarily as a helicopter base and a landing field for smaller military fixed-wing planes.

When Stanton Rogers landed in a DC-7, he was welcomed by the base commander and his staff. A limousine was standing by, waiting to drive Stanton to the Ashley home. He had telephoned Mary after the President's call.

'I promise to make my visit as brief as possible, Mrs Ashley. I plan to fly in Monday afternoon to see you, if that's all right?'

He's being so polite. And he's such an important man. Why is the President sending him to talk to me? 'That will be fine.' In a reflex action, Mary asked, 'Would you care to have dinner with us?'

He hesitated. 'Thank you.' *It's going to be a long, boring evening*, Stanton thought.

147

When Florence Schiffer heard the news, she was thrilled. 'The President's Foreign Affairs Adviser is coming to dinner *here*? That means you're going to accept the appointment!'

'Florence, it means nothing of the kind. I promised the President I would talk to him. That's all.'

Florence put her arms around Mary and hugged her. 'I just want you to do whatever makes you happy.'

'I know that.'

Stanton Rogers was a formidable man, Mary decided. Mary had seen him on *Meet the Press*, and had seen photographs of him in *Time* Magazine, but she thought: *He looks bigger in person*. He was polite, but there was something distant about him.

'Permit me to convey again the President's sincere regrets about your terrible tragedy, Mrs Ashley.'

'Thank you.'

She introduced him to Beth and Tim. Mary went into the kitchen to see how Lucinda was getting along with the dinner.

'Whenever you're ready,' Lucinda said, 'but he'll hate it.'

When Mary had told Lucinda that Stanton Rogers was coming to the house for dinner, and that she wanted Lucinda to make a pot roast, Lucinda had said, 'People like Mr Rogers don't eat pot roast.'

'Oh. What do they eat?'

'Châteaubriand and crêpes suzettes.'

'We're having pot roast.'

'All right,' Lucinda said stubbornly, 'but it's the wrong dinner.'

Along with the pot roast she had prepared creamed mashed potatoes, fresh vegetables and a salad. She had baked a pumpkin pie for dessert. Stanton Rogers finished everything on his plate. During dinner Mary and Stanton Rogers discussed the problems of the farmers.

'The farmers in the mid-west are caught in a terrible squeeze between low prices and overproduction,' Mary said earnestly. 'They're too poor to paint, and too proud to whitewash.'

They talked about the colourful history of Junction City, and Stanton Rogers finally brought the discussion around to Romania.

'What is your opinion of President Ionescu's government?' he asked Mary.

'There is no government in Romania, in the real sense of the word,' Mary replied. 'Ionescu is the government. He's in total control.'

'Do you think there will be a revolution there?'

'Not in the present circumstances. The only man powerful enough to depose him is Marin Groza, who's in exile in France.'

The questioning went on. She was an expert on the Iron Curtain countries, and Stanton Rogers was visibly impressed. Mary had the uncomfortable feeling that he had been examining her under a

149

microscope all evening. She was closer to the mark than she knew.

Paul was right, Stanton Rogers thought. *She really is an authority on Romania.* And there was something more. *We need the opposite of the Ugly American. She's beautiful. And she and the children make an all-American package that will sell.* Stanton found himself getting more and more excited by the prospect. *She can be more useful than she realizes.*

At the end of the evening, Stanton Rogers said, 'Mrs Ashley, I'm going to be frank with you. I was against the President appointing you to a post as sensitive as Romania. I told him as much. I tell you this now because I've changed my mind. I think you may very well make an excellent ambassador.'

Mary shook her head. 'I'm sorry, Mr Rogers. I'm no politician. I'm just an amateur.'

'As President Ellison pointed out to me, some of our finest ambassadors have been amateurs. That is to say, their experience was not in the Foreign Service. Walter Annenberg, our former Ambassador to the United Kingdom of Great Britain, was a publisher.'

'I'm not –'

'Arthur Burns, our former Ambassador to the Federal Republic of Germany, was an assistant professor, and John Kenneth Galbraith, our Ambassador to India, was also a professor. Mike

Mansfield started out as a reporter before he became a Senator and then was appointed our Ambassador to Japan. I could give you a dozen more examples. These people were all what you would call "amateurs". What they had, Mrs Ashley, was intelligence, a love for their country, and goodwill towards the people of the country where they were sent to serve.'

'You make it sound so simple.'

'As you're probably aware, you've already been investigated very thoroughly. You've been approved for a security clearance, you have no problem with the IRS, and there's no conflict of interest. According to Dean Hunter, you're an excellent teacher, and of course you're an expert on Romania. You've got a running start. And last, but not least, you have the kind of image the President wants to project in the Iron Curtain countries, where they're fed so much adverse propaganda about us.'

Mary listened, a thoughtful expression on her face. 'Mr Rogers, I want you and the President to know that I appreciate everything you've said. But I couldn't accept it. I have Beth and Tim to think about. I can't just uproot them like –'

'There's a fine school for diplomats' children in Bucharest,' Rogers informed her. 'It would be a wonderful education for Tim and Beth to spend time in a foreign country. They'd learn things they could never learn in school here.'

The conversation was not going the way Mary had planned.

'I don't – I'll think about it.'

'I'm staying in town overnight,' Stanton Rogers said. 'I'll be at the All Seasons Motel. Believe me, Mrs Ashley, I know what a big decision this is for you. But this programme is important not only to the President, but to our country. Please think about that.'

When Stanton Rogers left, Mary went upstairs. The children were waiting for her, wide awake and excited.

'Are you going to take the job?' Beth asked.

'We have to have a talk. If I did decide to accept it, it would mean that you would have to leave school and all your friends. You would be living in a foreign country where we don't speak the language, and you would be going to a strange school.'

'Tim and I talked about all that,' Beth said, 'and you know what we think?'

'What?'

'That any country would be really lucky to have you as an ambassador, Mom.'

She talked to Edward that night: *You should have heard him, darling. He made it sound as though the President really needed me. There are probably a million people who could do a better job than I could, but he was very flattering. Do you remember how you and I talked about how exciting it would be? Well, I have the chance again, and I don't*

152

know what to do. To tell you the truth, I'm terri-
fied. This is our home. How can I bear to leave
it? There's so much of you here. She found that
she was crying. *This is all I have left of you. Help*
me decide. Please help me . . .

She sat by the window, in her robe, looking out
at the trees shivering in the howling, restless wind.

At dawn she made her decision.

At nine o'clock in the morning, Mary telephoned
the All Seasons Motel and asked for Stanton
Rogers.

When he came on the line, she said, 'Mr Rogers,
would you please tell the President that I will be
honoured to accept his nomination for the ambassadorship.'

ELEVEN

This one's even more beautiful than the others, the guard thought. She did not look like a prostitute. She could have been a movie actress or a model. She was in her early twenties, with long blonde hair and a clear, milky complexion. She wore a designer dress.

Lev Pasternak came to the gate himself to conduct her to the house. The girl, Bisera, was a Yugoslavian, and it was her first trip to France. The sight of all the armed security guards made her nervous. *I wonder what I've got myself into?* All Bisera knew was that her pimp had handed her a round-trip plane ticket and told her she would be paid $2,000 for an hour's work.

Lev Pasternak knocked at a bedroom door and Groza's voice called out, 'Come in.'

Pasternak opened the door and ushered the girl inside. Marin Groza was standing at the foot of the bed. He had on a robe, and she could tell he was naked under it.

Lev Pasternak said, 'This is Bisera.' He did not mention Marin Groza's name.

'Good evening, my dear. Come in.'

Pasternak left, carefully closing the door behind him, and Marin Groza was alone with the girl.

She moved towards him and smiled seductively. 'You look comfortable. Why don't I get undressed and we can both be comfortable?' She started to get out of her dress.

'No. Keep your clothes on, please.'

She looked at him in surprise. 'Don't you want me to –?'

Groza walked over to the closet and selected a whip. 'I want you to use this.'

So that was it. A slave fetish. Strange. He did not look the type. *You never know*, Bisera thought. 'Sure, honey. Whatever turns you on.'

Marin Groza took off his robe and turned around. Bisera was shocked by the sight of his scarred body. It was covered with cruel welts. There was something in his expression that puzzled her, and when she realized what it was, she was even more perplexed. It was anguish. The man was in an enormous amount of pain. Why did he want to be whipped? She watched him as he walked over to a stool and sat on it.

'Hard,' he commented. 'Whip me very hard.'

'All right.' Bisera picked up the long leather whip. Sado-masochism was not new to her, but there was something different here that she did not understand. *Well, it's none of my business*, Bisera thought. *Take the money and run.*

She raised the whip and cracked it down against his naked back.

'Harder,' he urged. 'Harder.'

He flinched with pain as the tough leather beat against his skin. Once . . . and twice . . . and again . . . and again, harder and harder. The vision he had been waiting for came to him then. Scenes of his wife and his daughter being raped seared through his brain. It was a gang-rape, and the laughing soldiers went from the woman to the child, their pants pulled down, waiting in line for their turn. Marin Groza strained against the stool as though bound to it. As the whip fell again and again, he could hear the screams of his wife and daughter begging for mercy, choking on the men's penises in their mouths, being raped and sodomized at the same time, until the blood started pouring out and their cries finally trailed off.

And Marin Groza groaned, 'Harder!' And with each crack of the whip, he felt the sharp blade of the knife tearing into his genitals, castrating him. He was having difficulty breathing. 'Get – get –' His voice was a croak. His lungs felt paralysed.

The girl stopped, holding the whip in mid-air. 'Hey! Are you all right? I –?'

She watched as he toppled to the floor, his eyes open, staring at nothing.

Bisera screamed, '*Help! Help!*'

Lev Pasternak came running in, gun in hand. He saw the figure on the floor. 'What happened?'

Bisera was hysterical. 'He's dead. He's dead! I didn't do anything. I just whipped him like he told me to. I swear!'

The doctor, who lived in the villa, came into the room within seconds. He looked at Marin Groza's body, and bent down to examine him. The skin had turned blue, and the muscles were rigid.

He picked up the whip and smelled it.

'What?'

'Damn! Curare. It's an extract from a South American plant. The Incas used it on darts to kill their enemies. Within three minutes the entire nervous system is paralysed.'

The two men stood there, staring helplessly at their dead leader.

The news of Marin Groza's assassination was carried all over the world by satellite. Lev Pasternak was able to keep the sordid details away from the press. In Washington, D.C., the President had a meeting with Stanton Rogers.

'Who do you think is behind it, Stan?'

'Either the Russians or Ionescu. In the end, it comes to the same thing, doesn't it? They didn't want the status quo disturbed.'

'So we'll be dealing with Ionescu. Very well. Let's push the Mary Ashley appointment through as quickly as possible.'

157

'She's on her way here, Paul.'
'Good.'

On hearing the news, Angel smiled. *It happened sooner than I thought.*

At 10 p.m. the private phone rang and the Controller picked it up. 'Hello.'

He heard the sound of Neusa Muñez's guttural voice. 'Angel saw this mornin's paper. He say to depos't the money in his bank account.'

'Inform him that it will be taken care of immediately. And Miss Muñez, tell Angel how pleased I am. Also tell him that I may need him again very soon. Do you have a telephone number where I can reach you?'

There was a long pause, then: 'I guess so.' She gave it to him.

'Fine. If Angel –'

The line went dead.

Damn the stupid bitch.

The money was deposited in a numbered account in Zürich that morning, and one hour after it was received, it was transferred to a Saudi Arabian bank in Geneva. *A person can't be too careful these days,* Angel thought. *The god-damned bankers will cheat you every chance they get.*

TWELVE

It was more than packing up a household. It was packing up a life. It was bidding farewell to thirteen years of dreams, memories, love. It was saying a final goodbye to Edward. This had been their home, and now it would become merely a house again, occupied by strangers with no awareness of the joys and sorrows and tears and laughter that had happened within these walls.

Douglas and Florence Schiffer were delighted that Mary had decided to accept the post.

'You'll be fantastic,' Florence assured Mary. 'Doug and I will miss you and the kids.'

'Promise that you'll come to Romania to visit us.'

'Promise.'

Mary was overwhelmed by the practical details that had to be taken care of, the multitude of unfamiliar responsibilities. She made a list:

Call the storage company to pick up personal things that we're leaving.

Cancel milkman.

Cancel newspaper.

Give postman new mailing address.

Sign lease on house.

Arrange for insurance.

Change over utilities.

Pay all bills.

Don't panic!

An indefinite leave of absence from the University had been arranged with Dean Hunter.

'I'll have someone take over your undergraduate classes. That's no problem. But your seminar students are certainly going to miss you.' He smiled. 'I'm sure you'll do us all proud, Mrs Ashley. Good luck.'

'Thank you.'

Mary withdrew the children from their school. There were travel arrangements to be made and airline tickets to be bought. In the past, Mary had taken all the financial transactions for granted, because Edward had been there to handle them. Now there was no Edward, except in her mind and in her heart, where he would always be.

Mary was worried about Beth and Tim. In the beginning, they had been enthusiastic about living in a foreign country, but now that they were face to face with the reality, they were filled with apprehension. They each came to Mary separately.

'Mother,' Beth said, 'I can't just leave all my

friends. I may never see Virgil again. Could I stay here until the end of the semester?'

Tim said, 'I just got into little league. If I go away, they'll find another third baseman. Maybe we can go after next summer, when the season's over. Please, Mom!'

They're frightened. Like their mother. Stanton Rogers had been so convincing. But alone with her fears in the middle of the night, Mary thought: *I don't know anything about being an ambassador. I'm a Kansas housewife pretending to be some kind of statesman. Everyone's going to know I'm a fraud. I was insane ever to agree to this.*

Finally, miraculously, everything was ready. The house had been rented on a long lease to a family that had just moved to Junction City.

It was time to leave.

'Doug and I will drive you to the airport,' Florence insisted.

The airport where they would catch the six-passenger commuter plane to Kansas City, Missouri, was located in Manhattan, Kansas. In Kansas City, they would transfer to a larger plane to Washington, D.C.

'Just give me a minute,' Mary said. She walked upstairs to the bedroom she and Edward had shared for so many wonderful years. She stood there, taking a long, last look.

I'm leaving now, my dearest. I just wanted to

*say goodbye. I think I'm doing what you would
have liked me to do. I hope I am. The only thing
that really bothers me is that I have a feeling we
may never come back here. I feel as though I'm
deserting you. But you'll be with me wherever I
go. I need you now more than I've ever needed
you. Stay with me. Help me. I love you so much.
Sometimes I don't think I can stand it without you.
Can you hear me, darling? Are you there . . . ?*

Douglas Schiffer saw to it that their baggage was
checked onto the little commuter plane. When
Mary saw the plane sitting on the tarmac, she froze
in her tracks. 'Oh, my God!'

'What's the matter?' Florence asked.

'I – I've been so busy, I forgot all about it.'

'About what?'

'Flying! Florence, I've never been up in a plane
in my life! I can't go up in that little thing!'

'Mary – the odds are a million to one against
anything happening.'

'I don't like the odds,' Mary said flatly. 'We'll
take the train.'

'You can't. They're expecting you in Washington
this afternoon.'

'*Alive*. I'm not going to be any good to them
dead.'

It took the Schiffers fifteen minutes to persuade
Mary to board the plane. Half an hour later, she
and the children were strapped aboard Air Mid-
West Flight Number 826. As the motors revved up

and the plane began racing down the runway, Mary closed her eyes and gripped the arms of her seat. Seconds later, they were airborne.

'Mama –'

'Sh! Don't talk!'

She sat rigid, refusing to look out of the window, concentrating on keeping the plane in the air. The children were pointing out the sights below, having a wonderful time.

Children, thought Mary bitterly. *What do they know!*

At the Kansas City Airport, they changed to a DC-10 and took off for Washington, D.C. Beth and Tim were seated together, and Mary was across the aisle from them. An elderly lady sat next to Mary.

'To tell you the truth, I'm a little nervous,' Mary's seatmate confessed. 'I've never flown before.'

Mary patted her hand and smiled. 'There's nothing to be nervous about. The odds are a million to one against anything happening.'

BOOK TWO

THIRTEEN

When their plane landed at Washington's Dulles Airport, Mary and the children were met by a young man from the State Department.

'Welcome to Washington, Mrs Ashley. My name is John Burns. Mr Rogers asked me to meet you and see that you get to your hotel safely. I've checked you in at the Riverdale Towers. I think you'll all be comfortable there.'

'Thank you.'

Mary introduced Beth and Tim.

'If you'll give me your baggage claim checks, Mrs Ashley, I'll see that everything is taken care of.'

Twenty minutes later they were all seated in a chauffeur-driven limousine, heading towards the centre of Washington.

Tim was staring out of the car window, awed. 'Look!' he exclaimed. 'There's the Lincoln Memorial!'

Beth was looking out of the other window. 'There's the Washington Monument!'

Mary looked at John Burns in embarrassment. 'I'm afraid the children aren't very sophisticated,' she apologized. 'You see, they've never been away from –' She glanced out of the window, and her eyes widened. 'Oh, my goodness!' she cried. 'Look! It's the White House!'

The limousine moved up Pennsylvania Avenue, surrounded by some of the most stirring landmarks in the world. Mary thought excitedly: *This is the city that rules the world. This is where the power is. And in a small way, I'm going to be a part of it.*

As the limousine approached the hotel, Mary asked, 'When will I see Mr Rogers?'

'He'll be in touch with you in the morning.'

Pete Connors, head of KUDESK, the counter-intelligence section of the CIA, was working late, and his day was far from over. Every morning at 3 a.m. a team reported to prepare the President's daily intelligence checklist, collected from overnight cables. The report, codenamed 'Pickles', had to be ready by 6 a.m. so that it could be on the President's desk at the start of his day. An armed courier carried the list to the White House, entering at the west gate. Pete Connors had a renewed interest in the intercepted cable traffic coming from behind the Iron Curtain, because much of it concerned the appointment of Mary Ashley as the American Ambassador to Romania.

The Soviet Union was worried that President

Ellison's plan was a ploy to penetrate their satellite countries, to spy on them or seduce them.

The commies aren't as worried as I am, Pete Connors thought grimly. *If the President's idea works this whole country is going to be open house for their fucking spies.*

Pete Connors had been informed the moment Mary Ashley landed in Washington. He had seen photographs of her and the children. *They're going to be* perfect, Connors thought happily.

The Riverdale Towers, one block away from the Watergate Complex, is a small family hotel with comfortable, nicely decorated suites.

A bellhop brought up the luggage, and as Mary started unpacking, the telephone rang. Mary picked it up. 'Hello.'

A masculine voice said, 'Mrs Ashley?'

'Yes.'

'My name is Ben Cohn. I'm a reporter with the *Washington Post*. I wonder if we could talk for a few minutes.'

Mary hesitated. 'We just checked in and I'm –'

'It will only take five minutes. I really just wanted to say hello.'

'Well, I – I suppose –'

'I'm on my way up.'

Ben Cohn was short and stocky, with a muscular body and the battered face of a prize fighter. *He looks like a sports reporter*, Mary thought.

He sat in an easy chair across from Mary. 'Your first time in Washington, Mrs Ashley?' Ben Cohn asked.

'Yes.' She noticed that he had no notebook or tape recorder.

'I won't ask you the dumb question.'

She frowned. 'What's the "dumb question"?'

'"How do you like Washington?" Whenever a celebrity steps off an airplane somewhere, the first thing they're asked is, "How do you like this place?"'

Mary laughed. 'I'm not a celebrity, but I think I'm going to like Washington a lot.'

'You were a professor at Kansas State University?'

'Yes. I taught a course called "Eastern Europe: Today's Politics".'

'I understand that the President first learned about you when he read a book of yours on Eastern Europe. And the magazine articles.'

'Yes.'

'And the rest, as they say, is history.'

'I suppose it *is* an unusual way to –'

'Not that unusual. Jeane Kirkpatrick came to President Reagan's attention in the same way, and he made her Ambassador to the UN.' He smiled at her. 'So you see, there's precedent. That's one of the big buzz words in Washington. Precedent. Your grandparents were Romanian?'

'My grandfather. That's right.'

Ben Cohn stayed for another fifteen minutes, getting information on Mary's background.

Mary asked, 'When will this interview appear in the paper?' She wanted to be sure to send copies to Florence and Douglas and her other friends back home.

Ben Cohn rose and said evasively, 'I'm going to save it for now.' There was something about the situation that puzzled him. The problem was that he was not sure what it was. 'We'll be talking again later.'

After he left, Beth and Tim came into the living room. 'Was he nice, Mom?'

'Yes.' She hesitated, unsure. 'I think so.'

The following morning Stanton Rogers telephoned.

'Good morning, Mrs Ashley. It's Stanton Rogers.'

It was like hearing the voice of an old friend. *Maybe it's because he's the only person in town I know*, Mary thought. 'Good morning, Mr Rogers. Thank you for having Mr Burns meet us at the airport, and for arranging our hotel.'

'I trust it's satisfactory?'

'It's lovely.'

'I thought it would be a good idea if we met to discuss some of the procedures you'll be going through.'

'I would like that.'

'Why don't we make it lunch today at the Grand? It's not far from your hotel. One o'clock?'

'Fine.'

'I'll meet you in the downstairs dining room.'

It was starting.

Mary arranged for the children to have room service, and at one o'clock a taxi dropped her off at the Grand Hotel. Mary looked at it in awe. The Grand Hotel is its own centre of power. Heads of State and diplomats from all over the world stay there, and it is easy to see why. It is an elegant building, with an imposing lobby with Italian marble floors and gracious columns under a circular ceiling. There was a landscaped courtyard, with a fountain and an outdoor swimming pool. A marble staircase led down to the promenade restaurant, where Stanton Rogers was waiting for her.

'Good afternoon, Mrs Ashley.'

'Good afternoon, Mr Rogers.'

He laughed. 'That sounds so formal. What about Stan and Mary?'

She was pleased. 'That would be nice.'

Stanton Rogers seemed different somehow, and the change was hard for Mary to define. In Junction City there had been an aloofness about him, almost a resentment towards her. Now that seemed to have completely vanished. He was warm and friendly. *The difference is that he's accepted me*, Mary thought happily.

'Would you like a drink?'

'Thank you, no.'

They ordered lunch. The entrées seemed very

expensive to her. *It's not like the prices in Junction City*. Her hotel suite was $250 a day. *At that rate, my money's not going to last very long*, Mary thought.

'Stan, I don't want to seem rude, but can you tell me how much an ambassador is paid?'

He laughed. 'That's a fair question. Your salary will be sixty-five thousand dollars a year, plus a housing allowance.'

'When does that begin?'

'The moment you're sworn in.'

'And until then?'

'You'll be paid seventy-five dollars a day.'

Her heart sank. That would not even take care of her hotel bill, let alone all the other expenses.

'Will I be in Washington long?' Mary asked.

'About a month. We'll do everything we can to expedite your move. The Secretary of State has cabled the Romanian government for approval of your appointment. Just between us, there have already been private discussions between the two governments. There will be no problem with the Romanians, but you still have to pass the Senate.'

So the Romanian government is going to accept me, Mary thought wonderingly. *Perhaps I'm better qualified than I realized.*

'I've set up an informal consultation for you with the Chairman of the Senate Foreign Relations Committee. The next stop after that will be an open hearing of the full committee. They'll ask you questions about your background, your loyalty to this country, your perceptions of the job, and what you hope to accomplish.'

'What happens after that?'

'The committee votes, and when they turn in their report, the full Senate votes.'

Mary said slowly, 'Nominations have been voted down in the past, haven't they?'

'The President's prestige is on the line with this one. You'll have the full backing of the White House. The President is eager to push your appointment through as quickly as possible. Incidentally, I thought you and the children might like to do some sightseeing in the next few days, so I've arranged for a car and driver for you, and a private tour of the White House.'

'Oh! Thank you so much.'

Stanton Rogers smiled. 'My pleasure.'

The private tour of the White House was arranged for the following morning. A guide escorted them. They were taken through the Jacqueline Kennedy Rose Garden and the sixteenth-century-style American Garden containing a pool, trees and herbs for use in the White House kitchen.

'Just ahead,' the guide announced, 'is the East Wing. It houses military offices, Congressional liaisons to the President, a visitors' office, and the First Lady's office.'

They went through the West Wing and looked into the President's Oval Office.

'How many rooms have they got in this place?' Tim asked.

'There are one hundred and thirty-two rooms, sixty-nine closets, twenty-nine fireplaces and seventeen bathrooms.'

'They sure must go to the bathroom a lot.'

'President Washington helped supervise much of the construction of the White House. He is the only President who never resided here.'

'I don't blame him,' Tim muttered. 'It's too darned big.'

Mary nudged him, red-faced.

The tour took almost two hours, and by the end of it the Ashley family was exhausted and impressed.

This is where it all began, Mary thought. *And now I'm going to be a part of it.*

'Mom?'

'Yes, Beth?'

'You have a funny look on your face.'

The call from the President's office came the following morning.

'Good morning, Mrs Ashley. President Ellison wondered whether you could make yourself available this afternoon to meet with him?'

Mary swallowed. 'Yes, I – of course.'

'Would three o'clock be convenient?'

'That would be fine.'

'A limousine will be downstairs for you at two forty-five.'

* * *

Paul Ellison rose as Mary was ushered into the Oval Office. He walked over to shake her hand, grinned and said, 'Gotcha!'

Mary laughed. 'I'm glad you did, Mr President. This is a great honour for me.'

'Sit down, Mrs Ashley. May I call you Mary?'

'Please.'

They sat down on the couch.

President Ellison said, 'You're going to be my doppelgänger. Do you know what that is?'

'It's a kind of identical spirit of a living person.'

'Right. And that's us. I can't tell you how excited I was when I read your latest article, Mary. It was as though I were reading something I had written. There are a lot of people who don't believe our people-to-people plan can work, but you and I are going to fool them.'

Our people-to-people plan. *We're* going to fool them. *He's a charmer*, Mary thought. Aloud, she said, 'I want to do everything I can to help, Mr President.'

'I'm counting on you. Very heavily. Romania is the testing ground. Since Groza was assassinated, your job is going to be more difficult. If we can pull it off there, we can make it work in the other communist countries.'

They spent the next thirty minutes discussing some of the problems that lay ahead, and then Paul Ellison said, 'Stan Rogers will keep in close touch with you. He's become a big fan of yours.' He held out his hand. 'Good luck, doppelgänger.'

*   *   *

The next afternoon Stanton Rogers telephoned Mary. 'You have an appointment at nine o'clock tomorrow morning with the Chairman of the Senate Foreign Relations Committee.'

The committee on Foreign Relations has offices in the Russell Building, the oldest government building in Washington. A plaque in the hallway at the right side of the door reads: COMMITTEE ON FOREIGN RELATIONS SD-419.

The Chairman was a rotund, grey-haired man with sharp green eyes and the easy manner of a professional politician.

He greeted Mary at the door. 'Charlie Campbell. It's a pleasure to meet you, Mrs Ashley. I've certainly been hearing a lot about you.'

Good or bad? Mary wondered.

He led her to a chair. 'Some coffee?'

'No, thank you, Senator.' She was too nervous to hold a cup in her hand.

'Well, then, let's get right down to business. The President is eager to have you represent us in Romania. Naturally, we all want to give him our full support in every way possible. The question is – do you think you're qualified to handle that position, Mrs Ashley?'

'No, sir.'

Her answer caught him off guard. 'I beg your pardon?'

'If you mean have I had any diplomatic experience in dealing with foreign countries, then I'm not qualified. However, I've been told that one-third of the country's ambassadors are also people without previous experience. What I would bring to my job is a knowledge of Romania. I'm familiar with its economic and sociological problems and with its political background. I believe I could project a positive image of our country to the Romanians.'

Well, Charlie Campbell thought in surprise. *I expected a bubble-head.* In fact, Campbell had resented Mary Ashley even before meeting her. He had been given orders from the top to see that Mary Ashley got his committee's approval, no matter what they thought of her. A lot of snickering was going on in the corridors of power about what a gaffe the President had made by selecting an unknown hayseed from a place called Junction City, Kansas. *But, by God*, Campbell thought, *I think the boys may be in for a little surprise.*

Aloud, he said, 'The full Hearing Committee meets at nine o'clock Wednesday morning.'

The night before the hearing, Mary was in a panic. *Darling, when they question me about my experience, what am I going to tell them? That in Junction City I was homecoming queen, and that I won the ice skating contest three years in a row? I'm panicky. Oh, how I wish you were here with me.*

But once again, the irony struck her. If Edward were alive, *she* would not be here. *I'd be safe and*

*warm at home with my husband and children, where
I belong.*

She lay awake all night.

The hearing was held in the Senate Foreign
Relations Committee Room, with the full fifteen
members of the committee present, seated on a
dais in front of a wall that held four large world
maps. Along the left side of the room was the
press table, filled with reporters, and in the centre,
seats for 200 spectators. The corners were brightly
lit for television cameras. The room was filled
to overflowing. Pete Connors sat in a back row.
There was a sudden hush as Mary entered with
Beth and Tim.

Mary was wearing a dark, tailored suit and a
white blouse. The children had been forced out of
their jeans and sweaters and were in their Sunday
best.

Ben Cohn, seated at the press table, watched as
they came in. *Jesus*, he thought, *they look like a
Normal Rockwell cover.*

An attendant seated the children in a front row,
and Mary was escorted to the witness chair facing
the committee. She sat under the glare of the hot
lights, trying to conceal her nervousness.

The hearing began. Charlie Campbell smiled
down at Mary. 'Good morning, Mrs Ashley. We
thank you for appearing before this committee. We
will proceed to the questions.'

They started innocently enough.

'Name . . . ?'

'Widow . . . ?'

'Children . . . ?'

The questions were gentle and supportive.

'According to the biography we've been furnished, Mrs Ashley, for the last several years you've taught political science at Kansas State University. Is that correct?'

'Yes, sir.'

'You're a native of Kansas?'

'Yes, Senator.'

'Your grandparents were Romanian?'

'My grandfather. Yes, sir.'

'You've written a book and articles on rapprochement between the United States and Soviet bloc countries?'

'Yes, sir.'

'The latest article was printed in *Foreign Affairs* magazine and came to the attention of the President?'

'That's my understanding.'

'Mrs Ashley, would you kindly tell this committee what the basic premise of your article is?'

Her nervousness was rapidly disappearing. She was on sure ground now, discussing a subject on which she was an authority. She felt as though she were conducting a seminar at school.

'Several regional economic pacts currently exist in the world, and because they are mutually exclusive, they serve to divide the world into antagonistic and competitive blocs, instead of uniting it. Europe has the Common Market, the Eastern bloc has COMECON, and then there is the OECD, consisting of the free market countries and the non-aligned movement of third world states. My premise is very simple: I would like to see all the various and discrete organizations linked together by economic ties. Individuals who are engaged in a profitable partnership don't kill one another. I believe that the same principle applies to countries. I would like to see our country spearhead a movement to form a common market that includes allies and adversaries alike. Today, as an example, we're paying billions of dollars to store surplus grain in grain elevators while people in dozens of countries are starving. The one-world common market could solve that. It could cure inequities of distribution, at fair market prices for everyone. I would like to try to help make that happen.'

Senator Harold Turkel, a senior member of the Foreign Relations Committee, and a member of the opposition party, spoke up. 'I'd like to ask the nominee a few questions.'

Ben Cohn leaned forward in his seat. *Here we go.*

Senator Turkel was in his seventies, tough and abrasive, a noted curmudgeon. 'Is this your first time in Washington, Mrs Ashley?'

'Yes, sir. I think it's one of the most –'

'I suppose you've done a good deal of travelling?'

'Well, no. My husband and I had planned to travel, but –'

181

'Have you ever been to New York?'

'No, sir.'

'California?'

'No, sir.'

'Been to Europe?'

'No. As I said, we planned to –'

'Have you, in fact, ever been outside the State of Kansas, Mrs Ashley?'

'Yes. I gave a lecture at the University of Chicago and a series of talks in Denver and Atlanta.'

Turkel said drily, 'That must have been very exciting for you, Mrs Ashley. I can't recall when this committee has been asked to approve a less qualified candidate for an ambassadorial post. You expect to represent the United States of America in a sensitive Iron Curtain country, and you're telling us that your entire knowledge of the world comes from living in Junction City, Kansas, and spending a few days in Chicago and Denver and Atlanta. Is that true?'

Mary was aware of the television cameras focused on her, and she held back her temper. 'No, sir. My knowledge of the world comes from studying it. I have a Ph.D. in political science and I've been teaching at Kansas State University for five years, with an emphasis on the Iron Curtain countries. I'm familiar with the current problems of the Romanian people and what their government thinks of the United States, and why.' Her voice was stronger now. 'All they know about this country is what their propaganda machines tell them. I would like to go over there and try to convince them that the United States is not a greedy, war-hungry country. I would like to show them what a typical American family is like. I –'

She broke off, afraid she had gone too far in her anger. And then, to her surprise, the members of the committee started to applaud. All except Turkel.

The questioning went on.

One hour later, Charlie Campbell asked, 'Are there any more questions?'

'I think the nominee has expressed herself very clearly,' one of the senators commented.

'I agree. Thank you, Mrs Ashley. This session is adjourned.'

Pete Connors studied Mary thoughtfully for a moment, then quietly left as the members of the press swarmed around her.

'Was the President's appointment a surprise to you?'

'Do you think they're going to approve your appointment, Mrs Ashley?'

'Do you really believe that teaching about a country qualifies you to –'

'Turn this way, Mrs Ashley. Smile, please. One more.'

'Mrs Ashley –'

Ben Cohn stood apart from the others, watching and listening. *She's good,* he thought. *She has all the right answers. I wish to hell I knew the right questions.*

* * *

When Mary arrived back at the hotel, emotionally drained, Stanton Rogers was on the telephone.

'Hello, Madam Ambassador.'

She felt giddy with relief. 'You mean I *made* it? Oh, Stan. Thank you so much. I can't tell you how excited I am.'

'So am I, Mary.' His voice was filled with pride. 'So am I.'

When Mary told the children, they hugged her.

'I knew you'd make it!' Tim screamed.

Beth asked quietly, 'Do you think Daddy knows?'

'I'm sure he does, darling.' Mary smiled. 'I wouldn't be surprised if he gave the committee a little nudge . . .'

Mary telephoned Florence, and when she heard the news, she began to cry. 'Fantastic! Wait until I spread this around town!'

Mary laughed. 'I'll have a room at the Embassy ready for you and Douglas.'

'When do you leave for Romania?'

'Well, first the full Senate has to vote, but Stan says it's just a formality.'

'What happens next?'

'I have to go through a few weeks of briefing sessions in Washington, and then the children and I are on our way to Romania.'

'I can't wait to call the *Daily Union*!' Florence exclaimed. 'The town will probably put up a statue

to you. I've got to go now. I'm too excited to talk.
I'll call you tomorrow.'

Ben Cohn heard the results of the confirmation
hearing when he returned to his office. He was still
bothered. And he did not know why.

FOURTEEN

As Stanton Rogers predicted, the full Senate vote was a formality. Mary was voted in by a comfortable majority. When President Ellison heard the news, he said to Stanton Rogers, 'Our plan is under way, Stan. Nothing can stop us now.'

Stanton Rogers nodded. 'Nothing,' he agreed.

Pete Connors was in his office when he received the news. He immediately wrote out a message and encoded it. One of his men was on duty in the CIA cable room.

'I want to use the Roger Channel,' Connors said. 'Wait outside.'

The Roger Channel is the CIA's ultra-private cable system, available only for use by top-level executives. Messages are sent by a laser transmitter, on an ultrahigh frequency in a fraction of a second. When Connors was alone, he dispatched the cable. It was addressed to Sigmund.

*   *   *

During the next week, Mary called on the Deputy Secretary for Political Affairs, the head of the CIA, the Secretary of Commerce, the directors of the New York Chase Manhattan Bank, and several important Jewish organizations. Each of them had admonitions, advice and requests.

Ned Tillingast, at the CIA, was enthusiastic. 'It will be great to get our people back into action there, Madam Ambassador. Romania's been a blind spot for us since we became *personae non gratae*. I'll assign a man to your embassy as one of your attachés.' He gave her a meaningful look. 'I'm sure you'll give him your full cooperation.'

Mary wondered exactly what that meant. *Don't ask*, she decided.

The swearing-in ceremony of new ambassadors is customarily presided over by the Secretary of State, and there are usually twenty-five to thirty candidates sworn in at the same time. The morning the ceremony was to take place, Stanton Rogers telephoned Mary.

'Mary, President Ellison has asked that you be at the White House at noon. The President himself is going to swear you in. Bring Tim and Beth.'

The Oval Office was filled with members of the press. When President Ellison walked in with Mary and her children, television cameras began to turn and still cameras began to flash. Mary had spent the previous half-hour with the President, and he had been warm and reassuring.

'You're perfect for this assignment,' he told her, 'or I would never have chosen you. You and I are going to make this dream come true.'

And it does seem like a dream, Mary thought as she faced the battery of cameras.

'Raise your right hand, please.'

Mary repeated after the President: 'I, Mary Elizabeth Ashley, do solemnly swear that I will support and defend the Constitution of the United States against all enemies foreign and domestic, that I will bear true faith and allegiance to the same, that I take this obligation freely and without any mental reservation or purpose of evasion, that I will well and faithfully discharge the duties of the office on which I am about to enter, so help me God.'

And it was done. She was the Ambassador to the Socialist Republic of Romania.

The treadmill began. Mary was ordered to report to the European and Yugoslavian Affairs Section at the State Department, located in the Mall Building that overlooked the Washington and Lincoln Memorials. There she was assigned a small, temporary, box-like office next to the Romanian desk.

James Stickley, the Romanian desk officer, was a career diplomat with twenty-five years in the service. He was in his late fifties, of medium height, with a vulpine face and small, thin lips. His eyes were a pale, cold brown. He looked with disdain on the political appointees who were invading his world. He was considered the foremost expert on the Romanian desk, and when President Ellison had announced his plan to support an Ambassador to Romania, Stickley had been ecstatic, fully expecting that the post would be given to him. The news about Mary Ashley was a bitter blow. It was bad enough to have been passed over, but to have lost out to a political appointee – a nobody from Kansas – was galling.

'Can you believe it?' he asked Bruce, his closest friend. 'Half of our ambassadors are fucking appointees. That could never happen in England or France, chum. *They* use professional career officers. Would the Army ask an amateur to be a general? Well, overseas our fucking amateur ambassadors are generals.'

'You're drunk, Jimbo.'

'I'm gonna get drunker.'

He studied Mary Ashley now, as she sat across from his desk.

Mary was also studying Stickley. There was something mean-looking about him. *I wouldn't want to have him as an enemy*, Mary thought.

'You're aware that you're being sent to an extremely sensitive post, Mrs Ashley?'

'Yes, of course. I –'

'Our last Ambassador to Romania put one

wrong foot forward and the whole relationship exploded in our faces. It's taken us three years to get back in the door. The President would be damned mad if we blew it again.'

If I blew it, he means.

'We're going to have to make an instant expert out of you. We don't have a lot of time.' He handed her an armful of files. 'You can start by reading these reports.'

'I'll dedicate my morning to it.'

'No. In thirty minutes you're scheduled to begin a language course in Romanian. The course usually takes months, but I have orders to push you through the mill.'

Time became a blur, a whirlwind of activity that left Mary exhausted. Every morning she and Stickley went through the daily files of the Romanian desk together.

'I'll be reading the cables you send in,' Stickley informed her. 'They will be yellow copies for action, or white copies for information. Duplicates of your cables will go to Defence, the CIA, the USIA, the Treasury Department, and a dozen other departments. One of the first issues you'll be expected to resolve is Americans being held in Romanian prisons. We want their release.'

'What are they charged with?'

'Espionage, drugs, theft – anything the Romanians want to charge them with.'

Mary wondered how on earth one went about

getting a charge of espionage dismissed. *I'll find a way*.

'Right,' she said briskly.

'Remember – Romania is one of the more independent Iron Curtain countries. We have to encourage that attitude.'

Exactly.

Stickley said, 'I'm going to give you a package. Don't let it out of your hands. It's for your eyes only. When you've read it and digested it, I want you to return it to me personally tomorrow morning. Any questions?'

'No, sir.'

He handed Mary a thick manila envelope sealed with red tape. 'Sign for it, please.'

She sighed.

During the ride on the way back to the hotel, Mary clutched it to her lap, feeling like a character in a James Bond movie.

The children were dressed up and waiting for her.

Oh dear, Mary remembered. *I promised to take them out to a Chinese dinner and a movie.*

'Fellas,' she said. 'There's been a change of plans. We'll have to make our excursion another evening. Tonight we're going to stay in and have room service. I have some urgent work to do.'

'Sure, Mom.'

'Okay.'

And Mary thought: *Before Edward died, they*

*would have screamed like banshees. But they've
had to grow up. We've all had to grow up.*

She took them both in her arms. 'I'll make it
up to you,' she promised.

The material James Stickley had given her was
incredible. *No wonder he wants this right back*,
Mary thought. There were detailed reports on
every important Romanian official, from the
President to the Minister of Commerce. There
was a dossier on their sex habits, financial deal-
ings, friendships, personal traits and prejudices.
Some of the reading was lurid. The Minister of
Commerce, for example, was sleeping with his
mistress and his chauffeur, while his wife was
having an affair with her maid.

Mary was up half the night memorizing the
names and peccadilloes of the people with whom
she would be dealing. *I wonder if I'll be able to
keep a straight face when I meet them?*

In the morning, she returned the secret documents.

Stickley said, 'All right, now you know everything you should know about the Romanian
leaders.'

'And then some,' Mary murmured.

'There's something you should bear in mind: By
now the Romanians know everything there is to
know about *you*.'

'That won't get them far,' Mary said.

'No?' Stickley leaned back in his chair. 'You're

192

a woman, and you're alone. You can be sure they've already marked you as an easy target. They'll play on your loneliness. Every move you make will be watched and recorded. The Embassy and the Residence will be bugged. In communist countries, we're forced to use local staffs, so every servant in the Residence will be a member of the Romanian security police.'

He's trying to frighten me, Mary thought. *Well, it won't work*.

Every hour of Mary's day seemed to be accounted for, and most of the evenings. Besides Romanian language lessons, her schedule included a course at the Foreign Service Institute in Rosslyn, briefings at the Defence Intelligence Agency, meetings with the Secretary of the ISA – International Security Affairs – and with Senate committees. They all had demands, advice, questions.

Mary felt guilty about Beth and Tim. With Stanton Rogers' help, she had found a tutor for the children. In addition, Beth and Tim had met some other children living in the hotel, so at least they had playmates; still, she hated leaving them on their own so much.

Mary made it a point to have breakfast with them every morning before she went off to her 8 a.m. language course at the Institute. The language was impossible. *I'm surprised even Romanians can speak it*. She studied the phrases aloud:

'Good morning.'	*Bună Dimineaţa*
'Thank you.'	*Mulţumésc*
'You're welcome.'	*Cu Plăcére*
'I don't understand.'	*Nu Inteleg*
'Sir.'	*Domnule*
'Miss.'	*Domnisoara*

And none of the words was pronounced the way it was spelled.

Beth and Tim sat watching her struggle over her homework, and Beth grinned. 'This is our revenge for your making us learn the multiplication tables.'

James Stickley said, 'I want you to meet your military attaché, Madam Ambassador, Colonel William McKinney.'

Bill McKinney wore mufti, but his military bearing was like a uniform. He was a tall, middle-aged man with a seamed, weathered face.

'Madam Ambassador.' His voice was rough and gravelly, as though his throat had suffered an injury.

'I'm pleased to meet you,' Mary said.

Colonel McKinney was her first staff member, and meeting him gave her a sense of excitement. It seemed to bring her new position much closer.

'I look forward to working with you in Romania,' Colonel McKinney said.

'Have you been to Romania before?'

The Colonel and James Stickley exchanged a look.

'He's been there before,' Stickley replied.

Every Monday afternoon diplomatic sessions for new ambassadors were held in a conference room on the eighth floor of the State Department.

'In the Foreign Service, we have a strict chain of command,' the class was told. 'At the top is the Ambassador. Under him – (*under her*, Mary automatically thought) – is the DCM – the Deputy Chief of Mission. Under him – (*under her*) – are the political consular, economic consular, administrative consular, and public affairs consular. Then you have agriculture, commerce and the military attaché.' *That's Colonel McKinney*, Mary thought. 'When you are at your new posts, you will have diplomatic immunity. You cannot be arrested for speeding, drunken driving, burning down a house, or even for murder. When you die, no one can touch your body or examine any note you may have left. You don't have to pay your bills – the stores can't sue you.'

Someone in the class called out, 'Don't let my wife hear that!'

The instructor glanced at his watch. 'Before our next session, I suggest you study the Foreign Affairs Manual, Volume Two, Section Three Hundred, which talks about social relationships. Thank you.'

* * *

Mary and Stanton Rogers were having lunch at the Watergate Hotel.

'President Ellison would like you to do some public relations for him,' Rogers said.

'What kind of public relations?'

'We'll set up some national things. Press interviews, radio, television –'

'I've never – well, if it's important. I'll try.'

'Good. We'll have to get you a new wardrobe. You can't pose in the same dress twice.'

'Stan, that would cost a fortune! Besides, I don't have time to shop. I'm busy from early morning until late at night. If –'

'No problem. Helen Moody.'

'What?'

'She's one of Washington's top professional shoppers. Just leave everything to her.'

Helen Moody was an attractive, outgoing black woman who had been a successful model before she started her own personal shopping service. She appeared at Mary's hotel room early one morning and spent an hour going through her wardrobe.

'Very nice, for Junction City,' she said frankly, 'but we have to wow Washington, D.C. Right?'

'I don't have much money to –'

Helen Moody grinned. 'I know where the bargains are. And we'll do it fast. You're going to need a floor-length evening gown, a dress for cocktail parties and evening receptions, an afternoon dress for tea parties and lunch parties, a suit for street or office wear, a black dress, and an appropriate head covering for official mournings or funerals.'

The shopping took three days. When it was finished, Helen Moody studied Mary Ashley. 'You're a pretty lady, but I think we can do even better for you. I want you to see Susan at Rainbow for makeup and then I'll send you to Billy at Sunshine for your hair.'

A few evenings later Mary ran into Stanton Rogers at a formal dinner given at the Corcoran Gallery. He looked at Mary and smiled. 'You look absolutely ravishing.'

The media blitz began. It was orchestrated by Ian Villiers, Chief of Press Relations for the State Department. Villiers was in his late forties, a dynamic ex-newspaperman who seemed to know everybody in the media.

Mary found herself in front of the cameras on *Good Morning America, Meet the Press,* and *Firing Line.* She was interviewed by the *Washington Post,* the *New York Times,* and half a dozen other important daily papers. She did interviews for the London *Times, Der Spiegel, Oggi,* and *Le Monde. Time* magazine and *People* did feature articles on her and the children. Mary Ashley's photograph seemed to be everywhere, and whenever there was a news break about an event in some far-off corner of the world, she was asked for her comments. Overnight, Mary Ashley and her children became celebrities.

Tim said, 'Mom, it's really spooky seeing our pictures on the covers of all the magazines.'

'*Spooky* is the word,' Mary agreed.

Somehow she felt uneasy about all the publicity. She spoke to Stanton Rogers about it.

'Look on it as a part of your job. The President is trying to create an image. By the time you arrive in Europe, everyone there will know who you are.'

Ben Cohn and Akiko were lying in bed, naked. Akiko was a lovely Japanese girl, ten years younger than the reporter. They had met a few years earlier, when he was writing a story on models, and they had been together ever since.

Cohn was having a problem.

'What's the matter, baby?' Akiko asked softly. 'Would you like me to work on you some more?'

His thoughts were far away. 'No. I've already got a hard-on.'

'I don't see it,' she teased.

'It's in my mind, Akiko. I've got a hard-on for a story. There's something weird happening in this town.'

'So what else is new?'

'This is different. I can't figure it out.'

'Do you want to talk about it?'

'It's Mary Ashley. I've seen her on the covers of six magazines in the last two weeks, and she hasn't

198

even taken up her post yet! Akiko, someone is giving Mrs Ashley a movie-star build-up. She and her two kids are being splashed all over the newspapers and magazines. Why?'

'I'm supposed to be the one with the devious Oriental mind. I think you're complicating that which is very simple.'

Ben Cohn lit a cigarette and took an angry puff on it. 'You could be right,' he grumbled.

She reached down and began to stroke him. 'How about putting out that cigarette and lighting me . . . ?'

'There's a party being given for Vice President Bradford,' Stanton Rogers informed Mary, 'and I've arranged for you to be invited. It's on Friday night at the Pan American Union.'

The Pan American Union was a large, sedate building with a huge courtyard, and was frequently used for diplomatic functions. The dinner for the Vice President was an elaborate affair, with tables holding gleaming antique silverware and sparkling Baccarat glasses. There was a small orchestra. The guest list consisted of the capital's elite. Besides the Vice President and his wife, there were senators, ambassadors and celebrities from all walks of life.

Mary looked around at the glamorous gathering. *I must remember everything so I can tell Beth and Tim about it*, she thought.

* * *

When dinner was announced, Mary found herself at a table with an interesting mix of senators, State Department officials and diplomats. The people were charming and the dinner was excellent.

At eleven o'clock, Mary looked at her watch and said to the Senator on her right, 'I didn't realize it was so late. I promised the children I'd be back early.'

She rose and nodded to the people seated at her table. 'It's been lovely meeting you all. Good night.'

There was a stunned silence, and everyone in the huge banquet hall turned to watch Mary as she walked across the dance floor and exited.

'Oh, my God!' Stanton Rogers whispered. 'No one told her!'

Stanton Rogers had breakfast with Mary the following morning.

'Mary,' he said, 'this is a town that takes its rules seriously. A lot of them are stupid, but we all have to live by them.'

'Oh, oh. What did I do?'

He sighed. 'You broke rule number one: No one – but no one – ever leaves a party before the guest of honour. Last night it happened to be the Vice President of the United States.'

'Oh, dear.'

'Half the telephones in Washington have been ringing off the hook.'

'I'm sorry, Stan. I didn't know. Anyway, I had promised the children –'

'There are no children in Washington – only young voters. This town is about power. Never forget that.'

Money was proving to be a problem. Living expenses were horrendous. The price of everything in Washington seemed to Mary to be outrageous. She gave some laundry and pressing to the hotel's valet service, and when she got the bill, she was shocked. 'Five dollars and fifty cents to wash a blouse,' she said. 'And a dollar ninety-five for a brassière!' *No more*, she vowed. *From now on I'll do the laundry myself.*

She soaked her pantihose in cold water, and then put them in the freezer. They lasted much longer that way. She washed the children's socks and handkerchiefs and underpants along with her bras in the bathroom sink. She spread the handkerchiefs against the mirror to dry, and then carefully folded them so that they did not have to be ironed. She steamed out her dresses and Tim's trousers by hanging them on the shower curtain rack, turning the hot water of the shower on full force, and closing the bathroom door. When Beth opened the door one morning, she was hit by a wall of steam.

'Mother – what are you *doing*?'

'Saving money,' Mary informed her loftily. 'The laundry charges a fortune.'

'What if the President walked in? How would it look? He'd think we were Okies.'

201

'The President's not going to walk in. And close the bathroom door, please. You're wasting money.'

Okies, indeed! If the President walked in and saw what she was doing, he would be proud of her. She would show him the hotel laundry list and let him see how much she was saving by using a little yankee ingenuity. He would be impressed. *If more people in government had your imagination, Madam Ambassador, the economy of this country would be in a lot better shape than it is. We've lost the pioneering spirit that made this country great. Our people have gone soft. We rely too much on time-saving electrical appliances and not enough on ourselves. I would like to use you as a shining example to some of the spendthrifts in Washington who think this country is made of money. You could teach them all a lesson. As a matter of fact, I have a wonderful idea. Mary Ashley, I'm going to make you Secretary of the Treasury.*

Steam was seeping out from under the bathroom door. Dreamily, Mary opened the door. A cloud of steam poured into the living room.

There was the sound of the doorbell, and a moment later Beth said, 'Mother, James Stickley is here to see you.'

FIFTEEN

'The whole thing gets weirder and weirder,' Ben Cohn said. He was sitting up in bed, nude, his young mistress, Akiko Hadaka, at his side. They were watching Mary Ashley on *Meet the Press*.

She was saying, 'I believe that mainland China is heading for a more humane, individualistic communist society with its incorporation of Hong Kong and Macao.'

'Now what the fuck does that lady know about China?' Ben Cohn muttered. He turned to Akiko. 'You're looking at a housewife from Kansas who's become an expert on everything overnight.'

'She seems very bright,' Akiko said.

'Bright is beside the point. Every time she gives an interview, the reporters go crazy. It's like a feeding frenzy. How did she get on *Meet the Press*? I'll tell you how. Someone decided that Mary Ashley was going to be a celebrity. Who? Why? Charles Lindbergh never had a build-up like this.'

'Who's Charles Lindbergh?'

Ben Cohn sighed. 'That's the problem with the generation gap. There's no communication.'

Akiko said softly, 'There are other ways to communicate.'

She pushed him gently down on the bed and moved on top of him. She worked her way down his body, flicking her long, silken hair across his chest and his stomach and his groin, watching him grow hard. She stroked him and said, 'Hello, Arthur.'

'Arthur wants to get inside you.'

'Not yet. I'll be back to him.'

She rose and padded off to the kitchen. Ben Cohn watched her as she moved out of the room. He looked at the television set and thought: *That lady gives me shpilkes. There's a hell of a lot less there than meets the eye, and I'm damned well going to find out what it is.*

'Akiko!' he shouted. 'What're you doing? Arthur's falling asleep.'

'Tell him to wait up,' she called. 'I'll be right there.'

A few minutes later, she returned, carrying a dish filled with ice cream, whipped cream and a cherry.

'For God's sake,' he said. 'I'm not hungry. I'm horny.'

'Lie back.' She put a towel under him, took the ice cream from the dish and started spreading it around his testicles.

He yelled, 'Hey! That's cold.'

'Sh!' Akiko put the whipped cream over the ice cream and then put his penis in her mouth until it became turgid.

'Oh, my God,' Ben moaned. 'Don't stop.'

Akiko put the cherry on top of his now rigid penis. 'I love banana splits,' she whispered.

And as she began to eat it, Ben felt an incredible mixture of sensations, all of them wonderful. When he could stand it no longer, he rolled Akiko over and plunged inside her.

On the television set Mary Ashley was saying, 'One of the best ways to prevent war with countries opposed to the American ideology is to increase our trade with them . . .'

Later that evening, Ben Cohn telephoned Ian Villiers.

'Hi, Ian.'

'Benjie, my boy – what can I do for you?'

'I need a favour.'

'Name it, and you've got it.'

'I understand you're in charge of press relations for our new Ambassador to Romania.'

A cautious, 'Yes . . . ?'

'Who's behind her build-up, Ian? I'm interested in –'

'I'm sorry, Ben. That's State Department business. I'm just a hired hand. You might drop a note to the Secretary of State.'

Hanging up, Ben said, 'Why didn't he just tell me to go fuck myself?' He made a decision. 'I think

I'm going to have to go out of town for a few days.'

'Where are you going, baby?'

'Junction City, Kansas.'

As it turned out, Ben Cohn was in Junction City for only one day. He spent an hour talking to Sheriff Munster and one of his deputies, then drove a rental car to Fort Riley, where he visited the CID office. He caught a late afternoon plane to Manhattan, Kansas, and a connecting flight home.

As Ben Cohn's plane took off, a person-to-person telephone call was placed from the Fort to a number in Washington, D.C.

Mary Ashley was walking down the long corridor of the Foreign Service Building on her way to report to James Stickley when she heard a deep, male voice behind her say, 'Now *that's* what I call a perfect ten.'

Mary spun around. A tall stranger was leaning against a wall, openly staring at her, an insolent grin on his face. He was rugged-looking, dressed in jeans, T-shirt and tennis shoes, and he looked scruffy and unshaven. There were laugh lines around his mouth, and his eyes were a bright, mocking blue. There was an air of arrogance about him that was infuriating. Mary turned on her heel and angrily walked away, conscious of his eyes following her.

* * *

The conference with James Stickley lasted for more than an hour. When Mary returned to her office, the stranger was seated in her chair, his feet on her desk, looking through her papers. She could feel the blood rising to her face.

'What the devil do you think you're doing?'

The man gave her a long, lazy look and slowly got to his feet. 'I'm Mike Slade. My friends call me Michael.'

She said icily, 'What can I do for you, Mr Slade?'

'Nothing, really,' he said easily. 'We're neighbours. I work here in the department, so I thought I'd come by and say hello.'

'You've said it. And if you really are in the department, I assume you have your own desk. So in the future you won't have to sit at my desk and snoop.'

'God, it has a temper! I heard the Kansians, or whatever you people call yourselves, were supposed to be friendly folks.'

She gritted her teeth. 'Mr Slade, I'll give you two seconds to get out of my office before I call a guard.'

'I must have heard wrong,' he mumbled to himself.

'And if you really work in this department, I'd suggest you go home and shave and put on some proper clothing.'

'I used to have a wife who talked like that,' Mike Slade sighed. 'I don't have her any more.'

Mary felt her face getting redder. 'Out.'

He waved his hand at her. "Bye, honey. I'll be seeing you.'

Oh, no, Mary thought. *No, you won't.*

The whole morning was a series of unpleasant experiences. James Stickley was openly antagonistic. By noon, Mary was too upset to eat. She decided to spend her lunch hour riding around Washington, getting the anger out of her system.

Her limousine was sitting at the kerb in front of the Foreign Service Building.

'Good morning, Madam Ambassador,' the chauffeur said. 'Where would you like to go?'

'Anywhere, Marvin. Let's just drive around.'

'Yes, ma'am.' The car pulled smoothly away from the kerb. 'Would you like to see Embassy Row?'

'Fine.' Anything to get the taste of the morning out of her mouth.

He made a left turn at the corner and headed for Massachusetts Avenue.

'It begins here,' Marvin said as he turned onto the wide street. He slowed the car down and began to point out the various embassies.

Mary recognized the Japanese Embassy because of the rising sun flag in front of it. The Indian Embassy had an elephant over the door.

They passed a beautiful Islamic mosque. There were people in the front courtyard kneeling in prayer.

They reached the corner of 23rd Street and

passed a white stone building with pillars on each side of the three steps.

'That's the Romanian Embassy,' Marvin said. 'Next to it is –'

'Stop, please!'

The limousine swung to the kerb. Mary looked out of the car window at a plaque on the outside of the building. It read: EMBASSY OF THE SOCIALIST REPUBLIC OF ROMANIA.

On an impulse, Mary said, 'Wait here, please. I'm going inside.'

Her heart began to beat faster. This was going to be her first real contact with the country she had been teaching about – the country that was going to be her home for the next few years.

She took a deep breath and pressed the doorbell. Silence. She tried the door. It was unlocked. She opened it and stepped inside. The reception hall was dark and freezing cold. There was a red couch in an alcove and next to it two chairs placed in front of a small television set. She heard footsteps and turned. A tall, thin man was hurrying down the stairs.

'Yes, yes?' he called. 'What is it? What is it?'

Mary beamed. 'Good morning. I'm Mary Ashley. I'm the new Ambassador to Rom –'

The man slapped his hand to his face. 'Oh, my God!'

She was startled. 'What's wrong?'

'What's wrong is that we are not expecting you, Madam Ambassador.'

'Oh, I know that. I was just driving by and I –'

'Ambassador Corbescue is going to be terribly, terribly upset!'

'Upset? Why? I just thought I'd say hello and –'

'Of course, of course. Forgive me. My name is Gabriel Stoica. I am the Deputy Chief of Mission. Please let me put on the lights and some heat. We were not expecting guests, as you can see. Not at all.'

He was so obviously in a panic that all Mary wanted to do was leave, but it was too late. She watched as Gabriel Stoica ran around turning on overhead lights and lamps until the reception hall was brightly lit.

'It will take a few minutes for the heat to come on,' he apologized. 'We try to save as much on fuel costs as we can. Washington is very expensive.'

She wished she could have disappeared into the floor. 'If I had realized . . .'

'No, no! It is nothing, nothing. The Ambassador is upstairs. I will inform him you are here.'

'Don't bother –'

Stoica was racing upstairs.

Five minutes later, Stoica returned. 'Please come. The Ambassador is delighted that you are here. Delighted.'

'Are you sure that –?'

'He is waiting for you.'

He escorted Mary upstairs. At the top of the stairs was a conference room with fourteen chairs around a long table. Against the wall was a cabinet filled with crafts and sculptures from Romania, and on the wall was a relief map of Romania. There was a fireplace with the Romanian flag above it. Coming forward to greet her was Ambassador Radu Corbescue, in shirt sleeves, hastily pulling on a jacket. He was a tall, heavy-set man with a dark complexion. A servant was hurriedly turning on lights and adjusting the heating.

'Madam Ambassador!' Corbescue cried. 'What an unexpected honour! Forgive us for receiving you so informally. Your State Department did not notify us that you were coming.'

'It's my fault,' Mary said apologetically. 'I was in the neighbourhood and I –'

'It is a pleasure to meet you! A pleasure! We have seen so much of you on television and in newspapers and magazines. We have been very curious about the new Ambassador to our country. You will have some tea?'

'Well, I – if you're sure it isn't too much trouble.'

'Trouble? Of course not! I apologize because we have not prepared a formal luncheon for you. Forgive me! I am so embarrassed.'

I'm the one who's embarrassed, Mary thought. *What made me do this crazy thing? Dumb, dumb, dumb. I'm not even going to tell the children about this. It will be my secret 'til the grave.*

211

When the tea was brought, the Ambassador from Romania was so nervous that he spilled it. 'How clumsy of me! Forgive me!'

Mary wished he would stop saying that.

The Ambassador tried to make small talk, but that only made the situation worse. It was obvious that he was miserably uncomfortable. As soon as she discreetly could, Mary rose.

'Thank you so much, your Excellency. It was very nice meeting you. Goodbye.'

And she fled.

When Mary returned to the office, James Stickley immediately sent for her.

'Mrs Ashley,' he said coldly, 'would you mind explaining to me exactly what you thought you were doing?'

I guess it's not going to be a secret I'll carry to the grave, Mary decided. 'Oh. You mean about the Romanian Embassy? I – I just thought I'd drop in and say hello and –'

'This is not a cosy little back-home get-together,' Stickley snapped. 'In Washington, you don't just *drop in* on an embassy. When an Ambassador makes a call on another Ambassador, it's by invitation only. You've embarrassed the hell out of Corbescue. I had to talk him out of making a formal protest to the State Department. He believes that you went there to spy on him and catch him off guard.'

'What! Well, of all the –'

'Just try to remember you're no longer a private citizen – you're a representative of the United States government. The next time you have an impulse less personal than brushing your teeth, you'll check with me first. Is that clear – I mean *very* clear?'

Mary swallowed. 'That's fine.'

'Good.' He picked up the telephone and dialled a number. 'Mrs Ashley is with me now. Would you like to come in? Right.' He replaced the receiver.

Mary sat there in silence, feeling like a small child being chastised. The door opened and Mike Slade walked in.

He looked at Mary and grinned. 'Hi. I took your advice and shaved.'

Stickley looked from one to the other. 'You two have met?'

Mary was glaring at Slade. 'Not really. I found him snooping at my desk.'

James Stickley said, 'Mrs Ashley, Mike Slade. Mr Slade is going to be your Deputy Chief of Mission.'

Mary stared at him. '*He's what?*'

'Mr Slade is on the East European desk. He usually works out of Washington, but it's been decided to assign him to Romania as your Deputy Chief.'

Mary found herself springing out of her chair. 'No!' she protested. 'That's impossible.'

Mike said mildly, 'I promise to shave every day.'

Mary turned to Stickley. 'I thought an ambassador was permitted to choose her own Deputy Chief of Mission.'

'That is correct, but –'

'Then I am unchoosing Mr Slade. I don't want him.'

'Under ordinary circumstances, you would be within your rights, but in this case, I'm afraid you have no choice. The order came from the White House.'

Mary could not seem to avoid Mike Slade. The man was everywhere. She ran into him in the Pentagon, in the Senate dining room, in the corridors of the State Department. He was always dressed in either denims and a T-shirt or in sports clothes. Mary wondered how he got away with it in an environment that was so formal.

One day Mary saw him having lunch with Colonel McKinney. They were engaged in an earnest conversation, and Mary wondered how close the two men were. *Could they be old friends? And could they be planning to gang up on me? I'm getting paranoid*, Mary told herself. *And I'm not even in Romania yet.*

Charlie Campbell, head of the Senate Foreign Relations Committee, hosted a party in Mary's honour at the Corcoran Gallery. When Mary walked into the room and saw all the elegantly gowned women, she thought: *I don't even belong here. They look like they were all born chic.*

She had no idea how lovely she looked.

There were more than a dozen photographers

present, and Mary was the most photographed woman of the evening. She danced with half a dozen men, some married, and some unmarried, and was asked for her telephone number by almost all of them. She was neither offended nor interested.

'I'm sorry,' she said to each of them, 'my work and my family keep me too busy to think about going out.'

The idea of being with anyone but Edward was unthinkable. There could never be another man for her.

She was at a table with Charlie Campbell and his wife and half a dozen people from the State Department. The conversation turned to anecdotes about ambassadors.

'A few years ago in Madrid,' one of the guests recounted, 'hundreds of rioting students were clamouring for the return of Gibraltar in front of the British Embassy. As they were on the verge of breaking into the building, one of General Franco's ministers telephoned. "I'm deeply distressed to hear what's happening at your embassy," he said. "Shall I send more police?" "No," the Ambassador said, "just send fewer students."'

Someone asked, 'Wasn't it Hermes who was regarded by the ancient Greeks as the patron of ambassadors?'

'Yes,' came the rejoinder. 'And he was also the protector of vagabonds, thieves and liars.'

Mary was enjoying the evening tremendously. The people were bright and witty and interesting. She could have stayed all night.

The man next to her said, 'Don't you have to get up early for appointments tomorrow?'

'No,' Mary said. 'It's Sunday. I can sleep late.'

A little later, a woman yawned. 'Excuse me. I've had a long day.'

'So have I,' Mary said brightly.

It seemed to her that the room was abnormally quiet. She looked around, and everyone seemed to be staring at her. *What on earth –?* She glanced at her watch. It was 2.30 a.m. And with horror, she suddenly remembered something Stanton Rogers had told her: *At a dinner party, the guest of honour always leaves first.*

And *she* was the guest of honour! *Oh, my God,* Mary thought. *I'm keeping everybody up.*

She rose to her feet and said in a choked voice, 'Good night, everybody. It's been a lovely evening.'

She turned and hurried out of the door, and behind her she could hear the other guests scrambling to leave.

Next morning she ran into Mike Slade in the hallway. He grinned and said, 'I hear you kept half of Washington up Saturday night.'

His supercilious air infuriated her.

She brushed past him and went into James Stickley's office.

'Mr Stickley, I really don't think it would serve

216

the best interests of our embassy in Romania for Mr Slade and me to try working together.'

He looked up from the paper he was reading. 'Really? What's the problem?'

'It's his – his attitude. I find Mr Slade to be rude and arrogant. Frankly, I don't like Mr Slade.'

'Oh, I know Mike has his little idiosyncrasies, but –'

'*Idiosyncrasies?* He's a rhinestone in the rough. I'm officially requesting that you send someone else in his place.'

'Are you finished?'

'Yes.'

'Mrs Ashley, Mike Slade happens to be our top expert on East European affairs. Your job is to make friends with the natives. My job is to see to it that you get all the help I can give you. And his name is Mike Slade. I really don't want to hear any more about it. Do I make myself clear?'

It's no use, Mary thought. *No use at all.*

She returned to her office, frustrated and angry. *I could talk to Stan*, she thought. *He would understand. But that would be a sign of weakness. I'm going to have to handle Mike Slade myself.*

'Daydreaming?'

Mary looked up, startled. Mike Slade was standing in front of her desk, holding a large stack of memos.

'This should keep you out of trouble tonight,' he said. He laid them on her desk.

'*Knock* next time you want to come into my office.'

His eyes were mocking her. 'Why do I get the feeling you're not crazy about me?'

She felt her temper rising again. 'I'll tell you why, Mr Slade. Because I think you're an arrogant, nasty, conceited –'

He raised a finger. 'You're being tautological.'

'Don't you dare make fun of me.' She found herself yelling.

His voice dropped to a dangerous level. 'You mean I can't join the others? What do you think everyone in Washington is saying about you?'

'I don't really care what they're saying.'

'Oh, but you should.' He leaned over her desk. 'Everybody is asking what right you have to be sitting at an ambassador's desk. I spent four years in Romania, lady. It's a piece of dynamite ready to explode, and the government is sending in a dumb kid from the sticks to play with it.'

Mary sat there listening, gritting her teeth.

'You're an amateur, Mrs Ashley. If someone wanted to pay you off, they should have made you Ambassador to Iceland.'

Mary lost control. She sprang to her feet and slapped him hard across the face.

Mike Slade sighed. 'You're never stuck for an answer, are you?'

SIXTEEN

The invitation read: 'The Ambassador of the Socialist Republic of Romania requests your presence for cocktails and dinner at the Embassy, 1607 23rd Street, N.W., at 7.30 p.m., Black Tie, RSVP 232–6593.'

Mary thought of the last time she had visited that embassy and what a fool she had made of herself. *Well, that won't happen again. I'm past all that. I'm part of the Washington scene now.*

She put on one of the new outfits she had bought, a black, cut-velvet evening dress, with long sleeves. She wore black silk high-heel shoes and a pearl necklace.

Beth said, 'You look prettier than Madonna.'

Mary hugged her. 'I'm overwhelmed. You two have dinner in the dining room downstairs and then you may come up and watch television. I'll be home early. Tomorrow we're all going to visit President Washington's home at Mount Vernon.'

'Have a good time, Mom.'

The telephone rang. It was the desk clerk. 'Madam Ambassador, Mr Stickley is waiting for you in the lobby.'

I wish I could have gone alone, Mary thought. *I don't need him or anyone else to keep me out of trouble.*

The Romanian Embassy looked completely different from the last time Mary had seen it. There was a festive air about it that had been totally missing on her first visit. They were greeted at the door by Gabriel Stoica, the Deputy Chief of Mission.

'Good evening, Mr Stickley. How nice to see you.'

James Stickley nodded towards Mary. 'May I present our Ambassador to your country?'

There was no flicker of recognition on Stoica's face. 'It is a pleasure to meet you, Madam Ambassador. Please follow me.'

As they walked down the hallway, Mary noticed that all the rooms were brightly lit and well-heated. From upstairs she could hear the strains of a small orchestra. There were vases of flowers everywhere.

Ambassador Corbescue was talking to a group of people when he saw James Stickley and Mary Ashley approach.

'Ah, good evening, Mr Stickley.'

'Good evening, Ambassador. May I present the United States Ambassador to Romania?'

Corbescue looked at Mary and said tonelessly, 'I am happy to meet you.'

Mary waited for the twinkle in his eye. It never came.

There were a hundred people at dinner. The men wore dinner jackets and the women were beautifully gowned in dresses by Luis Estévez and Oscar de la Renta. The large table Mary had seen upstairs on her earlier visit had been augmented by half a dozen smaller tables around it. Liveried butlers circled the room with trays of champagne.

'Would you like a drink?' Stickley asked.

'No, thank you,' Mary said. 'I don't drink.'

'*Really?* That's a pity.'

She looked at him, puzzled. 'Why?'

'Because it's part of the job. At every diplomatic dinner party you attend, there will be toasts. If you don't drink, you'll offend your host. You have to take a sip now and then.'

'I'll remember,' Mary said.

She looked across the room, and there was Mike Slade. She did not recognize him for a moment. He was wearing a dinner jacket, and she had to admit that he was not unattractive in evening clothes. His arm was draped over a voluptuous blonde who was about to fall out of her dress. *Cheap*, Mary thought. *Just his taste. I wonder how many girl friends he has waiting for him in Bucharest?*

Mary remembered Mike's words: *You're an amateur, Mrs Ashley. If someone wanted to pay you off, they should have made you Ambassador to Iceland.* The bastard.

As Mary watched, Colonel McKinney, in full dress uniform, walked up to Mike. Mike excused himself from the blonde and walked over to a corner with the colonel. *I'm going to have to watch them both*, Mary thought.

A servant was passing by with champagne. 'I think I *will* have a glass,' Mary said.

James Stickley watched her as she drank it down. 'Okay. It's time to start working the room.'

'Working the room?'

'A lot of business gets done at these parties. That's why embassies give them.'

Mary spent the next hour being introduced to ambassadors, senators, governors and some of Washington's most powerful political figures. Romania had become a hot ticket, and nearly everyone of importance had managed to get an invitation to the Embassy dinner. Mike Slade approached James Stickley and Mary, holding the blonde in tow.

'Good evening,' Mike said genially. 'I'd like you to meet Debbie Dennison. This is James Stickley and Mary Ashley.'

It was a deliberate slap. Mary said coolly, 'It's *Ambassador* Ashley.'

Mike clapped his hand to his forehead. 'Sorry. *Ambassador* Ashley. Miss Dennison's father happens to be an Ambassador, too. He's a career diplomat, of course. He's served in half a dozen countries for the last twenty-five years.'

222

Debbie Dennison said, 'It's a wonderful way to grow up.'

Mike said, 'Debbie's been around a lot.'

'Yes,' Mary said evenly. 'I'm sure she has.'

Mary prayed she would not be seated next to Mike at dinner, and her prayers were granted. He was at another table, next to the half-naked blonde. There were a dozen people at Mary's table. Some of them were familiar faces she had seen on magazine covers and on television. James Stickley was seated across from Mary. The man to Mary's left spoke a mysterious language that Mary was unable to identify. To her right was a tall, thin, middle-aged blond man, with an attractive, sensitive face.

'I am delighted to be your dinner companion,' he said to Mary. 'I am an ardent fan of yours.' He spoke with a slight Scandinavian accent.

'Thank you.' *A fan of my what?* Mary wondered. *I haven't done anything.*

'I am Olaf Peterson. I am the Cultural Attaché from Sweden.'

'I'm very happy to meet you, Mr Peterson.'

'Have you been to Sweden?'

'No. To tell you the truth, I really haven't been anywhere.'

Olaf Peterson smiled. 'Then so many places have a treat in store for them.'

'Perhaps one day the children and I will visit your country.'

'Ah, you have children? How old are they?'

'Tim is ten and Beth is twelve. I'll show you.' Mary opened her purse and took out snapshots of the children. Across the table, James Stickley was shaking his head disapprovingly.

Olaf Peterson examined the snapshots. 'They are beautiful children!' he exclaimed. 'They take after their mother.'

'They have their father's eyes.'

They used to have mock arguments about which one of them the children resembled.

Beth is going to be a beauty, like you, Edward would say. *I don't know who Tim looks like. Are you sure he's mine?*

And their play-argument would end in love-making.

Olaf Peterson was saying something to her.

'I beg your pardon?'

'I said I read about your husband being killed in a motor accident. I am sorry. It must be very difficult for a woman to be alone without a man.' His voice was filled with sympathy.

Mary picked up the glass of wine in front of her and took a sip. It was cold and refreshing. She drained the glass. It was immediately refilled by a white-gloved waiter hovering behind the guests.

'When do you take up your post in Romania?' Peterson asked.

'I was told we'll be leaving within the next few weeks.' Mary picked up her wine glass. 'To Bucharest.' She drank. The wine was really quite delicious, and everyone knew that wine had a low alcoholic content.

When the waiter offered to fill her glass again, she nodded happily. She looked around the room at all the beautifully dressed guests speaking in a dozen different tongues and thought: *They don't have banquets like this in good old Junction City. No, sir. Kansas is as dry as a bone. Washington is as wet as a – what was Washington as wet as?* She frowned, trying to think.

'Are you all right?' Olaf Peterson asked.

She patted him on the arm. 'Great. I'm just great. I'd like another glass of wine, Olaf.'

'Certainly.'

He motioned to the waiter, and Mary's wine glass was refilled.

'At home,' Mary said confidentially, 'I never drank wine.' She lifted her glass and took a swallow. 'In fact, I never drank anything.' Her words were beginning to slur. 'That doesn' 'clude water, of course.'

Olaf Peterson was studying her, smiling.

At the centre table, Romanian Ambassador Corbescue rose to his feet. 'Ladies and gentlemen – distinguished guests – I would like to propose a toast.'

The ritual began. There were toasts to Alexandros Ionescu, the President of Romania. There were toasts to Madam Alexandros Ionescu. There were toasts to the President of the United States, and to the Vice President, to the Romanian flag and to the American flag. It seemed to Mary that there were thousands of toasts. She drank to every one of them. *I'm a 'bassador*, she reminded herself, *'s my duty*.

In the middle of the toasts, the Romanian Ambassador said, 'I am sure we would all like to hear a few words from the United States' charming new Ambassador to Romania.'

Mary raised her glass and started to drink a toast, when she suddenly realized she was being called upon. She sat there for a moment, then managed to get to her feet. She stood up, holding on to the table for support. She looked out at the throng of people and and waved. 'Hi, everybody. Having a good time?'

She had never felt happier in her life. Everyone in the room was so friendly. They were all smiling at her. Some were even laughing. She looked over at James Stickley and grinned.

'It's a great party,' Mary said. 'I'm delighted you could all come.' She sat down heavily and turned to Olaf Peterson. 'They put somethin' in my wine.'

He pressed her hand. 'I think what you need is a little fresh air. It is very stuffy in here.'

'Yeah. Stuffy. To tell you the truth, I'm feelin' a l'l dizzy.'

'Let me take you outside.'

He helped Mary to her feet, and to her surprise, she found it difficult to walk. James Stickley was engaged in an earnest conversation with his dinner partner and did not see Mary leave. Mary and Olaf

Peterson passed Mike Slade's table, and he was watching her with a frown of disapproval.

He's jealous, Mary thought. *They didn' ask him to make a speech.*

She said to Peterson, 'You know his problem, don' you? He wan's 'a be Ambassador. He can't stand it that I got the job.'

'Who are you talking about?' Olaf Peterson asked.

''s not importan'. He's not importan'.'

They were outside in the cold night air. Mary was grateful for the support of Peterson's arm. Everything seemed blurred.

'I have a limousine here somewhere,' Mary said.

'Let's send it away,' Olaf Peterson suggested. 'We'll go up to my place for a little nightcap.'

'No more wine.'

'No, no. Just a little brandy to settle your stomach.'

Brandy. In books, all the sophisticated people drank brandy. Brandy and soda. It was a Cary Grant kind of drink.

'With soda?'

'Of course.'

Olaf Peterson helped Mary into a taxi and gave the driver an address. When they stopped in front of a large apartment building, Mary looked at Peterson, puzzled. 'Where are we?'

'We're home,' Olaf Peterson said. He supported Mary as she stepped out of the taxi, holding on to her as she started to fall.

''m I drunk?' Mary asked.

'Of course not,' he said soothingly.

'I feel funny.'

Peterson led her into the lobby of the building and rang for the elevator. 'A little brandy will fix you up.'

They stepped into the elevator and he pressed a button.

'Did you know I'm a toeteetler? I mean – tee-totler?'

'No. I did not know that.'

''s a fact.'

Peterson was stroking her bare arm.

The elevator door opened, and Peterson helped Mary out of the elevator.

'Did anyone ever tell you the floor's uneven?'

'I'll have it taken care of,' Olaf promised.

He held her up with one hand while he fumbled for the key to his apartment and unlocked the door. They stepped inside. The apartment was dimly lit.

''s dark in here,' Mary said.

Olaf Peterson took her in his arms. 'I like the dark, don't you?'

Did she? She was not sure.

'You are a very beautiful woman, do you know that?'

'Thank you. You're a beaut'ful man.'

He led her to the couch and sat her down. She was feeling giddy. His lips pressed against hers, and she felt his hand sliding up her thigh.

'What're you doing?'

'Just relax, darling. It's going to feel lovely.'

It *did* feel lovely. His hands were very gentle, like Edward's.

'He was a won'erful doctor,' Mary said.

'I'm sure he was.' He pressed his body against hers.

'Oh, yes. 'never anyone needed an operation, they always asked for Edward.'

She was lying on the couch on her back, and soft hands had pushed her dress up and were gently massaging her. Edward's hands. Mary closed her eyes and felt his lips moving down her body – soft lips, and a gentle tongue. Edward had such a gentle tongue. It was blissful. And she wanted it never to stop.

'That's so good, my darling,' she said. 'Take me. Please take me.'

'I will. Now.' His voice was husky. Suddenly harsh. Not at all like Edward's voice.

Mary opened her eyes, and she was staring into the face of a stranger. As she felt the man start to thrust inside her, she screamed, 'No! Stop it!'

She rolled away from him and fell to the floor. She stumbled to her feet.

Olaf Peterson was staring at her. 'But –'

'No!'

She looked around the apartment wildly. 'I'm sorry,' she said. 'I made a mistake. I don't want you to think I –'

She turned and ran towards the door.

'Wait! Let me at least take you home.'

She was gone.

She walked down the deserted streets, bracing herself against the icy wind, filled with a deep, bruising mortification. There was no explanation for what she had done. And there was no excuse. She had disgraced her position. And in what a stupid way! She had got drunk in front of half the diplomatic corps in Washington, had gone to a stranger's apartment, and had almost let him seduce her. In the morning she was going to be the target for every gossip columnist in Washington.

Ben Cohn heard the story from three people who had attended the dinner at the Romanian Embassy. He searched through the columns of the Washington and New York newspapers. There was not one word about the incident. Someone had killed the story. It had to be someone very important.

Cohn sat in the small cubicle that the newspaper called an office, thinking. He dialled Ian Villiers' number. 'Hello, is Mr Villiers in?'

'Yes. Who's calling?'

'Ben Cohn.'

'One moment, please.' She was back on the line one minute later. 'I'm terribly sorry, Mr Cohn. Mr Villiers seems to have stepped out.'

'When can I reach him?'

'I'm afraid he's fully booked up all day.'

'Right.' He replaced the receiver and dialled the number of a gossip columnist who worked on another newspaper. Nothing happened in Washington without her knowing about it.

'Linda,' he said, 'how goes the daily battle?'

'Plus ça change, plus c'est la même chose.'

'Anything exciting happening around this gilded watering hole?'

'Not really, Ben. It's deadly quiet.'

He said casually, 'I understand the Romanian Embassy had a big wing-ding last night.'

'Did they?' There was a sudden caution in her voice.

'Uh huh. Did you happen to hear anything about our new Ambassador to Romania?'

'No. I've got to go now, Ben. I have a long distance call.'

The line went dead.

He dialled the number of a friend in the State Department. When the secretary put him through, he said, 'Hello, Alfred.'

'Benjie! What's cooking?'

'It's been a long time. I thought we might get together for lunch.'

'Fine. What are you working on?'

'Why don't I tell you about it when I see you?'

'Fair enough. My calendar is pretty light today. Do you want to meet me at the Watergate?'

Ben Cohn hesitated. 'Why don't we make it Mama Regina's in Silver Springs?'

'That's a little out of the way, isn't it?'

Ben said, 'Yes.'

There was a pause. 'I see.'

'One o'clock?'

'Fine.'

Ben Cohn was seated at a table in the corner when his guest, Alfred Shuttleworth, arrived. The host, Tony Sergio, seated him.

'Would you care for a drink, gentlemen?'

Shuttleworth ordered a martini.

'Nothing for me,' Ben Cohn said.

Alfred Shuttleworth was a sallow-looking, middle-aged man who worked in the European Section of the State Department. A few years earlier, he had been involved in a drunken driving accident that Ben Cohn had covered for his newspaper. Shuttleworth's career was at stake. Cohn had killed the story, and Shuttleworth had shown his appreciation by giving him news tips from time to time.

'I need your help, Al.'

'Name it, and you've got it.'

'I'd like the inside information on our new Ambassador to Romania.'

Alfred Shuttleworth frowned. 'What do you mean?'

'Three people called to tell me that she got so stoned at the Romanian Ambassador's party last night that she made a horse's ass of herself in front of Washington's who's who. Have you seen the morning papers today, or the early editions of the afternoon papers?'

'Yes. They mentioned the Embassy party, but there was no mention of Mary Ashley.'

'Exactly. *Silver Blaze*.'

'I beg your pardon?'

'Sherlock Holmes. The dog didn't bark. It was silent. So are the newspapers. Why would the gossip columnists skip over a juicy story like that? Someone had that story killed. Someone important. If it had been any other VIP who publicly disgraced herself, the press would have had a Roman holiday.'

'That doesn't necessarily follow, Ben.'

'Al, there's this Cinderella who comes out of nowhere, is touched by the magic wand of our President, and suddenly becomes Grace Kelly, Princess Di and Jacqueline Kennedy rolled into one. Now, I'll admit the lady is pretty – but she isn't *that* pretty. The lady is bright – but she isn't *that* bright. In my humble opinion, teaching a political science course at Kansas State University doesn't exactly qualify anyone to be the Ambassador to one of the world's hot spots. I'll tell you something else that's out of kilter. I flew to Junction City and talked to the sheriff there.'

Alfred Shuttleworth drained the remainder of his martini. 'I think I'd like another one. You're making me nervous.'

'Join the club.' Ben Cohn ordered a martini.

'Go on,' Shuttleworth said.

'Mrs Ashley turned down the President because her husband couldn't leave his medical practice. Then he was killed in a convenient auto accident. Voilà! The lady's in Washington, on her way to Bucharest. Exactly as someone had planned from the beginning.'

'Someone? Who?'

'That's the jackpot question.'

'Ben – what are you suggesting?'

'I'm not suggesting anything. Let me tell you what Sheriff Munster suggested. He thought it was peculiar that half a dozen witnesses showed up out of nowhere in the middle of a freezing winter night just in time to witness the accident. And do you want to hear something even more peculiar? They've all disappeared. Every one of them.'

'Go on.'

'I went over to Fort Riley to talk to the driver of the Army truck that killed Dr Ashley.'

'And what did he have to say?'

'Not much. He was dead. Heart attack. Twenty-seven years old.'

Shuttleworth was toying with the stem of his glass. 'I assume there's more?'

'Oh, yes. There's more. I went over to the CID office at Fort Riley to interview Colonel Jenkins, the officer in charge of the Army investigation, as well as being one of the witnesses to the accident. The colonel wasn't there. He's been promoted and transferred. He's a major-general now, overseas somewhere. No one seems to know where.'

Alfred Shuttleworth shook his head. 'Ben, I know you're a hell of a reporter, but I honestly think this time you've gone off the track. You're building a few coincidences into a Hitchcock scenario. People *do* get killed in auto accidents. People *do* have heart attacks, and officers *do* get promoted. You're looking for some kind of conspiracy where there is none.'

'Al, have you heard of an organization called Patriots for Freedom?'

'No. Is it something like the DAR?'

Ben Cohn said quietly, 'It's nothing like the DAR. I keep hearing rumours, but there's nothing I can pin down.'

'What kind of rumours?'

'It's supposed to be a cabal of high-level right wing and left wing fanatics from a dozen Eastern and Western countries. Their ideologies are diametrically opposed, but what brings them together is fear. The communist members think President Ellison's plan is a capitalist trick to destroy the Eastern bloc. The right wingers believe his plan is an open door that will let the communists destroy us. So they've formed this unholy alliance.'

'Jesus! I don't believe it.'

'There's more. Besides the VIPs, splinter groups from various national security agencies are said to be involved. Do you think you could check it out for me?'

'I don't know. I'll try.'

'I would suggest you do it discreetly. If the organization really exists, they won't be too thrilled to have anyone nosing around.'

'I'll get back to you, Ben.'

'Thanks. Let's order lunch.'

The spaghetti carbonara was superb.

Alfred Shuttleworth was sceptical about Ben Cohn's theory. *Reporters are always looking for sensational angles*, Shuttleworth thought. He liked Ben Cohn, but Shuttleworth had no idea how to go about tracking down a probably mythical organization. If it really did exist, it would be in some government computer. He himself had no access to the computers. *But I know someone who does*, Alfred Shuttleworth remembered. *I'll give him a call.*

Alfred Shuttleworth was on his second martini when Pete Connors walked into the bar.

'Sorry I'm late,' Connors said. 'A minor problem at the pickle factory.'

Pete Connors ordered a straight Scotch, and Shuttleworth ordered another martini.

The two men had met because Connors' girl friend and Shuttleworth's wife worked for the same company and had become friends. Connors and Shuttleworth were complete opposites; one was involved in deadly games of espionage, and the other functioned as a desk-bound bureaucrat. It was this dissimilarity that made them enjoy each other's company, and from time to time they exchanged useful information. When Shuttleworth had first met him, Pete Connors had been an amusing and interesting companion. Somewhere along the line, something had soured him. He had become a bitter reactionary.

Shuttleworth took a sip of his martini. 'Pete – I need a favour. Could you look up something for me in the CIA computer? It may not be in there, but I promised a friend I'd try.'

Connors smiled inwardly. *The poor schmuck probably wants to find out if someone is banging his wife.* 'Sure. I owe you a few. Who do you want to know about?'

'It's not a "who", it's a "what". And it probably doesn't even exist. It's an organization called Patriots for Freedom. Have you heard of it?'

Pete Connors carefully set down his drink. 'I can't say that I have, Al. What's the name of your friend?'

'Ben Cohn. He's a reporter for the *Post*.'

The following morning, Ben Cohn made a decision. He said to Akiko, 'I either have the story of the century, or I have nothing. It's time I found out.'

'Thank God!' Akiko exclaimed. 'Arthur's going to be very happy.'

Ben Cohn reached Mary Ashley at her office. 'Good morning, Ambassador. Ben Cohn. Remember me?'

237

'Yes, Mr Cohn. Have you written that story yet?'

'That's what I'm calling you about, Ambassador. I went to Junction City and picked up some information that I think will interest you.'

'What kind of information?'

'I'd rather not discuss it over the phone. I wonder if we could meet somewhere?'

'I have a ridiculously full schedule. Let me see . . . I have half an hour free on Friday morning. Would that be all right?'

Three days away. 'I guess it can wait until then.'

'Do you want to come up to my office?'

'There's a coffee shop downstairs in your building. Why don't we meet there?'

'All right. I'll see you Friday.'

They said goodbye and hung up. A moment later there was a third click on the line.

There was no way to get directly in touch with the Controller. He had organized and financed the Patriots for Freedom, but he never attended committee meetings, and he was completely anonymous. He was a telephone number – untraceable (Connors had tried) – and a recording that said, 'You have sixty seconds in which to leave your message.' The number was to be used only in case of emergency. Connors stopped at a public telephone booth to make the call. He talked to the recording.

The message was received at 6 p.m.

In Buenos Aires, it was 8 p.m.

The Controller listened to the message twice, then dialled a number. He waited for three full minutes before Neusa Muñez's voice came on.

'*Si?*'

The Controller said, 'This is the man who made arrangements with you before about Angel. I have another contract for him. Can you get in touch with him right away?'

'I don' know.' She sounded drunk.

He kept the impatience out of his voice. 'When do you expect to hear from him?'

'I don' know.'

Damn the woman. 'Listen to me.' He spoke slowly and carefully, as though addressing a small child. 'Tell Angel I need this done immediately. I want him to –'

'Wait a minute. I gotta go to the toilet.'

He heard her drop the phone. The Controller sat there, filled with frustration.

Three minutes later, she was back on the line. 'A lotta beer makes you pee,' she announced.

He gritted his teeth. 'This is very important.' He was afraid she was going to remember none of it. 'I want you to get a pencil and write this down. I'll speak slowly.'

That evening Mary attended a dinner party given by the Canadian Embassy. As she was leaving the office to go home and dress, James Stickley said, 'I would suggest that you *sip* the toasts this time.'

He and Mike Slade make a wonderful pair.

Now she was at the party, and she wished she were home with Beth and Tim. The faces at her table were unfamiliar. On her right was a Greek shipping magnate. On her left was an English diplomat.

A Philadelphia socialite dripping with diamonds said to Mary, 'Are you enjoying Washington, Madam Ambassador?'

'Very much, thank you.'

'You must be thrilled to have made your escape from Kansas.'

Mary looked at her, not understanding. 'Escape from Kansas?'

The woman went on. 'I've never been to middle America, but I imagine it must be dreadful. All those farmers and nothing but dreary fields of corn and wheat. It's a wonder you could bear it as long as you did.'

Mary felt a surge of anger, but she kept her voice under control. 'That corn and wheat you're talking about,' she said politely, 'feeds the world.'

The woman's tone was patronizing. 'Our automobiles run on gasoline, but I wouldn't want to live in the oilfields. Culturally speaking, I think one has to live in the East, don't you? Quite honestly now – in Kansas unless you're out harvesting in the fields all day, there really isn't anything to do, is there?'

The others at the table were all listening closely.

There really isn't anything to do, is there? Mary thought of August hayrides and county fairs and

240

exciting classical dramas at the University Theatre. Sunday picnics in Milford Park and softball tournaments, and fishing in the clear lake. The band playing on the green and town hall meetings and block parties and barn dances and the excitement of harvest time . . . winter sleigh rides and fourth of July fireworks rainbowing the soft, Kansas sky.

Mary said to the woman, 'If you've never been to middle America, you really don't know what you're talking about, do you? Because that's what this country is all about. America isn't Washington or Los Angeles or New York. It's thousands of small towns that you'll never even see or hear of that make this country great. It's the miners and the farmers and the blue collar workers. And yes, in Kansas we have ballets and symphonies and theatre. And, for your information, we raise a lot more than corn and wheat – we raise honest-to-God human beings.'

'You know, of course, that you insulted the sister of a very important senator,' James Stickley informed Mary the following morning.

'Not enough,' Mary said defiantly. 'Not enough.'

Thursday morning. Angel was in a bad mood. The flight from Buenos Aires to Washington, D.C., had been delayed because of a telephoned bomb threat. *The world isn't safe any more*, Angel thought angrily.

241

The hotel room that had been reserved in Washington was too modern, too – what was the word? *Plastic. That was it*. In Buenos Aires, everything was *auténtico*.

I'll finish this contract and get back home. The job is simple, almost an insult to my talent. But the money is excellent. I've got to get laid tonight. I wonder why killing always makes me horny.

Angel's first stop was at an electrical supply store, then a paint store, and finally a supermarket, where Angel's only purchase was six light bulbs. The rest of the equipment was waiting in the hotel room in two sealed boxes marked 'Fragile – Handle With Care'. Inside the first box were four carefully packed army-green hand grenades. In the second box was soldering equipment.

Working very slowly, with exquisite care, Angel cut off the top of the first grenade, then painted the bottom of it the same colour as the light bulbs. The next step was to scoop out the explosive from the grenade and replace it with a seismic explosive. When it was tightly packed, Angel added lead and metallic shrapnel to it. Angel shattered a light bulb against the table, preserving the filament and threaded base. It took less than a minute to solder the filament of the bulb to an electrically activated detonator. The final step was to insert the filament into a gel to keep it stable and then gently place it inside the painted grenade. When Angel was finished, it looked exactly like a normal light bulb.

Angel began to work on the remaining light bulbs. After that, there was nothing to do but wait for the phone call.

The telephone rang at eight o'clock that evening. Angel picked up the phone and listened, without speaking. After a moment, a voice said, 'He's gone.'

Angel replaced the receiver. Carefully, very carefully, the light bulbs were packed into an excelsior padded container and placed in a suitcase, along with all the scraps of discarded materials.

The taxi ride to the apartment building took seventeen minutes.

There was no doorman in the lobby, but if there had been, Angel was prepared to deal with him. The target apartment was on the fifth floor, at the far end of the corridor. The lock was an early model Schlage, childishly simple to manipulate. Angel was inside the dark apartment within seconds, standing stock still, listening. There was no one there.

It was the work of a few minutes to replace six light bulbs in the living room of the apartment. Afterwards, Angel headed for Dulles Airport to catch a midnight flight back to Buenos Aires.

It had been a long day for Ben Cohn. He had covered a morning press conference by the Secretary of State, a luncheon for the retiring Secretary of the Interior, and had been given an off-the-record briefing from a friend in the Defence Department. He had gone home to shower and change, and then left again to have dinner with a senior *Post* editor. It was almost midnight when he returned to his apartment building. *I have to prepare my notes for the meeting with Ambassador Ashley tomorrow*, Ben thought.

Akiko was out of town and would not be returning until tomorrow. *It's just as well. I can use the rest. But Jesus*, he thought with a grin, *the lady sure knows how to eat a banana split.*

He put the key in the lock and opened the door. The apartment was pitch black. He reached for the light switch and pressed it. There was a sudden bright flash of light, and the room exploded like an atomic bomb, splashing pieces of his body against the four walls.

The following day, Alfred Shuttleworth's wife reported him missing. He was never found.

SEVENTEEN

'We just received official word,' Stanton Rogers said. 'The Romanian government has approved you as the new Ambassador from the United States.'

It was one of the most thrilling moments of Mary Ashley's life. *Grandfather would have been so proud.*

'I wanted to bring you the good news in person, Mary. The President would like to see you. I'll take you over to the White House.'

'I – I don't know how to thank you for everything you've done, Stan.'

'I haven't done anything,' Rogers protested. 'It was the President who selected you.' He grinned. 'And I must say, he made the perfect choice.'

Mary thought of Mike Slade. 'There are some people who don't agree.'

'They're wrong. You can do more for our country over there than anyone else I can think of.'

'Thank you,' she said soberly. 'I'll try to live up to that.'

245

She was tempted to bring up the subject of Mike Slade. Stanton Rogers had a lot of power. Perhaps he could arrange to have Slade stay in Washington. *No*, Mary thought. *I mustn't impose on Stan. He's done enough already.*

'I have a suggestion. Instead of flying directly to Bucharest, why don't you and the children stop first in Paris and Rome for a few days? Tarom Airlines flies directly from Rome to Bucharest.'

She looked at him and said, 'Oh, Stan – that would be heaven! But would I have time?'

He winked. 'I have friends in high places. Let me work it out for you.'

Impulsively, she hugged him. He had become such a dear friend. The dreams she and Edward had talked about so often were about to come true. But without Edward. It was a bittersweet thought.

Mary and Stanton Rogers were ushered into the Green Room, where President Ellison was waiting for them.

'I want to apologize for the delay in setting things in motion, Mary. Stanton has told you that you've been approved by the Romanian government. Here are your credentials.'

He handed her a letter. She read it slowly:

Mrs Mary Ashley is herewith appointed to be Chief Representative of the President of the United States in Romania, and every

United States government employee there is herewith subject to her authority.

'This goes along with it.' The President handed Mary a passport. It had a black cover instead of the usual blue one. On the front, in gold letters, was printed 'Diplomatic Passport'.

Mary had been anticipating this for weeks, but now that the time had come, she could scarcely believe it.

Paris!

Rome!

Bucharest!

It seemed almost too good to be true. And for no reason, something that Mary's mother used to tell her popped into her mind: *If something seems to be too good to be true, Mary, it probably is.*

There was a brief item in the afternoon press that *Washington Post* reporter Ben Cohn had been killed by a gas explosion in his apartment. The explosion was attributed to a leaky stove.

Mary did not see the news item. When Ben Cohn did not show up for their appointment, Mary decided that the reporter had either forgotten, or was no longer interested. She returned to her office and went back to work.

The relationship between Mary and Mike Slade became steadily more irritating to her. *He's the most arrogant man I've ever met*, Mary thought. *I'm going to have to talk to Stan about him.*

Stanton Rogers accompanied Mary and the children to Dulles Airport in a State Department limousine. During the ride, Stanton said, 'The embassies in Paris and Rome have been alerted to your arrival. They'll see to it that the three of you are well taken care of.'

'Thank you, Stan. You've been wonderful.'

He smiled. 'I can't tell you how much pleasure it's given me.'

'Can I see the catacombs in Rome?' Tim asked.

Stanton warned, 'It's pretty scary down there, Tim.'

'That's why I want to see it.'

At the airport, Ian Villiers was waiting with a dozen photographers and reporters. They surrounded Mary and Beth and Tim, and called out all the usual questions.

Finally, Stanton Rogers said, 'That's enough.'

Two men from the State Department and a representative of the airline ushered the party into a private lounge. The children wandered off to the magazine stand.

Mary said, 'Stan – I hate to burden you with this, but James Stickley told me that Mike Slade is going to be my Deputy Chief of Mission. Is there any way to change that?'

He looked at her in surprise. 'Are you having some kind of problem with Slade?'

'Quite honestly, I don't like him. And I don't trust him – I can't tell you why. Isn't there someone who could replace him?'

Stanton Rogers said thoughtfully, 'I don't know Mike Slade well, but I know he has a magnificent record. He's served brilliantly in posts in the Middle East and Europe. He can give you exactly the kind of expertise you're going to need.'

She sighed. 'That's what Mr Stickley said.'

'I'm afraid I have to agree with him, Mary. Slade's a troubleshooter.'

Wrong. Slade's trouble. Period.

'If you have any problems with him, I want you to let me know. In fact, if you have problems with *anyone*, I want you to let me know. I intend to make sure that you get every bit of help I can give you.'

'I appreciate that.'

'One last thing. You know that all your communications will be copied and sent to various departments in Washington?'

'Yes.'

'Well, if you have any messages that you want to send to me without anyone else reading them, the code at the top of the message is three x's. I'll be the only one to receive that message.'

'I'll remember.'

The Charles de Gaulle Airport was something out of science fiction, a kaleidoscope of stone columns and what seemed to Mary like hundreds of escalators running wild. The airport was crowded with travellers.

'Stay close to me, children,' Mary urged.

When they got off the escalator, she looked around helplessly. She stopped a Frenchman passing by, and summoning up one of the few French phrases she knew, she asked haltingly, *'Pardon, monsieur, où sont les bagages?'*

In a heavy French accent, he said witheringly, 'Sorry, Madame. I don't speak English.' He walked away, leaving Mary staring after him.

At that moment, a well-dressed young American hurried up to Mary and the children.

'Madam Ambassador, forgive me! I was instructed to meet you at the plane, but I was delayed by a traffic accident. My name is Peter Callas. I'm with the American Embassy.'

'I'm really glad to see you,' Mary said. 'I think I'm lost.' She introduced the children. 'Where do we find our luggage?'

'No problem,' Peter Callas assured her. 'Everything will be taken care of for you.'

He was true to his word. Fifteen minutes later, while the other passengers were starting to wend their way through Customs and passport control, Mary, Beth and Tim were heading for the airport exit.

Inspector Henri Durand from the General Directorate of External Security, the French Intelligence

Agency, watched as they got into the waiting limousine. When the car pulled away, the Inspector walked over to a bank of phone booths and entered one. He closed the door, inserted a jeton, and dialled.

When a voice answered, he said, *'Veuillez dire à Thor que son paquet est arrivé à Paris.'*

When the limousine pulled up in front of the American Embassy, the French press was waiting in force.

Peter Callas watched out of the car window. 'My God! It looks like a riot.'

Waiting for them inside was Hugh Simon, the American Ambassador to France. He was a Texan, middle-aged, with inquisitive eyes in a round face, topped by a wave of bright red hair.

'Everyone's sure eager to meet you, Madam Ambassador. The press has been snapping at my heels all morning.'

Mary's press conference ran longer than an hour, and when it was over she was exhausted. Mary and the children were taken to Ambassador Simon's office.

'Well,' he said, 'I'm glad that's over. When I arrived here to take up this job, I think it got one paragraph on the back page of *Le Monde*.' He smiled. 'Of course, I'm not as pretty as you are.' He remembered something. 'I received a telephone call from Stanton Rogers. I have life and death instructions from the White House to see that you and Beth and Tim enjoy every moment that you're in Paris.'

'*Really* life and death?' Tim asked.

Ambassador Simon nodded. 'His words. He's very fond of you all.'

'We're very fond of him,' Mary assured him.

'I've arranged a suite for you at the Ritz. It's a lovely hotel off the Place de la Concorde. I'm sure you'll be quite comfortable there.'

'Thank you.' Then she added, nervously, 'Is it very expensive?'

'Yes – but not for you. Stanton Rogers has arranged for the State Department to pick up all your expenses.'

Mary said, 'He's incredible.'

'According to him, so are you.'

The afternoon and evening newspapers carried glowing stories of the arrival of the President's first ambassador in his people-to-people programme. The event was given full coverage on the evening television news programme, and in the morning papers the following day.

Inspector Durand looked at the pile of newspapers and smiled. Everything was proceeding as planned. The build-up was even better than expected. He could have predicted the Ashleys' itinerary during the next three days. *They'll go to all the mindless tourist places that Americans want to see*, he thought.

* * *

252

Mary and the children had lunch at the Jules Verne Restaurant in the Tour Eiffel, and later they went to the top of the Arc de Triomphe.

They spent the following morning gazing at the treasures of the Louvre, had lunch near Versailles, and dinner at the Tour d'Argent.

Tim stared out of the restaurant window at Notre-Dame and asked, 'Where do they keep the hunchback?'

Every moment in Paris was a joy. Mary kept thinking how much she wished Edward were there.

The next day after lunch, they were driven to the airport. Inspector Durand watched them as they checked in for their flight to Rome.

The woman is attractive – quite lovely, in fact. An intelligent face. Good body, great legs and derrière. I wonder what she would be like in bed? The children were a surprise. They were very well-mannered for Americans.

When the plane took off, Inspector Durand went to a telephone booth. '*Veuillez dire à Thor que son paquet est en route à Rome.*'

In Rome, the *paparazzi* were waiting at the Michelangelo Airport. As Mary and the children disembarked, Tim said, 'Look, Mom, they followed us!'

Indeed, it seemed to Mary that the only difference was the Italian accents.

The first question the reporters asked was, 'How do you like Italy . . . ?'

Ambassador Oscar Viner was as puzzled as Ambassador Simon had been.

'Frank Sinatra didn't get this big a reception. Is there something about you I don't know, Madam Ambassador?'

'I think I can explain,' Mary replied. 'It isn't *me* the press are interested in. They're interested in the President's people-to-people programme. We'll soon have representatives in every Iron Curtain country. It will be an enormous step towards peace. I think *that's* what the press is excited about.'

After a moment, Ambassador Viner said, 'A lot is riding on you, isn't it?'

Captain Caesar Barzini, the head of the Italian Secret Police, was also able to predict accurately the places Mary and her children would visit during their brief stay.

The captain assigned two men to watch the Ashleys, and each day when they reported back, it was almost exactly as he had anticipated.

'They had ice cream sodas at Doney's, walked along the Via Veneto, and toured the Colosseum.'

'They went to see the Trevi Fountain. Threw in coins.'

'Visited Terme di Caracalla and then the Catacombs. Boy became ill and was taken back to hotel.'

'Subjects went for a carriage ride in Borghese Park and walked along the Piazza Navona.'

Enjoy yourselves, Captain Barzini thought sardonically.

Ambassador Viner accompanied Mary and the children to the airport.

'I have a diplomatic pouch to go to the Romanian Embassy. Would you mind taking it along with your luggage?'

'Of course not,' Mary said.

Captain Barzini was at the airport to watch the Ashley family board the Tarom Airlines plane bound for Bucharest. He stayed until the plane took off, and then made a telephone call. 'I have a message for Balder. Everything went perfectly. The press coverage was tremendous.'

It was only after they were airborne that the enormity of what was about to happen really struck Mary Ashley. It was so incredible that she had to say it aloud. 'We're on our way to Romania, where I'm going to take up my post as Ambassador from the United States.'

Beth was looking at her strangely. 'Yes, Mother. We know that. That's why we're here.'

But how could Mary explain her excitement to them?

The closer the plane got to Bucharest, the more her excitement increased.

I'm going to be the best damned ambassador they've ever seen, she thought. *Before I'm finished, the United States and Romania are going to be close allies.*

The NO SMOKING sign flashed on, and Mary's euphoric dreams of great statesmanship evaporated.

We can't be landing already, Mary thought in a panic. *We just took off. Why is the flight so short?*

She felt pressure on her ears as the plane began to descend, and a few moments later the wheels touched the ground. *It's really happening,* Mary thought incredulously. *I'm not an ambassador. I'm a fake. I'm going to get us into a war. God help us. Dorothy and I should never have left Kansas.*

BOOK THREE

EIGHTEEN

Otopeni Airport, twenty-five miles from the heart of Bucharest, is a modern airport, built to facilitate the flow of travellers from nearby Iron Curtain countries, as well as to take care of the lesser number of Western tourists who visit Romania each year.

Inside the terminal were soldiers in brown uniforms, armed with rifles and pistols, and there was a stark air of coldness about the building that had nothing to do with the frigid temperature. Tim and Beth unconsciously moved closer to Mary. *So they feel it, too*, she thought.

Two men were approaching. One of them was a slim, athletic, American-looking man, and the other was older and dressed in an ill-fitting foreign-looking suit.

The American introduced himself. 'Welcome to Romania, Madam Ambassador. I'm Jerry Davis, your Public Affairs Consular. This is Tudor Costache, the Romanian Chief of Protocol.'

'It is a pleasure to have you and your children with us,' Costache said. 'Welcome to our country.'

In a way, Mary thought, *it's going to be my country, too.* '*Mulţumésc, domnule*,' Mary said.

'You speak Romanian!' Costache cried. '*Cu plăcére!*'

Mary hoped the man was not going to get carried away. 'A few words,' she replied hastily.

Tim said, '*Bună dimineaţa.*'

And Mary was so proud she could have burst. She introduced Tim and Beth.

Jerry Davis said, 'Your limousine is waiting for you, Madam Ambassador. Colonel McKinney is outside.'

Colonel McKinney. Colonel McKinney and Mike Slade. She wondered whether Slade was here, too, but she refused to ask.

There was a long line waiting to go through Customs, but Mary and the children were outside the building in a matter of minutes. There were reporters and photographers waiting again, but instead of the free-for-alls that Mary had encountered earlier, they were orderly and controlled. When they had finished, they thanked Mary and departed in a body.

Colonel McKinney, in Army uniform, was waiting at the kerb. He held out his hand. 'Good morning, Madam Ambassador. Did you have a pleasant trip?'

'Yes, thank you.'

'Mike Slade wanted to be here, but there was some important business he had to take care of.'

Mary wondered whether it was a redhead or a blonde.

A long, black limousine with an American flag on the right front wing pulled up. A cheerful-looking man in a chauffeur's uniform held the door open.

'This is Florian.'

The chauffeur grinned, baring beautiful white teeth. 'Welcome, Madam Ambassador. Master Tim. Miss Beth. It will be my pleasure to serve all of you.'

'Thank you,' Mary said.

'Florian will be at your disposal twenty-four hours a day. I thought we would go directly to the Residence, so you can unpack and relax. Later, perhaps you would like to drive around the city a bit. In the morning, Florian will take you to the American Embassy.'

'That sounds fine,' Mary said.

She wondered again where Mike Slade was.

The drive from the airport to the city was fascinating. They drove on a two-lane highway, heavily used by cars and lorries, but every few miles the traffic would be held up by little gypsy carts plodding along the road. On both sides of the highway were modern factories, next to ancient huts. The car passed farm after farm, with women working in the fields, colourful bandanas knotted around their heads.

They drove by Baneasa, Bucharest's domestic airport. Just beyond it, off the main highway, was a low, blue and grey, two-storey building with an ominous look about it.

'What is that?' Mary asked.

Florian grimaced. 'The Ivan Stelian Prison. That is where they put anyone who disagrees with the Romanian government.'

During the drive, Colonel McKinney pointed to a red button near the door. 'This is an emergency switch,' he explained. 'If you're ever in trouble – attacked by terrorists or whomever – just press this button. It activates a radio transmitter in the car that's monitored at the Embassy, and turns on a red light on the roof of the car. We're able to triangulate your position within minutes.'

Mary said fervently, 'I hope I'll never have to use it.'

'I hope so, too, Madam Ambassador.'

The centre of Bucharest was beautiful. There were parks and monuments and fountains everywhere one looked. Mary remembered her grandfather saying, 'Bucharest is a miniature Paris, Mary. They even have a replica of the Eiffel Tower.' And there it was. She was in the homeland of her forefathers.

The streets were crowded with people and buses and streetcars. The limousine honked its way through the traffic, the pedestrians scurrying out of the way, as the car turned into a small, tree-lined street.

'The Residence is just ahead,' the colonel said. 'The street is named after a Russian general. Ironic, eh?'

The Ambassador's Residence was a large and

beautiful, old-fashioned three-storey house surrounded by acres of lovely grounds.

The staff was lined up outside the Residence,
awaiting the arrival of the new Ambassador. When
Mary stepped out of the car, Jerry Davis made the
introductions.

'Madam Ambassador, your staff. Mihai, your
butler; Sabina, your social secretary; Rosica, your
housekeeper; Cosma, your chef; and Delia and
Carmen, your maids.'

Mary moved down the line, receiving their bows
and curtsies, thinking: *Oh, my God. What am I
going to do with all of them? At home I had Lucinda
come in three times a week to cook and clean.*

'We are very honoured to meet you, Madam
Ambassador,' Sabina, the social secretary, said.

They all seemed to be staring at her, waiting for
her to say something. She took a deep breath.
'*Bună ziua. Mulţumésc. Nu vorbésc –*' Every bit
of Romanian she had learned flew out of her head.
She stared at them, helplessly.

Mihai, the butler, stepped forward and bowed.
'We all speak English, ma'am. We welcome you
and shall be most happy to serve your every need.'

Mary sighed with relief. 'Thank you.'

There was iced champagne waiting inside the
house, along with a table loaded with tempting-
looking foods.

'That looks delicious!' Mary exclaimed. They were
watching her hungrily. She wondered whether she
should offer them anything. Did one do that with

servants? She did not want to start out by making a mistake. *Did you hear what the new American Ambassador did? She invited the servants to eat with her, and they were so shocked that they quit.*

Did you hear what the new American Ambassador did? She gorged herself in front of the starving servants and didn't offer them a bite.

'On second thoughts,' Mary said, 'I'm not hungry right now. I'll – I'll have something later.'

'Let me show you around,' Jerry Davis said.

They followed him eagerly.

The Residence was a lovely house. It was pleasant and charming, in an old-fashioned way. On the ground floor were an entry-way, a library filled with books, music room, living room, and a large dining room, with a kitchen and pantry adjoining. All the rooms were comfortably furnished. A terrace ran the length of the building outside the dining room, facing a large park.

Towards the rear of the house was an indoor swimming pool with an attached sauna, and dressing rooms.

'We have our own swimming pool!' Tim exclaimed. 'Can I go swimming?'

'Later, darling. Let's get settled in first.'

The *pièce de résistance* downstairs was the ballroom, built near the garden. It was enormous. Glistening Baccarat sconces lined the walls, which were done in flocked paper.

Jerry Davis said, 'This is where the Embassy parties are given. Watch this.' He pressed a switch on the wall. There was a grinding noise, and the ceiling began to split in the centre, opening up, until the sky became visible. 'It can also be operated manually.'

'Hey, that's neat!' Tim exclaimed.

'I'm afraid it's called the "Ambassador's folly",' Jerry Davis said apologetically. 'It's too hot to keep open in the summer and too cold in the winter. We use it in April and September.'

'It's still neat,' Tim insisted.

As the cold air started to descend, Jerry Davis pressed the switch again, and the ceiling closed.

'Let me show you to your quarters upstairs.'

They followed Jerry Davis up the staircase to a large, central hall with two bedrooms separated by a bathroom. Farther down the hallway were the master bedroom with a sitting room, a boudoir and bath; a smaller bedroom and bath; plus a sewing and utility room. There was a terrace on the roof, with its separate stairway.

Jerry Davis said, 'The third floor has servants' quarters, a laundry room, and a storage area. In the basement is a wine cellar, and the servants' dining and rest area.'

'It's – it's enormous,' Mary said.

The children were running from room to room.

'Which is my bedroom?' Beth asked.

'You and Tim can decide that between yourselves.'

'You can have this one,' Tim offered. 'It's frilly. Girls like frilly things.'

The master bedroom was lovely, with a queen-sized bed with a goose-down comforter, two couches around a fireplace, an easy chair, dressing table with an antique mirror, an armoire, a luxurious bathroom and a wonderful view of the gardens.

Delia and Carmen had already unpacked Mary's suitcases. On the bed was the diplomatic pouch that Ambassador Viner had asked her to bring to Romania. *I must take it to the Embassy tomorrow morning*, Mary thought. She walked over to pick it up, and took a closer look at it. The red seals had been broken and clumsily taped together again. *When could it have happened?* she wondered. *At the airport? Here? And who did it?*

Sabina came into the bedroom. 'Is everything satisfactory, ma'am?'

'Yes. I've never had a social secretary,' Mary confessed. 'I'm not sure exactly what it is you do.'

'It is my job to see that your life runs smoothly, Madam Ambassador. I keep track of your social engagements, dinners, luncheons, and so on. I also see that the house runs well. With so many servants, there are always problems.'

'Yes, of course,' Mary said, off-handedly.

'Is there anything I can do for you this afternoon?'

You can tell me about that broken seal, Mary thought. Aloud, she said, 'No, thank you. I think I'll rest a while.' She suddenly felt drained.

* * *

She lay awake most of that first night, filled with a deep, cold loneliness mingled with a growing feeling of excitement about starting her new job.

It's up to me now, my darling. I don't have anyone to lean on. I wish you were here with me, telling me not to be afraid, telling me I won't fail. I mustn't fail.

When she finally drifted off to sleep, she dreamed of Mike Slade saying: *I hate amateurs. Why don't you go home?*

The American Embassy in Bucharest, at 21 Soseava Kiseieff, is a white, semi-Gothic, two-storey building, with an iron gate in front, patrolled by a uniformed officer with a grey coat and a red hat. A second guard sits inside a security booth at the side of the gate. There is a *porte-cochère* for cars to drive through, and rose marble steps leading up to the lobby.

Inside, the lobby is ornate. It has a marble floor, two closed circuit television sets at a desk guarded by a Marine, and a fireplace with a firescreen on which is painted a dragon breathing smoke. The corridors are lined with portraits of Presidents. A winding staircase leads to the second floor, where a conference room and offices are located.

A Marine guard was waiting for Mary. 'Good morning, Madam Ambassador,' he said. 'I'm Sergeant Hughes. They call me Gunny.'

'Good morning, Gunny.'

'They're waiting for you in your office. I'll escort you there.'

'Thank you.'

She followed him upstairs to a reception room where a middle-aged woman sat behind a desk.

She rose. 'Good morning, Madam Ambassador. I'm Dorothy Stone, your secretary.'

'How do you do?'

Dorothy said, 'I'm afraid you have quite a crowd in there.'

She opened the office door, and Mary walked into the room. There were nine people seated around a large conference table. They rose as Mary entered. They were all staring at her, and Mary felt a wave of animosity that was almost palpable. The first person she saw was Mike Slade. She thought of the dream she had had.

'I see you got here safely,' Mike said. 'Let me introduce you to your department heads. This is Lucas Janklow, Administrative Consular; Eddie Maltz, Political Consular; Patricia Hatfield, your Economic Consular; David Wallace, Head of Administration; Ted Thompson, Agriculture. You've already met Jerry Davis, your Public Affairs Consular, David Victor, Commerce Consular, and you already know Colonel Bill McKinney.'

'Please be seated,' Mary said. She moved to the seat at the head of the table and surveyed the group. *Hostility comes in all ages, sizes and shapes*, Mary thought.

Patricia Hatfield had a fat body and an attractive face. Lucas Janklow, the youngest member of the team, looked and dressed Ivy League. The other men were older, grey-haired, bald, thin, fat. *It's going to take time to sort them all out.*

Mike Slade was saying, 'All of us are serving at your discretion. You can replace any of us at any time.'

That's a lie, Mary thought angrily, *I tried to replace you.*

The meeting lasted for fifteen minutes. There was general, inconsequential conversation. Mike Slade finally said, 'Dorothy will set up individual meetings for all of you with the Ambassador later in the day. Thank you.'

Mary resented his taking charge. When she and Mike Slade were alone, Mary asked, 'Which one of them is the CIA agent attached to the Embassy?'

Mike looked at her a moment and said, 'Why don't you come with me?'

He walked out of the office. Mary hesitated a moment, and then went after him. She followed him down a long corridor, past a rabbit warren of offices. He came to a large door with a Marine guard standing in front of it. The guard stepped aside as Mike pushed the door open. He turned and gestured for Mary to enter.

She stepped inside and looked around. The room was an incredible combination of metal and glass, covering the floor, the walls and the ceiling.

Mike Slade closed the heavy door behind them. 'This is the Bubble Room. Every embassy in an

Iron Curtain country has one. It's the only room in the Embassy that can't be bugged.'

He saw her look of disbelief.

'Madam Ambassador, not only is the Embassy bugged, but you can bet your last dollar that your Residence is bugged, and that if you go out to a restaurant for dinner, your table will be bugged. You're in enemy territory.'

Mary sank into a chair. 'How do you handle that?' she asked. 'I mean not ever being able to talk freely?'

'We do an electronic sweep every morning. We find their bugs and pull them out. Then they replace them, and we pull *those* out.'

'Why do we permit Romanians to work in the Embassy?'

'It's their playground. They're the home team. We play by their rules, or blow the ball game. They can't get their microphones into this room because there are Marine guards on duty in front of that door twenty-four hours a day. Now – what are your questions?'

'I just wondered who the CIA man was.'

'Eddie Maltz, your Political Consular.'

She tried to recall what Eddie Maltz looked like. Grey-haired and heavy. No, that was the Agriculture Consular. Eddie Maltz . . . Ah, he was the middle-aged one, very thin, a sinister face. Or did she think that now in retrospect because she was told he was CIA?

'Is he the only CIA man on the staff?'

'Yes.'

Was there a hesitation in his voice?

Mike Slade looked at his watch. 'You're due to present your credentials in thirty minutes. Florian is waiting for you outside. Take your Letter of Credence. You'll give the original to President Ionescu and put a copy in our safe.'

Mary found that she was gritting her teeth. 'I *know* that, Mr Slade.'

'He requested that you bring the children with you. I've sent a car for them.'

Without consulting her. 'Thank you.'

Headquarters for the Romanian government is a forbidding-looking building made of blocks of sandstone, in the centre of Bucharest. It is protected by a steel wall, with armed guards in front of it. There were more guards at the entrance to the building. An aide escorted Mary and the children upstairs.

President Alexandros Ionescu greeted Mary and the children in a long, rectangular-shaped room on the second floor. The President of Romania had a powerful presence. He was dark, with hawk-like features, and curly black hair. He had one of the most imperious noses she had ever seen. His eyes were blazing, mesmerizing.

The aide said, 'Your Excellency, may I present Madam Ambassador from the United States?'

The President took Mary's hand and gave it a lingering kiss. 'You are even more beautiful than your photographs.'

'Thank you, your Excellency. This is my daughter Beth and my son Tim.'

'Fine-looking children,' Ionescu said. He looked at her expectantly. 'You have something for me?'

Mary had almost forgotten. She quickly opened her purse and took out the Letter of Credence from President Ellison.

Alexandros Ionescu gave it a careless glance. 'Thank you. I accept it on behalf of the Romanian government. You are now officially the American Ambassador to my country.' He beamed at her. 'I have arranged a reception this evening for you. You will meet some of our people who will be working with you.'

'That's very kind of you,' Mary said.

He took her hand in his again and said, 'We have a saying here. "An ambassador arrives in tears because he knows he will be spending years in a foreign place, away from his friends, but when he leaves, he leaves in tears because he must leave his new friends in a country he has grown fond of." I hope you will grow to love our country, Madam Ambassador.' He massaged her hand.

'I'm sure I will.' *He thinks I'm just another pretty face*, Mary thought grimly. *I'll have to do something about that.*

Mary sent the children home and spent the rest of the day at the Embassy, in the large conference room, meeting with the section heads, the Political, Economic, Agriculture and Administrative Consulars, as well as the Commerce Consular. Colonel McKinney was present as the military attaché.

They were all seated around a long, rectangular table. Against the back walls were a dozen junior members of the various departments.

The Commerce Consular, a small, pompous man, spoke, rattling off a string of facts and figures. Mary was looking around the room, thinking: *I'll have to remember all their names.*

Then it was the turn of Ted Thompson, the Agriculture Consular. 'The Romanian Agriculture Minister is in worse trouble than he's admitting. They're going to have a disastrous crop this year, and we can't afford to let them go under.'

The Economic Consular, Patricia Hatfield, protested, 'We've given them enough aid, Ted. Romania's already operating under a favoured nations treaty. It's a GSP country.' She looked at Mary, covertly.

She's doing this deliberately, Mary thought, *trying to embarrass me.*

Patricia Hatfield said, patronizingly, 'A GSP country is –'

'– is a generalized system of preferences,' Mary cut in. 'We treat Romania as a less developed country so that they get import and export advantages.'

Hatfield's expression changed. 'That's right,' she said. 'We're already giving the store away and –'

David Victor, the Commerce Consular, interrupted, 'We're not giving it away – we're just trying to keep it open so we can shop there. They need

273

more credit in order to buy corn from us. If *we* don't sell it to them, they're going to buy it from Argentina.' He turned to Mary. 'It looks like we're going to lose out on soy beans. The Brazilians are trying to undercut us. I would appreciate it if you'd talk to the Prime Minister as soon as possible and try to make a package deal before we're shut out.'

Mary looked over at Mike Slade, who was seated at the opposite end of the table, slouched in his chair, doodling on a pad, seemingly paying no attention. 'I'll see what I can do,' Mary promised.

She made a note to send a cable to the head of the Commerce Department in Washington asking permission to offer more credit to the Romanian government. The money would come from American banks, but they would make the loans only with government approval.

Eddie Maltz, the Political Consular, as well as the CIA agent, spoke up. 'I have a rather urgent problem, Madam Ambassador. A nineteen-year-old American student was arrested last night for possession of drugs. That's an extremely serious offence here.'

'What kind of drugs did he have on him?'

'Her. It's a young girl. Marijuana. Just a few ounces.'

'What's the girl like?'

'Bright, a college student, rather pretty.'

'What do you think they'll do to her?'

'The usual penalty is a five-year prison sentence.'

My God, Mary thought. *What will she be like when she gets out?* 'What can we do about it?'

274

Mike Slade said lazily, 'You can try your charm on the head of *Securitate*. His name is Istrase. He has a lot of power.'

Eddie Maltz went on. 'The girl says she was framed, and she may have a point. She was stupid enough to have an affair with a Romanian policeman. After he fu – took her to bed, he turned her in.'

Mary was horrified. 'How could he?'

Mike Slade said drily, 'Madam Ambassador, here, we're the enemy – not them. Romania is playing patty cake with us, and we're all buddies, and it's smiles and hands across the sea. We let them sell to us and buy from us at bargain basement discounts, because we're trying to woo them away from Russia. But when it comes right down to it, they're still communists.'

Mary made another note. 'All right. I'll see what I can do.' She turned to the Public Affairs Consular, Jerry Davis. 'What are your problems?'

'My department is having trouble getting approvals for repairs on the apartments our Embassy staff live in. Their quarters are in a disgraceful condition.'

'Can't they just go ahead and have their own repairs made?'

'Unfortunately, no. The Romanian government has to approve all repairs. Some of our people are without heat, and in several of the apartments, the toilets don't work and there's no running water.'

'Have you complained about this?'

'Yes, ma'am. Every day for the last three months.'

'Then why –?'

'It's called harassment,' Mike Slade explained. 'It's a war of nerves they like to play with us.'

Mary made another note.

'Madam Ambassador, I have an extremely urgent problem,' Jack Chancelor, the head of the American Library said. 'Only yesterday some very important reference books were stolen from . . .'

Ambassador Ashley was beginning to get a headache.

The afternoon was spent in listening to a series of complaints. Everyone semed unhappy. And then there was the reading. On her desk was a blizzard of white paper. There were the English translations of newspaper items that had appeared the day before in Romanian papers and magazines. Most of the stories in the popular newspaper *Scinteia Tineretului*, were about the daily activities of President Ionescu, with three or four pictures of him on every single page. *The incredible ego of the man*, Mary thought.

There were other condensations to read: the *Romania Liberă*, the weekly *Flacăra* magazine, and *Magafinul*. And that was only the beginning. There was the wireless file and the summary of news developments reported in the United States. There was a file of the full texts of important American officials' speeches, a thick report on arms control negotiations, and an update on the state of the United States economy.

There's enough reading material in one day, Mary thought, *to keep me busy for years, and I'm going to get this every morning.*

But the problem that disturbed Mary most was the feeling of antagonism from her staff. That had to be handled immediately.

She sent for Harriet Kruger, her Protocol Officer.

'How long have you worked here at the Embassy?' Mary asked.

'Four years before our break with Romania, and now three glorious months.' There was a note of irony in her voice.

'Don't you like it here?'

'I'm a McDonald's and Coney Island girl. Like the song says, "Show Me the Way to Go Home".'

'May we have an off-the-record conversation?'

'No, ma'am.'

Mary had forgotten. 'Why don't we adjourn to the Bubble Room?' she suggested.

When Mary and Harriet Kruger were seated at the table in the Bubble Room, with the heavy door safely closed behind them, Mary said, 'Something just occurred to me. Our meeting today was held in the conference room. Isn't that bugged?'

'Probably,' Kruger said cheerfully. 'But it doesn't matter. Mike Slade wouldn't let anything be discussed that the Romanians aren't already aware of.'

Mike Slade again.

'What do you think of Slade?'

'He's the best.'

Mary decided not to express her opinion. 'The reason I wanted to talk to you is because I got the feeling today that the morale around here isn't very good. Everyone's complaining. No one seems happy. I would like to know whether it's because of me, or whether it's always that way.'

Harriet Kruger studied her for a moment. 'You want an honest answer?'

'Please.'

'It's a combination of both. The Americans working here are in a pressure cooker. We break the rules, and we're in big trouble. We're afraid to make friends with Romanians because they'll probably turn out to belong to the *Securitate*, so we stick with the Americans. We're a small group, so pretty soon that gets boring and incestuous.' She shrugged. 'The pay is small, the food is lousy, and the weather is bad.' She studied Mary. 'None of that is your fault, Madam Ambassador. You have two problems: The first is that you're a political appointee, and you're in charge of an embassy manned by career diplomats.' She stopped. 'Am I coming on too strong?'

'No, please go on.'

'Most of them were against you before you even got here. Career workers in an embassy tend not to rock the boat. Political appointees like to change things. To them, you're an amateur telling profes-

278

sionals how to run their business. The second problem is that you're a woman. Romania should have a big symbol on its flag: a male chauvinist pig. The American men in the Embassy don't like taking orders from a woman, and the Romanians are a lot worse.'

'I see.'

Harriet Kruger smiled. 'But you sure have a great publicity agent. I've never seen so many magazine cover stories in my life. How do you do it?'

Mary had no answer to that.

Harriet Kruger glanced at her watch. 'Oops! You're going to be late. Florian's waiting to take you home so you can change.'

'Change for what?' Mary asked.

'Haven't you looked at the schedule I put on your desk?'

'I'm afraid I haven't had time. Don't tell me I'm supposed to go to some party!'

'*Parties*. Three of them tonight. You have twenty-one parties altogether this week.'

Mary was staring at her. 'That's impossible. I have too much to –'

'It goes with the territory. There are seventy-five embassies in Bucharest, and on any given night, some of them are celebrating something.'

'Can't I say "no"?'

'That would be the United States saying "no" to them. They would be offended.'

Mary sighed. 'I guess I'd better go and change.'

* * *

The cocktail party that afternoon was held at the Romanian State Palace for a visiting dignitary from East Germany.

As soon as Mary arrived, President Ionescu walked over to her. He kissed her hand and said, 'I have been looking forward to seeing you again.'

'Thank you, your Excellency. I, too.'

She had a feeling he had been drinking heavily. She recalled the dossier on him: *Married. One son, fourteen, the heir apparent, and three daughters. Is a womanizer. Drinks a lot. A shrewd peasant mentality. Charming when it suits him. Generous to his friends. Dangerous and ruthless to his enemies.* Mary thought: *A man to beware of.*

Ionescu took Mary's arm and led her off to a deserted corner. 'You will find us Romanians interesting.' He squeezed her arm. 'We are a very passionate people.' He looked at her for a reaction, and when he got none, he went on. 'We are descendants of the ancient Dacians and their conquerors, the Romans, going back to the year AD 106. For centuries, we have been Europe's doormat. The country with rubber borders. The Huns, Goths, Avars, Slavs and Mongols wiped their feet on us, but Romania survived. And do you know how?' He leaned closer to her, and she could smell the liquor on his breath. 'By giving our people a strong, firm leadership. They trust me, and I rule them well.'

Mary thought of some of the stories she had heard. The arrests in the middle of the night, the kangaroo court, the atrocities, the disappearances.

As Ionescu went on talking, Mary looked over his shoulder at the people in the crowded room. There were at least two hundred, and Mary was sure they represented every embassy in Romania. She would meet them all soon. She had glanced at Harriet Kruger's appointment list and was interested to see that one of her first duties would be to make a formal duty call on every one of the seventy-five embassies. In addition to that, there were the multiple cocktail parties and dinners scheduled for six nights of the week.

When am I going to have time to be an ambassador? Mary wondered. And even as she thought it, she realized that all this was part of being an ambassador.

A man came up to President Ionescu and whispered in his ear. The expression on Ionescu's face turned cold. He hissed something in Romanian, and the man nodded and hurried off. The dictator turned back to Mary, oozing charm again. 'I must leave you now. I look forward to seeing you again soon.'

And Ionescu was gone.

NINETEEN

To get a head start on the crowded days that faced her, Mary had Florian pick her up at 6.30. During the ride to the Embassy, she read the reports and the communiqués from other embassies that had been delivered to the Residence during the night.

As Mary walked down the corridor of the Embassy, past Mike Slade's office, she stopped in surprise. He was at his desk, working. He was unshaven. She wondered if he had been out all night.

'You're in early,' Mary said.

He looked up. 'Morning. I'd like to have a word with you.'

'All right.' She started to walk in.

'Not here. Your office.'

He followed Mary through the connecting door to her office, and she watched as he walked over to an instrument in the corner of the room. 'This is a shredder,' Mike informed her.

'I know that.'

'Really? When you went out last night, you left

some papers on top of your desk. By now they've been photographed and sent to Moscow.'

'Oh, my God! I must have forgotten. Which papers were they?'

'A list of cosmetics, toilet paper, and other personal feminine things you wanted to order. But that's beside the point. The cleaning women work for the *Securitate*. The Romanians are grateful for every scrap of information they can get, and they're great at putting things together. Lesson number one: At night everything must be locked in your safe, or shredded.'

'What's lesson number two?' Mary asked coldly.

Mike grinned. 'The Ambassador always starts the day by having coffee with her Deputy Chief of Mission. How do you take yours?'

She had no desire to have coffee with this arrogant bastard. 'I – black.'

'Good. You have to watch your figure around here. The food is fattening.' He rose and started towards the door that led to his office. 'I make my own brew. You'll like it.'

She sat there, furious with him. *I have to be careful how I handle him*, Mary decided. *I want him out of here as quickly as possible.*

He returned with two steaming mugs of coffee and set them down on her desk.

'How do I arrange for Beth and Tim to start at the American school here?' Mary asked.

'I've already arranged it. Florian will deliver them mornings and pick them up afternoons.'

She was taken aback. 'I – thank you.'

'You should take a look at the school when you get a chance. It's a small school, about a hundred pupils. Each class has eight or nine students. They come from all over – Canadians, Israelis, Nigerians – you name it. The teachers are excellent.'

'I'll stop by there.'

Mike took a sip of his coffee. 'I understand that you had a nice chat with our fearless leader last night.'

'President Ionescu? Yes. He seemed very pleasant.'

'Oh, he is. He's a lovely fellow. Until he gets annoyed with somebody. Then he chops your head off.'

Mary said nervously, 'Shouldn't we talk about this in the Bubble Room?'

'Not necessary. I had your office swept for bugs this morning. It's clean. After the janitors and cleaning people come in, then watch out. By the way, don't let Ionescu's charm fool you. He's a dyed-in-the-wool son-of-a-bitch. His people despise him, but there's nothing they can do about it. The secret police are everywhere. It's the KGB and police force wrapped into one. The general rule of thumb here is that one out of every three persons works for *Securitate* or the KGB. Romanians have orders not to have any contact with foreigners. If a foreigner wants to have dinner at a Romanian's apartment, it has to be approved first by the State.'

Mary felt a shiver go through her.

'A Romanian can be arrested for signing a petition, criticizing the government, writing graffiti . . .'

Mary had read newspaper and magazine articles about repression in communist countries, but living in the midst of it gave her a feeling of unreality.

'They do have trials here,' Mary said.

'Oh, occasionally they'll have a show trial, where reporters from the West are allowed to watch. But most of the people arrested manage to have fatal accidents while they're in police custody. There are gulags in Romania that we're not allowed to see. They're in the Delta area, and in the Danube near the Black Sea. I've talked to people who have seen them. The conditions there are horrifying.'

'And there's no place they can escape to,' Mary said, thinking aloud. 'They have the Black Sea to the east, Bulgaria to the south, and Yugoslavia, Hungary and Czechoslovakia on their other borders. They're right in the middle of the Iron Curtain.'

'Have you heard about the Typewriter Decree?'

'No.'

'It's Ionescu's latest brainstorm. He ordered every typewriter and copy machine in the country registered. As soon as they were registered, he had them confiscated. Now Ionescu controls all the information that's disseminated. More coffee?'

'No, thanks.'

'Ionescu is squeezing the people where it hurts. They're afraid to strike because they know they'll be shot. The standard of living here is one of the lowest in Europe. There's a shortage of everything.

If the people see a line in front of a store, they'll join in and buy whatever it is that's for sale while they have the chance.'

'It seems to me,' Mary said slowly, 'that all these things add up to a wonderful opportunity for us to help them.'

Mike Slade looked at her. 'Sure,' he said drily. 'Wonderful.'

As Mary was going through some newly arrived cables from Washington that afternoon, she thought about Mike Slade. He was a strange man. Arrogant and rude, and yet: *I've arranged for the children's school. Florian will deliver them mornings and pick them up afternoons.* And he seemed to really care about the Romanian people and their problems. *He may be more complex than I thought*, Mary decided.

I still don't trust him.

It was by sheer accident that Mary learned of the meetings going on behind her back. She had left the office to have lunch with the Romanian Minister of Agriculture. When she arrived at the Ministry, she was told he had been called away by the President. Mary decided to return to the Embassy and have a working lunch. She said to her secretary, 'Tell Lucas Janklow, David Wallace and Eddie Maltz that I would like to see them.'

Dorothy Stone hesitated. 'They're in a conference, ma'am.'

There was something evasive in her tone.

'In a conference with whom?'

Dorothy Stone took a deep breath. 'With all the other consulars.'

It took a moment for it to sink in. 'Are you saying that there's a staff meeting going on without me?'

'Yes, Madam Ambassador.'

It was outrageous! 'I gather that this isn't the first time?'

'No, ma'am.'

'What else is going on here that I should know about and don't?'

Dorothy Stone took a deep breath. 'They're all sending out cables without your authorization.'

Forget about a revolution brewing in Romania, Mary thought. *There's a revolution brewing right here in the Embassy.* 'Dorothy – call a meeting of all department heads for three o'clock this afternoon. That means *everybody*.'

'Yes, ma'am.'

Mary was seated at the head of the table, watching as the staff entered the conference room. The senior members seated themselves at the conference table and the junior members took chairs against the wall.

'Good afternoon,' Mary said crisply. 'I won't take up much of your time. I know how busy you all are. It has come to my attention that senior staff meetings have been called without my knowledge or

287

sanction. From this moment on, anyone attending such a meeting will be instantly dismissed.' Out of the corner of her eye, she saw Dorothy taking notes. 'It has also come to my attention that some of you are sending cables without informing me. According to State Department protocol, each ambassador has the right to hire and fire any member of the Embassy staff at his or her discretion.' Mary turned to Ted Thompson, the Agriculture Consular. 'Yesterday, you sent an unauthorized cable to the State Department. I've made reservations for you on a plane leaving for Washington at noon tomorrow. You are no longer a member of this Embassy.' She looked around the room. 'The next time anyone in this room sends a cable without my knowledge, or fails to give me full support, that person will be on the next plane back to the United States. That's all, ladies and gentlemen.'

There was a stunned silence. Then, slowly, the people began to rise and file out of the room. There was an intrigued expression on Mike Slade's face as he walked out.

Mary and Dorothy Stone were alone in the room. Mary said, 'What do you think?'

Dorothy grinned. 'Neat, but not gaudy. That's the shortest and most effective staff meeting I've ever seen.'

'Good. Now it's time to enlighten the cable office.'

All messages sent from embassies in Eastern Europe are sent in code. They are typed on a special typewriter, read by an electronic scanner in the code room, and automatically encoded there. The codes are changed every day, and have five designations: Top Secret; Secret; Confidential; Limited Official Use; and Unclassified. The cable office itself was a barred, windowless back room filled with the latest electronic equipment, and was closely guarded.

Sandy Palance, the officer in charge, was seated in the cable room behind a cage. He rose as Mary approached. 'Good afternoon, Madam Ambassador. May I help you?'

'No. I'm going to help *you*.'

There was a puzzled look on Palance's face. 'Ma'am?'

'You've been sending out cables without my signature. That means they're unauthorized cables.'

He was suddenly defensive. 'Well, the consulars told me that –'

'From now on, if you are asked by anyone to send a cable that does not have my signature on it, it is to be brought directly to me. Is that understood?' There was steel in her voice.

Palance thought: *Jesus! They sure had this one pegged wrong.* 'Yes, ma'am. I understand.'

'Good.'

Mary turned and walked away. She knew that the cable room was used by the CIA to send messages through a 'black channel'. There was no way she could stop that. She wondered how many members of the Embassy were part of the CIA, and she wondered if Mike Slade had told her the whole truth about it. She had the feeling he had not.

That night, Mary made notes of the day's events, and jotted down the problems that needed to be acted upon. She put them at her bedside, on top of a small table. In the morning she went into the bathroom to shower. When she was dressed, she picked up her notes. They were in a different order. *You can be sure that the Embassy and the Residence are bugged.* Mary stood there for a moment, thinking.

At breakfast, when she and Beth and Tim were alone in the dining room, Mary said, in a loud voice, 'The Romanians are such a wonderful people. But I have a feeling they're far behind the United States in some ways. Did you know that a lot of the apartments our Embassy staff live in have no heat or running water, and that the toilets don't work?'

Beth and Tim were looking at her strangely.

'I suppose we'll have to teach the Romanians how to fix things like that.'

The following morning, Jerry Davis said, 'I don't know how you did it, but there are workmen all over the place, fixing up our apartments.'

Mary grinned. 'You just have to speak nicely to them.'

* * *

At the end of a staff meeting, Mike Slade said, 'You have a lot of embassies to pay respects to. You'd better get started today.'

She resented his tone. Besides, it was none of his business; Harriet Kruger was the Protocol Officer, and she was away from the Embassy for the day.

Mike went on. 'It's important that you call on the embassies according to priority. The most important –'

'– is the Russian Embassy. I know that.'

'I would advise you –'

'Mr Slade – if I need any advice from you about my duties here, I'll let you know.'

Mike let out a deep sigh. 'Right.' He rose. 'Whatever you say, Madam Ambassador.'

After her visit to the Russian Embassy, the rest of Mary's day was taken up with interviews, a senator from New York who wanted inside information about dissidents, and a meeting with the new Agriculture Consular.

As Mary was about to leave the office, Dorothy Stone buzzed her. 'There's an urgent call for you, Madam Ambassador. James Stickley from Washington.'

Mary picked up the telephone. 'Hello, Mr Stickley.'

Stickley's voice came burning over the wire. 'Would you mind telling me what in God's name you're doing?'

'I – I don't know what you mean.'

'*Obviously*. The Secretary of State has just received a formal protest from the Ambassador of Gabon about your behaviour.'

'Just a minute!' Mary replied. 'There's some mistake. I haven't even *talked* to the Ambassador of Gabon.'

'Exactly,' Stickley snapped. 'But you talked to the Ambassador of the Soviet Union.'

'Well – yes. I made my courtesy call this morning.'

'Aren't you aware that foreign embassies take precedence according to the date they presented their credentials?'

'Yes, but –'

'For your information, in Romania, Gabon is the first, the Estonian Embassy is last, and there are about seventy more embassies in between. Any questions?'

'No, sir. I'm sorry if I –'

'Please see that it doesn't happen again.'

When Mike Slade heard the news, he came into Mary's office. 'I tried to tell you.'

'Mr Slade –'

'They take things like that very seriously in the diplomacy business. As a matter of fact, in 1661 the attendants of the Spanish Ambassador in London attacked the French Ambassador's coach, killed the postilion, beat up the coachman and hamstrung two horses just to make sure that the

Spanish Ambassador's coach arrived first. I would suggest that you send a note of apology.'

Mary knew what she would be having for dinner. *Crow*.

Mary was disturbed by the comments she kept hearing about the amount of publicity she and the children were getting. 'There's even an article in *Pravda* about the three of you.'

At midnight Mary placed a call to Stanton Rogers. He would just be getting into his office. He came onto the line immediately.

'How's my favourite ambassador?'

'I'm fine. How are you, Stan?'

'Aside from a forty-eight-hour-day schedule, I can't complain. As a matter of fact, I'm enjoying every minute of it. How are you getting along? Any problems I can help you with?'

'It's not a problem, really. It's just something I'm curious about.' She hesitated, trying to phrase it so he would not misunderstand. 'I presume you saw the photograph of the children and me in *Pravda* last week?'

'Yes, it's wonderful!' Stanton Rogers exclaimed. 'We're finally getting through to them.'

'Do other ambassadors get as much publicity as I've been getting?'

'Frankly, no. But the boss decided to go all out with you, Mary. You're our showcase. President Ellison meant it when he said he was looking for the opposite of the ugly American. We've got you

293

and we intend to flaunt you. We want the whole world to get a good look at the best of our country.'

'I – I'm really flattered.'

'Keep up the good work.'

They exchanged pleasantries for a few more minutes and said goodbye.

So it's the President who's behind this build-up, Mary thought. *No wonder he's been able to arrange so much publicity.*

The inside of the Ivan Stelian Prison was even more forbidding than its exterior. The corridors were narrow, painted a dull grey. There was a jungle of crowded, black-barred cells downstairs and on an upper tier, patrolled by uniformed guards armed with machine guns. The stench in the crowded cell area was overpowering.

A guard led Mary to a small visitors' room at the rear of the prison.

'She's in there. You have ten minutes.'

'Thank you.' Mary stepped inside the room, and the door closed behind her.

Hannah Murphy was seated at a small, battle-scarred table. She was handcuffed, and wearing prison garb. Eddie Maltz had referred to her as a pretty, nineteen-year-old student. She looked ten years older. Her face was pale and gaunt, and her eyes were red and swollen. Her hair was uncombed.

'Hi,' Mary said. 'I'm the American Ambassador.'

Hannah Murphy looked at her and began to sob uncontrollably.

Mary put her arms around her and said, soothingly, 'Sh! It's going to be all right.'

'N-no it's not,' the girl moaned. 'I'm going to be sentenced next week. I'll die if I have to stay in this place five years. I'll die!'

Mary held her for a moment. 'All right, tell me what happened.'

Hannah Murphy took a deep breath, and after a few moments she said, 'I met this man – he was a Romanian – and I was lonely. He was nice to me and we – we made love. A girl friend had given me a couple of sticks of marijuana. I shared one with him. We made love again and I went to sleep. When I woke up in the morning, he was gone, but the police were there. I was naked. They – they stood around watching me get dressed and they brought me to this hell-hole.' She shook her head helplessly. 'They told me five years.'

'Not if I can help it.'

Mary thought of what Lucas Janklow had said to her as she was leaving for the prison. 'There's nothing you can do for her, Madam Ambassador. We've tried before. A five-year sentence for a foreigner is standard. If she were a Romanian, they'd probably give her life.'

Now Mary looked at Hannah Murphy and said, 'I'll do everything in my power to help you.'

Mary had examined the official police report on Hannah Murphy's arrest. It was signed by Captain Aurel Istrase, head of *Securitate*. It was brief and unhelpful, but there was no doubt of the girl's guilt. *I'll have to find another way*, Mary thought. *Aurel Istrase*. The name had a familiar ring. She thought back to the confidential dossier James Stickley had showed her in Washington. There had been something in there about Captain Istrase. Something about – she remembered.

Mary arranged to have a meeting with the captain the following morning.

'You're wasting your time,' Mike Slade told her bluntly. 'Istrase is a mountain. He can't be moved.'

Aurel Istrase was a short, swarthy man with a scarred face, a shiny, bald head and stained teeth. Earlier in his career, someone had broken his nose, and it had failed to heal properly. Istrase had come to the Embassy for the meeting. He was curious about the new American Ambassador.

'You wished to talk to me, Madam Ambassador?'

'Yes. Thank you for coming. I want to discuss the case of Hannah Murphy.'

'Ah, yes. The drug peddler. In Romania, we have strict laws about people who sell drugs. They go to jail.'

'Excellent,' Mary said. 'I'm pleased to hear that. I wish we had stricter drug laws in the United States.'

Istrase was watching her, puzzled. 'Then you agree with me?'

'Absolutely. Anyone who sells drugs deserves jail. Hannah Murphy, however, did not sell drugs. She offered to give some marijuana to her lover.'

'It is the same thing. If –'

'Not quite, Captain. Her lover was a lieutenant on your police force. He smoked marijuana, too. Has he been punished?'

'Why should he be? He was merely gathering evidence of a criminal act.'

'Your lieutenant has a wife and three children?'

Captain Istrase frowned. 'Yes. The American girl tricked him into bed.'

'Captain – Hannah Murphy is a nineteen-year-old student. Your lieutenant is forty-five. Now who tricked whom?'

'Age has nothing to do with this,' the captain said stubbornly.

'Does the lieutenant's wife know about her husband's affair?'

Captain Istrase stared at her. 'Why should she?'

'Because it sounds to me like a clear case of entrapment. I think we had better make this whole thing public. The international press will be fascinated.'

'There would be no point to that,' he said.

She sprang her ace. 'Because the lieutenant happens to be your son-in-law?'

'Certainly not!' the captain said angrily. 'I just want to see justice done.'

'So do I,' Mary assured him.

According to the dossier she had seen, the son-in-law specialized in making the acquaintance of young tourists – male or female – sleeping with them, suggesting places where they could trade in the black market or buy dope, and then turning them in.

Mary said in a conciliatory tone, 'I see no need for your daughter to know how her husband conducts himself. I think it would be much better for all concerned if you quietly released Hannah Murphy from jail, and I shipped her back to the States. What do you say, Captain?'

He sat there, fuming, thinking it over. 'You are a very interesting lady,' he said finally.

'Thank you. You're a very interesting man. I'll expect Miss Murphy in my office this afternoon. I'll see that she's put on the first plane out of Bucharest.'

He shrugged. 'I will use what little influence I have.'

'I'm sure you will, Captain Istrase. Thank you.'

The following morning a grateful Hannah Murphy was on her way home.

'How did you do it?' Mike Slade asked, unbelievingly.

'I followed your advice. I charmed him.'

TWENTY

The day Beth and Tim were to start school, Mary got a call at 5 a.m. from the Embassy that a NIACT – a night action cable – had come in and required an immediate answer. It was the start of a long and busy day, and by the time Mary returned to the Residence it was after 7 o'clock. The children were waiting for her.

'Well,' Mary asked, 'how was school?'

'I like it,' Beth replied. 'Did you know there are kids there from twenty-two different countries? This neat Italian boy kept staring at me all through class. It's a great school.'

'They've got a keen science laboratory,' Tim added. 'Tomorrow we're going to take some Romanian frogs apart.'

'It's so weird,' Beth said. 'They all speak English with such funny accents.'

'Just remember,' Mary told the children, 'when someone has an accent, it means that he knows one more language than you do. Well, I'm glad you had no problems.'

Beth said, 'No. Mike took care of us.'

'Who?'

'Mr Slade. He told us to call him Mike.'

'What does Mike Slade have to do with your going to school?'

'Didn't he tell you? He picked us up and drove Tim and me there and took us in and introduced us to our teachers. He knows them all.'

'He knows a lot of kids there, too,' Tim said. 'And he introduced us to them. Everybody likes him. He's a neat guy.'

A little too neat, Mary thought.

The following morning when Mike walked into Mary's office, she said, 'I understand you took Beth and Tim to school.'

He nodded. 'It's tough for youngsters trying to adjust in a foreign country. They're good kids.'

Did he have children? Mary suddenly realized how little she knew about Mike Slade's personal life. *It's probably better that way*, she decided. *He intends to see that I fail.*

She intended to succeed.

Saturday afternoon Mary took the children to the private Diplomatic Club, where members of the diplomatic community gathered to exchange gossip.

As Mary looked across the patio, she saw Mike Slade having a drink with someone, and when the woman turned, Mary realized that it was Dorothy Stone. Mary felt a momentary shock. It was as though her secretary were collaborating with the enemy. She wondered how close Dorothy and Mike Slade were. *I must be careful not to trust her too much*, Mary thought. *Or anyone.*

Harriet Kruger was seated at a table alone. Mary walked over. 'Do you mind if I join you?'

'I'd be delighted.' Harriet pulled out a package of American cigarettes. 'Cigarette?'

'Thank you, no. I don't smoke.'

'A person can't live in this country without cigarettes,' Harriet said.

'I don't understand.'

'Kent's One Hundred soft packs make the economy go around. I mean – literally. If you want to see a doctor, you give the nurse cigarettes. If you want meat from the butcher, a mechanic to fix your automobile, or an electrician to fix a lamp – you bribe them with cigarettes. I had an Italian friend who needed a small operation. She had to bribe the nurse in charge to use a new razor blade when she prepped her, and she had to bribe the other nurses to put on clean bandages after they had cleansed the wounds, instead of using all the old bandages again.'

'But why –?'

Harriet Kruger said, 'This country's short on bandages and every kind of medication you can name. It's the same everywhere in the Eastern bloc.

301

Last month there was a plague of botulism in East Germany. They had to get all their anti-serum from the West.'

'And the people have no way of complaining,' Mary commented.

'Oh, they have their ways. Haven't you heard of Bula?'

'No.'

'He's a mythical character the Romanians use to let off steam. There's a story about people standing in line for meat one day and the line was barely moving. After five hours, Bula gets mad and says, "I'm going over to the palace and kill Ionescu!" Two hours later, he comes back to the line and his friends ask, "What happened – did you kill him?" Bula says, "No. There was a long line there, too."'

Mary laughed.

Harriet Kruger said, 'Do you know what one of the biggest black market items here is? Our home video cassettes.'

'They like to watch our movies?'

'No – it's the commercials they're interested in. All the things we take for granted – washing machines, vacuum cleaners, automobiles, television sets – those things are out of their reach. They're fascinated by them. When the movie starts again, they go to the john.'

Mary looked up in time to see Mike Slade and Dorothy Stone leaving the club. She wondered where they were going.

* * *

When Mary came home at night after a hard, long day at the Embassy, all she wanted to do was bathe and change clothes and shed the day. At the Embassy every minute seemed to be filled, and she never had any time to herself. But she soon found that the Residence was just as bad. Wherever Mary went, there were the servants, and she had the uncomfortable feeling they were constantly spying on her.

One night she got up at 2 a.m. and went downstairs to the kitchen. As she opened the refrigerator, she heard a noise. She turned around, and Mihai, the butler, in his robe, and Rosica and Delia and Carmen were standing there.

'What can I get you, Madam?' Mihai asked.

'Nothing,' Mary said. 'I just wanted a little something to eat.'

Cosma, the chef, came in and said in a hurt voice, 'All Madam had to do was tell me she was hungry and I would have prepared something.'

They were staring at her reprovingly.

Mary said, 'I don't think I'm really hungry. Thank you.' And she fled back to her room.

The next day she told the children what had happened. 'Do you know,' she said to Tim and Beth, 'I felt like the second wife in *Rebecca*.'

'What's *Rebecca*?' Beth asked.

'It's a lovely book you'll read one day.'

When Mary walked into her office, Mike Slade was waiting for her.

'We have a sick kid you'd better take a look at,' he said.

He led her to one of the small offices down the corridor. On the couch was a white-faced young Marine, groaning in pain.

'What happened?' Mary asked.

'My guess is appendicitis.'

'Then we'd better get him to a hospital right away.'

Mike turned and looked at her. 'Not here.'

'What do you mean?'

'He has to be flown either to Rome or Zürich.'

'That's ridiculous,' Mary snapped. She lowered her voice, so the boy would not hear. 'Can't you see how sick he is?'

'Ridiculous or not, no one from an American embassy goes to a hospital in an Iron Curtain country.'

'But, why —?'

'Because we're vulnerable. We'd be at the mercy of the Romanian government and the *Securitate*. We could be put under ether, or given scopolamine – they could extract all kinds of information from us. It's a State Department rule – we fly him out.'

'Why doesn't our Embassy have its own doctor?'

'Because we're a "C" category embassy. We haven't the budget for our own doctor. An American doctor pays us a visit here once every three months. In the meantime, we have a pharmacist for minor aches and pains.' Mike walked over to a desk and picked up a piece of paper. 'Just sign this, and he's on his way. I'll arrange for a special plane to fly him out.'

'Very well.' Mary signed the paper. She walked over to the young Marine and took his hand in hers. 'You're going to be fine,' she said softly. 'Just fine.'

Two hours later, the Marine was on a plane to Zürich.

The following morning when Mary asked Mike how the young Marine was, he shrugged. 'They operated,' he said indifferently. 'He'll be all right.'

What a cold man, Mary thought. *I wonder if anything ever touches him.*

TWENTY-ONE

No matter what time in the morning Mary arrived at the Embassy, Mike Slade was always there ahead of her. She saw him at very few of the embassy parties, and she had a feeling he had his own private entertainment every night.

He was a constant surprise. One afternoon Mary agreed to let Florian take Beth and Tim ice-skating at Floreasca Park. Mary left the Embassy early to join them, and when she arrived, she saw that Mike Slade was with them. The three of them were skating together, obviously having a wonderful time. He was patiently teaching them figure eights. *I must warn the children about him*, Mary thought. But she was not sure exactly what the warning should be.

The following morning when Mary arrived at her office, Mike walked in. 'A codel is arriving in two hours. I thought –'

'A codel?'

'That's diplomatese for a congressional delegation. Four senators with their wives and aides. They'll expect you to meet with them. I'll set up an appointment with President Ionescu and have Harriet see that their shopping and sight-seeing are taken care of.'

'Thank you.'

'Some of my home-brewed coffee?'

'Fine.'

She watched him as he walked through the connecting door into his office. A strange man. Rough, rude. And yet, there was his patience with Beth and Tim.

When he returned with two cups of coffee, Mary said, 'Do you have children?'

The question caught Mike Slade off guard. 'I have two boys.'

'Where –?'

'They're in the custody of my ex-wife.' He abruptly changed the subject. 'Let's see if I can set up that appointment with Ionescu.'

The coffee was delicious. Mary was later to remember that this was the day she realized that having coffee with Mike Slade had become a morning ritual.

Angel picked her up in the evening at La Boca, near the waterfront, where she was standing with the other *putas*, dressed in a tight-fitting blouse and jeans that were cut off at the thighs, showing off her wares. She looked no older than fifteen.

She was not pretty, but that did not bother Angel.

'*Vámonos, querida*. We will entertain each other.'

The girl lived in a cheap, walk-up apartment nearby, consisting of one dirty room with a bed, two chairs, a lamp and a sink.

'Get undressed, *estrelita*. I want to see you naked.'

The girl hesitated. There was something about Angel that frightened her. But it had been a slow day, and she had to bring money to Pepe, or she knew she would be beaten. Slowly, she began to undress.

Angel stood watching. Off came the blouse and then the jeans. The girl was wearing nothing underneath. Her body was pale and thin.

'Keep your shoes on. Come over here and kneel down.'

The girl obeyed.

'Now this is what I want you to do.'

She listened, and looked up with frightened eyes. 'I've never done –'

Angel kicked her in the head. She lay on the floor, moaning. Angel picked her up by the hair and threw her on the bed. As the girl started to scream, Angel punched her hard across the face. She moaned.

'Good,' Angel said. 'I want to hear you moan.'

A huge fist slammed into her nose and broke it. When Angel was finished with her thirty minutes later, the girl lay on the bed, unconscious.

Angel smiled down at the battered figure of the girl and threw a few pesos on the bed. '*Gracias.*'

Mary spent every possible moment she could with the children. They did a lot of sight-seeing. There were dozens of museums and old churches to visit, but for the children the highlight was the trip to Braşov, to Dracula's castle, located in the heart of Transylvania, a hundred miles from Bucharest.

'The count was really a prince,' Florian explained on the drive up. 'Prince Vlad Tepes. He was a great hero who stopped the Turkish invasion.'

'I thought he just liked to suck blood and kill people,' Tim said.

Florian nodded. 'Yes. Unfortunately, after the war Vlad's power went to his head. He became a dictator and he impaled his enemies on stakes. The legend grew that he was a vampire. An Irishman, named Bram Stoker, wrote a book based on the legend. A silly book, but it has done wonders for tourism.'

Bram Castle was a huge, stone monument high in the mountains. They were all exhausted by the time they climbed the steep stone stairs leading to the castle. They went into a low-ceilinged room containing guns and ancient artefacts.

'This is where Count Dracula murdered his victims and drank their blood,' the guide said in a sepulchral voice.

The room was damp and eerie. A spiderweb brushed across Tim's face. 'I'm not scared of anything,' he said to his mother, 'but can we get out of here?'

Every six weeks an American Air Force C-130 plane landed at a small airfield on the outskirts of Bucharest. The plane was loaded with food and luxuries unavailable in Bucharest, that had been ordered by members of the American Embassy through the military commissary in Frankfurt.

One morning, while Mary and Mike Slade were having coffee, Mike said, 'Our commissary plane is due in today. Why don't you take a ride out to the airport with me?'

Mary started to say no. She had a great deal of work to do, and it seemed a pointless invitation. Still, Mike Slade was not a man given to wasting time. Her curiosity got the better of her.

'All right.'

They drove to the airfield, and on the way discussed various Embassy problems that had to be dealt with. The conversation was kept on a cool, impersonal level.

When they arrived at the airport, an armed Marine sergeant opened a gate to allow the limousine to pass through. Ten minutes later, they watched the C-130 land.

Behind the fence, on the boundary of the airport, hundreds of Romanians had gathered. They watched hungrily as the crew began unloading the aircraft.

'What is that crowd doing here?'

'Dreaming. They're looking at some of the things they can never have. They know we're getting steak and soap and perfume. A crowd is always here when the plane lands. It's some kind of mysterious underground telegraph.'

Mary studied the avid faces behind the fence. 'It's unbelievable.'

'That plane is a symbol to them. It's not just the cargo – it represents a free country that takes care of its citizens.'

Mary turned to look at him. 'Why did you bring me here?'

'Because I don't want you to get carried away by President Ionescu's sweet talk. This is the real Romania.'

Every morning when Mary rode to work, she noticed long queues of people outside the gates waiting to get into the consular section of the Embassy. She had taken it for granted that they were people with minor problems they hoped the consul could solve. But on this particular morning, she went to the window to take a closer look, and the expression she saw on their faces compelled her to go into Mike's office.

'Who are all those people waiting in line outside?'

Mike walked with her to the window. 'They're mostly Romanian Jews. They're waiting to file applications for visas.'

'But there's an Israeli Embassy in Bucharest. Why don't they go there?'

'Two reasons,' Mike explained. 'First of all, they think the United States government has a greater chance of assisting them to get to Israel than the Israeli government. And secondly, they think there's less of a chance of the Romanian security people finding out their intention if they come to us. They're wrong, of course.' He pointed out the window. 'There's an apartment house directly across from the Embassy that has several flats filled with agents using telescopic lenses, photographing everybody who goes in and out of the Embassy.'

'That's terrible!'

'That's the way they play the game. When a Jewish family applies for a visa to emigrate, they lose their green job cards and they're thrown out of their apartments. Their neighbours are instructed to turn their backs on them. Then it takes three to four years before the government will tell them whether they'll even get their exit papers, and the answer is usually "no".'

'Can't we do something about it?'

'We try all the time. But Ionescu enjoys playing a cat-and-mouse game with the Jews. Very few of them are ever allowed to leave the country.'

Mary looked out at the expressions of hope-lessness painted on their faces. 'There has to be a way,' Mary said.

'Don't break your heart,' Mike told her.

* * *

The time zone problem was exhausting. When it was daylight in Washington, it was the middle of the night in Bucharest, and Mary was constantly being awakened by telegrams and telephone calls at three and four in the morning. Every time a night cable came in, the Marine on duty at the Embassy would call the day officer, who would send a staff assistant to the Residence to awaken Mary. After that, she would be too keyed up to go back to sleep.

It's exciting, Edward. I really think I can make a difference here. Anyway, I'm trying. I couldn't bear to fail. Everyone is counting on me. I wish you were here to say 'you can do it, old girl'. I miss you so much. Can you hear me, Edward? Are you here somewhere where I can't see you? Sometimes not knowing the answer to that makes me crazy . . .

They were having their morning coffee.

'We have a problem,' Mike Slade began.

'Yes?'

'A delegation of a dozen Romanian church officials wants to see you. A church in Utah has invited them for a visit. The Romanian government won't issue them an exit visa.'

'Why not?'

'Very few Romanians are allowed to leave the country. They have a joke about the day Ionescu took power. He went to the east wing of the palace and saw the sun rising. "Good morning,

313

comrade sun," Ionescu said. "Good morning," the sun said. "Everyone is so happy that you are Romania's new President." That evening, Ionescu went to the west wing of the palace to watch the sun set. He said, "Good evening, comrade sun." The sun didn't answer. "How is it that you spoke to me so nicely this morning, and now you won't speak to me at all?" "I'm in the west now," the sun said. "You can go to hell." Ionescu is afraid that once they get out, the church officials will tell the government to go to hell.'

'I'll talk to the Foreign Minister and see what I can do.'

Mike rose. 'Do you like folk-dancing?' he asked.

'Why?'

'There's a Romanian dance company opening tonight. They're supposed to be pretty good. Would you like to go?'

Mary was taken by surprise. The last thing she had expected was for Mike to invite her out.

And now, even more incredibly, she found herself saying, 'Yes.'

'Good.' Mike handed her a small envelope. 'There are three tickets here. You can take Beth and Tim, courtesy of the Romanian government. We get tickets to most of their openings.'

Mary sat there, her face flushed, feeling like a fool. 'Thank you,' she said stiffly.

'I'll have Florian pick you up at eight o'clock.'

*   *   *

Beth and Tim were not interested in going to the theatre. Beth had invited a schoolmate for dinner.

'It's my Italian friend,' Beth said. 'Is it okay?'

'To tell you the truth, I've never really cared much for folk-dancing,' Tim added.

Mary laughed. 'All right. I'll let you two off the hook this time.'

She wondered if the children were as lonely as she was. She thought about who she could invite to go with her. She mentally ran down the list: Colonel McKinney, Jerry Davis, Harriet Kruger? There was no one she really wanted to be with. *I'll go alone*, she decided.

Florian was waiting for Mary when she stepped out of the front door.

'Good evening, Madam Ambassador.' He bowed and opened the car door.

'You seem very cheerful tonight, Florian.'

He grinned. 'I am always cheerful, Madam.' He closed the door and got behind the wheel. 'We Romanians have a saying: "Kiss the hand you cannot bite."'

Mary decided to take a chance. 'Are you happy living here, Florian?'

He studied her in the rear-view mirror. 'Shall I give you the official party line answer, Madam Ambassador, or would you like the truth?'

'The truth, please.'

'I could be shot for saying this, but no Romanian

is happy here. Only foreigners. You are free to come and go as you please. We are prisoners. There is not enough of anything here.' They were driving by a long queue of people in front of a butcher's shop. 'Do you see that? They will wait in line for three or four hours to get a lamb chop or two, and half the people in line will be disappointed. It is the same for everything. But do you know how many homes Ionescu has hidden away? Twelve! I have driven many Romanian officials to them. Each one is like a palace. Meanwhile, three or four families are forced to live together in tiny apartments without heat.' Florian stopped suddenly, as though afraid he had said too much. 'You will not mention this conversation, please?'

'Of course not.'

'Thank you. I would hate to have my wife become a widow. She is young. And Jewish. There is the anti-semitism problem here.'

Mary knew that already.

'There is a story about a store that was promised fresh eggs. At five o'clock in the morning, there was a long line waiting in the freezing cold. By eight o'clock, the eggs still had not come, and the line had grown longer. The owner said, "There will not be enough for everyone. The Jews can leave." At two in the afternoon, the eggs still had not arrived, and the line was even longer. The store owner said, "Non-party members leave." At midnight the line was still waiting in the freezing cold. No eggs. The owner locked the store and said,

"Nothing's changed. The Jews always get the best of everything."'

Mary did not know whether to laugh or cry. *But I'm going to do something about it*, she promised herself.

The folk theatre was on Rapsodia Romana, a bustling street filled with small stands selling flowers and plastic slippers and blouses and pens. The theatre was small and ornate, a relic of more halcyon days. The entertainment itself was boring, the costumes tawdry, and the dancers were awkward. The show seemed interminable, and when it was finally over, Mary was glad to esape into the fresh night air. Florian was standing by the limousine in front of the theatre.

'I'm afraid there will be a delay, Madam Ambassador. A flat tyre. And a thief has stolen the spare. I have sent for one. It should be here in the next hour. Would you like to wait in the car?'

Mary looked up at the full moon shining above. The evening was crisp and clear. She realized she had not walked the streets of Bucharest since she had arrived. She made a sudden decision.

'I think I'll walk back to the Residence.'

He nodded. 'It is a lovely evening for a walk.'

Mary turned and started walking down the street towards the Central Square. Bucharest was a fascinating, exotic city. On the street corners were arcane signs: *Tuten . . . Gospodina . . . Chimice . . .*

She strolled down the Avenue Mosilor and

turned into the Piata Rosetti, where there were red and tan trackless trollies, crammed with people. Even at this late hour, most of the shops were open, and there were queues at all of them. Coffee shops were serving *gogoase*, the delicious Romanian doughnuts. The sidewalks were crowded with late night shoppers carrying *pungas*, the string shopping bags. It seemed to Mary that the people were ominously quiet. They seemed to be staring at her, the women avidly eyeing the clothes she was wearing. She began to walk faster.

When she reached the corner of Calea Victoriei, she stopped, unsure of which direction to take. She said to a passer-by, 'Excuse me – could you tell me how to get –?'

He gave her a quick, frightened look and hurried off.

They're not supposed to talk to foreigners, Mary remembered.

How was she going to get back? She tried to visualize the way she had come with Florian. It seemed to her that the Residence was somewhere to the east. She began walking in that direction. Soon she was on a small side street, dimly lit. In the far distance, she could see a broad, well-lit boulevard. *I can get a taxi there*, Mary thought with relief.

There was the sound of heavy footsteps behind her, and she involuntarily turned. A large man in an overcoat was coming towards her, moving rapidly. Mary walked faster.

'Excuse me,' the man called out in a heavy Romanian accent. 'Are you lost?'

She was filled with relief. He was probably a policeman of some sort. Perhaps he had been following her to make sure she was safe.

'Yes,' Mary said gratefully. 'I want to go back to –'

There was the sudden roar of a motor, and the sound of a car racing up behind her, and then the squeal of brakes as the car screamed to a stop. The pedestrian in the overcoat grabbed Mary. She could smell his hot, fetid breath and feel his fat fingers bruising her wrist. He started pushing her towards the open door of the car. Mary was fighting to break free . . .

'Get in the car!' the man growled.

'No!' She was yelling, 'Help! Help me!'

There was a shout from across the street, and a figure came racing towards them. The man stopped, unsure of what to do.

The stranger yelled, 'Let go of her!'

He grabbed the man in the overcoat and pulled him away from Mary. She found herself suddenly free. The man behind the wheel started to get out of the car to help his accomplice.

From the far distance came the sound of an approaching siren. The man in the overcoat called out to his companion, and the two men leapt into the car, and it sped away.

A blue and white car with the word 'Militia' on the side, and a flashing blue light on top, pulled to a halt in front of Mary. Two men in uniform hurried out.

In Romanian, one of them asked, 'Are you all right?' And then in halting English, 'What happened?'

Mary was fighting to get herself under control. 'Two men – they – they t-tried to force me into their car. If – if it hadn't been for this gentleman –' She turned.

The stranger was gone.

TWENTY-TWO

She fought all night long, struggling to escape the men, waking in a panic, falling to sleep and waking again. She kept re-living the scene: The sudden footsteps hurrying towards her, the car pulling up, the man trying to force her into the car. Had they known who she was? Or were they merely trying to rob a tourist dressed in American clothes?

When Mary arrived at her office, Mike Slade was waiting for her. He brought in two cups of coffee and sat down across from her desk. 'How was the theatre?' he asked.

'Fine.' What had happened to her afterwards was none of his business.

'Did you get hurt?'

She looked at him in surprise. 'What?'

He said patiently, 'When they tried to kidnap you. Did they hurt you?'

'I – how do you know about that?'

His voice was filled with irony. 'Madam

Ambassador, Romania is one big, open secret. You can't take a bath without everyone knowing about it. It wasn't very clever of you to go for a stroll by yourself.'

'I'm aware of that now,' Mary said coldly. 'It won't happen again.'

'Good.' His tone was brisk. 'Did the man take anything from you?'

'No.'

He frowned. 'It makes no sense. If they had wanted your coat or purse, they could have taken them from you on the street. Trying to force you into a car means it was a kidnapping.'

'Who would want to kidnap me?'

'It wouldn't have been Ionescu's men. He's trying to keep our relations on an even keel. It would have to be some dissident group.'

'Or crooks who planned to hold me for ransom.'

'There are no kidnappings for ransom in this country. If they caught anyone doing that, there wouldn't be a trial – there would be a firing squad.' He took a sip of his coffee. 'May I give you some advice?'

'I'm listening.'

'Go home.'

'What?'

Mike Slade put down the cup. 'All you have to do is send in a letter of resignation, pack up your kids and go back to Kansas, where you'll be safe.'

She could feel her face getting red. 'Mr Slade,

I made a mistake. It's not the first one I've made, and it probably won't be the last one. But I was appointed to this post by the President of the United States, and until he fires me, I don't want you or anyone else telling me to go home.' She fought to keep control of her voice. 'I expect the people in this Embassy to work with me, not against me. If that's too much for you to handle, why don't *you* go home?' She was trembling with anger.

Mike Slade stood up. 'I'll see that the morning reports are put on your desk, Madam Ambassador.'

The attempted kidnapping was the sole topic of conversation at the Embassy that morning. *How had everyone found out?* Mary wondered. *And how had Mike Slade found out?* Mary wished she could have learned the name of her rescuer, so that she could have thanked him. In the quick glimpse she had had of him, she had got the impression of an attractive man, probably in his early forties, with prematurely grey hair. He had had a foreign accent – possibly French. If he was a tourist, he could have left Romania by now.

An idea kept gnawing at Mary, and it was hard to dismiss. The only person she knew of who wanted to get rid of her was Mike Slade. What if he had set up the attack to frighten her into leaving? He had given her the theatre tickets. He had known where she would be. She could not put it out of her mind.

Mary had debated whether to tell the children about the attempted kidnapping, and decided against it. She did not want to frighten them. She would simply see to it that they were never alone.

There was a cocktail party to attend at the French Embassy that evening in honour of a visiting French concert pianist. Mary was tired and nervous and would have given anything to have avoided it, but she knew she had to go.

She bathed and selected an evening gown, and as she reached for her shoes, she noticed that one shoe had a broken heel. She rang for Carmen.

'Yes, Madam Ambassador?'

'Carmen, would you please take this to a shoe-maker and have it repaired?'

'Certainly, Madam. Is there anything else?'

'No, that's all, thank you.'

When Mary arrived at the French Embassy, it was already crowded with guests. She was greeted at the entrance by the French Ambassador's aide, whom Mary had met on a previous visit to the Embassy. He took her hand and kissed it.

'Good evening, Madam Ambassador. It is so kind of you to come.'

'It was so kind of you to invite me,' Mary said. They both smiled at their empty phrases.

'Permit me to take you to the Ambassador.' He escorted her through the crowded ballroom, where she saw the familiar faces she had been seeing for weeks on end. Mary greeted the French Ambassador, and they exchanged pleasantries.

'You will enjoy Madame Dauphin. She is a remarkable pianist.'

'I'm looking forward to it,' Mary lied.

A servant passed by with a tray of glasses filled with champagne. Mary had learned by now to sip drinks at the various embassies. As she turned to greet the Australian Ambassador, she caught sight of the stranger who had rescued her from the kidnappers. He was standing in a corner talking to the Italian Ambassador and his aide.

'Please excuse me,' Mary said. She moved across the room towards the Frenchman.

He was saying, 'Of course, I miss Paris, but I hope that next year –' He broke off as he saw Mary approaching.

'Ah, the lady in distress.'

'You know each other?' the Italian Ambassador asked.

'We haven't been officially introduced,' Mary replied.

'Madam Ambassador, may I present Dr Louis Desforges.'

The expression on the Frenchman's face changed. '*Madam Ambassador?* I beg your pardon! I had no idea.' His voice was filled with embarrassment. 'I should have recognized you, of course.'

'You did better than that,' Mary smiled. 'You saved me.'

The Italian Ambassador looked at the doctor and said, 'Ah! So *you* were the one.' He turned to Mary. 'I heard about your unfortunate experience.'

'It would have been unfortunate if Dr Desforges hadn't come along. Thank you.'

Louis Desforges smiled. 'I'm happy that I was in the right place at the right time.'

The Ambassador and his aide saw a British contingent enter.

The Ambassador said, 'If you will excuse us, there is someone we have to see.'

The two men hurried off. Mary was alone with the doctor.

'Why did you run away when the police came?'

He studied her a moment. 'It is not good policy to get involved with the Romanian police. They have a way of arresting witnesses, then pumping them for information. I'm a doctor attached to the French Embassy here, and I don't have diplomatic immunity. I do, however, know a great deal about what goes on at our Embassy, and that information could be valuable to the Romanians.' He smiled. 'So forgive me if I seemed to desert you.'

There was a directness about him that was very appealing. In some way that Mary could not define, he reminded her a little bit of Edward. Perhaps because Louis Desforges was a doctor. But, no, it was more than that. He had the same openness that Edward had, almost the same smile.

'If you'll excuse me,' Dr Desforges said, 'I must go and become a social animal.'

'You don't like parties?'

He winced. 'I despise them.'

'Does your wife enjoy them?'

He started to say something, and then hesitated. 'Yes – she did. Very much.'

'Is she here this evening?'

'She and our two children are dead.'

Mary paled. 'Oh, my God. I'm so sorry. How –?'

His face was rigid. 'I blame myself. We were living in Algeria. I was operating undercover, fighting the terrorists.' His words became slow and halting. 'They found out my identity and blew up the house. I was away at the time.'

'I'm so sorry,' Mary said again. Hopeless, inadequate words.

'Thank you. There is a cliché that time heals everything. I no longer believe it.' His voice was bitter.

Mary thought about Edward and how much she still missed him. But this man had lived with his pain longer.

He looked at her and said, 'If you will excuse me, Madam Ambassador . . .' He turned and walked over to greet a group of arriving guests.

He reminds me a little of you, Edward. You'd like him. He's a very brave man. He's in a lot of pain,

*and I think that's what draws me to him. I'm in
pain, too, darling. Will I ever get over missing you?
It's so lonely here. There's no one I can talk to. I
desperately want to succeed. Mike Slade is trying
to get me to go home. I'm not going. But oh, how
I need you. Good night, my darling.*

The following morning, Mary telephoned Stanton
Rogers. It was wonderful to hear his voice. *It's like
a lifeline to home*, she thought.

'I'm getting some excellent reports on you,'
Stanton Rogers said. 'The Hannah Murphy story
made headlines here. You did an excellent job.'

'Thank you, Stan.'

'Mary, tell me about the attempted kidnapping.'

'I've talked to the Prime Minister and the head
of *Securitate*, and they have no clues at all.'

'Didn't Mike Slade warn you not to go out
alone?'

Mike Slade. 'Yes, he warned me, Stan.' *Shall I
tell him that Mike Slade told me to go home?* No,
she decided. *I'll handle Mr Slade in my own way.*

'Remember – I'm always here for you. Any time.'

'I know,' Mary said gratefully. 'I can't tell you
what it means to me.'

The telephone call made her feel much better.

'We have a problem. There's a leak somewhere in
our Embassy.'

Mary and Mike Slade were having a cup of
coffee before the daily staff meeting.

'How serious is it?'

'Very. Our Commerce Consular, David Victor, held some meetings with the Romanian Minister of Commerce.'

'I know. We discussed it last week.'

'Right,' Mike said. 'And when David went back for a second meeting, they were ahead of us on every counter-proposal we made. They knew exactly how far we were prepared to go.'

'Isn't it possible that they just figured it out?'

'It's possible, yes. Except that we discussed some new proposals, and they were ahead of us again.'

Mary was thoughtful for a moment. 'You think it's someone on the staff?'

'Not just *someone*. The last executive conference was held in the Bubble Room. Our electronics experts have traced the leak to there.'

Mary looked at him in surprise. There were only eight people allowed at the conferences in the Bubble Room, each an executive member of the Embassy.

'Whoever it is is carrying electronic equipment, probably a tape recorder. I suggest you call a conference meeting this morning in the Bubble Room and have the same group in. Our instruments will be able to pinpoint the guilty person.'

There were eight persons seated around the table in the Bubble Room. Eddie Maltz, the Political Consular and CIA agent, Patricia Hatfield, the Economic Consular, Jerry Davis, Public Affairs,

David Victor, Commerce Consular, Lucas Janklow, Administrative Consular, and Colonel William McKinney. Mary was at one end of the table, Mike Slade at the other.

Mary turned to David Victor. 'How are your meetings going with the Romanian Minister of Commerce?'

The Commerce Consular shook his head. 'Frankly, not as well as I had hoped. They seem to know everything I have to say before I say it. I come in with new proposals, and they've already prepared their arguments against them. It's as though they're reading my mind.'

'Maybe they are,' Mike Slade said.

'What do you mean?'

'They're reading somebody's mind in this room.' He picked up a red telephone on the table. 'Send him in.'

A moment later, the huge door was pushed open and a man dressed in civilian clothes entered, carrying a black box with a dial on it.

Eddie Maltz said, 'Wait a minute. No one is allowed in . . .'

'It's all right,' Mary said. 'We have a problem and this man is going to solve it.' She looked up at the newcomer. 'Please go ahead.'

'Right. I'd like everyone to stay just where you are, please.'

As the group watched, he walked over to Mike Slade and held the box close to him. The needle on the dial remained at zero. The man moved on to Patricia Hatfield. The needle remained still. Eddie Maltz was next, then Jerry Davis and Lucas Janklow. The needle remained still. The man moved to David Victor, and finally to Colonel McKinney, but the needle still did not move. The only person left was Mary. When he approached her, the needle began to swing wildly.

Mike Slade said, 'What the hell –' He got to his feet and went over to Mary.

'Are you sure?' Mike demanded of the civilian.

The dial was moving crazily.

'Talk to the machine,' the man said.

Mary rose in confusion.

'Do you mind if we break up this meeting?' Mike asked.

Mary turned to the others. 'That's it for now, thank you.'

Mike Slade said to the technician, 'You stay.'

When the others had left the room, Mike asked, 'Can you pinpoint where the bug is?'

'Sure can.' The man slowly moved the black box down, inches away from Mary's body. As it got closer to her feet, the dial began to move faster.

The civilian straightened up. 'It's your shoes.'

Mary stared at him incredulously. 'You're mistaken. I bought these shoes in Washington.'

Mike said, 'Would you mind taking them off?'

'I –' This whole thing was ridiculous. The machine had to be crazy. Or someone was trying to frame her. This could be Mike Slade's way of getting rid of her. He would report to Washington that she had been caught spying and giving information to the enemy. Well, he was not going to get away with it.

She stepped out of her shoes, picked them up and dropped them into Mike's hands. 'Here,' she said angrily.

He turned them over and examined them. 'Is this a new heel?'

'No, it's –' And then she remembered: *Carmen, would you please take this to a shoemaker and have it repaired?*

Mike was breaking open the heel of the shoe. Inside was a miniature tape recorder.

'We found our spy,' Mike said drily. He looked up. 'Where did you have this heel put on?'

'I – I don't know. I asked one of the maids to take care of it.'

'Wonderful,' he said sardonically. 'In the future, we'd all appreciate it, Madam Ambassador, if you would let your secretary handle things like that.'

There was a telex for Mary.

'Senate Foreign Affairs Committee has agreed to Romanian loan you requested. Announcement to be made tomorrow. Congratulations.

Stanton Rogers.'

Mike read the telex. 'That's good news. Negulesco will be tickled.'

Mary knew that Negulesco, the Romanian Finance Minister, was on shaky ground. This would make him a hero with Ionescu.

'They're not announcing this until tomorrow,' Mary said. She sat there, deep in thought. 'I want you to make an appointment for me with Negulesco this morning.'

'Do you want me to come along?'

'No. I'll do this alone.'

Two hours later, Mary was seated in the office of the Romanian Finance Minister. He was beaming. 'So you have good news for us, yes?'

'I'm afraid not,' Mary said regretfully. She watched his smile fade away.

'*What?* I understood that the loan was – how do you say? – "in the bag"?'

Mary sighed. 'So did I, Minister.'

'What happened? What went wrong?' His face was suddenly grey.

Mary shrugged. 'I don't know.'

'I promised our President –' He stopped, as the full implication of the news hit him. He looked at Mary and said in a hoarse voice, 'President Ionescu is not going to like this. Is there *nothing* you can do?'

Mary said earnestly, 'I'm as disappointed as you, Minister. The vote was going well until one of the senators learned that a Romanian church group that wanted to visit Utah was refused a visa. The Senator is a Mormon, and he was very upset.'

'A *church group*?' Negulesco's voice had risen an octave. 'You mean the loan was voted down because of a –?'

'That's my understanding.'

'But Madam Ambassador, Romania is *for* the churches. They have a great freedom here!' He was almost babbling now. 'We *love* the churches.'

Negulesco moved over to the chair next to Mary. 'Madam Ambassador – if I could arrange for this group to visit your country, do you think the Senate Finance Committee would approve the loan?'

Mary looked him in the eye and said, 'Minister Negulesco – I can guarantee it. But I would have to know by this afternoon.'

Mary sat at her desk, waiting for the phone call, and at 2.30 Negulesco called.

'Madam Ambassador – I have wonderful news! The church group is free to leave at any time! Now do you have any good news for me?'

Mary waited an hour and then called him back. 'I've just received a telex from our State Department. Your loan has been granted.'

TWENTY-THREE

Mary had been unable to get Dr Louis Desforges out of her mind. He had saved her life, and then disappeared. She was glad she had found him again. On an impulse, Mary went to the American Dollar Shop and bought a beautiful silver bowl for the doctor and had it sent to the French Embassy. It was a small enough gesture after what he had done.

That afternoon, Dorothy Stone said, 'There's a Dr Desforges on the phone. Do you wish to speak to him?'

Mary smiled. 'Yes.' She picked up the telephone. 'Good afternoon.'

'Good afternoon, Madam Ambassador.' The phrase sounded delightful in his French accent. 'I called to thank you for your thoughtful gift. I assure you that it was unnecessary. I was delighted that I was able to be of some service.'

'It was more than just some service.' Mary told him. 'I wish there were some way I could really show my appreciation.'

There was a pause. 'Would you –' He stopped.

'Yes?' Mary prompted.

'Nothing, really.' He sounded suddenly shy.

'Please.'

'Very well.' There was a nervous laugh. 'I was wondering if you might care to have dinner with me one evening, but I know how busy you must be and –'

'I would love to,' Mary said quickly.

'Really?'

She could hear the pleasure in his voice. 'Really.'

'Do you know the Taru Restaurant?'

Mary had been there twice. 'No.'

'Ah, splendid. Then I shall have the pleasure of showing it to you. You probably won't be free Saturday night –?'

'I have to go to a cocktail party at six o'clock, but we could have dinner after that.'

'Wonderful. I understand you have two small children. Would you care to bring them?'

'Thank you, but they're busy on Saturday night.'

She wondered why she had lied.

The cocktail party was at the Swiss Embassy. It was obviously one of the 'A' parties, because President Alexandros Ionescu was there.

When he saw Mary, he walked over to her. 'Good evening, Madam Ambassador.' He took her hand and held it longer than necessary. 'I want to tell you how pleased I am that your country has agreed to make us the loan we asked for.'

'And we're very pleased that you allowed the church group to visit the United States, your Excellency.'

He waved a hand carelessly. 'Romanians are not prisoners. Anyone is free to come and go as he pleases. My country is a symbol of social justice and democratic freedom.'

Mary thought of the long queues of people waiting to buy scarce food, and the mob at the airport, and the refugees desperate to leave.

'All power in Romania belongs to the people.'

There are gulags in Romania that we're not allowed to see.

Mary said, 'With all respect, Mr President, there are hundreds, perhaps thousands of Jews who are trying to leave Romania. Your government will not give them visas.'

He scowled. 'Dissidents. Trouble-makers. We are doing the world a favour by keeping them here where we can watch them.'

'Mr President –'

'We have a more lenient policy towards the Jews than any other Iron Curtain country. In 1967, during the Arab-Israeli war, the Soviet Union and every Eastern bloc country except Romania broke off diplomatic relations with Israel.'

'I'm aware of that, Mr President, but there are still –'

'Have you tasted the caviare? It is fresh Beluga.'

* * *

Dr Louis Desforges had offered to pick Mary up, but she had arranged for Florian to drive her to the Taru Restaurant. She telephoned ahead to inform Dr Desforges that she would be a few minutes late. She had to return to the Embassy to file a report on her conversation with President Ionescu.

Gunny was on duty. The Marine saluted her and unlocked the door. Mary walked into her office and turned on the light. She stood in the doorway, frozen. On the wall, someone had sprayed in red paint, GO HOME BEFORE YOU DIE. She backed out of the room, white-faced, and ran down the hall to the reception desk.

Gunny stood at attention. 'Yes, Madam Ambassador?'

'Gunny – wh – who's been in my office?' Mary demanded.

'Why, no one that I know of, ma'am.'

'Let me see your roster sheet.' She tried to keep her voice from quavering.

'Yes, ma'am.'

Gunny pulled out the Visitors' Access Sheet and handed it to her. Each name had the time of entry listed after it. She started at 5.30, the time she had left the office, and scanned the list. There were a dozen names.

Mary looked up at the Marine guard. 'The people on this list – were they all escorted to the offices they visited?'

'Always, Madam Ambassador. No one goes up

to the second floor without an escort. Is something wrong?'

Something was very wrong.

Mary said, 'Please send someone to my office to paint out that obscenity on the wall.'

She turned and hurried outside, afraid she was going to be sick. The telex could wait until morning.

Dr Louis Desforges was waiting for Mary when she arrived at the restaurant. He stood up as she approached the table.

'I'm sorry I'm late.' Mary tried to sound normal.

He pulled out her chair. 'That's perfectly all right. I received your message. You were very kind to join me.'

She wished now that she had not agreed to have dinner with him. She was too nervous and upset. She pressed her hands together to keep them from trembling.

He was observing her. 'Are you all right, Madam Ambassador?'

'Yes,' she said. 'I'm fine.' *Go Home Before You Die*. 'I think I'd like a straight Scotch, please.' She hated Scotch, but she hoped it would relax her.

The doctor ordered drinks, then said, 'It can't be easy being an ambassador – especially a woman in this country. Romanians are male chauvinists, you know.'

Mary forced a smile. 'Tell me about yourself.' Anything to take her mind off the threat.

'I am afraid there is not much to tell that is exciting.'

'You mentioned that you fought undercover in Algeria. That sounds exciting.'

He shrugged. 'We live in terrible times. I believe that every man must risk something so that in the end he does not have to risk everything. The terrorist situation is literally that – *terrifying*. We must put an end to it.' His voice was filled with passion.

He's like Edward, Mary thought. *Edward was always passionate about his beliefs.* Dr Desforges was a man who could not be easily swayed. He was willing to risk his life for what he believed in.

He was saying, '. . . If I had known that the price of my fighting would be the lives of my wife and children –' He stopped. His knuckles were white against the table. 'Forgive me. I did not bring you here to talk about my troubles. Let me recommend the lamb. They do it very well here.'

'Fine,' Mary said.

He ordered dinner and a bottle of wine, and they talked. Mary began to relax, to forget the frightening warning painted in red. She was finding it surprisingly easy to talk to this attractive Frenchman. In an odd way, it was like talking to Edward. It was amazing how she and Louis shared so many of the same beliefs and felt the same way about so many things. Louis Desforges was born in a small town in France, and Mary was born in a small town in Kansas, five thousand miles apart,

340

and yet their backgrounds were so similar. His father had been a farmer and had scrimped and saved to send Louis to a medical school in Paris.

'My father was a wonderful man, Madam Ambassador.'

'Madam Ambassador sounds so formal.'

'Mrs Ashley?'

'Mary.'

'Thank you, Mary.'

She smiled. 'You're welcome, Louis.'

Mary wondered what his personal life was like. He was handsome and intelligent. He could surely have all the women he wanted. She wondered if he were living with anyone.

'Have you thought of getting married again?'

He shook his head. 'No. If you had known my wife, you would understand. She was a remarkable woman. No one could ever replace her.'

That's how I feel about Edward, Mary thought. *No one can ever replace him*. He was so special. And yet everyone needed companionship. It was not really a question of replacing a loved one. It was finding someone new to share things with.

Louis was saying, '. . . so when I was offered the opportunity, I thought it would be interesting to visit Romania.' He lowered his voice. 'I confess I feel an evilness about this country.'

'Really?'

'Not the people. They are lovely. The government is everything I despise. There is no freedom here for anyone. The Romanians are virtual slaves.

341

If they want to have decent food and a few luxuries, they are forced to work for the *Securitate*. Foreigners are constantly spied upon.' He glanced around to make sure no one could overhear. 'I shall be glad when my tour of duty is over and I can return to France.'

Without thinking, Mary heard herself saying, 'There are some people who think *I* should go home.'

'I beg your pardon?'

And suddenly Mary found herself pouring out the story of what had happened in her office. She told him about the paint scrawled on her office wall.

'But this is horrible!' Louis exclaimed. 'You have no idea who did this?'

'No.'

Louis said, 'May I make an impertinent confession? Since I found out who you were, I have been asking questions. Everyone who knows you is very impressed with you.'

She was listening to him with intense interest.

'It seems that you have brought here an image of America that is beautiful and intelligent and warm. If you believe in what you are doing, then you must fight for it. You must stay. Do not let anyone frighten you away.'

It was exactly what Edward would have said.

Mary lay in bed, unable to sleep, thinking about what Louis had told her. *He was willing to die for*

what he believed in. Am I? I don't want to die,
Mary thought. *But no one is going to kill me. And
no one is going to scare me.*

She lay awake in the dark. Scared.

The following morning, Mike Slade brought in two
cups of coffee. He nodded at the wall where it had
been cleaned.

'I hear someone has been spraying graffiti on
your walls.'

'Have they found out who did it?'

Mike took a sip of coffee. 'No. I went through
the Visitors' List myself. Everyone is accounted
for.'

'That means it must have been someone here in
the Embassy.'

'Either that, or someone managed to sneak in
past the guards.'

'Do you believe that?'

Mike put down his coffee cup. 'Nope.'

'Neither do I.'

'What exactly did it say?'

'Go home before you die.'

He made no comment.

'Who would want to kill me?'

'I don't know.'

'Mr Slade, I would appreciate a straight answer.
Do you think I'm in any real danger?'

He studied her thoughtfully. 'Madam Ambassador,
they assassinated Abraham Lincoln, John Kennedy,
Robert Kennedy, Martin Luther King, and Marin

Groza. We're all vulnerable. The answer to your question is "yes".'

If you believe in what you are doing, then you must fight for it. You must stay. Do not let anyone frighten you away.

TWENTY-FOUR

At eight forty-five the following morning, as Mary was in the middle of a conference, Dorothy Stone came rushing into the office and said, 'The children have been kidnapped!'

Mary jumped to her feet. 'Oh, my God!'

'The limousine alarm just went off. They're tracking the car now. They won't get away.'

Mary raced down the corridor to the Communications Room. There were half a dozen men standing around a switchboard. Colonel McKinney was talking into a microphone.

'Roger,' he said. 'I have that. I'll inform the Ambassador.'

'What's happening?' Mary croaked. She could barely get the words out. 'Where are my children?'

The colonel said, reassuringly, 'They're fine, ma'am. One of them touched the emergency switch in the limousine by accident. The emergency light on top of the limousine flashed on, along with an SOS shortwave signal, and before the driver had

345

gone two blocks, four police cars closed in on them with sirens screaming.'

Mary sagged against the wall with relief. She had not realized how much tension she had been under. *It's so easy to understand*, she thought, *why foreigners living here finally turn to drugs or drink . . . or love affairs.*

Mary stayed with the children that evening. She wanted to be as close to them as possible. Looking at them, she wondered: *Are they in danger? Are we all in danger? Who would want to harm us?* She had no answer.

Three nights later Mary had dinner again with Dr Louis Desforges. He seemed more relaxed with her this time, and although the core of sadness she sensed within him was still there, he took pains to be attentive and amusing. Mary wondered if he felt the same attraction towards her that she felt towards him. *It wasn't just a silver bowl I sent him*, she admitted to herself, *it was an invitation.*

Madam Ambassador is so formal. Call me Mary. My God, was she actually pursuing him? And yet: *I owe him a lot – possibly my life. I'm rationalizing*, Mary thought. *That has nothing to do with why I wanted to see him again.*

They had an early dinner at the dining room on the roof of the Intercontinental Hotel, and when Louis took Mary back to the Residence, she asked, 'Would you like to come in?'

'Thank you,' he said. 'I would.'

The children were downstairs doing their homework. Mary introduced them to Louis.

He bent down before Beth and said, 'May I?' And he put his arms around her and hugged her. He straightened up. 'One of my little girls was three years younger than you. The other one was about your age. I'd like to think they would have grown up to be as pretty as you are, Beth.'

Beth smiled. 'Thank you. Where are –?'

Mary asked hastily, 'Would you all like some hot chocolate?'

They sat in the huge Embassy kitchen drinking the hot chocolate and talking.

The children were enchanted with Louis, and Mary thought she had never seen a man with so much hunger in his eyes. He had forgotten about her. He was focused entirely on the children, telling them stories about his daughters and anecdotes and jokes until he had them roaring with laughter.

It was almost midnight when Mary looked at her watch. 'Oh, no! You children should have been in bed hours ago. Scoot.'

Tim went over to Louis. 'Will you come and see us again?'

'I hope so, Tim. It's up to your mother.'

Tim turned to Mary. 'Well, Mom?'

She looked at Louis and said, 'Yes.'

* * *

Mary saw Louis to the door. He took her hand in his. 'I won't try to tell you what this evening has meant to me, Mary. There are no words.'

'I'm glad.' She was looking into his eyes, and she felt him moving towards her. She raised her lips.

'Good night, Mary.'

And he was gone.

The following morning when Mary walked into her office, she noticed that another side of the wall had been freshly painted. Mike Slade walked in with two cups of coffee.

'Morning.' He set a cup on her desk.

'Someone wrote on the wall again?'

'Yes.'

'What did it say this time?'

'It doesn't matter.'

'It doesn't matter!' she said furiously. 'It matters to *me*. What kind of security does this Embassy have? I won't have people sneaking into my office and making threats against my life. What did it say?'

'You want it verbatim?'

'Yes.'

'It said, "Leave now or die."'

Mary sank back into her chair, enraged. 'Will you explain to me how someone is able to walk into this Embassy, unseen, and write messages on my wall?'

'I wish I could,' Mike said. 'We're doing everything we can to track it down.'

'Well, "everything you can" is obviously not enough,' she retorted. 'I want a Marine guard posted outside my door at night. Is that understood?'

'Yes, Madam Ambassador. I'll pass the word to Colonel McKinney.'

'Never mind. I'll talk to him myself.'

Mary watched as Mike Slade left her office, and she suddenly wondered if he knew who was behind it.

And she wondered if it could be Mike Slade.

Colonel McKinney was apologetic. 'Believe me, Madam Ambassador, I'm just as upset about this as you are. I'll double the guard in the corridor and see that there's a twenty-four-hour watch outside your office door.'

Mary was not mollified. Someone inside the Embassy was responsible for what was happening.

Colonel McKinney was inside the Embassy.

Mary invited Louis Desforges to a small dinner party at the Residence. There were a dozen other guests, and at the end of the evening when the others had departed, Louis said, 'Do you mind if I go up and see the children?'

'I'm afraid they're sleeping by now, Louis.'

'I won't awaken them,' he promised. 'I would just like to look at them.'

Mary walked upstairs with him and watched as he stood in the doorway, silently staring at Tim's sleeping figure.

After a while, Mary whispered, 'Beth's room is this way.'

Mary led him to another bedroom down the hall, and opened the door. Beth was curled up around the pillow, the bed covers twisted around her. Louis walked quietly to the bed and gently straightened out the bedclothes. He stood there for a long moment, his eyes tightly closed. Then he turned and walked out of the room.

'They're beautiful children,' Louis said. His voice was husky.

They stood there, facing each other, and the air between them was charged. He was naked in his need.

It's going to happen, Mary thought. *Neither of us can stop it.*

And their arms were tightly around each other, and his lips were pressed hard against hers.

He pulled away. 'I shouldn't have come. You realize what I'm doing, don't you? I'm re-living my past.' He was quiet for a moment. 'Or perhaps it is my future. Who knows?'

Mary said softly, '*I* know.'

David Victor, the Commerce Consular, hurried into Mary's office. 'I'm afraid I have some very bad news. I just got a tip that President Ionescu is going to approve a contract with Argentina for a million and a half tons of corn and with Brazil for half a million tons of soy beans. We were counting heavily on those deals.'

'How far have the negotiations gone?'

'They're almost concluded. We've been shut out. I was about to send a telex to Washington – with your approval, of course,' he added hastily.

'Hold off a bit,' Mary said. 'I want to think about it.'

'You won't get President Ionescu to change his mind. Believe me, I've tried every argument I could think of.'

'Then we have nothing to lose if I give it a try.' She buzzed her secretary. 'Dorothy, set up an appointment with President Ionescu as quickly as possible.'

Alexandros Ionescu invited Mary to the palace for lunch. As she entered, she was greeted by Nicu, the President's fourteen-year-old son.

'Good afternoon, Madam Ambassador,' he said. 'I am Nicu. Welcome to the palace.'

'Thank you.'

He was a handsome boy, tall for his age, with beautiful black eyes and a flawless complexion. He had the bearing of an adult.

'I have heard very nice things about you,' Nicu said.

'I'm pleased to hear that, Nicu.'

'I will tell my father you have arrived.'

Mary and Ionescu sat across from each other in the formal dining room, just the two of them. Mary wondered where his wife was. She seldom appeared, even at formal functions.

The President had been drinking and was in a mellow mood. He lit a Snagov, the vile-smelling Romanian-made cigarette.

'I understand you have been doing some sight-seeing with your children.'

'Yes, your Excellency. Romania is such a beautiful country, and there is so much to see.'

He gave her what he thought was a seductive smile. 'One of these days you must let me show you my country.' His smile became a parody of a leer. 'I am an excellent guide. I could show you many interesting things.'

'I'm sure you could,' Mary said. 'Mr President, I was eager to meet with you today because there is something important I would like to discuss with you.'

Ionescu almost laughed aloud. He knew exactly why she had come. *The Americans wish to sell me corn and soy beans, but they are too late.* The American Ambassador would go away empty-handed this time. Too bad. Such an attractive woman.

'Yes?' he said innocently.

'I want to talk to you about sister cities.'

Ionescu blinked. 'I beg your pardon?'

'Sister cities. You know – like San Francisco and Osaka, Los Angeles and Athens, Washington and Beijing . . .'

'I – I don't understand. What does that have to do with –?'

'Mr President, it occurred to me that you could

get headlines all over the world if you made Bucharest a sister city of some American city. Think of the excitement it would create. It would get almost as much attention as President Ellison's people-to-people plan. It would be an important step towards world peace. Talk about a bridge between our countries! I wouldn't be surprised if it got you a Nobel Peace Prize.'

Ionescu sat there, trying to reorient his thinking. He said cautiously, 'A sister city in the United States? It is an interesting idea. What would it involve?'

'Mostly wonderful publicity for you. You would be a hero. It would be your idea. You would pay the city a visit. A delegation from Kansas City would pay *you* a visit.'

'Kansas City?'

'That's just a suggestion, of course. I don't think you'd want a big city like New York or Chicago – too commercial. And Los Angeles is already spoken for. Kansas City is middle-America. There are farmers there, like your farmers. People with down-to-earth values, like your people. It would be the act of a great statesman, Mr President. Your name would be on everyone's lips. No one in Europe has thought of doing this.'

He sat there, silent. 'I – I would naturally have to give this a great deal of thought.'

'Naturally.'

'Kansas City, Kansas, and Bucharest, Romania.' He nodded. 'We are a much larger city, of course.'

'Of course. Bucharest would be the big sister.'

'I must admit it is a very intriguing idea.'

In fact, the more Ionescu thought about it, the more he liked it. *My name will be on everyone's lips. And it will serve to keep the Soviet bear hug from becoming too tight.*

'Is there any chance of a rejection from the American side?' Ionescu asked.

'Absolutely none. I can guarantee it.'

He sat there, reflecting. 'When would this go into effect?'

'Just as soon as you're ready to announce it. I'll handle our end. You're already a great statesman, Mr President, but this would make you even greater.'

Ionescu thought of something else. 'We could set up a trade exchange with our sister city. Romania has many things to sell. Tell me – what crops does Kansas grow?'

'Among other things,' Mary said innocently, 'corn and soy beans.'

'You really made the deal? You actually fooled him?' David Victor asked incredulously.

'Not for a minute,' Mary assured him. 'Ionescu is too smart for that. He knew what I was after. He just liked the package I wrapped it in. You can go in and close the deal. Ionescu's already rehearsing his television speech.'

When Stanton Rogers heard the news, he telephoned

Mary. 'You're a miracle worker,' he laughed. 'We thought we'd lost that deal. How in the world did you do it?'

'Ego,' Mary said. 'His.'

'The President asked me to tell you what a really great job you're doing over there, Mary.'

'Thank him for me, Stan.'

'I will. By the way, the President and I are leaving for China in a few weeks. If you need me, you can get in touch with me through my office.'

'Have a wonderful trip.'

Over the swiftly moving weeks, the dancing March winds had given way to spring and then summer, and winter clothes were replaced by light, cool outfits. Trees and flowers blossomed everywhere, and the parks were greening. June was almost over.

In Buenos Aires, it was winter. When Neusa Muñez returned to her apartment, it was the middle of the night. The telephone was ringing. She picked it up. *'Si?'*

'Miss Muñez?' It was the gringo from the United States.

'Yeah.'

'May I speak with Angel?'

'Angel no here, *señor*. Wha' you wan'?'

The Controller found his irritation mounting. *What kind of man would be involved with a woman like this?* From the description Harry Lantz had given him before Lantz was murdered, she was not only dim-witted, she was very unattractive. 'I want you to give Angel a message for me.'

'Jus' a minute.'

He heard the phone drop, and waited.

Her voice finally came back on. 'Okay.'

'Tell Angel I need him for a contract in Bucharest.'

'Budapes'?'

Jesus! She was beyond anyone's endurance. 'Bucharest, Romania. Tell him it's a five million dollar contract. He has to be in Bucharest by the end of this month. That's three weeks from now. Do you have that?'

'Wait a minute. I'm writin'.'

He waited patiently.

'Okay. How many people Angel gotta kill for five million dollars?'

'A lot . . .'

The queues each day in front of the Embassy continued to disturb Mary. She discussed it again with Mike Slade.

'There must be something we can do to help those people get out of the country.'

'Everything's been tried,' Mike assured her. 'We've applied pressure, we've offered to sweeten the money pot – the answer is "no". Ionescu refuses to cut a deal. The poor bastards are stuck. He has no intention of letting them go. The Iron Curtain isn't just *around* the country – it's *in* the country.'

'I'm going to have a talk with Ionescu again.'

'Good luck.'

Mary asked Dorothy Stone to set up an appointment with the dictator.

A few minutes later, the secretary walked into Mary's office. 'I'm sorry, Madam Ambassador. No appointments.'

Mary looked at her, puzzled. 'What does that mean?'

'I'm not sure. Something weird is going on at the palace. Ionescu isn't seeing anybody. In fact, no one can even get into the palace.'

Mary sat there, trying to figure out what it could be. Was Ionescu preparing to make a major announcement of some kind? Was a coup imminent? Something important must be happening. Whatever it was, Mary knew she had to find out.

'Dorothy,' she said, 'you have contacts over at the Presidential Palace, don't you?'

Dorothy smiled. 'You mean the "old girl network"? Sure. We talk to one another.'

'I'd like you to find out what's going on there . . .'

An hour later, Dorothy reported back. 'I found out what you wanted to know,' she said. 'They're keeping it very hush-hush.'

'Keeping what hush-hush?'

'Ionescu's son is dying.'

Mary was aghast. 'Nicu? What happened?'

357

'He has botulism poisoning.'

Mary asked quickly, 'You mean there's an epidemic here in Bucharest?'

'No, ma'am. Do you remember the epidemic they had in East Germany recently? Apparently Nicu visited there and someone gave him some canned food as a gift. He ate some of it yesterday.'

'But there's an anti-serum for that!' Mary exclaimed.

'The European countries are out of it. The epidemic last month used it all up.'

'Oh, my God.'

When Dorothy left the office, Mary sat there thinking. It might be too late, but still . . . She remembered how cheerful and happy young Nicu was. He was fourteen years old – only a year older than Beth.

She pressed the intercom button and said, 'Dorothy, get me the Centre for Disease Control in Atlanta, Georgia.'

Five minutes later she was speaking to the director.

'Yes, Madam Ambassador, we have an anti-serum for botulism poisoning, but we haven't had any cases reported in the United States.'

'I'm not in the United States,' Mary told him. 'I'm in Bucharest. I need that serum immediately.'

There was a pause. 'I'll be happy to supply some,' the director said, 'but botulism poisoning works very rapidly. I'm afraid that by the time it gets there . . .'

'I'll arrange for it to get here,' Mary said. 'Just have it ready. Thank you.'

Ten minutes later, she was speaking to Air Force General Ralph Zukor in Washington.

'Good morning, Madam Ambassador. Well, this is an unexpected pleasure. My wife and I are big fans of yours. How are –?'

'General, I need a favour.'

'Certainly. Anything you want.'

'I need your fastest jet.'

'I beg your pardon?'

'I need a jet to fly some serum to Bucharest right away.'

'I see.'

'Can you do it?'

'Well, yes. I'll tell you what you have to do. You'll have to get the approval of the Secretary of Defence. There are some requisition forms for you to fill out. One copy should go to me and another copy to the Department of Defence. We'll send those on to –'

Mary listened, seething. 'General – let me tell you what *you* have to do. You have to stop talking and get that damned jet up in the air. If –'

'There's no way that –'

'A boy's life is at stake. And the boy happens to be the son of the President of Romania.'

'I'm sorry, but I can't authorize –'

'General, if that boy dies because some form hasn't been filled out, I promise you that I'm going to call the biggest press conference you've ever seen. I'll let you explain why you let Ionescu's son die.'

'I can't possibly authorize an operation like this without an approval from the White House. If –'

Mary snapped. 'Then get it. The serum will be waiting at Atlanta Airport. And, General – every single minute counts.'

She hung up, and sat there, silently praying.

General Ralph Zukor's aide said, 'What was that all about, sir?'

General Zukor said, 'The Ambassador expects me to send up an SR-71 to fly some serum to Romania.'

The aide smiled. 'I'm sure she has no idea of what's involved, General.'

'Obviously. But we might as well cover ourselves. Get me Stanton Rogers.'

Five minutes later the general was speaking to the President's Foreign Adviser. 'I just wanted to go on record with you that the request was made, and I naturally refused. If –'

Stanton Rogers said, 'General, how soon can you have an SR-71 airborne?'

'In ten minutes, but –'

'Do it.'

Nicu Ionescu's nervous system had been affected. He lay in bed, disoriented, sweating and pale, attached to a respirator. There were three doctors at his bedside.

President Ionescu strode into his son's bedroom. 'What's happening?'

'Your Excellency, we have communicated with our colleagues all over Eastern and Western Europe. There is no anti-serum left.'

'What about the United States?'

The doctor shrugged. 'By the time we could arrange for someone to fly the serum here –' He paused delicately. '. . . I'm afraid it would be too late.'

Ionescu walked over to the bed and picked up his son's hand. It was moist and clammy. 'You're not going to die,' Ionescu wept. 'You're not going to die.'

When the jet touched down at Atlanta International Airport, an Air Force limousine was waiting with the anti-botulism serum, packed in ice. Three minutes later, the jet was back in the air, on a northeast heading.

The SR-71 – the Air Force's fastest supersonic jet, flies at three times the speed of sound. It slowed down once to refuel over the mid-Atlantic. The plane made the four thousand miles to Bucharest flight in a little over two hours.

Colonel McKinney was waiting at the airport. An Army escort cleared the way to the Presidential Palace.

* * *

Mary had remained in her office all night, getting up-to-the-minute reports. The last report came in at 6 a.m.

Colonel McKinney telephoned. 'They gave the boy the serum. The doctors say he's going to live.'

'Oh, thank God!'

Two days later, a diamond and emerald necklace was delivered to Mary's office with a note:

> *I can never thank you enough.*
> *Alexandros Ionescu.'*

'My God!' Dorothy exclaimed when she saw the necklace. 'It must have cost half a million dollars!'

'At least,' Mary said. 'Return it.'

The following morning, President Ionescu sent for Mary.

An aide said, 'The President is waiting for you in his office.'

'May I see Nicu first?'

'Yes, of course.' He led her upstairs.

Nicu was lying in bed, reading. He looked up as Mary entered. 'Good morning, Madam Ambassador.'

'Good morning, Nicu.'

'My father told me what you did. I wish to thank you.'

Mary said, 'I couldn't let you die. I'm saving you for Beth one day.'

Nicu laughed. 'Bring her over and we'll talk about it.'

President Ionescu was waiting for Mary downstairs. He said without preamble, 'You returned my gift.'

'Yes, your Excellency.'

He indicated a chair. 'Sit down.' He studied her a moment. 'What do you want?'

Mary said, 'I don't make trades for children's lives.'

'You saved my son's life. I must give you something.'

'You don't owe me anything, your Excellency.'

Ionescu pounded his fist on the desk. 'I will not be indebted to you! Name your price.'

Mary said, 'Your Excellency, there is no price. I have two children of my own. I know how you must feel.'

He closed his eyes for a moment. 'Do you? Nicu is my only son. If anything had happened to him –' He stopped, unable to go on.

'I went upstairs to see him. He looks fine.' She rose. 'If there's nothing else, your Excellency, I have an appointment back at the Embassy.' She started to leave.

'Wait!'

Mary turned.

'You will not accept a gift?'

'No. I've explained –'

Ionescu held up a hand. 'All right, all right.' He

thought for a moment. 'If you were to make a wish, what would you wish for?'

'There is nothing –'

'You must! I insist! One wish. Anything you want.'

Mary stood there, studying his face, thinking. Finally she said, 'I wish that the restriction on the Jews waiting to leave Romania could be lifted.'

Ionescu sat there listening to her words. His fingers drummed on the desk. 'I see.' He was still for a long time. Finally he looked up at Mary. 'It shall be done. They will not all be allowed out, of course, but – I will make it easier.'

When the announcement was made public two days later, Mary received a telephone call from President Ellison himself.

'By God,' he said, 'I thought I was sending over a diplomat, and I got a miracle worker.'

'I was just lucky, Mr President.'

'It's the kind of luck I wish all my diplomats had. I want to congratulate you, Mary, on everything you've been doing over there.'

'Thank you, Mr President.'

She hung up, feeling a warm glow.

'July is just around the corner,' Harriet Kruger told Mary. 'In the past, the Ambassador always gave a Fourth of July party for the Americans living in Bucharest. If you'd prefer not to –'

'No. I think it's a lovely idea.'

'Fine. I'll take care of all the arrangements. A lot of flags, balloons, an orchestra – the works.'

'Sounds wonderful. Thank you, Harriet.'

It would eat into the Residence expense account, but it would be worth it. *The truth is*, Mary thought, *I miss home.*

Florence and Douglas Schiffer surprised Mary with a visit.

'We're in Rome,' Florence screamed over the telephone. 'Can we come and see you?'

Mary was thrilled. 'How soon can you get here?'

'How does tomorrow grab you?'

When the Schiffers arrived at Otopeni Airport the following day, Mary was there to meet them with the Embassy limousine. There was an excited exchange of hugs and kisses.

'You look fantastic!' Florence said. 'Being an ambassador hasn't changed you a bit.'

You'd be surprised, Mary thought.

On the ride back to the Residence, Mary pointed out the sights, the same sights she had seen for the first time only four months earlier. Had it been only four months? It seemed an eternity.

'This is where you live?' Florence asked, as they drove into the gates of the Residence, guarded by a Marine. 'I'm impressed.'

Mary gave the Schiffers a tour of the Residence.

'My God!' Florence exclaimed. 'A swimming

pool, a theatre, a thousand rooms, and your own park.'

They were seated in the large dining room, having lunch and gossiping about their neighbours in Junction City.

'Do you miss the place at all?' Douglas wanted to know.

'Yes.' And even as she said it, Mary realized how far she had come from home. Junction City had meant peace and security, an easy, friendly way of life. Here, there was fear and terror and obscene threats scrawled on her office walls in red paint. *Red, the colour of violence.*

'What are you thinking?' Florence asked.

'What? Oh, nothing. I was just daydreaming. What are you two lovely people doing in Europe?'

'I had to attend a medical convention in Rome,' Douglas said.

'Go on – tell her the rest,' Florence prompted.

'Well, the truth is, I wasn't sure I wanted to go, but we were concerned about you and wanted to find out how you were doing. So here we are.'

'I'm so glad.'

'I never thought I'd know such a big star,' Florence sighed.

Mary laughed. 'Florence, being an ambassador doesn't make me a star.'

'Oh, that's not what I'm talking about.'

'What *are* you talking about?'

'Don't you really know?'

'Know what?'

'Mary, there was a big article about you in *Time* last week, with a picture of you and the children. You're being written about in all the magazines and newspapers at home. When Stanton Rogers gives news conferences about foreign affairs, he uses you as a shining example. The President talks about you. Believe me, your name is on everyone's lips.'

'I guess I've been out of touch,' Mary said. She remembered what Stanton had said: *The President ordered the build-up.*

'How long can you stay?' Mary asked.

'I'd love to stay forever, but we planned three days here and then we're on our way back home.'

Douglas asked, 'How *are* you getting along, Mary? I mean about – you know – Edward?'

'I'm getting better,' Mary said slowly. 'I talk to him every night. Does that sound crazy?'

'Not really.'

'It's still hell. But I try. I try.'

'Have you – er – met anyone?' Florence asked delicately.

Mary smiled. 'As a matter of fact, maybe I have. You'll meet him at dinner tonight.'

The Schiffers took to Dr Louis Desforges immediately. They had heard that the French were aloof and snobbish, but Louis proved to be friendly and warm and outgoing. He and Douglas got into long discussions about medicine. It was one of her happiest evenings since she had come to Bucharest. For a brief time, she felt safe and relaxed.

At eleven o'clock, the Schiffers retired upstairs to the guest room that had been prepared for them. Mary was downstairs saying good night to Louis.

He said, 'I like your friends very much. I hope I shall see them again.'

'They liked you, too. They're leaving for Kansas in a couple of days,' Mary said.

He studied her. 'Mary – you're not thinking of leaving?'

'No,' Mary said. 'I'm staying.'

He smiled. 'Good.' He hesitated, then said quietly, 'I am going away to the mountains for the weekend. I would like it very much if you came with me.'

'Yes.'

It was as simple as that.

She lay in the dark talking to Edward that night. *Darling, I'll always, always love you, but I mustn't need you any more. It's time I started a new life. You'll always be a part of that life, but there has to be someone else, too. Louis isn't you, but he's Louis. He's strong, and he's good, and he's brave.*

That's as close as I can come to having you. Please understand, Edward. Please . . .

She sat up in bed and turned on the bedside light. She stared at her wedding ring for a long time, then she slowly slipped it off her finger.

It was a circle that symbolized an ending, and a beginning.

Mary took the Schiffers on a whirlwind tour of Bucharest, and saw to it that their days were filled. The three days passed too quickly, and when the Schiffers left, Mary felt a sharp pang of loneliness, a sense of being totally isolated from her roots, adrift once again in an alien and dangerous land.

Mary was having her usual morning coffee with Mike Slade, discussing the day's agenda.

When they finished, Mike said, 'I've been hearing rumours.'

Mary had heard them, too. 'About Ionescu and his new mistress? He seems to –'

'About you.'

She felt herself stiffen. 'Really? What kind of rumours?'

'It seems that you're seeing a lot of Dr Louis Desforges.'

Mary felt a flare of anger. 'Whom I see is no one's business.'

'I beg to differ with you, Madam Ambassador. It's the business of everyone in the Embassy. We have a strict rule against getting involved with foreigners, and the doctor is a foreigner. He also happens to be an enemy agent.'

Mary was almost too stunned to speak. 'That's absurd!' she sputtered. 'What do *you* know about Dr Desforges?'

'Think about how you met him,' Mike Slade suggested. 'The damsel in distress and the knight in shining armour. That's the oldest trick in the world. I've used it myself.'

'I don't give a damn what you've done and what you haven't done,' Mary retorted. 'He's worth a dozen of you. He fought against terrorists in Algeria, and they murdered his wife and children.'

Mike said mildly, 'That's interesting. I've been examining his dossier. Your doctor never had a wife or children.'

TWENTY-FIVE

They stopped for lunch at Timisoara, on their way up to the Carpathian Mountains. The inn was called Hunter's Friday, and was decorated in the period atmosphere of a medieval wine cellar.

'The speciality of the house is game,' Louis told Mary. 'I would suggest the venison.'

'Fine.' She had never eaten venison. It was delicious.

Louis ordered a bottle of Zghihara, the local white wine. There was an air of confidence about Louis, a quiet strength that gave Mary a feeling of security.

He had picked her up in town, away from the Embassy. 'It's better not to let anyone know where you are going,' he said, 'or it will be on the tongues of every diplomat in town.'

Too late, Mary thought wryly.

Louis had borrowed the car from a friend at the French Embassy. It had black and white oval CD licence plates.

Mary knew that licence plates were a tool for the police. Foreigners were given licence plates that started with the number twelve. Yellow plates were for officials.

After lunch, they started out again. They passed farmers driving primitive home-made wagons cut from limbs of trees that were twisted together, and caravans of gypsies.

Louis was a skilful driver. Mary studied him as he drove, thinking of Mike Slade's words: *I've been examining his dossier. Your doctor never had a wife or children. He's an enemy agent.*

She did not believe Mike Slade. Every instinct told her he was lying. It was not Louis who had sneaked into her office and scribbled those words on the walls. It was someone else who was threatening her. She trusted Louis. *No one could have faked the emotion I saw on his face when he was playing with the children. No one is that good an actor.*

The air was getting noticeably thinner and cooler, and the vegetation and oak trees had given way to ash trees and spruce and fir.

'There's wonderful hunting here,' Louis said. 'You can find wild boar, roebuck, wolves, and black chamois.'

'I've never hunted.'

'Perhaps one day I can take you.'

The mountains ahead looked like pictures she had seen of the Swiss Alps, their peaks covered by mists and clouds. Along the roadside they passed forests and green meadows dappled with grazing cows. The icy clouds overhead were the colour of steel, and Mary felt that if she reached up and touched them, they would stick to her fingers, like cold metal.

It was late afternoon when they reached their destination, Cioplea, a lovely mountain resort that was built like a miniature chalet. Mary waited in the car while Louis registered for both of them.

An elderly porter showed them to their suite. It had a good-sized, comfortable living room, simply furnished, a bedroom, bathroom, and a terrace with a breathtaking view of the mountains.

'For the first time in my life,' Louis sighed, 'I wish I were a painter.'

'It *is* a beautiful view.'

He moved closer to her. 'No. I mean I wish I could paint you.'

She found herself thinking: *I feel like a seventeen-year-old on a first date. I'm nervous.*

He took her in his arms and held her tightly. She buried her head against his chest, and then Louis' lips were on hers, and he was exploring her body, and he moved her hand down to his male hardness, and she forgot everything except what was happening to her.

There was a frantic need in her that went far beyond sex. It was a need for someone to hold her, to reassure her, to protect her, to let her know that she was no longer alone. She needed Louis to be inside her, to be inside him, to be one with him.

They were in the large, double bed, and she felt his tongue feather down her naked body, into the soft depths of her, and then he was inside her, and she screamed aloud with a feral, passionate cry before she exploded into a thousand glorious Marys. And again, and again, until the bliss became almost too much to bear.

Louis was an incredible lover, passionate and demanding, tender and caring. After a long, long time, they lay spent, contented. She nestled in his strong arms, and they talked.

'It's so strange,' Louis said. 'I feel whole again. Since Renée and the children were killed, I've been a ghost, wandering around lost.'

I, too, Mary thought.

'I missed her in all the important ways, and in ways I had never thought of. I felt helpless without her. Silly, trivial things. I did not know how to cook a meal, or do my laundry, or even make my bed properly. We men take so much for granted.'

'Louis, I felt helpless, too. Edward was my umbrella, and when it rained and he wasn't there to protect me, I almost drowned.'

They slept.

They made love again, slowly and tenderly now, the fire banked, the flame slower, more exquisite.

It was almost perfect. *Almost.* Because there was

a question Mary wanted to ask, and she knew she dared not: *Did you have a wife and children, Louis?*

The moment she asked that question, she knew everything between them would be over forever. Louis would never forgive her for doubting him. *Damn Mike Slade*, she thought. *Damn him.*

Louis was watching her. 'What were you thinking about?'

'Nothing, darling.'

What were you doing in that dark side street when those men tried to kidnap me, Louis?

They dined that evening on the outdoor terrace, and Louis ordered *Cemurata*, the strawberry liqueur made in the nearby mountains.

Saturday they went on a tram to a mountain peak. When they returned, they swam in the indoor pool, made love in the private sauna, and played bridge with a geriatric German couple on their honeymoon.

In the evening, they drove to Eintrul, a rustic restaurant in the mountains, where they had dinner in a large room with an open fireplace with a roaring fire. There were wooden chandeliers hanging from the ceiling, and hunting trophies on the wall over the fireplace. The room was lit by candlelight, and through the windows they could look at the snow-covered hills outside. A perfect setting, with the perfect companion.

*　*　*

And finally, too soon, it was time to leave.

Time to go back to the real world, Mary thought. And what was the real world? A place of threats and kidnapping and horrible graffiti written on her office walls.

The drive back was pleasant and easy. The sexual tension on the drive up had given way to an easy, relaxed feeling of togetherness. Louis was so comfortable to be with.

As they neared the outskirts of Bucharest, they drove by fields of sunflowers, their faces moving towards the sun.

That's me, Mary thought happily. *I'm finally moving into the sunlight.*

Beth and Tim were eagerly awaiting their mother's return.

'Are you going to marry Louis?' Beth asked.

Mary was taken aback. They had put into words what she had not dared allow herself to think.

'Well – are you?'

'I don't know,' she said carefully. 'Would you mind if I did?'

'He's not Daddy,' Beth answered slowly, 'but Tim and I took a vote. We like him.'

'So do I,' Mary replied happily. 'So do I.'

There were a dozen red roses with a note: *Thank you for you.*

She read the card. And wondered if he had sent flowers to Renée. And wondered if there had been a Renée and two daughters. And hated herself for it. *Why would Mike Slade make up a terrible lie like that?* There was no way she could ever check it. And at that moment, Eddie Maltz, the Political Consular and CIA agent, walked into her office.

'You're looking fit, Madam Ambassador. Have a good weekend?'

'Yes, thank you.'

They spent some time discussing a colonel who had approached Maltz about defecting.

'He'd be a valuable asset to us. He'll be bringing some useful information with him. I'm sending a black cable out tonight, but I wanted you to be prepared to receive some heat from Ionescu.'

'Thank you, Mr Maltz.'

He rose to leave.

On a sudden impulse, Mary said, 'Wait. I – I wonder if I could ask you for a favour?'

'Certainly.'

She found it unexpectedly awkward to continue. 'It's – personal and confidential.'

'Sounds like our motto,' Maltz smiled.

'I need some information on a Dr Louis Desforges. Have you heard of him?'

'Yes, ma'am. He's attached to the French Embassy. What would you like to know about him?'

This was going to be even more difficult than she had imagined. It was a betrayal. 'I – I'd like to know whether Dr Desforges was once married and had two children. Do you think you could find out?'

'Will twenty-four hours be soon enough?' Maltz asked.

'Yes, thank you.'

Please forgive me, Louis.

A short time later, Mike Slade walked into Mary's office. 'Morning.'

'Good morning.'

He put a cup of coffee on her desk. Something in his attitude seemed subtly changed. Mary was not sure what it was, but she had a feeling that Mike Slade knew all about her weekend. She wondered whether he had spies following her, reporting on her activities.

She took a sip of the coffee. Excellent, as usual. *That's one thing Mike Slade does well*, Mary thought.

'We have some problems,' he said.

And for the rest of the morning, they became involved in a discussion that included more Romanians who wanted to emigrate to America, the Romanian financial crisis, a Marine who had got a Romanian girl pregnant, and a dozen other topics.

At the end of the meeting, Mary was more tired than usual.

Mike Slade said, 'The ballet is opening tonight. Corina Socoli is dancing.'

Mary recognized the name. She was one of the prima ballerinas in the world.

'I have some tickets, if you're interested.'

'No, thanks.' She thought of the last time Mike had given her tickets for the theatre, and what had happened. Besides, she was going to be busy. She was invited to dinner at the Chinese Embassy and was meeting Louis at the Residence afterwards. It would not do for them to be seen too much together in public. She knew that she was breaking the rules by having an affair with a member of another embassy. *But this is not a casual affair.*

As Mary was dressing for dinner, she opened her closet to take out a dinner gown and found that the maid had washed it instead of having it cleaned. It was ruined. *I'm going to fire her*, Mary thought furiously. *Except that I can't. Their damned rules.*

She felt suddenly exhausted. She sank down on the bed. *I wish I didn't have to go out tonight. It would be so nice just to lie here and go to sleep. But you have to, Madam Ambassador. Your country is depending on you.*

She lay there, fantasizing. She would stay in bed instead of going to the dinner party. The Chinese Ambassador would greet his other guests, anxiously waiting for her. Finally, dinner would be announced. The American Ambassador had not arrived. It was a deliberate insult. China had lost face. The Chinese

Ambassador would send a black cable, and when his Prime Minister read it, he would be furious. He would telephone the President of the United States to protest. 'Neither you nor anyone else can force my ambassador to go to your dinners,' President Ellison would yell. The Prime Minister would scream, 'No one can talk to me that way. We have our own atomic bombs now, Mr President.' The two leaders would press the nuclear buttons together, and destruction would rain on both countries.

Mary sat up and thought wearily, *I'd better go to the damned dinner.*

The evening was a blur of the same familiar diplomatic corps faces. Mary had only a hazy recollection of the others at her table. She could not wait to get home.

As Florian was driving her back to the Residence, Mary smiled dreamily: *I wonder if President Ellison realizes I prevented an atomic war tonight?*

The following morning when Mary went to the office, she was feeling worse. Her head ached, and she was nauseated. The only thing that made her feel better was the visit from Eddie Maltz.

The CIA agent said, 'I have the information you requested. Dr Louis Desforges was married for thirteen years. Wife's name, Renée. Two daughters, ten and twelve, Phillipa and Geneviève. They were murdered in Algeria by terrorists, probably as an act of vengeance against the doctor, who was fighting them in a covert operation. Do you need any further information?'

'No,' Mary said happily. 'That's fine. Thank you.'

Over morning coffee, Mary and Mike Slade discussed a forthcoming visit from a college group.

'They'd like to meet President Ionescu.'

'I'll see what I can do,' Mary said. Her voice was slurred.

'You okay?'

'I'm just tired.'

'What you need is another cup of coffee. It will perk you up. No pun intended.'

By late afternoon, Mary was feeling worse. She called Louis and cancelled their dinner engagement. She felt too ill to see anybody. She wished that the American doctor were in Bucharest. Perhaps Louis would know what was wrong with her. *If I don't get over this, I'll call him.*

Dorothy Stone had the nurse send up some Tylenol from the pharmacy. It did not help.

Mary's secretary was concerned. 'You really look awful, Madam Ambassador. You should be in bed.'

'I'll be fine,' Mary mumbled.

The day had a thousand hours. Mary met with the students, some Romanian officials, an American banker, an official from the USIS – the United States Information Service – and sat through an endless dinner party at the Dutch Embassy. When she finally arrived home, she fell into bed.

She was unable to sleep. She felt hot and feverish, and she was caught up in a series of nightmares. She was running down a maze of corridors, and every time she turned a corner, she ran into someone writing obscenities in blood. She could only see the back of the man's head. Then Louis appeared, and a dozen men tried to pull him into a car. Mike Slade came running down the street yelling, 'Kill him. He has no family.'

Mary woke up in a cold sweat. The room was unbearably hot. She threw off the covers and was suddenly chilled. Her teeth began to chatter. *My God*, she thought, *what's wrong with me?*

She spent the remainder of the night awake, afraid to go to sleep again, afraid of her dreams.

It took all of Mary's willpower to get up and go to the Embassy the following morning. Mike Slade was waiting for her.

He looked at her critically and said, 'You don't look too well. Why don't you fly to Frankfurt and see our doctor there?'

'I'm fine.' Her lips were dry and cracked, and she felt completely dehydrated.

Mike handed her a cup of coffee. 'I have the new commerce figures here for you. The Romanians are going to need more grain than we thought. Here's how we can capitalize on it . . .'

She tried to pay attention, but Mike's voice kept fading in and out.

Somehow she managed to struggle through the day. Louis called twice. Mary told her secretary to tell him she was in meetings. She was trying to conserve every ounce of strength she had left to keep working.

When Mary went to bed that evening, she could feel that her temperature had climbed. Her whole body ached. *I'm really ill*, she thought. *I feel as though I'm dying*. With an enormous effort she reached out and pulled the bellcord. Carmen appeared.

She looked at Mary in alarm. 'Madam Ambassador! What –?'

Mary's voice was a croak. 'Ask Sabina to call the French Embassy. I need Dr Desforges . . .'

Mary opened her eyes and blinked. There were two blurred Louis figures standing there. He moved to her bedside. He bent down and took a close look at her flushed face. 'My God, what's happening to you?' He felt her forehead. It was hot to the touch. 'Have you taken your temperature?'

'I don't want to know.' It hurt to talk.

Louis sat down on the edge of the bed. 'Darling, how long has this been going on?'

'A few days. It's probably just a virus.'

Louis felt her pulse. It was weak and thready. As he leaned forward, he smelled her breath. 'Have you eaten something today with garlic?'

She shook her head. 'I haven't eaten anything in two days.' Her voice was a whisper.

He leaned forward and gently lifted her eyelids. 'Have you been thirsty?'

She nodded.

'Pain, muscle cramps, vomiting, nausea?'

All of the above, she thought wearily. Aloud she said, 'What's the matter with me, Louis?'

'Do you feel like answering some questions?'

She swallowed. 'I'll try.'

He held her hand. 'When did you start feeling this way?'

'The day after we got back from the mountains.' Her voice was a whisper.

'Do you remember having anything to eat or drink that made you feel ill afterwards?'

She shook her head.

'You just kept feeling worse every day?'

She nodded.

'Do you eat breakfast here at the Residence with the children?'

'Usually, yes.'

'And the children are feeling well?'

She nodded.

'What about lunch? Do you eat lunch at the same place every day?'

'No. Sometimes I eat at the Embassy, sometimes

I have meetings at restaurants.' Her voice was a whisper.

'Is there any one place you regularly have dinner or anything you regularly eat?'

She felt too tired to carry on this conversation. She wished he would go away. She closed her eyes.

He shook her gently. 'Mary, stay awake. Listen to me.' There was an urgency in his voice. 'Is there any person you eat with constantly?'

She blinked up at him sleepily. 'No.' Why was he asking all these questions? 'It's a virus,' she mumbled. 'Isn't it?'

He took a deep breath. 'No. Someone is poisoning you.'

It sent a bolt of electricity through her body. She opened her eyes wide. 'What? I don't believe it.'

He was frowning. 'I would say it was arsenic poisoning, except that arsenic is not for sale in Romania.'

Mary felt a sudden tremor of fear. 'Who – who would be trying to poison me?'

He squeezed her hand. 'Darling, you've got to think. Are you sure there's no set routine you have, where someone gives you something to eat or drink every day?'

'Of course not,' Mary protested weakly. 'I told you, I –' *Coffee. Mike Slade. My own special brew.* 'Oh, my God!'

'What is it?'

She cleared her throat and managed to say,

'Mike Slade brings me coffee every morning. He's always there waiting for me.'

Louis stared at her. 'No. It couldn't be Mike Slade. What reason would he have for trying to kill you?'

'He – he wants to get rid of me.'

'We'll talk about this later,' Louis said urgently. 'The first thing we have to do is treat you. I'd like to take you to the hospital here, but your Embassy will not permit it. I'm going to get something for you. I'll be back in a few minutes.'

Mary lay there, trying to grasp the meaning of what Louis had told her. *Arsenic. Someone is feeding me arsenic. What you need is another cup of coffee. It will make you feel better. I brew it myself.*

She drifted off into unconsciousness and was awakened by Louis' voice. 'Mary!'

She forced her eyes open. He was at her bedside, taking a syringe out of a small bag.

'Hello, Louis. I'm glad you could come,' Mary mumbled.

Louis felt for a vein in her arm and plunged the hypodermic needle in. 'I'm giving you an injection of Bal. It's an antidote for arsenic. I'm going to alternate it with Penicillamine. I'll give you another one in the morning. Mary?'

She was asleep.

The following morning, Dr Louis Desforges gave Mary an injection, and another one in the evening.

The effects of the drugs were miraculous. One by one, the symptoms began to disappear. The following day, Mary's temperature and vital signs were almost completely normal.

Louis was in Mary's bedroom, putting the hypodermic needle in a paper sack, where it would not be seen by a curious staff member. Mary felt drained and weak, as though she had gone through a long illness, but all the pain and discomfort were gone.

'This is twice you've saved my life.'

Louis looked at her soberly. 'I think we'd better find out who's trying to take it.'

'How do we do that?'

'I've been checking around at the various embassies. None of them carries arsenic. I have not been able to find out about the American Embassy. I would like you to do something for me. Do you think you will feel well enough to go to work tomorrow?'

'I think so.'

'I want you to go to the pharmacy in your Embassy. Tell them you need a pesticide. Say that you're having trouble with the insects in your garden. Ask for Antrol. That's loaded with arsenic.'

Mary looked at him, puzzled. 'What's the point?'

'My hunch is that the arsenic had to be flown into Bucharest. If it is anywhere, it will be in the Embassy pharmacy. Anyone who checks out a

poison must sign for it. When you sign for the
Antrol, see what names are on the sheet . . .'

Gunny escorted Mary through the Embassy door.
She walked down the long corridor to the pharmacy, where the nurse was working behind the
cage.

She turned as she saw Mary. 'Good morning,
Madam Ambassador. Are you feeling better?'

'Yes, thank you.'

'Can I get you something?'

Mary took a nervous breath. 'My – my gardener
tells me he's having trouble with insects in the
garden. I wondered whether you might have something to help – like Antrol?'

'Why, yes. As a matter of fact, we do have some
Antrol,' the nurse said. She reached towards a back
shelf and picked up a can with a poison label on
it. 'An infestation of ants is very unusual for this
time of year.' She put a form in front of Mary.
'You'll have to sign for it, if you don't mind. It
has arsenic in it.'

Mary was staring at the form placed in front of
her. There was only one name on it.

Mike Slade.

TWENTY-SIX

When Mary tried to telephone Louis Desforges to tell him what she had learned, his line was busy. He was talking to Mike Slade. Dr Desforges' first instinct had been to report the murder attempt, except that he could not believe Slade was responsible. And so, Louis had decided to telephone Slade himself.

'I have just left your ambassador,' Louis Desforges said. 'She is going to live.'

'Well, that's good news, doctor. Why shouldn't she?'

Louis' tone was cautious. 'Someone has been poisoning her.'

'What are you talking about?' Mike demanded.

'I think perhaps you know what I'm talking about.'

'Hold it! Are you saying that you think *I'm* responsible? You're wrong. You and I had better have a private talk. Some place where we can't be overheard. Can you meet me tonight?'

'At what time?'

'I'm tied up until nine o'clock. Why don't you meet me a few minutes later, at Baneasa Woods? I'll meet you at the fountain and explain everything then.'

Louis Desforges hesitated. 'Very well. I will see you there.' He hung up and thought: *Mike Slade cannot possibly be behind this.*

When Mary tried to telephone Louis again, he had left. No one knew where to reach him.

Mary and the children were having dinner at the Residence.

'You really look a lot better, Mother,' Beth said. 'We were worried.'

'I feel fine,' Mary assured her. And it was the truth. *Thank God for Louis!*

Mary was unable to get Mike Slade out of her mind. She could hear his voice saying: *Here's your coffee. I brewed it myself.* Slowly killing her. She shuddered.

'Are you cold?' Tim asked.

'No, darling.'

She must not involve the children in her nightmares. *Perhaps I should send them back home for a while?* Mary thought. *They could stay with Florence and Doug.* And then she thought: *I could go with them.* But that would be cowardly, a victory for Mike Slade, and whoever he was working with. There was only one person she could think of who could help her. Stanton Rogers. Stanton would know what to do about Mike.

But I can't accuse him without proof, and what proof do I have? That he made coffee for me every morning?

Tim was talking to her. '. . . so we said we'd ask if we could go with them.'

'I'm sorry, darling. What did you say?'

'I said Nikolai asked us if we could go out camping with him and his family next weekend.'

'No!' It came out more harshly than she had intended. 'I want you both to stay close to the Residence.'

'What about school?' Beth asked.

Mary hesitated. She could not keep them prisoners here, and she did not want to alarm them.

'That's fine. As long as Florian takes you there and brings you back. No one else.'

Beth was studying her. 'Mother, is anything wrong?'

'Of course not,' Mary said quickly. 'Why do you ask?'

'I don't know. There's something in the air.'

'Give her a break,' Tim said. 'She had the Romanian flu.'

That's an interesting phrase, Mary thought. *Arsenic poisoning – the Romanian flu.*

'Can we watch a movie tonight?' Tim asked.

'*May* we watch a movie tonight,' Mary corrected him.

'Does that mean "yes"?'

Mary had not planned on running a movie, but she had spent so little time with the children lately that she decided to give them a treat.

'It means "yes".'

'Thank you, Madam Ambassador,' Tim shouted. 'I get to pick the movie.'

'No, you don't. You picked the last one. Can we see *American Graffiti* again?'

American Graffiti. And suddenly Mary knew what proof she might show Stanton Rogers.

At midnight, Mary asked Carmen to call a taxi.

'Don't you want Florian to drive you?' Carmen asked. 'He's –'

'No.'

This was something that had to be done secretly.

When the taxi arrived a few minutes later, Mary got in. 'The American Embassy, please.'

The taxi driver replied, 'It is closed at this hour. There is no one –' He turned around and recognized her. 'Madam Ambassador! This is a great honour.' He began to drive. 'I recognized you from all your pictures in our newspapers and magazines. You are almost as famous as our great leader.'

Others in the Embassy had commented about all the publicity she was receiving in the Romanian press.

The driver was chattering on. 'I like Americans. They are good-hearted people. I hope your President's people-to-people plan works. We Romanians are all for it. It is time the world had peace.'

She was in no mood for a discussion of any kind.

When they arrived at the Embassy, Mary indicated a place marked: *Parcare cu Locuri Rezervate*. 'Pull in there, please, and come back for me in an hour. I'll be returning to the Residence.'

'Certainly, Madam Ambassador.'

A Marine guard was moving towards the taxi. 'You can't park there, it's res –' He recognized Mary, and saluted. 'Sorry. Good evening, Madam Ambassador.'

'Good evening,' Mary said.

The Marine walked her to the entrance and opened the door for her. 'Can I help you?'

'No. I'm going to my office for a few minutes.'

'Yes, ma'am.' He watched her walk down the hall.

Mary turned the lights on in her office and looked at the walls where the obscenities had been washed away. She walked over to the connecting door that led to Mike Slade's office and entered. The room was in darkness. She turned on the lights and looked around.

There were no papers on his desk. She began searching through the drawers. They were empty, except for brochures and bulletins and timetables. Innocent things that would be of no use to a snooping cleaning woman. Mary's eyes scrutinized the office. It had to be here somewhere. There was no other place he could have kept it, and it was unlikely that he would carry it around with him.

She opened the drawers and started examining

their contents again, slowly and carefully. When she came to a bottom drawer, she felt something hard at the back, behind a mass of papers. She pulled it out and held it in her hand, staring at it.

It was a can of red spray paint.

At a few minutes after nine, Dr Louis Desforges was waiting in Baneasa Woods, near the fountain. He wondered if he had done the wrong thing by not reporting Mike Slade. *No*, he thought. *First I must hear what he has to say. If I made a false accusation, it would destroy him.*

Mike Slade suddenly appeared out of the darkness.

'Thanks for coming. We can clear this up very quickly. You said on the telephone you thought someone was poisoning Mary Ashley.'

'I *know* it. Someone was feeding her arsenic.'

'And you think I'm responsible?'

'You could have put it in her coffee, a little bit at a time.'

'Have you reported this to anyone?'

'Not yet. I wanted to talk to you first.'

'I'm glad you did,' Mike said. He took his hand out of his pocket. In it was a .475 calibre Magnum pistol.

Louis stared. 'What – what are you doing? Listen to me! You can't –'

Mike Slade pulled the trigger, and watched the Frenchman's chest explode into a red cloud.

TWENTY-SEVEN

In the American Embassy, Mary was in the Bubble Room telephoning Stanton Rogers' office on the secure line. It was one o'clock in the morning in Bucharest, and 8 a.m. in Washington, D.C., Mary knew that Stanton Rogers' secretary always arrived at the office early.

'Mr Rogers' office.'

'This is Ambassador Ashley. I know that Mr Rogers is in China with the President, but it's urgent that I speak to him as soon as possible. Is there any way I can reach him there?'

'I'm sorry, Madam Ambassador. His itinerary is very flexible. I have no telephone number for him.'

Mary felt her heart plummet. 'When will you hear from him?'

'It's difficult to say. He and the President have a very busy schedule. Perhaps someone in the State Department could help you?'

'No,' Mary said dully. 'No one else can help me. Thank you.'

She sat in the room alone, staring at nothing, surrounded by the most sophisticated electronic equipment in the world, and none of it of any use to her. Mike Slade was trying to murder her. She *had* to let someone know. But who? Whom could she trust? The only one who knew what Slade was trying to do was Louis Desforges.

Mary tried the number at his residence again, but there was still no answer. She remembered what Stanton Rogers had told her: *If you want to send me any messages you don't want anyone else to read, the code at the top of the cable is three x's.*

Mary hurried back to her office and wrote out an urgent message addressed to Stanton Rogers. She placed three x's at the top. She took out the black code book from a locked drawer in her desk, and carefully encoded what she had written. At least if anything happened to her now, Stanton Rogers would know who was responsible.

Mary walked down the corridor to the Communications Room.

Eddie Maltz, the CIA agent, happened to be behind the cage.

'Good evening, Madam Ambassador. You're working late tonight.'

'Yes,' Mary said. 'There's a message I'd like sent off. I want it to go out right away.'

'I'll take care of it personally.'

'Thank you.' She handed him the message and

headed for the front door. She desperately wanted to be close to her children.

In the Communications Room, Eddie Maltz was decoding the message Mary had handed him. When he was finished, he read it through twice, frowning. He walked over to the shredder, threw the message in, and watched it turn into confetti.

Then he placed a call to Floyd Baker, the Secretary of State, in Washington. Code Name: *Thor*.

It took Lev Pasternak two months to follow the circuitous trail that led to Buenos Aires. SIS and half a dozen other security agencies around the world had helped identify Angel as the killer. Mossad had given him the name of Neusa Muñez, Angel's mistress. They all wanted to eliminate Angel. To Lev Pasternak, Angel had become an obsession. Because of Pasternak's failure, Marin Groza had died, and Pasternak could never forgive himself for that. He could, however, make atonement. And he intended to.

He did not get in touch with Neusa Muñez directly. He located the apartment building where she lived and kept a watch on it, waiting for Angel to appear. After five days, when there was no sign of him, Pasternak made his move. He waited until the woman left, and after fifteen minutes walked upstairs, picked the lock on her door, and entered the apartment. He searched it swiftly and thoroughly. There were no photographs, memos or addresses that could lead him to Angel. Pasternak discovered the suits in the closet. He examined the Herrera labels, took one of the jackets off the hanger and tucked it under his arm. A minute later, he was gone, as quietly as he had entered.

The following morning Lev Pasternak walked into Herrera's. His hair was dishevelled and his clothes wrinkled, and he smelled of whisky.

The manager of the men's shop came up to him and said disapprovingly. 'May I help you, *señor*?'

Lev Pasternak grinned sheepishly. 'Yeah,' he said. 'Tell you the truth, I got as drunk as a skunk last night. I got inna card game with some South American dudes in my hotel room. I think we all got a little drunk, pal. Anyway, one of the guys – I don't remember his name – left his jacket in my room.' Lev held up the jacket, his hand unsteady. 'It had your label in it, so I figured you could tell me where to return it to him.'

The manager examined the jacket. 'Yes, we tailored this. I would have to look up our records. Where can I reach you?'

'You can't,' Lev Pasternak mumbled. 'I'm on my way to 'nother poker game. Got a card? I'll call you.'

'Yes.' The manager handed him his card.

'You're not gonna steal that jacket, are you?' Lev asked drunkenly.

'Certainly not,' the manager said indignantly.

Lev Pasternak clapped him on the back and said, 'Good. I'll call you later this afternoon.'

That afternoon when Lev called from his hotel room, the manager said, 'The name of the gentleman we made the jacket for is *Señor* H. R. de Mendoza. He has a suite at the Aurora Hotel, Suite Four Seventeen.'

Lev Pasternak checked to make sure that his door was locked. He took a suitcase out of the closet, carried it to the bed and opened it. Inside was a .45 SIG-Saur pistol with a silencer, courtesy of a friend in the Argentinian secret service. Pasternak checked again to make sure the gun was loaded and that the silencer was secure. He put the suitcase back in the closet, and went to sleep.

At 5 a.m., Lev Pasternak was silently moving down the deserted fourth floor corridor of the Aurora Hotel. When he reached 417, he looked around to make sure no one was in sight. He reached down to the lock and quietly inserted a wire. When he heard the door click open, he pulled out the pistol.

He sensed a draught as the door across the hall opened, and before Pasternak could swing around, he felt something hard and cold pressing against the back of his neck.

'I don't like being followed,' Angel said.

Lev Pasternak heard the click of the trigger a second before his brain was torn apart.

* * *

399

Angel was not sure whether Pasternak was alone, or working with someone, but it was always nice to take extra precautions. The telephone call had come, and it was time to move. First Angel had some shopping to do. There was a good lingerie shop on Pueyerredón, expensive, but Neusa deserved the best. The inside of the shop was cool and quiet.

'I would like to see a négligé, something very frilly,' Angel said.

The female clerk stared.

'And a pair of panties with a split in the crotch . . .'

Fifteen minutes later, Angel walked into Frenkel's. The shelves were filled with leather purses, gloves and briefcases.

'I would like a briefcase, please. Black.'

The El Aljire in the Sheraton Hotel was one of the finest restaurants in Buenos Aires. Angel sat down at a table in the corner, and placed the new briefcase on the table. The waiter came up to the table.

'Good afternoon.'

'I'll start with the *Centolla Pargo*, and after that the *Parrillada* with *Ensalada de Berros*. I'll decide on my dessert later.'

'Certainly.'

'Where are the rest rooms?'

'In the rear, through the far door and to your left.'

Angel got up from the table and walked towards the rear of the restaurant, leaving the briefcase in sight on the table. There was a narrow corridor with two small doors, one marked *Hombres*, and the other marked *Señoras*. At the end of the corridor were double doors leading to the noisy, steamy kitchen. Angel pushed one of the doors open and stepped inside. It was a scene of frantic activity, with chefs and souschefs bustling around, trying to keep up with the urgent demands of the lunch hour. Waiters moved in and out of the kitchen with loaded trays. The chefs were screaming at the waiters, and the waiters were screaming at the bus boys.

Angel moved, threading across the room, and stepped out through a back door leading to an alley. A five-minute wait to make sure that no one had followed.

There was a taxi at the corner. Angel gave the driver an address on Humberto 1°, alighted a block away, and hailed another taxi.

'*Donde, por favor?*'

'*Aeropuerto.*'

There would be a ticket for London waiting there. Tourist. First class was too conspicuous.

Two hours later, Angel watched the city of Buenos Aires disappear beneath the clouds, like some celestial magician's trick, and concentrated on the assignment ahead, thinking about the instructions that had been given.

Make sure the children die with her. Their deaths must be spectacular.

Angel did not like to be told how to fulfil a contract. Only amateurs were stupid enough to give advice to professionals. Angel smiled. *They will all die, and it will be more spectacular than anyone bargained for.*

Angel slept, a deep, dreamless sleep.

London's Heathrow Airport was crowded with summer tourists, and the taxi ride into Mayfair took more than an hour. The lobby of the Churchill was busy with guests checking in and out.

A bellboy took charge of Angel's three pieces of luggage.

The tip was modest, nothing that the bellboy would remember later. Angel walked over to the bank of hotel elevators, waited until a car was empty, then stepped inside.

When the elevator was on its way, Angel pressed the fifth, seventh, ninth and tenth floors, and got off at the fifth floor. Anyone who might be watching from the lobby would be confused.

A rear service staircase led to an alley, and five minutes after checking into the Churchill, Angel was in a taxi and on the way back to Heathrow.

The passport read H. R. de Mendoza. The ticket was on Tarom Airlines to Bucharest. Angel sent a telegram from the airport:

ARRIVING WEDNESDAY.
H. R. de Mendoza

It was addressed to Eddie Maltz.

Early the following morning, Dorothy Stone said, 'Stanton Rogers' office is on the line.'

'I'll take it,' Mary said eagerly. She snatched up the phone. 'Stan?'

She heard his secretary's voice, and wanted to weep in frustration. 'Mr Rogers asked me to call you, Madam Ambassador. He's with the President and unable to get to a telephone, but he asked me to see that you get anything you need. If you'll tell me what the problem is –?'

'No,' Mary said, trying to keep the disappointment out of her voice. 'I – I have to speak to him myself.'

'I'm afraid that won't be until tomorrow. He said he would call you as soon as he was able to.'

'Thank you. I'll be waiting for his call.' She replaced the receiver. There was nothing to do but wait.

Mary kept trying to telephone Louis at his home. No answer. She tried the French Embassy. They had no idea where he was.

'Please have him call me as soon as you hear from him.'

Dorothy Stone said, 'There's a call for you, but she refuses to give her name.'

'I'll take it.' Mary picked up the phone. 'Hello, this is Ambassador Ashley.'

A soft, female voice with a Romanian accent said, 'This is Corina Socoli.'

The name registered instantly. She was a beautiful young girl in her early twenties, Romania's prima ballerina.

'I need your help,' the girl said. 'I have decided to defect.'

I can't handle this today, Mary thought. *Not now*. She said, 'I – I don't know if I can help you.' Her mind was racing. She tried to remember what she had been told about defectors.

Many of them are Soviet plants. We bring them over, they feed us a few innocuous bits of information or misinformation. Some of them become moles. The real catches are the high-level intelligence officers or scientists. We can always use those. But otherwise, we don't grant political asylum unless there's a damned good reason.

Corina Socoli was sobbing now. 'Please! I am not safe staying where I am. You must send someone to get me.'

Communist governments set some cute traps. Someone posing as a defector asks for help. You bring them into the Embassy, and then they scream that they've been kidnapped. It gives them an excuse to take measures against targets in the United States.

'Where are you?' Mary asked.

There was a pause. Then, 'I suppose I must trust

you. I am at the Roscow Inn at Moldavia. Will you come for me?'

'I can't,' Mary said. 'But I'll send someone to get you. Don't call on this phone again. Just wait where you are. I –'

The door opened, and Mike Slade walked in. Mary looked up in shock. He was moving towards her.

The voice at the other end of the phone was saying, 'Hello? Hello?'

'Who are you talking to?' Mike asked.

'To – to Dr Desforges.' It was the first name that came to her mind. She replaced the receiver, terrified.

Don't be ridiculous, she told herself. *You're in the Embassy. He wouldn't dare do anything to you here.*

'Dr Desforges?' Mike repeated slowly.

'Yes. He's – he's on his way over to see me.'

How she wished it were true!

There was a strange look in Mike Slade's eyes. Mary's desk lamp was on, and it threw Mike's shadow against the wall, making him grotesquely large and menacing.

'Are you sure you're well enough to be back at work?'

The cold-blooded nerve of the man. 'Yes. I'm fine.'

She desperately wanted him to leave, so that she could escape. *I must not show him I'm frightened.*

He was moving closer to her. 'You look tense.

Maybe you should take the kids and go out to the lake district for a few days.'

Where I'll be an easier target.

Just looking at him filled her with such a fear that she found it hard to breathe. Her intercom phone rang. It was a lifesaver.

'If you'll excuse me . . .'

'Sure.'

Mike Slade stood there a moment, staring at her, then turned and left, taking his shadow with him. Almost sobbing with relief, Mary picked up the telephone. 'Hello?'

It was Jerry Davis, the Public Affairs Consular. 'Madam Ambassador, I'm sorry to disturb you, but I'm afraid I have some terrible news for you. We just received a police report that Dr Louis Desforges has been murdered.'

The room began to swim. 'Are you – are you sure?'

'Yes, ma'am. His wallet was found on his body.'

Sensory memories flooded through her, and a voice over the telephone was saying: *This is Sheriff Munster. Your husband has been killed in a car accident.* And all the old sorrows came rushing back, stabbing at her, tearing her apart.

'How – how did it happen?' Her voice was strangled.

'He was shot to death.'

'Do they – do they know who did it?'

'No, ma'am. The *Securitate* and the French Embassy are investigating.'

She dropped the receiver, her mind and body numb, and leaned back in her chair, studying the ceiling. There was a crack in it. *I must have that repaired*, Mary thought. *We mustn't have cracks in our Embassy. There's another crack. Cracks everywhere. Cracks in our lives, and when there is a crack, evil things get in. Edward is dead. Louis is dead.* She could not bear to think of that. She searched for more cracks. *I can't go through this pain again*, Mary thought. *Who would want to kill Louis?*

The answer immediately followed the question. *Mike Slade.* Louis had discovered that Slade was feeding Mary arsenic. Slade probably thought that with Louis dead, no one could prove anything against him.

A sudden realization struck her and filled her with a new terror. *Who were you talking to? Dr Desforges.* And Mike must have known that Dr Desforges was dead.

She stayed in her office all day, planning her next move. *I'm not going to let him drive me away. I'm not going to let him kill me. I have to stop him.* She was filled with rage such as she had never known before. She was going to protect herself and her children. And she was going to destroy Mike Slade.

Mary placed another urgent call to Stanton Rogers.

'I gave him your message, Madam Ambassador. He will return your call as soon as possible.'

*   *   *

She could not bring herself to accept Louis' death. He had been so warm, so gentle, and now he was lying in some morgue, lifeless. *If I had gone back to Kansas*, Mary thought dully, *Louis would be alive today*.

'Madam Ambassador . . .'

Mary looked up. Dorothy Stone was holding an envelope out to her.

'The guard at the gate asked me to give you this. He said it was delivered by a young boy.'

The envelope was marked *Personal, for the Ambassador's Eyes Only*.

Mary tore open the envelope. The note was written in a neat, copperplate handwriting. It read:

Dear Madam Ambassador:
    Enjoy your last day on earth.

It was signed 'Angel'.

Another one of Mike's scare tactics, Mary thought. *It won't work. I'll keep well away from him*.

Colonel McKinney was studying the note. He shook his head. 'There are a lot of sickies out there.' He looked up at Mary. 'You were scheduled to make an appearance this afternoon at the ground-breaking ceremony for the new Library addition. I'll cancel it and –'

'No.'

'Madam Ambassador, it's too dangerous for you to –'

'I'll be safe.' She knew now where the danger lay, and she had a plan to avoid it. 'Where's Mike Slade?' she asked.

'He's in a meeting at the Australian Embassy.'

'Please get word to him that I wish to see him right away.'

'You wanted to talk to me?' Mike Slade's tone was casual.

'Yes. There's something I want you to do.'

'I'm at your command.'

His sarcasm was like a slap.

'I received a telephone call from someone who wants to defect.'

'Who is it?'

She had no intention of telling him. He would betray the girl. 'That's not important. I want you to bring this person in.'

Mike frowned. 'Is this someone the Romanians want to keep?'

'Yes.'

'Well, that could lead to a lot of –'

She cut him short. 'I want you to go to the Roscow Inn at Moldavia and pick her up.'

He started to argue, until he saw the expression on her face. 'If that's what you want. I'll send –'

'No.' Mary's voice was steel. 'I want you to go. I'm sending two men with you.'

With Gunny and another Marine along, Mike would not be able to play any tricks. She had told Gunny not to let Mike Slade out of his sight.

Mike was studying Mary, puzzled. 'I have a heavy schedule. Tomorrow would probably –'

'I want you to leave immediately. Gunny is waiting for you in your office. You're to bring the defector back here to me.' Her tone left no room for argument.

Mike nodded slowly. 'All right.'

Mary watched him go, with a feeling of relief so intense that she felt giddy. With Mike out of the way, she would be safe.

She dialled Colonel McKinney's number. 'I'm going ahead with the ceremony this afternoon,' she informed him.

'I strongly advise against it, Madam Ambassador. Why would you want to expose yourself to unnecessary danger when –?'

'I have no choice. I'm representing our country. How would it look if I hid in a closet every time someone threatened my life? If I do that once, I'll never be able to show my face again. I might as well go home. And Colonel – I have no intention of going home.'

TWENTY-EIGHT

The ground-breaking ceremony for the new American Library addition was scheduled to be held at four o'clock in the afternoon at Alexandru Sahia Square, in the large vacant lot next to the main building of the American Library. By 3 p.m., a large crowd had already gathered. Colonel McKinney had had a meeting with Captain Aurel Istrase, head of *Securitate*.

'We shall certainly give your Ambassador maximum protection,' Istrase assured him.

Istrase had been as good as his word. He ordered all automobiles removed from the square, so that there was no danger of a car bomb, police were stationed around the entire area, and a sharpshooter was on the roof of the library building.

At a few minutes before four, everything was in readiness. Electronic experts had swept the entire area and had found no explosives. When all the checks had been completed, Captain Aurel Istrase said to Colonel McKinney, 'We are ready.'

411

'Very well.' Colonel McKinney turned to an aide. 'Tell the Ambassador to come ahead.'

Mary was escorted to the limousine by four Marines who flanked her as she got into the car.

Florian beamed, 'Good afternoon, Madam Ambassador. It is going to be a big, beautiful new library, no?'

'Yes.'

As he drove, Florian chattered on, but Mary was not listening. She was thinking of the laughter in Louis' eyes, and the tenderness with which he had made love to her. She dug her fingernails into her wrists, trying to make the physical pain replace the anguish inside. *I must not cry*, she told herself. *Whatever I do, I must not cry. There is no more love*, she thought wearily, *only hate. What's happening to the world?*

When the limousine reached the dedication site, two Marines stepped up to the car door, looked around carefully, and opened the door for Mary.

'Good afternoon, Madam Ambassador.'

As Mary walked towards the lot where the ceremony was to take place, two armed members of the *Securitate* walked in front of her, and two behind her, shielding her with their bodies. From the roof top, the sniper alertly scanned the scene below.

The onlookers applauded as the Ambassador stepped into the centre of the small circle that had been cleared for her. The crowd was a mixture of

Romanians, Americans and attachés from other embassies in Bucharest. There were a few familiar faces, but most of the people were strangers.

Mary looked over the crowd and thought: *How can I make a speech? Colonel McKinney was right. I should never have come here. I'm miserable and terrified.*

Colonel McKinney was saying, 'Ladies and gentlemen, it is my honour to present the Ambassador from the United States.'

The crowd applauded.

Mary took a deep breath, and began. 'Thank you . . .'

She had been so caught up in the maelstrom of events of the past week that she had not prepared a speech. Some deep wellspring within her gave her the words. She found herself saying, 'What we are doing here today may seem a small thing, but it is important because it is one more bridge between our country and all the countries of Eastern Europe. The new building we are dedicating here today will be filled with information about the United States of America. Here, you will be able to learn about the history of our country, both the good things and the bad things. You will be able to see pictures of our cities and factories and farms . . .'

Colonel McKinney and his men were moving through the crowd slowly. The note had said 'Enjoy your last day on earth.' When did the killer's day end? 6 p.m.? Nine o'clock? Midnight?

'. . . but there is something more important for you to find out than what the United States of America *looks* like. When this new building is finished, you can finally know what America *feels* like. We are going to show you the spirit of the country.'

On the far side of the square, a car suddenly raced past the police barrier and screamed to a stop at the kerb. As a startled policeman moved towards it, the driver jumped out of the car and began running away. As he ran, he pulled a device from his pocket and pressed it. The car exploded, sending out a shower of metal into the crowd. None of it reached the centre where Mary was standing, but the spectators began milling around in panic, trying to flee, to get away from the attack. The sniper on the roof raised his rifle and put a bullet through the fleeing man's heart before he could escape. He shot him twice more to make sure.

It took the Romanian police an hour to clear the crowd away from Alexandru Sahia Square and remove the body of the would-be assassin. The fire department had put out the flames of the burning car. Mary was driven back to the Embassy, shaken.

'Are you sure you wouldn't prefer to go to the Residence and rest?' Colonel McKinney asked her. 'You've just been through a horrifying experience that –'

'No,' Mary said stubbornly. 'The Embassy.'

That was the only place where she could safely talk to Stanton Rogers. *I must talk to him soon*, Mary thought, *or I'll go to pieces*.

The strain of everything that was happening to her was unbearable. She had made sure that Mike Slade was safely out of the way, yet an attempt had still been made on her life. So he was not working alone.

Mary wished desperately that Stanton Rogers would telephone.

At six o'clock, Mike Slade walked into Mary's office. He was furious.

'I put Corina Socoli in a room upstairs,' he said curtly. 'I wish to hell you'd told me who it was I was picking up. You've made a big mistake. We have to return her. She's a national treasure. There's no way the Romanian government will ever allow her out of the country. If –'

Colonel McKinney hurried into the office. He stopped short as he saw Mike.

'We have an identification on the dead man. He's the Angel, all right. His real name is H. R. de Mendoza.'

Mike was staring at him. 'What are you talking about?'

'I forgot,' Colonel McKinney said. 'You were away during all the excitement. Didn't the Ambassador tell you someone tried to kill her today?'

Mike turned to look at Mary. 'No.'

'She received a death warning from Angel. He tried to assassinate her at the ground-breaking ceremony this afternoon. One of Istrase's snipers got him.'

Mike stood there, silently, his eyes fixed on Mary.

Colonel McKinney said, 'Angel seems to have been on everybody's "Most Wanted List".'

'Where's his body?' Mike asked.

'In the morgue at police headquarters.'

The body was lying on a stone slab, naked. He had been an ordinary looking man, medium height, with unremarkable features, a naval tattoo on one arm, a small, thin nose that went with his tight mouth, very small feet, and thinning hair. His clothes and belongings were piled on a table.

'Mind if I have a look?'

The police sergeant shrugged. 'Go ahead. I'm sure he won't mind.' He snickered at his joke.

Mike picked up the jacket and examined the label. It was from a shop in Buenos Aires. The leather shoes also had an Argentinian label. There were piles of money next to the clothing, some Romanian lei, a few French francs, some English pounds, and at least ten thousand dollars in Republic of Argentina pesos – some in the new ten peso notes, and the rest in the devalued Un Million de Peso notes.

Mike turned to the sergeant. 'What do you have on him?'

'He flew in from London on Tarom Airlines two days ago. He checked into the Intercontinental Hotel under the name of de Mendoza. His passport shows his home address as Buenos Aires. It is forged.'

The policeman moved in to take a closer look at the body. 'He does not look like an international killer, does he?'

'No,' Mike agreed. 'He doesn't.'

Two dozen blocks away, Angel was walking past the Residence, fast enough so as not to attract the attention of the four armed Marines guarding the front entrance, and slowly enough to absorb every detail of the front of the building. The photographs that had been sent were excellent, but Angel believed in personally checking out every detail. Near the front door was a fifth guard in civilian clothes, holding two Doberman pinschers on leashes.

Angel grinned at the thought of the charade that had been played out in the town square. It had been child's play to hire a junkie for the price of a noseful of cocaine. *Throw everyone off guard. Let them sweat.* The big event was yet to come. *For five million dollars, I will give them a show they will never forget. What do the television networks call them? Spectaculars. They will get a spectacular in living colour.*

There will be a Fourth of July celebration at the Residence, the voice had said. *There will be balloons, a Marine band, entertainers*. Angel smiled and thought: *A five million dollar spectacular*.

Dorothy Stone hurried into Mary's office. 'Madam Ambassador – you're wanted right away in the Bubble Room. Mr Stanton Rogers is calling from Washington.'

'Mary – I can't understand a word you're saying. Slow down. Take a deep breath and start again.'

My God, Mary thought. *I'm babbling like a hysterical ninny*. There was such a mixture of violent emotions churning in her that she could barely get the words out. She was terrified and relieved and angry, all at the same time, and her voice came out in a series of choked words.

She took a deep, shuddering breath. 'I'm sorry, Stan – didn't you get my cable?'

'No. I've just returned. There was no cable from you. What's wrong back there?'

Mary fought to control her hysteria. *Where should I begin?* She took a deep breath. 'Mike Slade is trying to murder me.'

There was a shocked silence. 'Mary – you really can't believe –'

'It's true. I know it is. I met a doctor from the French Embassy – Louis Desforges. I became ill, and he found out I was being poisoned with arsenic. Mike was doing it.'

This time Stanton Rogers' voice was sharper. 'What makes you think that?'

'Louis – Dr Desforges – figured it out. Mike Slade made coffee for me every morning with arsenic in it. I have proof that he got hold of the arsenic. Last night, Louis was murdered, and this afternoon someone working with Slade tried to assassinate me.'

This time the silence was even longer.

When Stanton Rogers spoke again, his tone was urgent. 'What I'm going to ask you is very important, Mary. Think carefully. Could it have been anyone besides Mike Slade?'

'No. He's been trying to get me out of Romania from the very beginning.'

Stanton Rogers said crisply, 'All right. I'm going to inform the President. We'll handle Slade. In the meantime, I'll arrange extra protection for you there.'

'Stan – Sunday night I'm giving a Fourth of July party at the Residence. The guests have already been invited. Do you think I should cancel it?'

There was a thoughtful silence. 'As a matter of fact, the party might be a good idea. Keep a lot of people around you. Mary – I don't want to frighten you any more than you already are, but I would suggest that you do not let the children out of your sight. Not for a minute. Slade might try to get at you through them.'

She felt a shudder go through her. 'What's behind all this? Why is he doing this?'

'I wish I knew. It makes no sense. But I'm

damned well going to find out. In the meantime, keep as far away from him as you possibly can.'

Mary said grimly, 'Don't worry. I will.'

'I'll be in touch with you.'

When Mary hung up, it was as though an enormous burden had been lifted from her shoulders. *Everything's going to be all right*, she told herself. *The children and I are going to be fine.*

Eddie Maltz answered on the first ring.

The conversation lasted for ten minutes.

'I'll make sure everything is there,' Eddie Maltz promised.

Angel hung up.

Eddie Maltz thought: *I wonder what the hell Angel needs all that stuff for.* He looked at his watch. *Forty-eight hours to go.*

The moment Stanton Rogers finished talking to Mary, he placed an emergency call to Colonel McKinney.

'Bill, Stanton Rogers.'

'Yes, sir. What can I do for you?'

'I want you to pick up Mike Slade. Hold him in close custody until you hear from me.'

When the colonel spoke, there was an incredulous note in his voice. 'Mike Slade?'

'I want him held and isolated. He's probably armed and dangerous. Don't let him talk to anyone.'

'Yes, sir.'

'I want you to call me back at the White House as soon as you have him.'

'Yes, sir.'

Stanton Rogers' phone rang two hours later. He snatched up the receiver. 'Hello?'

'It's Colonel McKinney, Mr Rogers.'

'Do you have Slade?'

'No, sir. There's a problem.'

'What problem?'

'Mike Slade has disappeared.'

TWENTY-NINE

Sofia, Bulgaria
Saturday, July 3rd
In a small, nondescript building on Prezviter Kozma 32, a group of Eastern Committee members was meeting. Seated around the table were powerful representatives from Russia, China, Czechoslovakia, Pakistan, India and Malaysia.

The chairman was speaking: 'We welcome our brothers and sisters on the Eastern Committee who have joined us today. I am happy to tell you that we have excellent news from the Committee. Everything is now in place. The final phase of our plan is about to be successfully concluded. It will happen tomorrow night at the American Ambassador's Residence in Bucharest. Arrangements have been made for international press and television coverage.'

Code name Kali spoke. 'The American Ambassador and her two children –?'

'Will be assassinated, along with a hundred or so other Americans. We are all aware of the grave risks, and the holocaust that may follow. It is time to put the motion to a vote.' He started at the far end of the table. 'Brahma?'

'Yes.'

'Vishnu?'

'Yes.'

'Ganesha?'

'Yes.'

'Yama?'

'Yes.'

'Indra?'

'Yes.'

'Krishna?'

'Yes.'

'Rama?'

'Yes.'

'Kali?'

'Yes.'

'It is unanimous,' the chairman declared. 'We owe a particular vote of thanks to the person who has helped so much to bring this about.' He turned to the American.

'My pleasure,' Mike Slade said.

The decorations for the Fourth of July party were flown into Bucharest on a C-120 Hercules, late Saturday afternoon, and were trucked directly to a United States government warehouse. The cargo consisted of one thousand red, white and blue balloons, packed in flat boxes, three steel cylinders of helium to blow up the balloons, two hundred and fifty rolls of confetti, party favours, noisemakers, a dozen banners, and six dozen miniature American flags. The cargo was unloaded in the warehouse at 8 p.m. Two hours later, a jeep arrived with two oxygen cylinders stamped with US Army markings. The driver placed them inside.

At 1 a.m., when the warehouse was deserted, Angel appeared. The warehouse door had been left unlocked. Angel walked over to the cylinders, examined them carefully, and went to work. The first task was to empty the three helium tanks until each was only one third full. After that, the rest was simple.

On the morning of the Fourth of July, the Residence was in a state of chaos. Floors were being scrubbed, chandeliers dusted, rugs cleaned. Every room contained its own series of distinctive noises. There was hammering, as a podium at one end of the ballroom was being built for the band, the whir of vacuum cleaners in the hallways, sounds of cooking from the kitchen.

At four o'clock that afternoon, a United States Army truck pulled up at the service entrance of the Residence and was stopped. The guard on duty said to the driver, 'What have you got in there?'

'Goodies for the party.'

'Let's take a look.'

The guard inspected the inside of the truck. 'What's in the boxes?'

'Some helium and balloons and flags and stuff.'

'Open them.'

Fifteen minutes later, the truck was passed through. Inside the compound a corporal and two Marines began to unload the equipment and carry it into a large storage room off the main ballroom.

As they began to unpack, one of the Marines said, 'Look at all these balloons! Who the hell is going to blow them up?'

At that moment, Eddie Maltz walked in, accompanied by a stranger wearing Army fatigues.

'Don't worry,' Eddie Maltz said. 'This is the age of technocracy.' He nodded towards the stranger. 'Here's the one that's in charge of the balloons. Colonel McKinney's orders.'

One of the Marine guards grinned at the stranger. 'Better you than me.'

The two Marines left.

'You have an hour,' Eddie Maltz told the stranger. 'Better get to work. You've got a lot of balloons to blow up.'

Maltz nodded to the corporal and walked out.

The corporal walked over to one of the cylinders. 'What's in these babies?'

'Helium,' the stranger said curtly.

As the corporal stood watching, the stranger picked up a balloon, put the tip to the nozzle of a cylinder for an instant, and as the balloon filled, tied off the tip. The balloon floated to the ceiling. The whole operation took no more than a second.

'Hey, that's great,' the corporal smiled.

In her office at the Embassy, Mary Ashley was finishing up some action telexes that had to be sent out immediately. She desperately wished the party could have been called off. There were going to be more than two hundred guests. She hoped Mike Slade was caught before the party began.

Tim and Beth were under constant supervision at the Residence. *How could Mike Slade bear to harm them?* Mary remembered how much he had seemed to enjoy playing with them. *He's not sane.*

Mary rose to put some papers in the shredder – and froze. Mike Slade was walking into her office through the connecting door. Mary opened her mouth to scream.

'Don't!'

She was terrified. There was no one near enough to save her. He could kill her before she could call for help. He could escape the same way he had come in. How had he got past the guards? *I must not show him how frightened I am.*

'Colonel McKinney's men are looking for you. You can kill me,' Mary said defiantly, 'but you'll never escape.'

'You've been listening to too many fairy tales. Angel's the one who's trying to kill you.'

'You're a liar. Angel is dead. I saw him shot.'

'Angel is a professional from Argentina. The last thing he would do is walk around with Argentinian labels in his clothes, and Argentinian pesos in his pocket. The slob the police killed was an amateur who was set up.'

Keep him talking. 'I don't believe a word you're saying. *You* killed Louis Desforges. You tried to poison me. Do you deny that?'

Mike studied her for a long moment. 'No, I don't deny it. You'd better hear the story from a friend of mine.' He turned towards the door to his office. 'Come in, Bill.'

Colonel McKinney walked into the room. 'I think it's time we all had a chat, Madam Ambassador . . .'

In the Residence storage room, the stranger in Army fatigues was filling the balloons under the watchful eye of the Marine corporal.

Boy, that's one ugly customer, the corporal thought to himself. *Whew!*

The corporal could not understand why the white balloons were being filled from one cylinder, the red balloons from a second cylinder, and the blue ones from a third. *Why not use each cylinder until it's empty?* the corporal wondered. He was tempted to ask, but he did not want to start a conversation. *Not with this one.*

Through the open door that led to the ballroom, the corporal could see trays of hors d'oeuvres being carried out of the kitchen into the ballroom and set on tables along the sides of the room. *It's going to be a great party*, the corporal thought.

Mary was seated in her office, facing Mike Slade and Colonel McKinney.

'Let's start at the beginning,' Colonel McKinney said. 'On inauguration day when the President announced that he wanted to open relations with every Iron Curtain country, he exploded a bombshell. There's a faction in our government that's convinced that if we get involved with Romania, Russia, Bulgaria, Albania, Czechoslovakia, etc., the communists will destroy us. On the other side of the Iron Curtain, there are communists who believe that our President's plan is a trick – a Trojan Horse to bring our capitalist spies into their countries. A group of powerful men on both sides had formed a super-secret alliance called Patriots for Freedom. They decided the only way to destroy the President's plan was to let him start it, and then sabotage it in such a dramatic way that it would never be tried again. That's where you came into the picture.'

'But – why me? Why was I chosen?'

'Because the packaging was important,' Mike said. 'You were perfect. Adorable you, from middle-America, with two adorable kids – all that was missing was an adorable dog and an adorable cat. You were exactly the image they needed – the Ambassador with sizzle – Mrs America with two squeaky clean kids. They were determined to have you. When your husband got in the way, they murdered him and made it look like an accident so you wouldn't have any suspicions and refuse the post.'

'Oh, my God!' The horror of what he was saying was appalling.

'Their next step was your build-up. Through the "old-boy" network, they used their press connections around the world and saw to it that you became everyone's darling. Everybody was rooting for you. You were the beautiful lady who was going to lead the world down the road to peace.'

'And – and now?'

Mike's voice gentled. 'Their plan is to assassinate you and the children as publicly and as shockingly as possible – to sicken the world so much that it would put an end to any further ideas of détente.'

Mary sat there in stunned silence.

'That states it bluntly,' Colonel McKinney said quietly, 'but accurately. Mike is with the CIA. After your husband and Marin Groza were murdered, Mike started to get on the trail of the Patriots for Freedom. They thought he was on their side, and they invited him to join. We talked the idea over with President Ellison, and he gave his approval. The President has been kept abreast of every development. His over-riding concern has been that you and your children be protected. He didn't dare discuss what he knew with you or anyone else, because Ned Tillingast, the head of the CIA, had warned him there were high-level leaks.'

Mary's head was spinning. She said to Mike, 'But – you tried to kill me.'

He sighed. 'Lady, I've been trying to save your life. I tried every way I knew to get you to take the kids and go home where you'd be safe.'

'But – you poisoned me.'

'Not fatally. I wanted to get you just sick enough so that you'd have to leave Romania. Our doctors were waiting for you. I couldn't tell you the truth because it would have blown the whole operation, and we would have lost our one chance to catch them. Even now, we don't know who put the organization together. He never attends meetings. He's known only as the Controller.'

'And Louis?'

'The doctor was one of them. He was Angel's back-up. He was an expert with explosives. They assigned him here so he could stay close to you. A phoney kidnapping was set up and you were rescued by Mr Charm.' He saw the expression on Mary's face. 'You were lonely and vulnerable, and they worked on that. You weren't the first one to fall for the good doctor.'

Mary remembered something. *The smiling chauffeur. No Romanian is happy, only foreigners. I would hate to have my wife become a widow.*

She said slowly, 'Florian was in on it. He used the flat tyre as an excuse to get me out of the car.'

'We'll have him picked up.'

430

Something was bothering Mary. 'Mike – why did you kill Louis?'

'I had no choice. The whole point of their plan was to murder you and the children as spectacularly as possible in full public view. Louis knew I was a member of the Committee. When he figured out that I was the one poisoning you, he became suspicious of me. That wasn't the way you were supposed to die. I had to kill him before he exposed me.'

Mary sat there, listening as the pieces of the puzzle fell into place. The man she had distrusted had poisoned her to keep her alive, and the man she thought she loved had saved her for a more dramatic death. She and her children had been used. *I was the Judas goat*, Mary thought. *All the warmth that everyone showed me was phoney. The only one who was real was Stanton Rogers. Or was he –?*

'Stanton –' Mary began. 'Is he –?'

'He's been protective of you all the way,' Colonel McKinney assured her. 'When he thought Mike was the one trying to kill you, he ordered me to arrest him.'

Mary turned to look at Mike. He had been sent over here to protect her, and all the time she had looked on him as the enemy. Her thoughts were in a turmoil.

'Louis never had a wife or children?'

'No.'

Mary remembered something. 'But – I asked Eddie Maltz to check, and he told me that Louis was married and had two daughters.'

Mike and Colonel McKinney exchanged a look.

'He'll be taken care of,' McKinney said. 'I sent him to Frankfurt. I'll have him picked up.'

'Who is Angel?' Mary asked.

Mike answered. 'He's an assassin from South America. He's probably the best in the world. The Committee agreed to pay him five million dollars to kill you.'

Mary listened to the words in disbelief.

Mike went on. 'We know he's in Bucharest. Ordinarily, we'd have everything covered – airports, roads, railway stations – but we don't have a single description of Angel. He uses a dozen different passports. No one has ever talked directly to him. They deal through his mistress, Neusa Muñez. The different groups in the Committee are so compartmentalized that I haven't been able to learn who's been assigned to help him here, or what Angel's plan is.'

'What's to stop him from killing me?'

'Us.' It was Colonel McKinney talking. 'With the help of the Romanian government, we've taken extraordinary precautions for the party tonight. We've covered every possible contingency.'

'What happens now?' Mary asked.

Mike said carefully, 'That's up to you. Angel was ordered to carry out the contract at your party tonight. We're sure we can catch him, but if you and the children aren't at the party . . .' His voice trailed off.

'Then he won't try anything.'

'Not today. Sooner or later, he'll try again.'

'You're asking me to set myself up as a target.'

Colonel McKinney said, 'You don't have to agree, Madam Ambassador.'

I could end this now. I could go back to Kansas with the children and leave this nightmare behind. I could pick up my life again, go back to teaching, live like a normal human being. No one wants to assassinate school teachers. Angel would forget about me.

She looked up at Mike and Colonel McKinney and said, 'I won't expose my children to danger.'

Colonel McKinney said, 'I can arrange for Beth and Tim to be spirited out of the Residence and taken back here under escort.'

Mary looked at Mike for a long time. Finally she spoke. 'How does a Judas goat dress?'

THIRTY

At the Embassy, in Colonel McKinney's office, two dozen Marines were being given their orders.

'I want the Residence guarded like Fort Knox,' Colonel McKinney snapped. 'The Romanians are being cooperative. Ionescu is having his soldiers cordon off the square. No one gets through the line without a pass. We'll have our own checkpoints at every entrance to the Residence. Everyone going in or out will have to pass through a metal detector. The building and grounds will be completely surrounded. We'll have snipers on the roof. Any questions?'

'No, sir.'

'Dismissed.'

There was a tremendous feeling of excitement in the air. Huge spotlights ringed the Residence, lighting up the sky. The crowd was kept moving by a detachment of American MPs and Romanian police. Plainclothesmen mingled with the multitude, looking for anything suspicious. Some of them moved around with trained police dogs sniffing for explosives.

The press coverage was enormous. There were photographers and reporters from a dozen countries. They had all been carefully checked, and their equipment searched before they were allowed to enter the Residence.

'A cockroach couldn't sneak into this place tonight,' the Marine officer in charge of security boasted.

In the storage room, the Marine corporal was getting bored watching the person in Army fatigues filling up the balloons. He pulled out a cigarette and started to light it.

Angel yelled, 'Put that out!'

The Marine looked up, startled. 'What's the problem? You're filling those with helium, aren't you? Helium doesn't burn.'

'Put it out! Colonel McKinney said no smoking here.'

The Marine grumbled, 'Shit.' He dropped the cigarette and put it out with the sole of his shoe.

Angel watched to make sure there were no sparks left, then turned back to the task of filling each balloon from a different cylinder.

It was true that helium did not burn, but none

of the cylinders was filled with helium. The first tank was filled with propane, the second tank with white phosphorus, and the third with an oxygen-acetylene mix. Angel had left just enough helium in each tank the night before to make the balloons rise.

Angel was filling the white balloons with propane, the red balloons with oxygen-acetylene, and the blue balloons with white phosphorus. When the balloons were exploded, the white phosphorus would act as an incendiary for the initial gas discharge, drawing in oxygen so that all breath would be sucked out of the body of everybody within fifty yards. The phosphorus would instantly turn to a hot, searing, molten liquid, falling on everyone in the room. The thermal effect would destroy the lungs and throat, and the blast would flatten an area of a square block. *It's going to be beautiful.*

Angel straightened up and looked at the colourful balloons floating against the ceiling of the storage room. 'I am finished.'

'Okay,' the corporal said. 'Now all we have to do is push these babies out into the ballroom and let the guests have some fun.' The corporal called over four guards. 'Help me get these balloons out there.'

One of the guards opened wide the doors to the ballroom. The room had been decorated with American flags and red, white and blue bunting. At the far end was the raised stand for the band.

The ballroom was already crowded with guests helping themselves at the buffet tables set up along both sides of the room.

'It's a lovely room,' Angel said. *In one hour, it will be filled with burnt corpses.* 'Could I take a picture of it?'

The corporal shrugged. 'Why not? Let's go, fellas.'

The Marines pushed past Angel and started shoving the inflated balloons into the ballroom, watching as they floated to the ceiling high above.

'Easy,' Angel warned. 'Easy.'

'Don't worry,' a Marine called. 'We won't break your precious balloons.'

Angel stood in the doorway, staring at the riot of colours ascending in a rising rainbow, and smiled. One thousand of the lethal little beauties nestled against the ceiling. Angel took a camera from a pocket and stepped into the ballroom.

'Hey! You're not allowed in here,' the corporal said.

'I just want to take a picture to show my daughter.'

I'll bet that's some looking daughter, the corporal thought sardonically. 'All right. But make it quick.'

Angel glanced across the room at the entrance. Ambassador Mary Ashley was entering with her two children. Angel grinned. Perfect timing.

437

When the corporal turned his back, Angel quickly set the camera down under a cloth-covered table, where it could not be seen. The motor-driven automatic timing device was set for a one-hour delay. Everything was ready.

The Marine was approaching.

'I'm finished,' Angel said.

'I'll have you escorted out.'

'Thank you.'

Five minutes later, Angel was outside the Residence, strolling down Alexandru Sahia Street.

In spite of the fact that it was a hot and humid night, the area outside the American Embassy Residence had become a madhouse. Police were fighting to keep back the hundreds of curious Romanians who kept arriving. Every light in the Residence had been turned on, and the building blazed against the black night sky.

Before the party began, Mary had taken the children upstairs.

'We have to have a family conference,' she said. She felt she owed them the truth.

They sat listening, wide-eyed, as their mother explained what had been happening, and what might be about to happen.

'I'll see to it that you're in no danger,' Mary said. 'You'll be taken out of here, where you'll be safe.'

'But what about you?' Beth asked. 'Someone is trying to kill you. Can't you come with us?'

'No, darling. Not if we want to catch this man.'

Tim was trying not to cry. 'How do you know they'll catch him?'

Mary thought about that for a moment, and said, 'Because Mike Slade said so. Okay, fellas?'

Beth and Tim looked at each other. They were both white-faced, terrified. Mary's heart went out to them. *They're too young to have to go through this*, she thought. *Anyone is too young to have to go through this.*

She dressed carefully, wondering if she was dressing for her death. She chose a full-length, formal red silk chiffon gown and red silk high-heel sandals. She studied her reflection in the mirror. Her face was pale. *Mirror, mirror, on the wall – am I going to live or die tonight?*

Fifteen minutes later, Mary, Beth and Tim entered the ballroom. They walked across the floor, greeting guests, trying to conceal their nervousness. When they reached the other side of the room, Mary turned to the children. 'You have homework to do,' she said loudly. 'Back to your rooms.'

She watched them leave, a lump in her throat, thinking: *I hope to God Mike Slade knows what he's doing.*

There was a loud crash, and Mary jumped. She spun round to see what was happening, her pulse racing. A waiter had dropped a tray and was picking up the broken plates. Mary tried to stop the pounding of her heart. How was Angel planning to assassinate her? She looked around the festive ballroom, but there was no clue.

The moment the children left the ballroom, they were escorted to a service entrance by Colonel McKinney.

He said to the two armed Marines waiting at the door, 'Take them to the Ambassador's office. Don't let them out of your sight.'

Beth held back. 'Is mother really going to be all right?'

'She's going to be just fine,' McKinney promised. And he prayed that he was right.

Mike Slade watched Beth and Tim leave, then went to find Mary.

'The children are on their way. I have to do some checking. I'll be back.'

'Don't leave me.' The words came out before she could stop herself. 'I want to go with you.'

'Why?'

She looked at him and said honestly, 'I feel safer with you.'

Mike grinned. 'Now that's a switch. Come on.'

Mary followed him, staying close behind him. The orchestra had begun playing, and people were dancing. The repertoire was American songs, mostly from Broadway musicals. They played the score from *Oklahoma* and *South Pacific, Annie Get Your Gun*, and *My Fair Lady*. The guests were enjoying themselves tremendously. Those who were not dancing were helping themselves from the silver trays of champagne being offered or from the buffet tables.

The room looked spectacular. Mary raised her head, and there were the balloons, a thousand of them – red, white and blue – floating against the pink ceiling. It was a festive occasion. *If only death were not a part of it*, she thought.

Her nerves were so taut that she was ready to scream. A guest brushed against her, and she braced herself for the prick of a deadly needle. Or was Angel going to shoot her in front of all these people? Or stab her? The suspense of what was about to happen was unbearable. In the midst of the laughing, chattering guests, she felt naked and vulnerable. Angel could be anywhere. He could be watching her this minute.

'Do you think Angel is here now?' Mary asked.

'I don't know,' Mike said. And that was the most frightening thing of all. He saw the expression on her face. 'Look, if you want to leave –'

'No. You said I'm the bait. Without the bait, he won't spring the trap.'

He nodded and squeezed her arm. 'Right.'

Colonel McKinney was approaching. 'We've done a thorough search, Mike. We haven't been able to find a thing. I don't like it.'

'Let's take another look around.' Mike signalled to four armed Marines standing by, and they moved up next to Mary. 'Be right back,' Mike said.

Mary swallowed nervously. 'Please.'

Mike and Colonel McKinney, accompanied by two guards with sniffer dogs, searched every upstairs room in the Embassy Residence.

'Nothing,' Mike said.

They talked to a Marine guarding the back staircase.

'Did any strangers come up here?'

'No, sir. It's your average quiet Sunday night.'

Not quite, Mike thought bitterly.

They moved towards a guest room down the hall. An armed Marine was standing guard. He saluted the colonel and stood aside to let them enter. Corina Socoli was lying on the bed, reading a book in Romanian. Young and beautiful and talented; the Romanian national treasure. Could she be a plant? Could she be helping Angel?

Corina looked up. 'I am sorry I am going to miss the party. It sounds like such fun. Ah, well. I will stay here and finish my book.'

'Do that,' Mike said. He closed the door. 'Let's try the downstairs again.'

They returned to the kitchen.

'What about poison?' Colonel McKinney asked. 'Would he use that?'

Mike shook his head. 'Not photogenic enough. Angel's going for the big bang.'

'Mike, there's no way anyone could get explosives into this place. Our experts have gone over it, the dogs have gone over it – the place is clean.

He can't hit us through the roof, because we have fire power up there. It's impossible.'

'There's one way.'

Colonel McKinney looked at Mike. 'How?'

'I don't know. But Angel does.'

They searched the library and the offices again. Nothing. They passed the storage room where the corporal and his men were shoving out the last of the balloons, watching them as they floated to the ceiling.

'Pretty, huh?' the corporal said.

'Yeah.'

They started to walk on. Mike stopped. 'Corporal, where did these balloons come from?'

'From the US air base in Frankfurt, sir.'

Mike indicated the helium cylinders. 'And these?'

'Same place. They were escorted to our warehouse per your instructions, sir.'

Mike said to Colonel McKinney, 'Let's start upstairs again.'

They turned to leave. The corporal said, 'Oh, Colonel – the person you sent forgot to leave a time slip. Is that going to be handled by military payroll or civilian?'

Colonel McKinney frowned. 'What person?'

'The one you authorized to fill the balloons.'

Colonel McKinney shook his head. 'I never – who said I authorized it?'

'Eddie Maltz. He said you –'

Colonel McKinney said, '*Eddie Maltz?* I ordered him to Frankfurt.'

Mike turned to the corporal, his voice urgent. 'What did this man look like?'

'Oh, it wasn't a man, sir. It was a woman. To tell you the truth, I thought she looked weird. Fat and ugly. She had a funny accent. She was pock-marked and had kind of a puffy face.'

Mike said to McKinney, excitedly, 'That sounds like Harry Lantz's description of Neusa Muñez that he gave the Committee.'

The revelation hit them both at the same time.

Mike said slowly, 'Oh, my God! Neusa Muñez is Angel!' He pointed to the cylinders. 'She filled the balloons from these?'

'Yes, sir. It was funny. I lit a cigarette, and she screamed at me to put it out. I said, "Helium doesn't burn," and she said –'

Mike looked up. 'The balloons! The explosives are in the balloons!'

The two men stared at the high ceiling, covered with the spectacular red, white and blue balloons.

'She's using some kind of a remote control device to explode them.' He turned to the corporal. 'How long ago did she leave?'

'I guess about an hour ago.'

Under the table, unseen, the timing device had six minutes left on the dial.

Mike was frantically scanning the huge room. 'She

444

could have put it anywhere. It could go off at any second. We could never find it in time.'

Mary was approaching. Mike turned to her. 'You've got to clear the room. Fast! Make an announcement. It will sound better coming from you. Get everybody outside.'

She was looking at him, bewildered. 'But – why? What's happened?'

'We found our playmate's toy,' Mike said grimly. He pointed. 'Those balloons. They're lethal.'

Mary was looking up at them, horror on her face. 'Can't we take them down?'

Mike snapped, 'There must be a thousand of them. By the time you start pulling them down, one by one –'

Her throat was so dry she could hardly get the words out. 'Mike – I know a way.'

The two men were staring at her.

'The Ambassador's folly. The roof. It slides open.'

Mike tried to control his excitement. 'How does it work?'

'There's a switch that –'

'No,' Mike said. 'Nothing electrical. A spark could set them all off. Can it be done manually?'

'Yes.' The words were tumbling out. 'The roof is divided in half. There's a crank on each side that –' She was talking to herself.

The two men were frantically racing upstairs. When they reached the top floor, they found the door opening onto a loft, and hurried inside. A wooden ladder led to a catwalk above that was used by workmen to clean the ceiling of the ball-room. A crank was fastened to the wall.

'There must be another one on the other side,' Mike said.

He started across the narrow catwalk, pushing his way through the sea of deadly balloons, struggling to keep his balance, trying not to look down at the mob of people far below. A current of air pushed a mass of balloons against him, and he slipped. One foot went off the catwalk. He began to fall. He grabbed the boards as he fell, hanging on. Slowly, he managed to pull himself up. He was soaked in perspiration. He inched his way along the rest of the way. Fastened to the wall was the crank.

'I'm ready,' Mike called to the colonel. 'Careful. No sudden moves.'

'Right.'

Mike began turning the crank very slowly.

Under the table, the timer was down to two minutes.

Mike could not see Colonel McKinney because of the balloons, but he could hear the sound of the other crank being turned. Slowly, very slowly, the roof started to slide open. A few balloons lifted by the helium drifted into the night air, and as the roof opened farther, more balloons began to escape. Hundreds of them poured through the opening, dancing into the star-filled night, drawing oohs and ahs from the unsuspecting guests below, and the people out in the street.

On the ground floor there were 45 seconds left on the remote control timer. A cluster of balloons caught on the edge of the ceiling, just out of Mike's reach. He strained forward, trying to free them. They swayed, just beyond his fingertips. Carefully, he moved out on the catwalk with nothing to hold onto, and strained to push them free. *Now!*

Mike stood there, watching the last of the balloons escape. They soared higher and higher, painting the velvet night with their vivid colours, and suddenly the sky exploded.

There was a tremendous roar, and the tongues of red and white flames shot high into the air. It was a Fourth of July celebration such as had never been seen before. Below, everyone applauded.

Mike watched, drained, too tired to move. It was over.

The round-up was timed to take place simultaneously, in far-flung corners of the world.

Floyd Baker, the Secretary of State, was in bed with his mistress when the door burst open. Four men came into the room.

'What the hell do you mean by –?'

One of the men pulled out an identification card. 'FBI, Mr Secretary. You're under arrest.'

Floyd Baker stared at them unbelievingly. 'You must be mad. What's the charge?'

'Treason, Thor.'

General Oliver Brooks, Odin, was having breakfast at his club when two FBI agents walked up to his table and arrested him.

Sir Alex Hyde-White, KBE, MP, Freyr, was being toasted at a parliamentary dinner when the club steward approached him. 'Excuse me, Sir Alex. There are some gentlemen outside who would like a word with you . . .'

In Paris, in the Chambre des Députés de la République Française, a deputy, Balder, was called off the floor and arrested by the DGSE.

In the parliament building in New Delhi, the speaker of the Lok Sabha, Vishnu, was bundled into a limousine and taken to jail.

In Rome, the Deputy of the Camera dei Deputati, Tyr, was in a Turkish bath when he was arrested.

The sweep went on:

In Mexico and Albania and Japan, high officials were arrested and held in jails. A member of the

Bundestag in West Germany; a deputy in the Nationalrat in Austria; the Vice Chairman of the Presidium of the Soviet Union.

The arrests included the president of a large shipping company, and a powerful union leader. A television evangelist and the head of an oil cartel.

Eddie Maltz was shot while trying to escape.

Pete Connors committed suicide while FBI agents were trying to break down the door to his office.

Mary and Mike Slade were seated in the Bubble Room, receiving reports from around the world.

Mike was on the telephone. 'Vreeland,' he said. 'He's an MP in the South African government.' He replaced the receiver and turned to Mary. 'They've got most of them. Except for the Controller and Neusa Muñez – Angel.'

'No one knew that Angel was a woman?' Mary marvelled.

'No. She had all of us fooled. Lantz described her to the Patriots for Freedom Committee as a fat, ugly moron.'

'What about the Controller?' Mary asked.

'No one ever saw him. He gave orders by telephone. He was a brilliant organizer. The Committee was broken up into small cells, so that one group never knew what the other was doing.'

* * *

Angel was furious. In fact, she was more than furious. She was like an enraged animal. The contract had gone wrong somehow, but she had been prepared to make up for it.

She had called the private number in Washington, and using her dull, listless voice, had said, 'Angel say to tell you not to worry. There was som' mistake, but he weel take care of it, meester. They will all die nex' time, and –'

'There won't be a next time,' the voice had exploded. 'Angel bungled it. He's worse than an amateur.'

'Angel tol' me –'

'I don't give a damn what he told you. He's finished. He won't get a cent. Just tell the son-of-a-bitch to keep away. I'll find someone else who knows how to do the job.'

And he had slammed the phone down.

The gringo bastard. No one had ever treated Angel like that and lived to talk about it. Pride was at stake. The man was going to pay. Oh, how he would pay!

The private phone in the Bubble Room rang. Mary picked it up. It was Stanton Rogers.

'Mary! You're safe! Are the children all right?'

'We're all fine, Stan.'

'Thank God it's over. Tell me exactly what happened.'

'It was Angel. She tried to blow up the Residence and –'

450

'You mean *he*.'

'No. Angel is a woman. Her name is Neusa Muñez.'

There was a long, stunned silence. '*Neusa Muñez*? That fat, ugly moron was *Angel*?'

Mary felt a sudden chill go through her. She said slowly, 'That's right, Stan.'

'Is there anything I can do for you, Mary?'

'No. I'm on my way to see the children. I'll talk to you later.'

She replaced the receiver and sat there, dazed.

Mike looked at her. 'What's the matter?'

She turned to him. 'You said that Harry Lantz told only some Committee members what Neusa Muñez looked like?'

'Yes.'

'Stanton Rogers just described her.'

When Angel's plane landed at Dulles Airport, she went to a telephone booth and dialled the Controller's private number.

The familiar voice said, 'Stanton Rogers.'

Two days later, Mike, Colonel McKinney and Mary were seated in the Embassy conference room. An electronics expert had just finished de-bugging it.

'It all fits together now,' Mike said. 'The Controller *had* to be Stanton Rogers, but none of us could see it.'

'But why would he want to kill me?' Mary

asked. 'In the beginning, he was *against* my being appointed ambassador. He told me so himself.'

Mike explained. 'Once he realized what you and the children symbolized, everything clicked. After that, he *fought* for you to get the nomination. That's what threw us off the track. He was behind you all the way, seeing to it that you got a build-up in the press, making sure you were seen in all the right places by the right people.'

Mary shuddered. 'Why would he want to get involved with –?'

'Stanton Rogers never forgave Paul Ellison for being President. He felt cheated. He started out as a liberal, and he married a right-wing reactionary. My guess is that his wife turned him around.'

'Have they found him yet?'

'No. He's disappeared. But he can't hide for very long.'

Stanton Rogers' head was found in a Washington garbage dump two days later. His eyes had been torn out.

THIRTY-ONE

President Paul Ellison was calling from the White House. 'I'm refusing to accept your resignation.'

'I'm sorry, Mr President, but I can't –'

'Mary, I know how much you've been through, but I'm asking you to remain in your post in Romania.'

I know how much you've been through. Did anyone have any idea? She had been so unbelievably naïve when she arrived, filled with such ideals and high hopes. She was going to be the symbol and spirit of her country. She was going to show the world how wonderful Americans really were; and all the time she had been a cat's-paw. She had been used by her President, her government, by everyone around her. She and her children had been placed in mortal danger. She thought of Edward, and of how he had been murdered, and of Louis and his lies and his death. She thought of the destruction Angel had sown.

I'm not the same person I was when I came

here, Mary thought. *I was an innocent. I've grown up the hard way, but I've grown up. I've managed to accomplish something here. I got Hannah Murphy out of prison, and I made our grain deal. I saved the life of Ionescu's son, and I got the Romanians their bank loan. I rescued some Jews.*

'Hello. Are you there?'

'Yes, sir.' She looked across her desk at Mike Slade, who was slouched back in his chair, studying her.

'You've done a truly remarkable job,' the President said. 'We're all terribly proud of you. Have you seen the newspapers?'

She did not give a damn about the newspapers.

'You're the person we need over there. You'll be doing our country a great service, my dear.'

The President was waiting for an answer. Mary was thinking, weighing her decision. *I've become a damned good ambassador, and there's so much more that still has to be done here.*

She said, finally, 'Mr President, if I did agree to stay, I would insist that our country give sanctuary to Corina Socoli.'

'I'm sorry, Mary. I've already explained why we can't do that. It would offend Ionescu and –'

'He'll get over it. I know Ionescu, Mr President. He's using her as a bargaining chip.'

There was a long, thoughtful silence. 'How would you get her out of Romania?'

'An Army cargo plane is due to arrive in the morning. I'll send her out in that.'

There was a pause. 'I see. Very well. I'll square it with State. If that's all –?'

Mary looked over at Mike Slade again. 'No, sir. There's one thing more. I want Mike Slade to stay here with me. I need him. We make a good team.'

Mike was watching her, a private smile on his lips.

'I'm afraid that's impossible,' the President said firmly. 'I need Slade back here. He already has another assignment.'

Mary sat there, holding the phone, saying nothing.

The President went on. 'We'll send you someone else. You can have your choice. Anyone you want.'

Silence.

'We really do need Mike here, Mary.'

Mary glanced over at Mike again.

The President said, 'Mary? Hello? What is this – some kind of blackmail?'

Mary sat, silently waiting.

Finally, the President said grudgingly, 'Well, I suppose if you really need him, we might spare him for a little while.'

Mary felt her heart lighten. 'Thank you, Mr President. I'll be happy to stay on as Ambassador.'

The President had a final parting shot. 'You're a hell of a negotiator, Madam Ambassador. I have some interesting plans in mind for you when you're finished there. Good luck. And stay out of trouble.'

The line went dead.

Mary slowly replaced the receiver. She looked

across at Mike. 'You're going to be staying here. He told me to stay out of trouble.'

Mike Slade grinned. 'He has a nice sense of humour.' He rose and moved towards her. 'Do you remember the day I met you and called you a perfect ten?'

How well she remembered. 'Yes.'

'I was wrong. *Now* you're a perfect ten.'

She felt a warm glow. 'Oh, Mike . . .'

'Since I'm staying on, Madam Ambassador, we'd better talk about the problem we're having with the Romanian Commerce Minister.' He looked into her eyes and said softly, 'Coffee?'

EPILOGUE

Alice Springs, Australia
The chairman was addressing the Committee. 'We have suffered a setback, but because of the lessons we have learned, our organization will become even stronger. Now it is time to take a vote. Aphrodite?'

'Yes.'

'Athene?'

'Yes.'

'Cybele?'

'Yes.'

'Selene?'

'Considering the horrible murder of our former Controller, shouldn't we wait until –?'

'Yes, or no, please?'

'No.'

'Nike?'

'Yes.'

'Nemesis?'

'Yes.'

'The motion is carried. Please observe the usual precautions, ladies . . .'